S0-BSL-656

RANDOM HOUSE

LARGE PRINT

# Praise for
# The Hope of Refuge

"What a beautiful story of hope and renewal! Cindy Woodsmall's **The Hope of Refuge** is an honest and moving portrayal that rings with authenticity. It warmed my heart long after I finished reading and reminded me that new beginnings are possible, truth frees, and love can make all things new, if only we can learn to trust again."

—MARLO SCHALESKY, award-winning author of **If Tomorrow Never Comes** and **Beyond the Night**

"Cindy Woodsmall's **The Hope of Refuge** takes the reader on an emotional journey into the heart of Amish country and the heart of a very human heroine. A compelling novel of love lost and found with realistic characters from two very different worlds which become, beautifully, one."

—KAREN HARPER, **New York Times** best-selling author of **Deep Down**

# Praise for Cindy Woodsmall

"A skillfully written story of forgiveness and redemption. Woodsmall's authentic characters illustrate beautifully how wounded souls can indeed be mended."
—SUSAN MEISSNER, author of
**The Shape of Mercy** and
**White Picket Fences**

"Cindy Woodsmall writes **real**—real people, real conflicts, real emotions. When you open her book, you enter her world and live the story with the characters."
—KIM VOGEL SAWYER, author of
**Where Willows Grow** and
**Waiting for Summer's Return**

"Reaching deep into the heart of the reader, Cindy Woodsmall pens a beautifully lyrical story…. She paints a vivid backdrop of Amish and Mennonite cultures with fascinating detail and memorable clarity. Fans of this genre will be thrilled to discover this new author."
—TAMERA ALEXANDER, best-selling author of **Rekindled**

"Like the stitches on a well-loved quilt, love and faith hold together Cindy Woodsmall's **When the Soul Mends,** the brilliantly written third story in the Sisters of the Quilt series. With deft plotting and characters that seem to jump off the page, this novel offers the timeless truth that forgiveness is the balm which heals all wounds and a blanket for the soul."

—KATHLEEN Y'BARBO, author of
**The Confidential
Life of Eugenia Cooper**

"What a vibrant, strong, emotional story!"

—GAYLE ROPER, author of
**Fatal Deduction** and the
Seaside Seasons series

"Cindy Woodsmall's characters wrapped themselves around my heart and wouldn't let go."

—DEBORAH RANEY, author of
**A Vow to Cherish** and
**Remember to Forget**

# The HOPE of REFUGE

# The HOPE of REFUGE

A NOVEL

# CINDY WOODSMALL

RANDOM HOUSE
LARGE PRINT

Copyright © 2009 by Cindy Woodsmall

Published in the United States of America by Random House Large Print in association with Crown Publishing Group, New York. Distributed by Random House, Inc., New York.

Cover design: Mark D. Ford
Cover Photos: Girls, Jim Celuch; Background, Dale Yoder

The Library of Congress has established a Cataloging-in-Publication record for this title.

ISBN: 978-0-7393-7733-8

www.randomhouse.com/largeprint

FIRST LARGE PRINT EDITION

10  9  8  7  6  5  4  3  2  1

This Large Print edition published in accord with the standards of the N.A.V.H.

## To Justin, Adam, and Tyler

The Hope of Refuge **shares the story of several moms—their strengths, weaknesses, joys, and sorrows. I** dedicate this book to you because **each of you woke a different part of me before I even felt you move inside me. When I held you in my arms, it seemed my very DNA shifted. Without conscious effort, you stirred me with a challenge to be your mom—to become more than I ever was before. I found strength where weakness had once been. As you grew, you stumbled on weaknesses I hadn't known existed. But because of you, I discovered that life had a euphoric side. And I learned that where I ended—where my strength, wisdom, and determination failed— God did not. For Him and for each of you, I am eternally grateful…**

# Prologue

"Mama, can you tell me yet?" Cara held her favorite toy, stroking the small plastic horse as if it might respond to her tender touch. The brown ridges, designed to look like fur, had long ago faded to tan.

Mama held the well-worn steering wheel in silence while she drove dirt roads Cara had never seen before. Dust flew in through the open windows and clung to Cara's sweaty face, and the vinyl seat was hot to the touch when she laid her hand against it. Mama pressed the brake pedal, slowing the car to a near stop as they crossed another bridge with a roof over it. A covered bridge, Mama called it. The bumpiness of the wooden planks jarred

Cara, making her bounce like she was riding a cardboard box down a set of stairs.

Mama reached across the seat and ran her hand down the back of Cara's head, probably trying to smooth out one of her cowlicks. No matter how short Mama cut her hair, she said the unruly mop always won the battle. "We're going to visit a . . . a friend of mine. She's Amish." She placed her index finger on her lips. "I need you to do as the mother of Jesus did when it came to precious events. She treasured them in her heart and pondered them. I know you love our diary, and since you turned eight, you've been determined to write entries about everything, but you can't—not this time. No drawing pictures or writing about any part of this trip. And you can't ever tell your father, okay?"

Sunlight bore down on them again as they drove out of the covered bridge. Cara searched the fields for horses. "Are we going to your hiding place?"

Cara had a hiding place, one her mother had built for her inside the wall of the attic. They had tea parties in there sometimes when there was money for tea bags and sugar. And when Daddy needed quiet, her mother would silently whisk her to that secret room. If her mama didn't return for her by nightfall, she'd sleep in there, only sneaking out for a minute if she needed to go to the bathroom.

Mama nodded. "I told you every girl needs a fun place she can get away to for a while, right?"

Cara nodded.

"Well, this is mine. We'll stay for a couple of days, and if you like it, maybe we'll move here one day—just us girls."

Cara wondered if Mama was so tired of the bill collectors hounding her and Daddy that she was thinking of sneaking away and not even telling him where she was going. The familiar feeling returned—that feeling of her insides being Jell-O on a whirlybird ride. She clutched her toy horse even tighter and looked out the window, imagining herself on a stallion galloping into a world where food was free and her parents were happy.

After they topped another hill, her

mother slowed the vehicle and pulled into a driveway. Mama turned off the car. "Look at this place, Cara. That old white clapboard house has looked the same since I was a child."

The shutters hung crooked and didn't have much paint left on them. "It's really small, and it looks like ghosts live here."

Her mama laughed. "It's called a **Daadi Haus,** which means it's just for grandparents once their children are grown. It only has a small kitchen, two bedrooms, and a bathroom. This one has been here for many years. You're right—it does look dilapidated. Come on."

Seconds after Cara shut the passenger door, an old woman stepped out from between tall rows of corn. She stared at them as if they were aliens, and Cara wondered if her mama really did know these people. The woman wore a long burgundy dress and no shoes. The wrinkles covering her face looked like a road map, with the lines taking on new twists as she frowned. Though it was July and too hot for a toboggan cap, she wore a white one.

**"Grossmammi Levina, ich bin kumme bsuche. Ich hab aa die Cara mitgebrocht."**

Startled, Cara looked up at her mama. What was she saying? Was it code? Mama wasn't even good at pig Latin.

The old woman released her apron, and several ears of corn fell to the ground. She hurried up to Mama. "Malinda?"

Tears brimmed in Mama's eyes, and she nodded. The older woman squealed, long and loud, before she hugged Mama.

A lanky boy came running from the rows. "Levina, **was iss letz**?" He stopped short, watching the two women for a moment before looking at Cara.

As he studied her, she wondered if she looked as odd to him as he did to her. She hadn't seen a boy in long black pants since winter ended, and she'd never seen one wear suspenders and a straw hat. Why would he work in a garden in a Sunday dress shirt?

He snatched up several ears of corn the woman had dropped, walked to a wooden wheelbarrow, and dumped them.

Cara picked up the rest of the ears and followed him. "You got a name?"

"Ephraim."

"I can be lots of help if you'll let me."

"Ya ever picked corn before?"

Cara shook her head. "No, but I can learn."

He just stood there, watching her.

She held out her horse to him. "Isn't she a beauty?"

He shrugged. "Looks a little worn to me."

Cara slid the horse into her pocket.

Ephraim frowned. "Can I ask you a question?"

She nodded.

"Are you a boy or a girl?"

The question didn't bother her. She got it all the time at school from new teachers or ones who didn't have her in their classes. They referred to her as a young man until they realized she wasn't a boy. Lots of times it worked for her, like when she slipped right past the teacher who was the lavatory monitor and went into the boys' bathroom to teach Jake Merrow a lesson about stealing her milk money. She got her money back, and he never told a soul that a girl gave him a fat lip. "If I say I'm a boy, will you let me help pick corn?"

Ephraim laughed in a friendly way. "You know, I used to have a worn horse like the one you showed me. I kept him in my pocket too, until I lost him."

Cara shoved the horse deeper into her pocket. "You lost him?"

He nodded. "Probably down by the creek where I was fishing. Do you fish?"

She shook her head. "I've never seen a creek."

"Never seen one? Where are you from?"

"New York City. My mama had to borrow a car for us to get beyond where the subway ends."

"Well, if you're here when the workday is done, I'll show you the creek. We got a rope swing, and if your mama will let you, you can swing out and drop into the deep part. How long are you here for?"

She looked around the place. Her mama and the old woman were sitting under a shade tree, holding hands and talking.

Across the road was a barn, and she could see a horse inside it. Green fields went clear to the horizon. She took a deep breath. The air smelled delicious, like dirt, but not city dirt. Like growing-food dirt. Maybe this was where her horse took her when she dreamed. The cornstalks reached for the sky, and her chest felt like little shoes were tap-dancing inside it. She should have known that if her mama liked something, it was worth liking.

"Until it's not a secret anymore, I think."

# One

**Twenty years later**

Sunlight streamed through the bar's dirty windows as the lunch crowd filled the place. Cara set two bottles of beer on the table in front of the familiar faces.

The regulars knew the rules: all alcoholic drinks were paid for upon delivery. One of the men held a five-dollar bill toward her but kept his eyes on the television. The other took a long drink while he slid a hundred-dollar bill across the table.

She stared at the bill, her heart pounding with desire. If earning money as a waitress wasn't hard enough, Mac kept most of their tips. The money the customer slid across the table wasn't just cash but power.

It held the ability for her to fix Lori something besides boiled potatoes next week and to buy her a pair of shoes that didn't pinch her feet.

**Would the customer even notice if I shortchanged him from such a large amount?**

Lines of honesty were often blurred by desperation. Cara loathed that she couldn't apply for government help and that she had to uproot every few months to stay a few steps ahead of a maniac. Moving always cost money. Fresh security deposits on ever-increasing rents. Working time lost as she searched for another job—each one more pathetic than the one before it. Mike had managed to steal everything from her but mere existence. And her daughter.

"I'll get your change." **All of it.** She took the money.

"Cara." Mac's gruff voice sailed across the room. From behind the bar he motioned for her. "Phone!" He shook the receiver at her. "Kendal says it's an emergency."

Every sound echoing inside the

wooden-and-glass room ceased. She hurried toward him, snaking around tables filled with people.

"Keep it short." Mac passed the phone to her and returned to serving customers.

"Kendal, what's wrong?"

"He found us." Her friend's usually icy voice shook, and Cara knew she was more frightened than she'd been the other times. **How could he after all we've done to hide?** "We got a letter at our new place?"

"No. Worse." Kendal's words quaked. "He was here. Broke the lock and came inside looking for you. He ransacked the place."

"He what?"

"He's getting meaner, Cara. He ripped open all the cushions, turned mattresses, emptied drawers and boxes. He found your leather book and . . . and insisted I stay while he made himself at home and read through it."

"We've got to call the police."

"You know we can't . . ." Kendal dropped the sentence, and Cara heard her crying.

They both knew that going to the police would be a mistake neither of them would survive.

One of the waitresses plunked a tray of dirty dishes onto the counter. "Get off the phone, princess."

Cara plugged her index finger into her ear, trying desperately to think. "Where's Lori?"

"I'm sure they moved her to after-school care." Through the phone line Cara heard a car door slam. They didn't own a car.

A male voice asked, "Where to?"

Cara gripped the phone tighter. "What's going on?"

Kendal sobbed. "I'm sorry. I can't take this anymore. All we do is live in fear and move from one part of New York to another. He's . . . he's not after me."

"You know he's trying to isolate me from everyone. Please, Kendal."

"I . . . I'm sorry. I can't help you anymore," Kendal whispered. "The cab's waiting."

Disbelief settled over her. "How long ago did he break in?"

From behind Cara a shadow fell across the bar, engulfing her. "Hi, Care Bear."

She froze. Watching the silhouette, she noted how tiny she was in comparison.

Mike's thick hand thudded a book onto the bar beside her. He removed his hand, revealing her diary. "I didn't want to do it this way, Care Bear. You know that about me. But I had to get inside your place to try to find answers for why you keep running off."

She swallowed a wave of fear and faced him but couldn't find her voice.

"Johnny's been dead for a while. Now you're here . . . with me." His massive body loomed over her. "I'd be willing to forget that you ever picked that loser. We could start fresh. Come on, beautiful, I can help you."

**Help me?** The only person Mike wanted to help was himself—right into her bed.

"Please . . . leave me alone."

His steely grin unnerved her, and silence fell in the midst of the bar's noise. Thoughts of how to escape him exploded in her mind like fireworks shooting out in all directions. But before she could focus, they disappeared into the darkness, leaving only trails of smoke. Fear seemed to take on its own life form, one threatening to stalk her forever.

He tapped her diary. "I know it all now, even where you'd hide if you ran again, which is **not** happening, right?" The threatening tone in his voice was undeniable, and panic stole her next breath. "I know your daughter just as well as you do now. What happens if I show up one day after school with a puppy named Shamu?"

Cara's legs gave way. Without any effort he held her up by her elbow.

After she'd spent years of hide-and-seek in hopes of protecting Lori, now he knew Lori's name, her school, her likes and dislikes. Shaking, she looked around for help. Bottles of various sizes and shapes filled the bar's shelves. The television blared. Blank faces stared at it. The man who had given her the hundred-dollar bill glanced at her before turning to another waitress.

Apathy hung in the air, like smog in

summer, reminding her that there was no help for people like her and Lori. On a good day there were distractions that made them forget for a few hours. Even as her mind whirled, life seemed to move in slow motion. She had no one.

"You know how I feel about you." His voice softened to a possessive whisper, making her skin crawl. "Why do you gotta make this so tough?" Mike ran his finger down the side of her neck. "My patience is gone, Care Bear."

Where could she hide now? Somewhere she could afford that he wouldn't know about and couldn't track her to. A piece of a memory—washed in colorless fog—wavered before her like a sheet on a clothesline.

An apron. A head covering. An old woman. Rows of tall corn.

He dug his fingers into her biceps. Pain shot through her, and the disjointed thoughts disappeared. "Don't you dare leave again. I'll find you. You know I can . . . every time." His eyes reflected that familiar mixture of spitefulness and uncertainty as he willed her to do his bidding. "I call the shots. Not you. Not dear old Johnny. Me."

But maybe he didn't. A tender sprig of hope took root. If she could latch on to that memory—if it was even real—she might have a place to go. Somewhere Mike couldn't find her and she wouldn't owe anyone her life in exchange for food and shelter. Doubts rippled through her, trying to dislodge her newfound hope. It was probably a movie she'd watched. Remembering any part of her life, anything true, before her mama died seemed as impossible as getting free of Mike. She'd been only eight when her mother was killed by a hit-and-run driver as she crossed a street. Things became so hard after that, anything before seemed like shadows and blurs.

As she begged for answers, faint scenes appeared before her. A kitchen table spread with fresh food. A warm breeze streaming through an unfamiliar window. Sheets flapping on a clothesline. Muffled laughter as a boy jumped into a creek.

Was it just a daydream? Or was it somewhere she'd once been, a place she couldn't reach because she couldn't remember?

Her heart raced. She had to find the answer.

Mike pulled the phone from her hand, a sneer overriding the insecurity he tried hard to cover. "You're more afraid of one thing than anything else. And I know what that is." He eased the receiver into its cradle and flipped the diary open. "If you don't want nothing to cause the social workers to take her . . ." He tapped his huge finger on a photo of Lori. "Think about it, Care Bear. And I'll see you at your place when your shift is over." He strode out the door.

Cara slumped against the counter. No matter how hard she tried, she landed in the same place over and over again—in the clutches of a crazy man.

In spite of the absurdity of it, she longed for a cigarette. It would help her think and calm her nerves.

Clasped in her fist was the cash the two

men had given for their drinks. She rubbed it between her fingers. If she slipped out the back door, no one at Mac's would have a clue where she went. She could pick up Lori and disappear.

# Two

Ephraim and Anna Mary gently swayed back and forth in his yard. Chains ran from the large oak tree overhead and attached to the porch swing. The metal chain felt cool inside his palm, and the new spring leaves rustled overhead. He held out his free hand to Anna Mary. Without a word she smiled and slid her soft hand into his.

This small sanctuary where they sat was surrounded by tall hedges on three sides. The fourth side was open and had a view of a pasture, livestock, and a large pond. The hiddy—as he called it—afforded privacy that was hard to come by on Mast property. Ephraim had created the concealed area when he returned to the farm nine years ago, appreciating that his family wouldn't enter unless invited.

Storm clouds moved across the night sky, threatening to block his view of the stars and the clear definition of the crescent moon. Even without his telescope, he could pick out the Sea of Crisis and to its left the Sea of Fertility.

Anna Mary squeezed his hand. "What are you thinking about?"

"The gathering thunderhead." He gestured toward the southwest. "See it? In a few minutes it'll ruin my stargazing, but the spring showers will be just what the corn seed needs."

She angled her head, watching him. "I don't understand what you see night after night of looking at the same sky."

During the few evenings she joined him out here, she paid little attention to the awesome display spread out across the heavens. Her interest in an evening like this was to try to get inside his head. She wasn't one to say plain out what she thought or wanted, but she prodded him to talk. It tended to grate on his nerves, but he understood.

"Vastness. Expanse beyond the darkness. Each star is a sun, and its light shines like day where it is. I see our God, who has more to Him than we can begin to understand."

She squeezed his hand. "You know what I see? A man who is growing restless with the life he's chosen."

Inside the Amish ways that had called him home years ago, he'd found peace. But at twenty-four she wanted promises. He'd been four years younger than she was now when he began moving about the country, free of all Amish restraints. But when he was twenty-three, his stepmother had called, telling him his **Daed** was ill and the family needed him.

He had to come home. His Daed had caught a virus that moved into his heart and severely damaged it. Ephraim needed to take over his father's cabinetry business and provide for his Daed, pregnant stepmother, and a houseful of younger siblings.

It didn't matter that part of the reason he had left was because he disagreed with his father remarrying so soon after his mother died. And here he was, nine years later, still not quite fitting into the role forced upon him.

The sound of a horse and buggy pulling onto the gravel driveway caused him to stand and head that way. Anna Mary followed closely behind. As they crossed through the small opening of hedges, he saw his sister and Mahlon pulling the rig to a stop.

Deborah held up a plate covered in aluminum foil. "Birthday cake." She showed him a knife, clearly hopeful of celebrating this long-awaited day. Mahlon stepped out of the carriage and helped Deborah down.

Ephraim had known today was on its way, but it was hard to believe the time had come to give her what she wanted.

Two years ago, at nineteen, she'd come to him, wanting to talk about marrying Mahlon. Since it wasn't Amish tradition for a girl to ask for her father's blessing, let alone a brother's, it'd surprised him. But he'd found himself unwilling to lie to her and yet unable to tell her his concerns, so he had simply told her she needed to wait. Then he'd grabbed his coat and headed for the door . . . and away from Deborah's mounting frustrations.

But she'd followed him. "Ephraim, we aren't finished talking about this."

He'd slid into his jacket. "Actually, I think we are."

The disappointment in her face had been hard for him to ignore.

"Until when?" she'd asked.

Convinced a couple of years would be enough, he'd said, "When you turn twenty-one."

If she'd decided to ignore him on the matter, he couldn't have stopped her. But she'd thought his only reason for telling her to wait was that the family needed her, so she'd done as he'd wanted without question. Today she turned twenty-one, and she'd just spent most of the day celebrating her good fortune with Mahlon and his mother, Ada. Sometimes Ephraim wasn't sure who Deborah loved the most—Mahlon or Ada.

But his sister stood in front of him now, hoping he'd say she was free to marry during the next wedding season. He glanced to Anna Mary, who waited quietly. Her eyes radiated trust in him and hope for Deborah and Mahlon.

Ephraim had two sisters between his and Deborah's age, but they'd married a few years back and moved to Amish communities in other states. When it came to marriage, no one had interfered with their desires.

In spite of his remaining reservations, Ephraim motioned. "**Kumm** then, and I'll light a fire and brew us some coffee. Then we'll talk."

Deborah passed the cake to Mahlon and mumbled something about the dessert that made Anna Mary laugh softly.

A horn tooted, causing all of them to pause. A car pulled into the driveway behind Mahlon's carriage, and Robbie rolled down the window. "Hey, I took my truck in like we talked about, but the mechanic has to keep it for a few days. Do I need to rent one to drive you to a job tomorrow?"

Ephraim shook his head. "No. Mahlon and I'll load a wagon and hitch horses to it. We're putting in cabinets at the Wyatt place about three miles from here. I have work lined up at the shop for you and Grey."

"Ah, you must've known."

"**Ya.** When you mentioned the mechanic, I rearranged the schedule. It seems every time you get work done to make your truck run better, it doesn't run at all for a while. If it's not ready by Tuesday afternoon, we'll have to rent one. We've got a job in Carlisle on Wednesday. You know, I never have mechanical problems like this when I take my horse in to the smithy."

A toothy grin covered Robbie's face. "The truck should be ready before then. I gave the mechanic the shop's phone number and told him to call us as soon as it's ready." Robbie motioned toward Mahlon. "So you'll go with the big boss, and I'm working with the foreman. They don't intend for us to have any horsing-around time, do they?"

"They never do," Mahlon scoffed.

Robbie laughed and started backing out of the driveway. "I'll see you guys in the morning."

"Sure thing." Ephraim turned his attention back to the group. "Anyone besides me ready for some cake?"

Deborah smoothed the folds of her apron. "Well . . . I'm more interested in talking to you about what we came here for."

Ephraim nodded. Mahlon had set his cabinetry work aside and left the shop hours earlier than usual today. Unfortunately, it seemed that Mahlon found it too easy to leave work behind and go do whatever pleased him on any given day, regardless of how much Ephraim needed him. But his sister's love for Mahlon never wavered, and it was time Ephraim trusted her instinct.

Mahlon looked a bit unsure of himself. "She's twenty-one today."

"So she is." Ephraim shook his hand, silently assuring him he'd ask for no further delays. "Then it's time plans were made."

Deborah threw her arms around Ephraim's neck. **"Denki."**

Her thank-you was unnecessary, but he returned the hug. **"Gern gschehne."**

She released him and hugged Anna Mary, both of them smiling and whispering excitedly.

"Ephraim?" His stepmother's voice called to him.

He looked back toward his Daed's house and saw Becca crossing the field that separated their home from his. Between business and family, some days he didn't get a break. But he'd put boundaries around parts of his life, and that helped. Of his family members, only Deborah was allowed to enter his home at will, because she tended to ask for very little and always did something helpful—like cook supper or wash dishes.

"Is Simeon with you?" Becca hollered.

"I haven't seen him since before suppertime." But he knew he wasn't far. His brother had a secret—an innocent kind that eight-year-old boys liked to keep.

She continued toward them, and they moved to meet her halfway.

"He's been missing since then." Her hands shook with nervousness as she wiped them on her apron. "This is the third time in two weeks he's disappeared like this. You have to put a stop to this, Ephraim, before he lands your father in the hospital again. He just doesn't seem to understand how frail his Daed is."

"Does Daed know he's missing?"

Becca shook her head. "Not yet. I hope to keep it from him. And when Simeon gets home, I'm tempted to send him to bed without supper."

"Don't say anything to Daed. Simeon's not far. When I find him, I'll see to it he doesn't do this again."

"Denki." Without another word she left.

Mahlon looked across the property. "You want help, Ephraim?"

"No sense in that. Just stay here and help Deborah get a fire going in the cookstove and a pot of coffee on to percolate." He looked to Anna Mary. "I'll be back shortly."

"If you don't take too long, we'll save you some cake." Anna Mary cocked an eyebrow, mocking a threat. He suppressed a smile and mirrored her raised eyebrow.

He started to leave when he thought of something. He pulled a large handkerchief from his pocket. "Can I take a piece of that with me?"

"Does this mean you're planning on being gone too long?" Anna Mary removed the aluminum foil.

His eyes met hers, and he chuckled.

Deborah cut a slice of cake and laid it in the handkerchief. "Here you go."

"Denki."

Mahlon chuckled. "You gonna bribe the boy to come home?"

"Something like that." Ephraim slid the squishy stuff into his baggy pocket. "Be back soon." He strode off toward the back fields.

He walked between the rows of freshly planted corn and onto what he still referred to as Levina's land. Although she'd not been related to his family, Levina had always been like a grandmother to him. When she passed away, he bought the old place, mostly because it connected to the property where he'd built his home.

Under the gentle winds of the night, thoughts of his life before his father's illness nagged at him. When he'd been called to come home, it gave him a reason to leave a world that offered as many different types of imprisonment as it did freedoms. But what bothered him was that each year since he'd returned, his family seemed to need him more, not less.

When he walked down Levina's old driveway, his attention lingered on the conjoined trees that stood nearby—full of majesty and recollections. Habit dictated that he run his hand across the bark as he passed by. Just one touch caused a dozen memories.

Flickers of dim light shone through the slits in the abandoned barn, and he was confident he'd found his brother—half brother, actually. After he crossed the road, he pushed against the barn door, causing it to creak as he opened it.

With a lap full of puppies, Simeon glanced up. "Ephraim, look. I've been working with 'em today, and I've spotted a really good one for ya."

"And I spotted a **Mamm** who's ready to send you to bed without your supper. It's after dark, Sim. What are ya thinking? If she finds out what's causing you to run off, she'll haul these dogs out of here. And the pound is just as likely to kill them as find them a home."

"The mama dog is missing." Simeon picked up the smallest puppy and hugged it. "I saw somebody outside the barn while I was walking this way. He took off when he spotted me. You think he stole the mama?"

"Makes no sense to take an old mama dog and leave the pups." Ephraim placed the puppy in the haystack where Simeon had made a little bed for the mutts. "Look, don't pull another stunt like this—staying out past dark and making your Mamm worry—or I'll put these pups in the auction myself. Got it?" Even though he was twenty-four years older than Simeon, he hated it when he had to sound like a parent. He should be a brother and a friend, but his role was more than just a provider.

Simeon's eyes filled with tears, and he nodded.

Ephraim picked up the lantern. "Now, let's go."

His brother's shoulders drooped as they left the barn. Without another word Simeon headed for the edge of the road to cross it. Ephraim went toward the back pasture.

"Ephraim?"

He paused. "Well, come on. We can't find the mama dog going that way. I just came from there."

Simeon wiped his eyes with the back of his hands.

Ephraim pulled the handkerchief out of his pocket. "I brought cake. If we get anywhere near her, I'll bet she'll get a whiff of this and come running."

# Three

The noise and busyness of the Port Authority Bus Terminal raked a feeling of déjà vu over Cara. She'd been in the building plenty of times before, but this time she sensed . . . something odd.

With her diary clutched in one arm and her other hand holding her daughter's hand, she walked past shops, restaurants, and ticket counters. The strange feeling grew stronger as she stepped on the escalator and began the descent to the subway level.

Suddenly it was her father holding her hand, not Lori. Memories unrolled inside her. A set of escalators taking her and her dad deeper into the belly of the city. A brown paper bag, the top of it scrunched like a rope inside her hand. They kept going and going—hundreds, maybe thousands, of people all around her not caring one bit that her mom had died last week. Her father went into a café and set her on a chair. **"Dry your tears, Cara. You'll be fine. I promise."**

He pulled the map out of his jacket pocket, the one he had drawn for her the night before and had gotten her to help him color. He spread it out on the table. **"See, this is right where you are, New York City's bus station. A woman is coming for you. Her name is Emma Riehl. The bus will take you and her southwest. You'll probably change buses in Harrisburg and keep heading west for another hour or so. Right here."** His huge finger tapped the paper.

She must have said something odd because he gaped at her, and then he ordered a drink. He drank until his words slurred, then he walked her to a bench and demanded she stay put, promising Emma was coming.

And he left.

The terror of watching him walk away faded as the hours passed. Afraid Emma might show up and leave without her if she didn't stay put, she left the spot where her father had set her only long enough to go to the bathroom when she absolutely had to.

Later she fell asleep, and a man in a uniform woke her. He had a woman beside him, and she hoped it was Emma. But it wasn't, and they took her to a place where rows of metal bunk beds were half-filled with mean kids who'd never had anybody show up for them either.

Feeling Lori tug at her hand, she looked down into her innocent brown eyes.

"Are we looking for Kendal, Mom?"

She shook her head. Her days of meeting up with her friend were over. Kendal's complete abandonment earlier today had been a long time in coming. They'd been close once, starting when they'd shared the same foster-care home for a while, but over the last few years, Kendal had stolen from, lied to, and argued with her a lot. Since they were all each other had in the way of family, Cara had refused to give up. But—

Lori pointed to a picture. "Are we going somewhere on a bus?"

"Yes."

"What about Kendal?"

"It's just the two of us this time."

"But . . ."

"Shh." Cara gently placed one arm around Lori's shoulders as they continued walking. Memories of Kendal mocked her, and she felt like an idiot for trying to keep them together as long as she had. She'd always figured life with Kendal was as much like family as she'd ever have. One doesn't get to pick their family or choose who rescues them. But Kendal had done just that. At nineteen years old she'd opened the grubby door to her tiny, shabby apartment and dared to give a fifteen-year-old runaway food and shelter. The gesture had filled Cara with hope. Without her, she had little chance of making it on her own and no chance of escaping Mike's grip. But it'd been easier back then to ignore

Kendal's weaknesses—men and drugs. It'd always seemed that she and Kendal were like a lot of siblings in a real family—extreme opposites.

Her attention shifted to the diary resting on her arm. Maybe the faded words her mother had written to her more than twenty years ago had kept her from seeking men or drugs to help numb the ache inside her—maybe not. But she'd read the beautiful entries ten thousand times over the years and couldn't separate herself from the woman her mother hoped she'd become.

A middle-school teacher once said that Cara's mother's diary sparked her love of dissecting books for understanding. It probably had, and she was a good student, but then life changed, and books and schooling faded in comparison to survival knowledge. That's where Kendal came in.

As one thought strung to another, Cara realized somewhere inside her, beyond her fear and jumbled thoughts, it hurt for Kendal to give up the way she had. No last-minute message of encouragement for either her or Lori. No whisper of wanting to

37

once Cara worked free of Mike
just a final good-bye. And **after**
packed and hailed a taxi.

The numbness gave way to grief, and in some odd way that Cara couldn't understand, it seemed right to be inside this place—the building where her father had abandoned her.

"Mom," Lori elongated the word, half whining and half demanding, "I want to know where we're going."

Cara thought for a moment. They needed to get out of the city, but their traveling funds were limited. "Jersey, I think. We're fine and safe, so no worrying, okay?" The words didn't leave her mouth easily.

She had no real answers. But she knew one thing—any life she could give Lori would be immeasurably better than foster care, where she'd have to live with strangers who were paid to pretend they cared.

It seemed unfair that Cara had spent all her life trying to be good, always aiming to live in a way her dead mother would be proud of, just to fall victim to Mike's power to find her time and again. Maybe that's what had made her and Lori an easy target for him.

Regardless of whatever she needed to do—lie, cheat, or steal—no one was separating her from her daughter.

Needing a few moments to think, she moved to an empty table outside Au Bon Pain. She opened her diary and thumbed through it, looking for signs of a life she wasn't sure ever existed. The frayed leather binding and bulging pages were hints to how much she loved this book. She didn't write everyday stuff in it. This book was used mostly for sharing things between mom and daughter—first her and her mother and now her and Lori. It made her sick to think of Mike reading her mother's thoughts and hopes for her, the special things they'd done, and Cara's most treasured memories with Lori.

Standing in front of him less than an hour ago, she'd envisioned rows of tall corn, heard a boy's laughter, and remembered feeling welcomed by an old woman in a black apron and white head covering. But her treasured journal revealed none of it. Why?

Lori pulled a baggie of stale cookies from her backpack—the kind that had ingredients dogs shouldn't eat, but they were tasty enough and were always able to remove the worst of the hunger. With Mike probably watching and waiting outside her apartment—maybe inside it—she and Lori would leave New York with the clothes they were wearing, whatever that school-bag held, and the diary.

Cara flipped page after page, skimming the entries written by her mother. She'd had this book since she was younger than Lori. With one exception every available spot had been written on. Each line had two rows of writing squeezed in. The margins were filled with tiny words and drawings. Even the insides of the book's covers were written on. There were places where she'd taped and stapled clean paper onto existing pages before filling them with words too. Only one spot, about three inches high and four inches long, remained blank.

Her mother's instructions written above that space told her never to write in that spot but to remember. A sadness she'd grown to hate moved into her chest as she read her mother's words.

**Don't write inside the area I've marked. When the time is right, my beloved one, I'll fill in the blank.**

**Beloved one.** The phrase twisted her insides as it'd done for what seemed like forever. Had her mother ever loved her like it sounded?

Obviously her mother couldn't fulfill her plan, and Cara had no recollection of what she might have been talking about. According to the date on the entry, her mother wrote those words when Cara was five. She raised her head and skimmed her index finger over the spot.

Demanding the emotional nonsense to cease, she buried her head in her hands, trying to gain control of her feelings.

Lori smacked her palm on the blank spot of the diary. "What's that?"

Cara brushed off the specks of cookie that'd fallen from her daughter's hand onto the page. "An empty place my mother said not to write in."

"Why?"

Cara shrugged. "I don't know."

"Can I sign my name there?"

She hesitated for a moment before sliding the book toward Lori. "Sure, why not?"

Lori dug into her book bag and came up with a pencil. She began trying to write in cursive. At seven, Lori's marks were more swirls than real letters. Cara eyed the few leftover cookies, but she refused to eat one. Money was limited, and Lori might need those before Cara found another job.

The good thing about waitressing was it came with immediate money. She'd have to wait for her paycheck, but she'd make tips the very day she started. Time and again the need for immediate food money after they moved kept her waitressing—that and the fact that being a tenth-grade dropout didn't qualify her for much. But she was capable of more. She knew that. Her school years had proved it. Got great grades, skipped the third grade, and always landed at the top of her classes. But she'd probably never get a chance to prove she wasn't who others thought—a poor quitter with no potential.

"Mom, look!"

Cara glanced while closing the baggie of cookies. Her daughter had given up on cursive and made a thick, double-edged L. Then she'd filled the middle part with light sketching. "Very pretty, Lori."

"No, Mom, look."

She moved the book closer, seeing that letters had shown up under the shading.

"Oh, that's from words written on the opposite page." She slid the book to Lori.

**The time is long past, my beloved . . .** Like a whisper, her mother's voice floated into her mind from nowhere.

"Wait, Lori. Stop writing." Cara pulled the book in front of her. Through the light gray coloring of pencil, she saw part of a word. "Let me see your pencil for a minute."

"No." Lori jerked the book away from her. "It's my spot. You said so."

Cara resisted the desire to overreact. "Okay. You're right. I gave it to you." She placed the cookies into the backpack and zipped it up. "If you look at the date on that entry, you can see that I was a couple of years younger than you are now when your grandma wrote that." She pointed to the words her mother had written above the blank space. "Maybe it's nothing. Or maybe your grandma hid a secret in the diary. But . . . if you'd rather write your name . . ."

Lori pulled the book closer, inspecting the blank space. "You think she wanted to tell me something?"

"No, kiddo. How could she? She didn't know you. But we should still figure out what she wrote."

Lori's brows furrowed. "Let's do it together."

Cara nodded. "Good idea. We need to run the pencil over the whole area very, very lightly, or we might scratch out the message rather than make it visible."

Lori passed her the pencil. "I already went first. It's your turn."

Relieved, Cara took the pencil and

began lightly rubbing the lead over the page. Words that had been there since before her mother died suddenly appeared on the page. It looked like an address. The street numbers were hidden under the heavy-handedness of her daughter's artwork, but the road, town, and state were clear.

Mast Road, Dry Lake, Pennsylvania

"What's it say, Mom?"

Hope trickled in, and tears stung her eyes. Lori had no one but her, a single mom who'd been an orphan. She had no support system. She wanted . . . no, she ached to give Lori some sort of life connections, a relative or friend of Cara's mother, something that spoke of the things life was supposed to be made of—worthy relationships. Maybe this was the answer. It had to be better than Jersey. "It says where we're going."

"Where's that?"

Cara closed the book. "As close to Dry Lake, Pennsylvania, as a bus route goes." She put the backpack over one shoulder

and held her hand out for Lori. "You discovered a secret I didn't know was there.
Come on. We've got bus tickets to buy."

In a blur of confusion and fears, Cara
bought tickets to Shippensburg, Pennsylvania. The man at the ticket counter said
they were heading for the heart of Amish
country. When she shrugged, he told her
they were easy to spot—wore clothing that
looked like something from the eighteen
hundreds and traveled by horse and buggy.

With the tickets in hand, they boarded
one bus, rode for hours, had a long delay at
another station, and then boarded another
bus. Now it was night again. Between pur-
chasing bus tickets and food, she had little
money left. The uncertainty scared her,
and it stole all sense of victory for getting
free of Mike and discovering the long-held
secret in her diary.

While Lori slept, Cara studied each
passing town, hoping something would
look familiar.

Hours of light mist turned into pelting
rain, making it difficult to see the land-

marks. Her eyelids ached with heaviness. She blinked hard and sat up straighter, concentrating on each thing they passed.

Spattering drops smacked the window endlessly. She wiped the fog from the glass, studying the water-colored world. As the bus pulled into a Kmart parking lot, the bus driver said, "Shippensburg. Shippensburg, Pennsylvania."

A peculiar feeling crawled over her. An elderly woman stood and made her way to the front of the bus.

The idea of waking Lori from a safe, dry sleep to enter a rainy, unknown world was ridiculous. She had a few dollars left. Maybe she could pay to ride farther.

"Shippensburg?" The driver looked in the rearview mirror, giving each passenger a chance to get off.

She clutched the armrests, assuring herself any good mother would stay put. When the doors to the bus began to close, Cara jumped to her feet, signaling her intention to get off here.

She stuffed her diary into Lori's backpack and lifted her sleeping child into her arms. She stopped next to the bus driver. "Any idea how to get to Dry Lake?"

"Follow this road for a few blocks." He pointed in front of the bus. "When you get to Earl Street, go right. It'll be about six miles."

"Thanks."

"There's a nice motel straight ahead, Shippen Place Hotel. Only hotel I know of near here."

"Thanks." Cold rain stung her face as she stepped off the bus. Since she didn't have enough money for a fancy hotel, she'd have to find somewhere free to stay for the night.

Lori lifted her head off Cara's shoulder, instantly whining. "No, Mom. I want to go home."

"Shh." Cara eased Lori's head against her shoulder and placed the backpack against her little girl's cheek, trying to shield her from the rain. "Listen, kid, you've got to trust me. Remember?"

Lori wrapped her little hands around

the back of Cara's neck, whimpering. Within seconds her daughter fell asleep again, deaf to the sound of the rain beating a pattern against her backpack like a tapping on a door.

# Four

Through the window behind the kitchen sink, Deborah watched as broad streaks of sunlight broke through the remaining thick clouds. She continued slicing large hunks of stew meat into bite-size pieces—all the while her mind on Mahlon.

Since her birthday the day before yesterday, she and Mahlon had made the rounds throughout the district, telling their family and friends about their plans to marry in the fall. She didn't think she'd ever had so much fun as they'd had Thursday night, popping into homes to share good news. Nothing would be announced officially until October when the bishop "published" all the couples who were to be married. He'd make a declaration of everyone who would marry that wedding season, but they had to make plans long before then. And she'd ordered an engagement present for Mahlon—one she'd spent a year saving for. She'd give it to him just as soon as her order arrived at the dry goods store.

Her heart raced with anticipation of the coming months. She tossed the freshly cut stew meat into a skillet to brown before she began washing the breakfast dishes. The desire to get done with her morning chores and go to Mahlon's pushed her to hurry. Beds were made, laundry washed and hung out to dry, and she and Becca had cooked breakfast for the family. The items left on her to-do list grew smaller by the hour. Mahlon had taken off work until after lunchtime today so they could start on their plans, and she didn't want to waste a minute of it.

Becca walked into the kitchen, carrying a twin on each hip. Her round, rosy cheeks gave her an appearance of sturdy health. As her brown hair gave way to more and more gray and she picked up a few extra pounds with each pregnancy, she no longer looked like the much-younger second wife of twelve years ago. She looked like and felt like a mom to a large, ever-growing family.

"How many houses do you and Mahlon have lined up to look at today?" Becca placed Sadie and Sally behind the safety gate of their playroom before moving to the stove.

"There are only two inside Dry Lake. Maybe three, because there's one that belongs to **Englischers** that might fall inside our district lines."

She lifted the lid off the meat and stirred it with a spatula. "Ya? Where's that one?"

"About half a mile from Mahlon's place."

"On the right or left?"

"Left. Their last name is Everson."

She shrugged. "That might be Yoder's district. If it is, they have their church Sundays on our between Sundays. It'll make finding time to visit with your family harder. Your Daed won't like that."

"Ya, I know. Mahlon's determined to find a place in Dry Lake, but he said we may have to settle for something in Yoder's district."

"Do you like that home more than the others?"

Deborah dried her hands. "It doesn't matter to me where we live." She went to the refrigerator and pulled out carrots, onions, and potatoes. "I'd be perfectly content to move into the home where he and Ada live now."

"It's small, but it seems like that'd be a great place to start out." Becca turned the eye to the stove to low, poured a quart of water over the meat, and replaced the lid on the skillet.

Deborah rinsed the carrots and potatoes before placing them on the chopping block. "Ya, but Mahlon says the landlord wants his daughter to live there. He has for nearly a year."

"Oh, that's right. I remember now. They rent their place. It was a shame the way Ada had to sell their house after Mahlon's Daed died." Becca grabbed a dry dishtowel and began emptying the dish drainer. "The community wanted to keep that from happening, but too many of us were dealing with our own losses. Besides, Ada was determined not to burden anyone."

While peeling potatoes, Deborah felt old grief wash over her. It didn't hurt like it used to, but it always stung. Thirteen years ago she lost her mother in the same accident in which Mahlon lost his father. Becca's husband died too and six others from their community. All in one fatal van accident. The Amish of Dry Lake had hired three Englischer drivers to take them to a wedding in Ohio. They were caravaning when one of the vehicles crashed. No one made it to the wedding. At the time there had been thirty families in their district, and nine of them lost a loved one. It'd taken Deborah years to push past feeling that they were cursed.

Becca placed the last plate in the cabinet. "So, will Ada live with you and Mahlon?"

"Ya. It's not Mahlon's favorite plan, but he can't afford two places, one for us and one for her. I don't know why the idea bothers him. Ada will be nothing but a blessing all her days."

"Which will be a lot of days, because she's young. What, forty-three?"

Deborah nodded.

Becca laid the dishtowel on her shoulder. "It seems odd to me that she's never remarried, but as long as you don't mind sharing a home with her, there will be peace in the house."

"The hardest part of living with Ada will be that both of us love to cook. I'm hoping one of the places has a huge kitchen. And then we can both have a workspace, and we could have some cookoffs, and may the youngest cook win."

Becca giggled. "Ada better watch out. It seems to me she's spent years teaching all her best cooking secrets to an ambitious young woman."

For the first time in quite a while, Deborah recalled her one-time dream of owning an Amish restaurant. But they lived too far away from the flow of tourists for it to be practical. Although Hope Crossing had a more touristy Amish community, her family always needed her to live at home to help out. Besides, she'd been in love with Mahlon since she was ten, and she couldn't imagine living elsewhere. But his mother gave her a way to do the next best thing— bake desserts for profit. Ada had taught her how to make all sorts of sweets, and together they made baked goods for a bakery that sent a driver to fetch the items three days a week.

"Anytime you need a kitchen to bake in, you're more than welcome to come here." One side of Becca's mouth curved into a smile. "Of course, what's cooked here stays here."

Deborah chuckled. "But not for long . . . before it's eaten."

Becca laughed. "Go fetch your horse. Maybe Ephraim will leave the shop long enough to help you hitch it to the carriage."

"You sure?"

One of the twins started wailing as if she'd pinched a finger or the other one had taken a toy.

Becca glanced into the room before she wagged her finger at Deborah. "You better go while the going is good. Your sister Annie has a good bit to learn to be the kind of help you are, but at fourteen and with you marrying this fall, it's time she gets more practice, no?"

Deborah nodded. "Mahlon said if the grounds aren't too wet today, we'll lay plow to the garden again late this afternoon when he and Ephraim get back from a job."

"He's right. What we've planted isn't enough to help provide food for a wedding feast come fall. So while you're out, go by the dry goods store and pick up more seeds, especially packages of celery and carrots. And buy the crates so we can get seedlings started first. We'll need a lot more veggies than usual come fall."

Deborah's cheeks ached from smiling. "This is simply too exciting."

Becca's eyes filled with tears. "Ya, it is. I can't even begin to tell you how excited I am for you. You'll be missed something fierce, but your Daed and I are really happy for you. I'm surprised you've waited this long."

Deborah wouldn't tell her that Ephraim had quietly but firmly said they had to wait. At the time, Becca and Daed had six children under the age of thirteen, and the twins were just a couple of months old. With Daed's health issues, he wasn't much help.

But Annie would graduate in just a few weeks, so she'd be able to help Becca full-time.

With exhilaration pulsing through her, she headed for the pasture to chase down her horse. Mahlon would be surprised when she arrived more than an hour ahead of schedule.

Before she got to the cattle gate, a wagonload of her girlfriends called to her as they pulled into her driveway: Rachel, Linda, Nancy, Lydia, Frieda, Esther. And Lena. They were talking and laughing softly among themselves while waving to her. Lena's smile was enough on its own to stir happiness. But her cousin never left anything at just a grin. She loved laughing and making people laugh. The birthmark across her cheek never dampened her spirits, and Deborah thought she was the most beautiful of any of them, but at twenty-three Lena had never had a man ask to take her home from a singing.

Lena brought the rig to a stop. "We came to help you get your chores done."

"Ya," Nancy said. "That way there's no chance of you having to cancel looking at houses with Mahlon."

"Becca said I'm through for today."

Raised eyebrows soon gave way to broad smiles.

"Then come on." Lena motioned. "We'll take a spin around the block . . . and play a trick on Anna Mary before we drop you off at Mahlon's."

When Deborah climbed into the wagon, Lydia patted a store-bought sack of pebbles. "We've got a good plan. And Lena just happens to have some inside information, like the fact that Anna Mary hasn't had time to repot her indoor plants, but she's purchased a bag of soil."

The girls began reminiscing about

past pranks they'd pulled on each other. When they arrived near Anna Mary's, Lena brought the rig to a stop. Two girls stayed with the wagon while the rest of them snuck past the house and to the shed. They took Anna Mary's bag of potting soil and replaced it with the sack of rocks. Soon they were on their way to Mahlon's, everyone guessing how long it would be before Anna Mary discovered the switch.

Deborah sat up front with Lena. "If she thinks she bought the wrong stuff, Lena and I should try to go with her to return it. Then one of us can pull another switch while she's loading other things."

The girls broke into fresh laughter.

"And yet you look so innocent," Lena quipped.

Deborah pushed the tie to her prayer **Kapp** behind her shoulder. "Not just me, dear cousin. You do too. It's how we get away with such antics, ya?"

As Lena turned onto the road that led to Mahlon's home, Deborah spotted a car coming from the opposite direction. She thought little of it until it pulled onto the side of the road twenty yards from Mahlon's place. A car door opened, and an Amish man got out. It wasn't until the man closed the car door and walked around to the driver's side that she recognized Mahlon. Even at this distance she could tell who it was by the way he carried himself—his slow, easy pace. With all the silly banter and laughter in the wagon, not one of her friends seemed to notice the vehicle or Mahlon. He stood outside the driver's window talking to whoever was inside. Then he stepped away, waved, and started walking through the field toward his home.

Like watching children performing a play at school, memories of their friendship ran through her mind—years of shared lunches, games at recess, and walks to and from school together. It all began when she'd been in fourth grade and he in sixth.

They'd borne each other's grief since the day they'd both lost a parent. They had learned to accept their loss together, learned to laugh afresh, and figured out how to trust in life again. Together they'd weathered change after change as they'd gone through their teen years. He'd been in New York City on September 11, 2001, and she'd been the one he shared his trauma with, his confusion and sense of helplessness, his hidden desire for revenge, and his recurring nightmares.

Quiet.

Deep.

And . . . secretive?

The car he'd gotten out of passed the wagon, revealing a man about Mahlon's age, wearing a military uniform of some type. When she looked to where she'd last seen Mahlon, he was nowhere in sight. As Rachel pulled into his driveway, Deborah realized he'd probably gone up the wooden steps that ran along the outside of his home and led straight to his bedroom—the private entrance she thought he never used.

She climbed down, waved to her friends, and headed for the front door.

What was going on? His quietness worked against them sometimes. It wasn't always easy to know his thoughts. But through the years she'd carried his secrets.

Few others, if any, knew that the weight of becoming the provider for himself and his mother before he graduated at thirteen had silently panicked him or that after 9/11 he'd struggled to accept the Old Ways.

She tapped on the screen door and then went inside.

Ada placed the flatiron on the stove, stepped around the ironing board, and hugged her. "**Gut** morning."

"Gut morning, Ada. Where's Mahlon?"

"Still asleep. I don't know when the last time was that he needed me to wake him, so I refuse to start now. Besides, with all the work to set up for the auction tomorrow and all he hopes to get done today, I figure he needs every minute of rest he can squeeze in."

Hoping her face didn't reveal how much was going through her mind, Deborah drew a shaky breath. "Do you mind if I go up and wake him?"

"Not a bit."

As she began climbing the narrow steps, she heard water start running overhead. His home consisted of a small kitchen and sitting area downstairs and two small bed-rooms and a bath upstairs. A hint of steam escaped under the bathroom door.

She tapped on the door. "Mahlon?"

"Hey, Deb. I'm in the shower. You're here early. I'll be out in a few."

He didn't sound any different. She heard no hint of guilt.

"Okay." Rather than go downstairs, she went into his room. It looked like a single man's room and not much different from the last time she'd seen it, when he was a teen. Clean clothes were stacked on his dresser, dirty ones piled in a corner. Parts of a newspaper lay beside his chair—each folded in a way that let her know which sections he'd read and which he'd chosen to ignore. A wad of cash on his nightstand caught her eye, and she went to it.

He came into the room, buttoning his shirt. His face and what she could see of his chest were still wet, reminding her of the boy he'd once been. "You're just full of sur-prises today. First you're here early, and then you're in my room." The smile on his face didn't hide the circles under his eyes. He pulled his suspenders over his shoulders and tucked his shirt into his pants. "Something wrong?"

Weighing her emotions against what she knew of him, she refused to sound stressed or harsh. "I'm not sure."

"Well, tell me, and if there is, I'll see what I can do to fix it." His eyes radiated something she couldn't define, but she knew that tone in his voice. The one that hinted of forced patience, usually when life doled out responsibilities he resented.

"You don't have to fix anything. I'm not part of what you consider your lot in life." When he didn't smile or chuckle or assure her she was the best part of his life, she felt suddenly unsure. "Am I?"

He shook his head. "You know better than that. I'm hungry. Are you?"

Hurt that he'd evaded the question, she tried to catch his eye but couldn't. She'd seen him dodge questions from his mother a hundred times, but she'd always thought he confided everything in her.

She went to the nightstand and pointed at the money. "Are you working a second job?"

"No. I wouldn't have time even if I had the desire. Your brother has me logging too much overtime. I'd wanted us to have all day together, but I could only get off until after lunch."

Without saying a word about the money, he turned his back to her and went to his dresser.

"If you're just working one job, then where were you coming from when I saw you get out of that man's car?"

He kept his back to her for several moments. "Oh, is that what this is about?" After pulling a pair of socks out of a drawer, he sat on his bed with his back still to her. "Eric Shriver is home on leave, so we spent some time together. That's all."

"I didn't realize he was back in the States." Nor did she know that Mahlon still considered Eric a friend to spend time with. They'd become friends about six years ago when he and Ephraim installed a set of kitchen cabinets for Eric's parents.

But Mahlon had chosen to lay that friendship aside when he joined the faith. Or had he? Was he friends with a soldier?

After he put on his shoes, he stood. "He came home last week. So, you looking forward to house hunting this morning?"

Realizing he didn't want to talk about his time with Eric, she chose not to push, but the hurt from earlier spread through her.

He studied her before moving in closer. "It was nothing, Deb. He came up here last night and wanted to talk, so I went with him."

"You've been out all night . . . just talking?"

"Hey, you two," Ada called. "The Realtor just pulled up."

"Be down in a minute." He placed his hands on her shoulders. "Is my Deb showing a bit of insecurity? Because if she is, I want to ignore our beliefs, get a camera, and take a photo during this rare event."

She rolled her eyes. "I don't doubt your love or faithfulness—only your good sense, which has been in question on occasion."

He brushed his lips against her cheek. "I have you, which means my good sense is amazing."

"Well . . . now, that's true."

Laughing, he released her. "You've never been short on friends, so you can't really understand how Eric feels. But I've never made friends easily either, so the two of us are a little alike. Should I cut him out simply because while he's been serving in Iraq, I joined a church that believes in nonresistance?" He grabbed a comb off his dresser and ran it through his brown hair, yanking at the curls with annoyance.

In his first few years of knowing Eric, she wondered at times if Mahlon would join the faith. Sometimes their bond seemed to defy more than the religious and political boundaries that separated them. It ignored reason. But she knew if she pushed Mahlon on the topic, he'd grow quieter than quiet. And that didn't help either of them.

She moved in front of him. "If I don't have you, I'll always be short on friends. So I guess I can understand how Eric feels.

But it seems odd for two people who look at life so differently to want to spend time together."

"In certain areas it surprises me how much we see things alike. Besides, isn't being different part of friendship? I certainly don't feel like you do about cooking or kitchens or new dresses."

Choosing to trust his judgment, she put her arms around his waist. "But I think you'd look so good in one of my newly sewn dresses."

He dropped the comb and pulled her close. "You could get away with about any insult as you stand in my bedroom wrapped in my arms . . ." He bent and kissed her. "But we'd better go." He took her by the hand and led her down the steps.

Five

Doubting herself, Cara kept walking, searching for Mast Road, hoping something would look familiar. It'd be dark again soon, and they were no better off now than when they left New York more than forty hours ago. Time seemed lost inside a fog of stress and lack of food and sleep, but the days were clearly marked in her mind. She'd left the city Wednesday around midnight, got off the second bus late on Thursday, and currently the Friday afternoon sun was beginning to dip behind the treetops.

Last night's rain had soaked her clothing, and now the insides of her thighs were raw. Her legs were so weak she kept tripping. She longed for a hot bath and a bed.

But it didn't look like that would happen anytime soon.

Her thin, snug-around-the-waist sweater-shirt was still damp against her skin, but she'd managed to buy a couple of items that her daughter could change in to. After getting off the bus, she'd carried Lori for nearly a mile before spotting a run-down gas station that sold liquor and groceries and even had a rack with overpriced T-shirts, sweatshirts, and hoodies.

The place didn't have the feel of country life, as she'd imagined. It had a roughness about it that felt very familiar, one that matched New York City. A group of six men, all drunk, based on the number of beer cans and whiskey bottles strewn around them, sat on a porch across the road from the store, playing beat-up guitars and watching her every move.

As she stepped into the store, the bell on the door jingled loudly and woke Lori. She wriggled to get down. When Cara released her, Lori scowled, stomping her feet. "I'm all wet! How'd I get all wet?" Her shrieks pierced the air as she threw herself onto the floor—hunger and exhaustion controlling her.

The man behind the register looked from Lori to Cara, disgust written on his face. He appeared ready to throw them out. When Cara left the store with a small-adult hoodie and socks for Lori, along with bagels, milk, and toiletries, the men across the street had whistled, howled, and made rude comments. Thankfully not one of them budged from their spot on the porch. They were probably too smashed to stand up, which was good, because their mannerisms didn't suggest good-natured catcalls. They were capable of malice. She saw the truth carved in their features, and she wasted no time getting herself and Lori out of sight. About a mile down the road, she found an old shed, and they stayed there last night.

After a day of walking through Dry Lake, Lori's feet had blisters. Cara didn't know anything to do but take off her shoes and let her walk in her socks.

Feeling lost and overwhelmed, Cara studied her surroundings. This was just like her—doing something with absolute hope, only to find that reality trumped it every single time. Like the blood flowing through her veins, anger circled round and round her insides. If having to uproot and travel like this wasn't enough to make her lash out, the nicotine withdrawal made her a hundred times more irritable. But so far she'd kept her grumpiness tucked deep inside.

The craving for a cigarette tormented her. Her addiction to smokes had started at fifteen, and unlike the rest of life, it came easy. The fact that she rarely paid to indulge in the habit had made getting hooked even easier. At work some of her regulars offered her a cigarette as she waited their tables. She'd slide it into her waitress pouch for later use. Almost nightly other customers left a half-empty pack by accident or as a tip. If she had four to five bucks to spend on a pack right now, she would. Of course the money for the cigarettes was only one of the issues. The other? Lori was with her, and she didn't know her mother smoked. When Lori was young and asked about the smoky smell clinging to her mom, Cara had shrugged it off as the fault of waitressing in a place that allowed smoking. Her daughter hadn't asked about the smell in years.

"My feet still hurt," Lori whined. "And look, I got blood on my socks."

"It's from the blisters. Do you need me to carry you?"

She shook her head. "But the pebbles on the road are hurting me, Mom."

"I know, sweetie. I'll figure something out soon."

Lori held her hand and fell into silence again as they kept walking. At the bottom of the hill, another road intersected with this one. Should she go down it in search of Mast Road or keep going straight?

She didn't know. Whenever she spotted someone or passed a home, she didn't dare stop to ask. People would think nothing of a mother and child going for a walk on a beautiful spring day in mid-May. But their curiosity would turn against her once she asked where a certain road was. It'd begin a peppering of questions. Are you lost? Who are you looking for? Did your car break down? Where do you live? What are you doing on foot?

No, she couldn't ask.

Lori tugged at her hand. "That road starts with an M, Mom."

"Does it?" Cara blinked, trying to focus in spite of a pounding headache.

**Mast Road.**

Her weariness dampened almost all the relief she felt at finding the road. The search for this sign had begun before dawn. Most of the roads in Dry Lake were long and hilly, but they'd at least found the one they'd been searching for—although she had no idea what the place had in store for them, if anything.

They'd barely gone a hundred feet on Mast Road when she noticed a man on foot, leading a horse-drawn carriage to the front of a home. He went inside for a moment and came back out with a woman and five children. They all got into the rig. To travel like that, they probably were

Amish. As they drove past her, she noticed a little girl inside the buggy who was a year or so older than Lori.

**Her shoes would fit Lori—without pinching her feet.**

As Cara approached the house, she saw only a screen door between her and the inside of the home. "Let's knock on that door."

"What for?"

"Just to see if someone's home."

"Mom, look." Lori pointed at a beer bottle lying in the ditch.

"That's nasty, babe. Let's keep moving."

Lori pulled her hand free and grabbed it. "It looks like brown topaz, like our teacher at school showed us."

"Come on, kid, give me a break. It's an empty beer bottle." Cara took it from her.

"Don't throw it."

Unwilling to provoke her daughter's taxed emotions, she nodded and held on to it.

As they went up the porch stairs, Cara set the bottle on a step. She knocked and waited. When no one answered, she banged on it really hard. "Hello?" She heard no sounds. "Let's go in for a minute."

"But, Mom—"

"It's okay. No one's home, but if they were here, they'd give us some Band-Aids and some shoes that fit you, right?"

"Yeah, I think so. But I don't want to go in."

Leaving Lori near the front door, she hurried through the house, scavenging for clean socks, bandages, ointment, and shoes. With two pairs of shoes, a bottle of peroxide, a box of bandages, fresh socks, and a tube of ointment for her daughter's blisters in hand, Cara hurried out the door, tripping as she went. The items scattered across the porch.

Lori had the beer bottle in her hand, and Cara snatched it from her and set it back down on the porch. "I think one of these pairs will fit. Try this set on, and let's get out of here. Can you wait until later for us to clean the blisters and wrap them?"

"I think so."

"That's my girl."

While helping Lori slip into the shoes, Cara looked around the yard. A man stood at an opened cattle gate, watching them. Her heart raced. How long had he been standing there? But he didn't seem interested in confronting her. Based on the description from the man at the ticket counter, this guy might be Amish. He appeared to be past middle age and had on a dress shirt and pants, straw hat, and suspenders.

Keeping an eye on him, she left one pair of shoes on the porch and gathered up the rest of the items and shoved them into the backpack. "Will those do?"

"Yeah, but my feet still hurt."

She glanced at the man, who remained stock-still, watching her.

"I'll put medicine and Band-Aids on later. We need to go."

Cara tripped as she stood, knocking the beer bottle down the steps. Without meaning to, she cursed.

Wordlessly, the man continued to stare at them.

Cara took Lori's hand and hurried down the steps and toward the road.

"Mom, wait. You forgot the beer bottle."

"Lori, shh. Come on." She elongated the last word, and Lori obeyed.

The man seemed unable to move other than rubbing his left shoulder. "Malinda?"

Her heart stopped as her mother's name rode on the wind.

He blinked and opened his mouth to speak, but he said nothing.

"Daed?" A young woman called to him.

He turned to glance behind him. Cara couldn't see who called to him, but based on her voice, she was close. The man looked back to Cara. "It makes no difference who you are, we don't need thieves, drunks, or addicts around here."

"But I'm not—"

He wasted no time getting inside the pasture and shutting the noisy metal gate, ending Cara's attempt to defend herself.

Part of Cara wanted another chance to explain herself and ask questions or at least follow them as they turned their backs to her and headed through the field. Why had he called her by her mother's name? But she feared he might lash out and scare Lori if she dared to ask questions. It would do no one any good if her search for answers began badly. Awash in emotions, she took Lori by the hand and continued down the road. Did she look like her mother had? Did that man know her mom?

"Mom, what'd that man say to you?"

Unwilling to tell her the truth, Cara improvised. "Something about monks and leaves being in the attic . . . maybe?"

She giggled. "I think he's confused."

"I think you're right. I'm feeling a little confused myself. How do the shoes feel?"

"Pretty good. Thanks. I might not need those Band-Aids."

"You're one tough little girl, you know that?" Cara bent and kissed the top of Lori's head.

She'd thought it could mean a sense of connection for herself and Lori to meet people who knew her mother . . . but now it felt like a mistake. Her mother's past was hidden to her, and the man looked horrified to think she might be Malinda.

They walked on and on, putting more than a mile between them and that man. While trying to sort through his reaction, she studied the land. Another barn in need of paint stood a few hundred feet ahead of them, but not one thing felt familiar. Her arms and shoulders ached from the miles she'd toted Lori. Surely they'd covered nearly every mile of Dry Lake—every road, paved and dirt. As they walked Mast Road, she had no hint of what to do now.

She tripped again, and it seemed that stumbling got easier as the day wore on. Whatever they were going to do for shelter, Cara had to find an answer soon. There wasn't a house in sight, but perhaps they could sleep in that slightly lopsided barn.

As they approached the old building, Cara spotted something of interest on the other side of the road. Holding on to Lori's hand, she crossed over. Walking up a short gravel driveway, she noticed a huge garden planted beside it. Ahead of her lay a bare foundation with only a rock chimney still standing. She stepped onto the concrete floor and walked to the fireplace. The stone hearth had a rusted crane and black kettle.

"That pot looks like a witch's cauldron, huh, Mom? Like in **Harry Potter.**"

Cara ran her fingers along the metal. "It's for cooking over an open fire. The house that used to be here must've been hundreds of years old."

Something niggled at her but nothing she could make sense of.

Lori tugged at her mother's hand. "Look at that tree. I've always wanted to climb a tree, Mom. Remember?"

She remembered.

"I think I can climb that one."

"Maybe so." With reality pressing in on her, Cara tried to hold on to the positive. They were free of Mike. She had Lori. Still, she had no idea how she'd start over and pull together a life for them with no help, no money, and no belongings.

After interlacing her fingers, she gave Lori a boost up to the lowest branch. If nothing else, she'd finally given Lori one of her lifelong hopes—a tree to climb. This one did seem perfect for climbing—large but with a thick branch within five feet of the ground.

Cara looked across the land, wondering if she'd used what little money they had on absolute foolishness. She should be somewhere looking for work, not chasing after shadows of things that once were.

She knew the reality—all children raised in foster care harbor the belief that they have a relative somewhere out there who loves them. She was no exception. Each night after her mother had died, she'd gone to bed hoping a loved one would stumble upon the truth of her existence and come for her. At first she'd been foolish enough to hope her father would come. But as the years passed, she realized that he'd never wanted her. So the fantasy changed into the dream that a relative she'd never met would show up for her one day. By the time she turned fourteen, she refused to give in to that longing. Life hurt less that way. But the desire to have one relative who cared never truly went away. She wished it would. Maybe then the ache inside would ease.

"Look, Mom. It has a spot to ride it like a horse. And that knot thing looks sorta like a horse's head."

Cara glanced. A dip in the branch where Lori sat made a perfect spot for straddling it and pretending she was riding a horse. "It does, doesn't it? All you need is a set of reins."

"How'd you know, Mom?"

Cara turned from looking at the field. "How'd I know what?"

Lori held up a set of rusted chains. They were small, probably from a swing set.

"How'd ya know there were reins here?" Lori tugged at the chains that were wrapped around the part of the branch that looked like a horse's head. "Parts of them have grown into the tree, but they work."

Cara returned to the tree, running her hands over the mossy bark. She recalled the pieces of memory that came to her when Mike had showed up at her workplace—

an old woman, rows of tall corn, a kitchen table filled with food, sheets flapping in the wind. As she studied the tree and the land around her, she began to sense that maybe her fragmented thoughts weren't her imagination or parts of an old movie she'd once seen.

## Six

Deborah held her father's arm, guiding him up the gentle slope. Their home sat just beyond the ridge of the field, but maybe this wasn't the easiest route to take. "You're pale and shaking. What possessed you to go for such a long walk today?" He didn't answer, and she tried again. "Kumm, let's go home."

He pulled back, stopping both of them. "Did you see that woman and child coming out of the Swareys' home?"

"No." Deborah slid her arm through his, trying to encourage him to keep moving toward home. "Do you know her?"

Her father's feet were planted firm, and it seemed she couldn't coax him into budging.

He looked to the heavens before closing his eyes. "But it can't be her. She'd be much older by now, and her daughter is seven or eight years older than you."

"Who, Daed?"

He massaged his shoulder as if it ached from deep within. "Your mother loved her so. Never once believed the ban against her was fair—not even when she came back eight years later with a child. When she returned with her daughter, I'd been a preacher only a short time." He gave a half shrug, rubbing the area below his collarbone.

"Daed, what are you talking about?"

He turned and headed for the cattle gate. "It can't be her. A ghost . . . a mirage—that's all it could be. Or"—he quickened his pace—"another one sent in her place to finish destroying what little she left intact."

"Daed." Deborah took him by the arm again, gently tugging on him to go the other way. "You're scaring me, talking such nonsense. Let's go home."

He pointed a finger at her. "I may suffer

under a chronic illness, but I'm not a child."

Feeling the sting of his correction, she nodded and released his arm. They came to the gate, and he waited as Deborah opened it. They went through it, and then she locked it back, her heart racing with fear.

She held her tongue, trying to piece together what he might be talking about.

"Even as a newly appointed preacher, I . . . still don't think I was wrong." He walked a bit faster as he mumbled. "But Pontius Pilate never thought he was either. Rueben swears she has a way about her—a deceiving, sultry, manipulative way. Who should know better than the man who'd been engaged to her? What else could I do? What else should I have done?"

"What are you talking about?"

"And that woman I just saw was stealing from the Swareys and drunk. She wasn't Malinda. Couldn't be."

"Who's Malinda, Daed?"

"You keep the children close to home. I have to warn our people."

He wasn't making any sense. And even though the temperature was barely sixty and a breeze blew, he had beads of sweat across his brow. When he stumbled a bit, she tucked her arm through his, helping him keep his balance.

"**Liewi** Deborah." He patted her arm, calling her "dear." "It's not easy being the daughter of a preacher, is it?"

Concerned that he still wasn't making much sense, she tried to encourage him to turn around and head toward home. There weren't many phones in the district, but the bishop had approved one for the cabinetry business.

He took a few steps and then paused. "Whether I'm right or wrong in a thing, only God knows. But decisions, tough ones that have the power to help or ruin, have to be made to protect our beliefs."

"I understand. You're just and caring and do your best. I've always believed that."

He nodded. "I hope you always do."

He staggered, and she did what she could to keep him from falling. "Daed?"

His legs buckled, and he fell to his knees.

"Daed!"

❦

Cara tried to think of a plan while Lori played in the tree. That man calling her Malinda haunted her, and she knew the memory wouldn't fade anytime soon. The sound of horses' hoofs striking the pavement made her jump. "Come on, sweetie. We'd better get off this property." **Or at least not look like we're trespassing.**

"Not yet, Mom, please." Lori wrapped her legs firmly around the branch and held on tight to the chains.

"Lori, we need to move. Now."

"I am moving. Watch me." She spurred the tree and mimicked all the motions of riding a horse.

The sound of the real horses' clopping grew louder. She couldn't see a rig just yet, but it'd top that hill soon.

"Lori." Cara narrowed her eyes, giving another sharp look. "Now."

Lori huffed, but she hung on to the tree with her arms, lowering her legs as close to the ground as she could. Cara wrapped her hands around her daughter's tiny waist. "Okay, drop."

Lori did.

"Come on. We need to keep walking, like we're just out for a stroll, okay?" They hurried to the far side of the road near the old barn.

Her daughter tugged on her hand, stopping her. "Did you hear that?"

**What, the sound of me failing you?**

Lori's brown eyes grew large. "I hear puppies." She pulled at her mom's hand, trying to hurry her. "It's coming from that building."

The whole plot looked abandoned, from the empty foundation to the dilapidated barn, and Cara thought maybe it was a better idea to get off the road and totally out of sight. The two ran to the barn door. As they ducked inside, Cara spotted two horses heading their way, pulling a buckboard. That meant she and Lori might have been seen too. She closed the door and peeked through the slats, hoping the rig passed on by.

"Mom, look!"

Her daughter was sitting in the middle of a litter of six puppies, all excited to have her attention.

"Shh." Cara peered out the slit of the slightly open barn door, trying to see where the horses and rig had gone. She didn't hear any clopping sounds.

"Excuse me." A male voice called out to her.

She jolted and looked in the other direction. Two men sat in the horse-drawn wagon, staring at the barn.

"Stay here," Cara whispered firmly before stepping outside.

Ephraim held the girl's stare, feeling as if he'd seen her somewhere before. She certainly wasn't someone he'd met while doing cabinetry work. With her short crop of blond hair, tattered jeans, a tight sweater-shirt that didn't quite cover her belly, he'd remember if he'd been in her house.

But those brown eyes . . . Where had he ever seen eyes that shade of golden bronze . . . or ones filled with that much attitude? On one hand, she gave off an aura of a bit of uncertainty, perhaps an awareness that she wasn't on her own property. But there was something else, something . . . cynical and cold.

She stepped away from the barn. "Is there a problem?"

"I was wondering the same thing. You're on private property."

"Yeah, I didn't figure this was a national park or anything. I'm just looking around. The old place has character."

"Thanks, but it being old is a cause for potential danger. I'd prefer you kept moving."

"I bet you would. I'm sure you're real concerned about my safety."

The sensation of remembering her made his chest tingle. Maybe she was one of the fresh-air teens from New York the

Millers sponsored each summer. They usually didn't arrive until mid-June, but . . . "Are you from around here?"

A bit of surprise overtook the hardness in her eyes for a moment. "Is that the Amish version of 'Haven't we met before?' "

Ephraim's face burned at the hint that he was coming on to her. He removed his hat, propped his elbow on his leg, and leaned forward. "It was the polite version of 'I want you off my property.' But if you're a newcomer to the area who's out for a walk, I was willing to be nice about it."

She raised an eyebrow, and he got the feeling she was holding back from telling him what she really thought. He'd had enough experience with her kind of Englischer women from his days of living and working among them to know that her restraint wasn't out of respect as much as self-serving interest.

She dipped her fingertips into the front pockets of her jeans. "Like I said, we just stopped in for a minute. I didn't think a brief look around would cause such a fuss."

Slipping his hat back on his head, he considered his words. Dry Lake had plenty of teen troubles sometimes, and in his caution he was probably coming across more harsh than he should. "I . . . I—"

Deborah screamed. Ephraim scanned the area and spotted her running toward them and motioning. "It's Daed. Hurry!"

Ready to dismiss the unusual stranger, he slapped the reins against the horse's back and the rig took off.

# Seven

Cara slid through the barely open barn door while keeping her eye on the horse and wagon as it headed down the road. The man who did the talking was every bit as cold and personable as winter with a tattered coat. She'd seen it too many times before—good-looking, strong men as unfeeling and heartless as the dead. "Come on, sweetie. We've got to go."

"No, Mom. Come look."

One glance at Lori erased a bit of stress and fatigue. It felt odd to grin, but the furry black pups, already weighing about five pounds, were sprawled across her daughter's lap, sleeping soundly while she petted them.

Lori gazed up at her. "We can't leave. They like me."

Was that a trace of awe and excitement in her daughter's eyes and voice?

Cara knelt beside her and stroked a puppy. "They're real nice, Lorabean, but we can't stay here. Heartless Man might come back."

"Please, Mom." Lori's brown eyes reflected a desire so strong, so hopeful, as if every empty promise the Santas of the world offered at Christmas could be salvaged by granting her this one request.

Cara sat cross-leggedly, wondering what it could possibly hurt to give Lori a few hours with the puppies. Besides, they had to sleep somewhere tonight. Glancing around the place, she noticed rusted pitchforks, ten-gallon tubs, and moldy bales of hay. A decaying wagon sat in a corner with painter's tarps, ropes, and a watering can. The tin roof had sections missing.

The barn side of a silo caught her attention. She went over to it and tugged on the door, almost falling when it finally opened.

Clearly the door had been closed for a long time. If the man came back, she and Lori could hide inside. He'd never think to look in there. When they were on the road, they'd crossed a small bridge not far from here, so the creek had to run nearby. That meant water to drink, wash up in, and brush their teeth with. If she could get the two days' worth of traveling grime washed off of her and Lori, she might be able to sleep—even if she was in a dirty barn.

A piece of tin standing against the wall rattled and shifted. An older dog walked out from behind it. After one glimpse at Cara, the mama dog lowered her head and tucked her tail between her legs.

Cara knelt, motioning for her. "I know just how you feel. But you can't go around acting like it." The old dog came to her and stood still while Cara rubbed her short black hair. "If you act all sad and dumped on, people get meaner. Don't you know that by now?"

The dog wagged her tail. As if sensing their mom's presence, the puppies woke and started whining and going to her. She licked Cara's hand and then moved to a corner and lay down, letting the pups nurse.

"What're they doing, Mom?"

Cara pulled the sack of bagels out of Lori's backpack. "They're nursing. That means they're getting milk from their mother."

"Did I nurse?"

Cara passed her a bagel. "It was free food. What do you think?"

Lori wiped her hands on her dress. "If I only eat half of my bagel, can I share it with the mama dog?"

"Your part **is** half of a bagel, so, no, you can't share any of it. She'll be fine. We should be so lucky as to scavenge like a dog and not get sick."

"You know what?"

Cara shrugged. "I don't want to play guessing games, okay?"

"If I ever had more food than I needed, I'd give it to other hungry boys and girls."

Cara rolled her eyes. "As if." The sarcasm in her tone ran deep within her; Cara knew that all too well.

Remembering how she used to dream of jumping on a horse and riding into a world that had people who loved her and flowed with tables of food, Cara stared at her half of the bagel. "Never be afraid to hope, Lorabean. Never."

Deborah continued to shake as Ephraim pulled into the driveway. Daed sat beside her, with Mahlon on the other side of him, as they rode on the back of the wagon with their legs dangling. She and Mahlon held on to her Daed so he wouldn't fall out as the wagon bumped along. His ashen face tortured her.

**Dear God, don't take him! Please.** The phrase screamed inside her. The loss of her mother had nearly destroyed her whole family. She couldn't stand losing someone else. Not after Daed and Becca had spent years building a new family while giving strength to the one they each already had.

Mahlon jumped off the back of the wagon before it came to a complete stop.

His eyes locked on hers, saying he cared and he understood. She knew he did. He always had, and she relied on his quiet strength.

Becca ran out the door. "Abner?"

"He's had a spell." Deborah choked on tears she refused to shed.

"Call the doctor, and call for a driver." Becca spoke in a whisper that didn't hide her panic.

Ephraim was already halfway to the shop.

"I'm fine now." Daed waved his arm for everyone to let go of him. "Stop fussing over me."

They released him.

"But you will be seen by the doctor, Abner. You must," Becca pleaded.

"I said I'm fine."

Deborah stood in front of him. "You were talking nonsense, Daed. And you had sharp chest pains." She wiped her fingers across his forehead. "You're still sweating."

He held her gaze. "I'll be okay. I just need to rest."

"Please." Deborah gently squeezed his

arm. "I need you to go to the hospital to be sure of what's going on. Not tomorrow or later in the week. Right now."

He slowly reached for her face and cradled her cheeks in the palms of his rough hands. "Okay. But don't let the young ones slip off while we're gone. You keep them close to home. Away from that drunken thief. And lock the doors." His raspy breathing came in shallow spurts, and his hands trembled. "Once I get to the hospital, those doctors'll want to keep me at least one night. They always do."

Deborah placed her hands over his. "Mahlon will stay and help Ephraim get ready for the auction. And Ada will fill in for Becca. The community can do the auction on schedule even without you giving out instructions left and right."

Daed gave a nod.

Becca stepped forward. "Kumm." She took Daed's arm and helped him into the house.

"He'll be okay." Mahlon came up behind her and placed his hands on her shoulders. "It's probably another incident that's easily fixed. You remember last year when he'd taken in too much salt and had a fluid overload."

"He never had any pain with that."

"No, but anyone with his kind of heart condition has times when his medication needs to be adjusted. We know that from past experiences. I'm sure it's something the doctors can solve."

"He kept saying that he saw a woman coming out of the Swarey home and that she'd stolen things from them and was drunk. I didn't see anyone. Then he started mumbling about a ghost and Mamm having loved her and maybe he'd been wrong, like Pontius Pilate." She swallowed, trying to hold in her emotions. "I couldn't do anything to help him."

"He'll be fine, Deb." He moved in front of her. "You did everything right." Mahlon's deep, soft voice strengthened her. "You used the power of his love for you to get him to do what's needed."

She moved to a lawn chair and sat. "I . . . I just don't know if I can handle losing him."

"Deb." His back stiffened, and frustration flickered in his eyes. "Don't do this. He'll be fine. And of course you can deal with whatever happens. What other choice do you have—to fall apart? That only makes everyone else need to carry you."

Fear for her Daed took a step back as offense lurched forward. But she knew where he was coming from and why, so she took a breath and gained control of herself. "You're right. I didn't mean . . . It's just that sometimes life is so scary, and about the time you can deal with one thing, something else happens."

He dipped his head for a moment before he looked her in the eye. "I know. But there's a difference between being concerned for someone and taking on all the anxiety of their what-ifs. You pull so hard for everyone to win, for everyone to be healthy and safe. Just . . . don't . . ."

He sounded as if he had more to say. It seemed to her that she deserved an apology, not a lecture, so she waited. A car horn blasted, and she knew the driver had arrived to take Daed to the hospital.

# Eight

Thunder rumbled, waking Cara. Her head spun with pain, and she wished she had a smoke and a cup of coffee to ease the effects of her lack of both. Darkness surrounded her, but what little sky she could see through the missing parts of the roof indicated the sun's rays were just below the horizon. The ragged canvas she'd placed over her and Lori didn't keep the chill out. Puppies covered a good bit of Lori, so in spite of the dirt and grime, she was at least warm.

Odors from the hay, the dirt floor, and the aging barn drifted through the air. She saw herself as a young girl swinging on a rope from a loft and dropping into a mound of hay. Could she have been in this barn before?

The mama dog raised her head and laid it on Cara's leg. She patted her, wondering what the day would bring and where they'd sleep tonight. Longing for basic human comforts, she missed having a toilet, shower, and clean clothes.

As she stood and knocked musty hay and dirt off herself, her tiny, pathetic apartment in the South Bronx took on a luster it'd never had before. It had hot water. A kitchen. A bathroom. A front door with keys that said she had the right to be there. She pulled a black beetle from her shirt. And the bugs stayed mostly on the floor during the night, not in her bed.

Trying to think how best to handle today, she slipped out the back of the barn through a narrow hole where a couple of vertical slats used to be. The cool May air smelled of rain. Her eyes burned from lack of sleep or maybe from the layer of moldy dust that covered her. A desire to go to the creek and wash up pulled at her, but she stayed put. The sun slowly climbed over the horizon. Birds sang. Dew covered the field. She'd never seen a sunrise like this.

Rays of light danced on the droplets of water that covered the fields.

When she heard a noise, she squeezed through the opening again and saw a young boy standing next to Lori and holding a pup.

"I got to hide 'em," he whispered. "My brother's gonna sell 'em at the auction today."

Cara moved forward. "He's on his way here?"

The boy turned. "Not yet. He'll probably wait till they start selling livestock to come get 'em."

"We gotta hide them, Mom. Simeon said they're too young to leave their mama."

In spite of her inclination to get out of there quickly, something about this scenario felt familiar—the boy's straw hat, collared shirt, suspenders, dress pants.

Simeon pulled a handkerchief out of his pocket and laid it on the ground before unfolding it. The mama dog wasted no time gobbling up the tidbits of food.

"What's an auction?" Lori asked.

"It's where you can buy all sorts of things. We always have it at our place because we're the only ones with enough parking space and a huge building to keep the rain out. We got whopper tents with just roofs and no sides set up, too, so some of the selling can go on there while some's going on inside the shop. And there's enough food to feed everybody." Simeon told where he lived and where his brother's house was, and he rambled about a meeting that would take place at his house tomorrow night and how his brother lived alone. He went on and on as if he'd forgotten what he'd come here to do.

"Simeon!" a male voice hollered.

The little boy's eyes widened. "That's my brother."

Cara grabbed Lori's arm, scooped up the backpack, and hurried into the silo. While closing the door to it, she placed her index finger over her lips, hoping Simeon wouldn't tell.

The boy jerked the door open. "What about hiding the puppies?"

"They'll make too much noise." She

closed the door, but the scowl on his face made her wonder if he'd give them away.

"Simeon Mast."

She recognized the man's voice. Simeon's brother and Heartless Man were one and the same. Cara held her breath. Trespassing and loitering were punishable by law. It wouldn't be much of a crime, but it'd be enough that the officials would start digging into her life and soon discover she had no money, no place to live, and a daughter in tow.

"Mom," Lori whispered, "there's food at the auction, and I'm hungry."

Cara gently placed her hand over Lori's mouth. "Shh." How could she explain that lack of money, not lack of supply, stood between them and the goods? After buying food and clothes at that store in Shippensburg, they had thirty-two cents left. If she dug through Lori's backpack, she might find enough change to buy her a little something.

The dark, dank hole crawled with creepy things. What was she doing living like this?

The question made her long to get back at Mike. He'd dogged her moves off and on for more than a decade. He should be in a dark hole with creepy things, not her.

The man's voice grew louder, as if he was heading straight for the silo. "Of course I'm not taking the pups to the auction." He sounded as if he were leaning against the silo. "We'll find homes for them in a few weeks when they're old enough. But with Daed in the hospital and all your sisters busy with the auction work, you need to be my shadow. Now, come on before I lose my patience."

Silence reigned for a bit, and then the barn door slammed shut. She waited a couple of moments, then eased the silo's hatch open and helped Lori get out. Simeon's brother must've brought a pan of food with him, and the mama dog's tail wagged as she ate.

The sounds of many horses' hoofs grabbed Cara's attention, and she peeked through the barn door. A long row of horse-drawn buggies lined the road, all heading east. Cars moved around them, driving in the same direction.

"Simeon said over a thousand people will be at the auction," Lori said. "Can we go too? Please?"

If they went and if she found a little more money, she might be able to buy a hot dog or something to help ease Lori's hunger. Besides, if this place had any answers for her foggy memories or why that man had called her by her mother's name, she was more likely to learn of them by going to a communitywide event than by traveling down quiet roads with her daughter. Since the auction was open to everyone, it couldn't hurt for them to show up.

Cara grabbed the backpack. "Let's slip out the back and freshen up in the creek first. We can't go looking like we slept in a barn."

The special-event tent over Deborah's head promised to keep out the threatening rain as she spread frosting on a tray of cinnamon buns. She and Ada had been baking since two a.m., and now they were almost ready for the hundreds of customers to begin arriving. Six warming trays were lined up, filled with breakfast food—scrambled eggs, sausage, bacon, biscuits, scrapple, and breakfast breads.

Lists of what else needed doing filled her thoughts, but she wanted a chance to talk to Mahlon. Between her baking hundreds of biscuits and cinnamon rolls for today's auction and her younger siblings needing her, she hadn't caught more than a glimpse of him since the driver had arrived last night.

"Hey, Little Debbie." Jonathan's familiar voice made her turn.

She laughed at the sight of Mahlon's cousin standing before her in the usual Amish attire but with the add-on of a white chef's apron and knee-high waders covered in mud.

He rolled his eyes. "Hey, be nice. My makeshift cooking area is a muddy mess."

"You be nice. Anything I make should

be better than a store-bought snack cake. So knock off the nickname thing."

He stuck out his hand, offering to shake hers. "Deal."

She peered at his palm, checking for a buzzer.

He smiled and showed her his empty hand before lowering it. Jonathan usually made some gentle but humorous remark about her name. Maybe some Amish somewhere used the name Deborah, but no one in her life knew of them. She'd been named after her mother's Englischer midwife.

She lifted her leg slightly, glancing at the hem of her dress. It already had spatters of mud. "I know at the end of today, I'll be doing my best to scrub mud out of all our clothing."

"Ya, you will. You should have worn a dark-colored dress. Did you get the change drawer?"

"Not yet. I'd forgotten, actually."

"Nothing like an annoying friend to remind you of things you haven't done." He chuckled. "I can't go get it. I've got sausages cooking. But if you need anything cooked, give me a holler."

"Denki."

It seemed odd that Jonathan and Mahlon were first cousins when the only similarity was the color of their eyes. Jonathan's lighthearted openness was quite a contrast to Mahlon's silent depth. Figuring Mahlon out didn't come easily. But he drew her—as if she were a parched land and he were a deep well of cool water.

Something so faint it almost didn't exist brushed her awareness, and she turned to find Mahlon at the edge of the tent, watching her. How she wished she could fully know what was behind those hazel eyes. A river most likely, a wide and deep one, teeming with thoughts and emotions that went deeper than most people experienced on their most reflective day.

He nodded a quiet hello, and she went to him. The apology she'd wanted from him last night reflected in his eyes.

"Morning." His deep, caring voice caused her skin to tingle. He slid his hand into hers and squeezed it. "Any more updates on your Daed?"

"Becca called the shop around ten o'clock last night. The doctors are pretty sure it wasn't a heart attack. That's the good news." She shrugged, not sure she understood the rest well enough to explain it decently. "It appears he had a spasm in the rib cage muscle. Fluid has built up throughout his body again, including around his heart and lungs. The doctor said that caused the shortness of breath and some of the chest discomfort. They're giving him meds that'll reduce the swelling. But none of that explains his odd behavior and mumbling about seeing a ghost."

"When will he get to come home?"

"Right now they're saying Tuesday. Becca asked me to have the driver come get me that day. She needs some things picked up at the pharmacy and grocery store, and she's too worn out and scattered to think it all through by herself."

Mahlon studied something behind her, and she turned.

Israel Kauffman walked beside Mahlon's mother, carrying a twenty-pound package of raw sausage. He was quite a looker for a man in his midforties—thin yet robust, with lots of shiny brown hair and a smile that never ended. Whatever he said to Ada made her laugh. Ada was only slightly younger, and both were widowed, so it seemed to Deborah they'd make a nice couple, but as far as she knew, they never saw each other outside of districtwide or communitywide events.

Israel took the meat around back of the temporary wall they'd installed, where Jonathan manned the sausage skillets in the makeshift kitchen. Deborah took Mahlon by the hand and moved back to her work station. She handed him a cinnamon roll to eat, and then she began making egg-and-bacon biscuits.

Ada went to the washbowl and scrubbed her hands. "I told Israel we've been at your house baking biscuits and cinnamon buns since two a.m. You know what he had the nerve to say?"

Deborah shook her head.

"That we'd better make more because he could eat all of that by himself before noon."

Deborah chuckled. "He won't have a hole in his stomach after all that, but he sure will in his pocket."

Jonathan rounded the corner with a tray of cooked sausages. He set them next to the warming tray and began moving them into it. "I know we have all the fixings for different kinds of sausage biscuits, but do you know how to make a sausage roll?"

Deborah shrugged. "Not sure that I do."

"You push it."

Laughing, she glanced to Mahlon, who didn't react at all. He had seemed so unsettled the last few days. Then again, their week had been packed with ups and downs since Ephraim gave his blessing on their wedding plans three days ago. He could just be tired.

She placed a sausage-and-egg biscuit in a wrapper and then tore off another piece of plastic wrap. "We need to assemble and wrap as many different kinds of meat-and-egg biscuits as we can. They sell the fastest."

Jonathan lifted the now-empty container. "You want the fresh vat of scrambled eggs?"

"Please."

"I'll bring it quicklike, but I'm not turning it over to you until I get some of your best brewed coffee." He tipped his hat and bowed, a broad smile saying he was teasing.

Deborah grabbed the coffee grinder, added fresh beans, and turned the crank. "You bring me the eggs, and I'll make the exchange."

"Yes ma'am." He disappeared.

Mahlon touched her shoulder. "I'll check on you in a few hours. I need to go."

The few seconds that passed between them as she looked in his eyes assured her that, despite whatever weighed on him, he adored her. "Maybe tomorrow we can go for a long, quiet ride—just the two of us."

"Doubtful with Becca gone and you running the household, but I sure will love it if we can."

She continued getting the place ready for the first customers—unloading paper plates and napkins into their bins, filling the salt and pepper shakers and condiment bottles.

"It's about to get wild, Deborah." Jonathan came around the corner with the huge container of steaming scrambled eggs. He nodded at the crowds parking their vehicles in the mowed fields. They'd soon form a line for Deborah and Ada's breakfast food, one that wouldn't end until nearly lunchtime.

# Nine

Cara and Lori followed the horse-and-buggy line heading for the auction. Thankfully they weren't the only ones walking, so they didn't stick out . . . too much. None of the women had on jeans. She seemed to be in the land of dresses and skirts and hair long enough to be pulled back. There didn't seem to be much point in that. If they were going to pull their hair back all the time, why not just cut it off?

After walking half a mile, she saw cars parked in a field on one side of the road. Buggies sat in a different field with a fenced pasture holding the unharnessed horses. Several portable potties and sinks were set up, clearly brought in for the occasion. Up ahead she spotted a huge farmhouse near the road. Half a block away sat what appeared to be an industrial-size warehouse.

"Smell that food, Mom?"

The aroma filled the air, making her mouth water. Even more appealing than the delectable smell of food was the aroma of coffee—a heavenly scent. But unless she found a bit of money buried inside Lori's book bag, they'd have to be content with the stale half bagel and creek water they'd had for breakfast. "Maybe we can get something later. We just ate. We're fine for now."

The sky began to release some of its threatening downpour. She and Lori hurried to the nearest tent, huddling under it with a lot of others aiming to keep dry. She studied the lay of the land. At the back of the property, some two or three city blocks away and almost hidden behind rows of bushes and trees, sat another building— perhaps someone's home, but she couldn't tell. If it was a house, it was probably the one Simeon had told them belonged to his brother. It looked like there was a shortcut back to the barn if she went through the field and past the building behind the trees. When she left here, she'd try going that way.

From inside the warehouse came the sound of a man's quick words as he auctioned an item. With a gentle tug she led Lori into the oversize structure. It seemed to be divided into stations. A man selling potted plants stood in the first section. Next was another makeshift kitchen area with benches and tables near it. Cara guessed lunch would be sold there later.

A huge wagon full of miscellaneous stuff sat in the middle of the building with people surrounding it. Two men dressed exactly like Simeon and his brother—navy blue pants; a solid-color, collared shirt; suspenders; and a straw hat—stood on the wagon. The auctioneer bent down and grabbed something beside him. "Who'll bid on this?" Frowning, he held up an old cardboard box of items. "What is this, anyway?"

Those around the wagon tittered with laughter. The auctioneer's helper shrugged, took it from him, and passed him a large hand-painted watering pot. "Ah, something I can sell. It's Mother's Day tomorrow. This would go great with some of the potted plants being sold in station one."

Lori's eyes grew wide. "It's Mother's Day tomorrow?"

Cara nodded.

Lori's eyes filled with tears. "But . . . but I was making something for you at school."

She knelt beside her daughter. "I have you. If all mothers had a daughter like you, there wouldn't be a need for such a thing as Mother's Day."

The hurt in Lori's eyes faded. "Really?"

Cara swiped her finger over her heart, making a crisscross. "I promise."

"I painted you a picture."

"I bet it's so gorgeous it'd brighten up the saddest mom's heart. I think the teacher will give it to Sherry's mom. If anybody deserves a gift because their kid isn't one, it'd be her." Cara didn't know the woman, but she'd seen how her daughter behaved at school and sassed the teacher over every little thing.

Lori smiled and wrapped her arms

around her neck and held on. Cara lifted her as she snuggled against her shoulder.

"Mom, I want to go home."

"I know, kiddo." Cara walked past the crowds to the back of the building. Rows of various types of lawn chairs were lined up facing a wall of racks filled with quilts. A table near the racks had a sign that read "Quilt Sale Starts at Noon."

She moved to an empty chair and rocked her daughter. There'd been too many quick changes this week, along with too much walking and too little food. She stroked her daughter's wavy hair, soothing her until she completely relaxed. Lori's back rested against Cara's chest, and she quietly watched people.

The rain fell harder, but under the roof of the building, the auctioneers kept calling for bids. No one seemed to notice Cara. Amish women with clipboards and pens looked at tags on the quilts and made notes. They moved a few quilts from one area to another, speaking in a language Cara didn't understand. She closed her eyes and dozed, odd images floating in and out of her mind.

A kitchen table spread with fresh food. A warm embrace from a woman her mother called Levina. Two trees side by side. She climbed one, and some boy climbed the other. He called to her as she straddled a thick branch as if it were a horse and pretended to ride far, far away.

Her mother's laughter filled her. **"Levina, ich bin kumme . . ."**

Cara jerked awake. An Amish woman stood near her, speaking to another Amish woman. The language . . . Wasn't it the same her mother had spoken to . . . to . . . What was the woman's name, the one she'd just dreamed of?

She couldn't remember, but she needed to know some things about her childhood. It shouldn't matter—not at twenty-eight years old. But it did. And she didn't intend to leave Dry Lake until she had some explanations. When she worked out a few things and was able to answer where she and her daughter lived, if anyone asked her, she'd begin searching for information.

Simeon's brother stood near the front of the room. Thankfully he hadn't spotted her. The desire to leave nudged her, but outside the rain poured. She and Lori would be soaked by the time they returned to the barn or found fresh shelter. Then they'd be stuck in wet clothes all through the day and night.

An auctioneer moved to the desk near the quilts. "We're waiting on the runners to get back with fresh pages, and then we'll begin."

She decided it'd be best to let Lori remain on her lap and hope Simeon's brother didn't notice her. Even if he did, it was a community auction. She had as much right to be here as any other non-Amish person.

The aroma of grilled chicken filled the air. Her stomach rumbled. She'd never seen so much home-cooked food in one place. She searched through Lori's backpack and came up with a dime.

**Great. Now we have forty-two cents. Not enough to buy Lori anything.**

Women attached one end of a quilt to a long dowel that was connected to ropes and a pulley. Simeon's brother hoisted the quilt up high so everyone could see what they were bidding on. When that quilt sold, he lowered it and moved to the other side, where several women had another quilt attached to a second dowel and pulley.

He helped the women regardless of their age, looks, or weight, smiling as he shared a few words with each of them. He hurried from raising one quilt to the next so they never had to hoist the heavy blankets themselves. She'd never seen a man act so protective over something as nonthreatening as a little heavy work.

The selling of quilts went on for hours. Lori moved to a chair beside Cara and sang softly and flipped through a children's magazine from her backpack, wiling away time the way tired children did. The rain slowed. Cara hoped the storm would be gone before much longer.

The auctioneer told bits of history about some of the quilts, his voice coming through the battery-operated mike clipped to his shirt. "Emma Riehl began this next quilt twenty years ago."

**Emma Riehl?**

The man's voice turned to garbled nonsense as the name Emma Riehl echoed throughout Cara.

Suddenly she was in the bus station again, walking through the long passageways, her father holding her hand.

**"Where are we going?"**

**"Not we, just you."**

**"You're gonna leave me here?"**

**"No. I'll stay until Emma Riehl arrives. She'll be here soon."**

Lori tapped her on the arm. "Mom, I'm hungry."

Cara's thoughts didn't slow, but she came to herself to realize afresh the delicious smells that permeated every breath they took. "I know, Lorabean. But all we have left is forty-two cents. That's not enough to buy anything. I'm sorry."

When Lori nodded and wiped unspilled tears from her eyes, Cara thought her heart might break.

"I gotta go to the bathroom."

Cara eyed the Amish women, wondering if one of them was Emma. "Can you wait?"

"No."

"You sure? I just need a few more—"

"I gotta go now."

"Okay. Okay." Cara weaved through the crowd, holding Lori's hand. She looked for the nearest Porta Potti, then they stood in line, waiting.

**Emma Riehl?** The oddity of this coincidence combined with that man calling her by her mother's name convinced her that, whatever it took, she'd not leave this area until she had some answers.

After their turn in a rest room, they washed their hands at the portable sinks and headed back to the quilt sale.

As they passed a tent with food, Lori tugged on Cara's hand. "Mom, please. Can we buy half of something with that money?"

An Amish woman behind a register looked at them.

"I still have a bagel in the backpack."

Lori stared up at her. "I'm hungry for real food, Mom."

Cara bent over and whispered, "I told you. We don't have enough money."

Lori nodded.

"Wait," a voice called.

Cara turned to see a young Amish woman holding a plate out to her.

"Deborah?" A man called.

"Ya?" the woman answered.

"Where's the aluminum foil?"

"In the box under the register." Deborah extended the plate closer to them. "The rain is keeping our numbers for the auction a little low this year. Is there any chance you could help me out by eating some of the leftover food?"

Lori squealed. "Please, Mom? Please?"

The plate held two huge biscuits loaded with steaming scrambled eggs and sausage. "The eggs and meat are hot off the grill." She smiled, leaving Cara no doubt that she knew Lori had been asking for food.

"Thank you."

"Yes!" Lori did a little jig.

The young woman chuckled. "I think she likes the idea. Come. You can choose a drink to go with it. We have white milk, chocolate milk, orange juice—"

"Orange juice? I love orange juice!" Lori's whole face glowed.

Cara's eyes misted. "Thank you."

Deborah nodded. "Come this way." She poured Lori a glass of juice. She held a foam cup out to Cara. "Coffee?"

Cara pulled out what little change she had in her pocket and handed it to Deborah. "Yes, please." She elongated the last word, making the woman laugh.

Deborah hesitated. Then she took the money.

Cara carefully balanced the plate of food and cup of coffee. "Can you carry your drink without spilling it?"

Lori nodded, thanking the woman half a dozen times.

Cara chuckled. "Thanks again."

"No problem."

They made their way back to Cara's chair in the auction building. Unlike when they'd left, several chairs were empty now, as were the quilt racks.

"We got hot, delicious food, so this is a pretty good day, huh, Mom?"

Wishing she could promise tomorrow would also be like this, Cara nodded. "Yes, it is." But Emma Riehl's quilt had been purchased, and any chance she had to spot which Amish woman might be Emma was gone with it.

While they ate and drank, the auctioneer unfolded a letter-size piece of paper. "This is a contract from a woman who is willing to clean someone's house one day a week for three months. Who'll start the bidding?"

When there was no response, a burly man held up a business card and hollered, "I'm willing to bid for an Amish woman to clean house, cook, and help take care of my wife five days a week until she's on her feet again. Any takers?"

There was a lot of murmuring and jokes, but no one volunteered.

When the burly man stood, it was clear he wasn't Amish. "We could probably get by on someone coming only four hours a day. We'd pay forty dollars each time. Surely there's someone."

Two women behind Cara agreed the

pay wasn't bad but said they couldn't find that kind of time to take on another job. She desperately wanted to raise her hand, but if she stood, the auctioneer would ask for her name and where she lived. Every employer wanted an address, and the closeness of this community meant they'd know if she lied. Just from spending the afternoon watching, she had decided that everyone here knew each other. If she could talk to this man alone, she might get away with a lie.

"Okay, I'll raise my offer. Four hours a day at fifty dollars. I'll pay in cash at the end of each workday." The man searched the room. "Come on. I'm like the rest of you, barely eking out a living, and that's good money."

No one raised a hand. Cara began to wonder if there were hidden reasons no one volunteered.

He tossed his business card on a nearby table. "If anyone changes their mind, that has my phone number and address."

Cara stared at the card, longing to snatch it up. All she needed was one break.

If she could get on her feet without going outside the law, she could apply to the government for help—if she still needed it. And stop living in fear of losing Lori.

She felt someone watching her. Turning, she saw Simeon's brother staring at her. Her nerves shot pinpricks of heat through her. She'd bet he wanted to question her, and she knew without being told that he had the power to ruin her fresh start. Clearly she had to get out of here.

"Let's go." Cara slid the strap to Lori's backpack over her shoulder and gathered their trash.

"I still got half a cup of juice left. Isn't that cool?"

"Yeah, now come on." But Cara was the one who didn't budge. The man's card lay on the table, begging for her to grab it.

An image floated through her mind again.

Her father tapped the hand-drawn map. **"See where I've drawn this horse and buggy? That's where you're going. It's where your mother never should have left. It did things to her . . . to us."**

**"I'm going to Levina's?"**

Her father stared hard at her before he emptied the glass of its golden drink. **"You know about her?"**

**"I met her."**

He ordered another drink and then another before he stood and led her to a bench seat elsewhere in the station. **"Stay put, Cara Atwater, right here, and don't you budge. Emma will come get you."**

Cara closed her eyes, trying to ward off the pain of being abandoned. Twice. Her father had left. And Emma Riehl never showed.

"You okay, Mom?"

She opened her eyes and forced another smile. "Sure, Lorabean." When she looked up, she met Simeon's brother's eyes. Defiance welled, and she held his gaze. She wasn't leaving, not yet. The man could just choke on his stinginess over his moldy hay and half-fallen barn, but she wasn't running.

Hiding? Yes. Running? Not yet. Not until she had answers.

Simeon hurried up to him, talking and stealing his attention.

The crowds pressed in around the table where the card lay. "Stay close and keep quiet." Cara eased from her chair and melted into the crowd. She reached through the gaps between people and grabbed the card. No one seemed to feel her arms moving past theirs. "Let's go."

On her way out of the huge shop, she saw a counter where a makeshift kitchen had been set up. She paused, watching as a woman slid two hamburgers onto buns and added the fixings before she placed them in a white lunch bag and set them on the counter. Cara sidled up to the spot and snatched the bag. She slid it into the book bag without even Lori noticing what she was doing. But when she glanced up, she saw Simeon's brother on the other side of the room, watching her. Resisting the urge to make a rude gesture, she ducked out the side entrance.

# Ten

Cara tossed a pebble into the water. Lori sat on the creek bank, drawing in the mud with a stick. A piece of tarp from the barn lay on the ground under her, keeping her clothes dry after yesterday's earth-soaking rain.

Homeless on Mother's Day. What a joke. Since Simeon's brother had walked into the barn yesterday, she couldn't even let Lori play with the puppies today like she wanted. From now until they found a place to live, she'd have to stay away from the barn until late at night. She'd looked for other outbuildings to sleep in, but they were too close to homes where people lived.

Year in and year out the longing to give

Lori a sense of self-worth, to let her know she had someone who adored her, kept Cara trying. She'd come here wanting to find ties to her past, friends or family of her mother's, but even if she did, would it make a difference for Lori?

Maybe getting out of New York only meant a chance for a clean break and a fresh start.

She played with the card the burly man had thrown on the table—Richard Howard on Runkles Road. Even though today was Sunday, she and Lori had gone to his place earlier. Lori would have to go to work with her, so she took her to the interview. After walking through most of Dry Lake while looking for Mast Road, she easily remembered how to get to that road. Once there, the man had led her into his wife's bedroom for an interview. Ginny Howard had broken her femur and was in a hip cast. Her husband had used up all his sick leave at work to stay home with her. He was desperate for help, even if Cara wasn't Amish, and wanted her to come work for him, but Ginny felt differently. She said if Cara put on some decent clothes, she might consider hiring her. Cara figured Mr. Howard must be more anxious for her to work out than his wife knew, or he wouldn't have told her to come back tonight before bedtime if she got the right clothes.

He'd reminded her that he would pay fifty dollars in cash at the end of each workday. With a bit of luck and that money in her pocket, she might find a room to rent in someone's home within a few days. Although she'd only be paid for four hours, she told him that if he hired her, she'd stay until he returned home from work each day. He was excited about that idea, but she hadn't offered out of the kindness of her heart. She knew it'd be easier to work at his home all day than to get off near lunchtime and try to stay out of sight until it was safe to return to the barn.

On her way back from the Howards, Cara had scoped out some "decent" clothes hanging to dry in Simeon's yard. She'd seen that woman who had given them food during the auction hanging the clothes on the line, and Cara would rather not take anything from her. If she snatched a few things and returned them later, would that be stealing? She'd have to wait until after dark.

Something in her ached to understand the connection between her mother and Emma Riehl. If this Emma was the same Emma who'd failed to come for her, why did she leave her at a bus station? What kind of person did that?

The longing to know was as deep and controlling as the desire to talk to her mom had been during those lonely nights in foster care.

As dusk settled over the place, she knew it was time to carry out her plan. "Come on, Lorabean."

Lori stood, dusting off the backside of her dress. "If we had a fishing pole, I could catch us a fish, and we could cook it."

Cara tucked the last bagel into the backpack. Like the two previous ones, it'd have to be soaked in water before being eaten, or they'd break a tooth. But those hamburgers she'd taken from the auction were delicious. She would have saved hers for Lori to eat today, but she was afraid it might spoil and make her daughter sick. "Do you really think so?"

"Yep."

"Then I'll have to get us a fishing pole." She held out her hand for Lori, and they began following the creek bed. Going this way would keep them out of sight until dark. Then they could use the road. "So, what are we going to cook your catch in?"

"Maybe one of those grills the men in hats were cooking chicken on yesterday."

Cara chuckled. "Those things must've held a hundred pounds of chicken."

"Then I'll have to catch a hundred pounds of fish."

"I like the way you think, kiddo."

"Mom? What are we gonna do now?"

"Borrow a few things, I think." Leading Lori across the back field, she spotted Simeon's brother's house. She studied the dark, quiet place. After she snatched a dress, she'd get a few things from his house.

Disappointed in how much time it'd taken them to get here, she hoped the single line of laundry hadn't been taken inside for the day. She continued on. Past the privacy bushes and trees, she saw Simeon's house and the workshop. Gauging distance like she did in New York, she guessed the houses sat about two north-south city blocks apart—about five hundred feet. Inside New York thousands of people would live between these two houses, yet here no other houses were in sight.

Near a tree grove a rock jutted from the ground. She led Lori in that direction. "I need you to stay on this rock until I get back, okay?"

"I guess so."

"There's no guessing. You wait right here, and don't budge until I come back for you."

"Okay."

"Promise?"

As she placed her daughter on the rock, Lori crossed her heart with her finger.

Cara eased around the perimeter of the property until she could see the clothesline. The same outfits still hung on the line. It seemed none had been added or removed. She focused on the row of dresses, two of which looked like they might fit. She moved across the yard slowly, hiding in the shadows and noticing everything she could. A child's red wagon lay in the gutter near the street. A reel mower sat under a nearby tree. The house buzzed with the voices of what had to be dozens of people. The driveway had six buggies, all attached to horses. She suspected busyness worked better for thievery. When people were distracted, they often didn't see right where they looked.

She snatched a dress and moved back into the shadows. No one seemed to notice.

Her next plan made her more nervous. Simeon had said that his brother lived alone and that he'd be at his Daed's house tonight. Simeon had also said this place was never locked. As long as Simeon's brother didn't return unexpectedly, she should be home free.

After snaking her way across the field and through his privacy bushes, she stood on the man's porch. The front door was open, leaving only the screen door. She tiptoed inside, looking for the refrigerator. It took just a few seconds to spot it.

When she opened it, she couldn't believe her eyes. The thing was absolutely packed with food. She grabbed the first container she could, set it on the counter, and opened the lid just to make sure it wasn't filled with raw meat. The aroma of grilled chicken filled her nostrils. Perfect. She took a can of soda and a few napkins. Stuffing them inside the dress, she scanned the dark room—a bathroom, a living room, and a bedroom. Once inside the bedroom, she looked through a chest of drawers and discovered several flashlights. She took one and went to the closet. At the bottom of a stack of quilts, she grabbed what looked like an old store-bought blanket.

"Hey, Ephraim," a man yelled, startling her. "You're not leaving for the night, are you?"

With her arms full, she hurried out the back door. Two men stood in the middle of the field between the two houses, talking. She scurried back to the rock, thrilled at the treasures in her arms, her heart pounding with adrenaline.

"Hey, Lorabean, guess what I have?" She held up the clear container.

"Food." She clapped her hands.

Cara opened it. "All the grilled chicken a girl can eat. We need to walk and eat at the same time, though, or it'll get too late for me to go on that interview." Cara pulled the dress on over her head and peeled out of her jeans. "I saw a little red wagon in a ditch. I'll spread this blanket in the bottom of it, and you can ride while you eat. Deal?"

"We're gonna steal?"

"No, honey. We'll bring it back before anyone even knows we borrowed it."

Lori licked her fingers. "This is delicious. Want some?"

"Just a bite." Her stomach ached with hunger, and she could've eaten the whole container by herself, but she'd settle for the bit of meat on a chicken wing. "You can have four legs, but after that, we'll seal the container tight and anchor it in the creek. That'll keep the rest cool enough so it won't spoil." She tucked her jeans in the backpack. "Come on."

❦

With Monday's workday behind him, Ephraim set up his telescope in the hiddy. He tried to focus on the stars glistening in the dark sky, but frustration at that girl's brazenness to walk into his house last night and steal from him had his attention much more than the heavens. She fit his Daed's description of the drunken thief he'd seen—the one his Daed had warned the community to watch out for. Ephraim had yet to figure out what she'd stolen from him. But he'd seen her arms filled with something.

Mars had come into view high in the western sky. Around midnight it'd set in the northwest. Since he wasn't taking an eye off his home tonight, he'd probably be here for that too, if he could concentrate long enough to see it.

Because he'd witnessed her leaving his house with an armload of things last night, he'd gone to the barn half a dozen times today, thinking she might be there. He'd ridden through various parts of Dry Lake, but he'd not seen her. He would have a few choice words for her when she did show up. And she would. Thieves returned to easy prey, and he knew his place must look like easy prey.

If his uncle hadn't called to him while coming across the field that separated his place from his Daed's, he would have confronted her right then. But he didn't want any disturbing news getting back to his Daed and Becca.

A faint sound drifted through the air, and he eased to the entryway of the hiddy. He saw nothing, so he started walking around the property, searching the place. Near the edge of the cornfield closest to his home, he saw what appeared to be a little girl sitting on a rock. The thief had to be here somewhere too. Realizing her target might be his father's house, he hurried through the trees and across the field. He saw her at the clothesline, but she had on a dress this time. An Amish one.

He eased up behind her and cleared his throat. Without hesitation she took off running. "Stop." He tore after her and grabbed her arm.

She yanked, trying to free herself. He twisted her arm behind her. "I'm not going to hurt you."

"Don't bank on me promising you the same." She ground out the words as she lowered her body, taking him with her, and then threw back her head, smacking him in the mouth.

"Ow!" He dug his fingers into both her arms and pinned them, wrestling her to the ground. Blood dripped from his lip onto her back. "I'm trying to be easy. Would you just stop?"

She squirmed, cursing at him and trying to throw him off. "Let me go!"

"When you calm down, then we'll negotiate."

For her size her strength astounded him. Her salty language—exactly what he expected from a thief.

Ephraim's mouth ached all the way across his face. "Either you stop fighting and talk to me, or I'll call the police, and you can talk to them."

To his shock she became perfectly still. He released one arm and held on to the other as he stood, helping her stand with him. She was probably five foot three and couldn't weigh much over a hundred pounds. "You've been stealing from us."

"I suppose that was your dress I took?"

"Cute. But it wasn't yours."

"I didn't steal it."

He wiped blood from his mouth. "It wasn't yours, and you took it. Is there a new definition for the word **steal** that I'm not familiar with?"

"I brought money back."

"Sure you did."

"You can argue with me about it or go look for yourself. It's on the clothesline."

Still holding on to her arm, he walked to the spot. A ten-dollar bill hung from the line, pinned securely.

Moonlight shone across her face, revealing her beauty. He saw something else too—the confidence of a woman, and suddenly she didn't look as young to him.

With her size and defiant stance and the jeans and a shirt that showed her stomach, he'd assumed she was a teen. But the way she held her own, staring at him with a certain assurance, he truly looked at her for the first time. "So giving money after taking things that weren't for sale is okay?"

"Lofty words coming from someone whose mommy and daddy gave him everything he needed his whole life."

"And what else has your little sister seen you steal?"

She stilled, but she didn't answer him.

"Speak up. What else did you take?"

She studied him, looking rather awed by his question. "You've got so much you don't even know what's missing?"

Somehow he was losing this argument. How was that possible? "Tell me what you took."

"Just some food and a blanket."

"You planning on paying me back too?"

She didn't respond, but he knew the answer. So why did she return to leave money only for Deborah?

"Where do your folks . . . do you live?"

She opened her mouth but then seemed to change her mind.

"Well?"

"I won't borrow anything else, and I'll never set foot on this place again. I promise. Just let me go."

He figured that answer was the best he'd get from her. Whatever was going on, he didn't have it in him to call the police. After all, she had brought money to replace the missing dress and taken items from him he'd never miss.

He released her. "Go."

She paused, staring at him as if he'd done something she didn't expect. Then she took off running.

Ephraim turned to look at his Daed's house. The dim shine of kerosene lamps barely left a glow on the lawn. Daed and Becca would be home tomorrow, and he intended to keep things calm around here.

She stole food and a blanket? He tumbled that thought around.

Was it possible this young woman and

her sister were using Levina's, or rather **his,** barn as a hangout . . . or maybe even as a place to sleep?

Wondering if his brother knew either of the girls' names, he headed for the house. Once inside he went to the sink, grabbed a clean rag, and ran cool water over it. Placing it on his bleeding lip, he sighed. Why did she have to show up now? Her presence would only make it more difficult to keep things peaceful and quiet for his Daed.

She knew how to hit a bull's-eye when arguing. But that didn't make her right. Stealing was stealing. Ephraim went into the living room. Annie and Simeon were in the middle of a game of checkers.

"Simeon, do you know the names of those girls you said were in the barn looking at the puppies?"

"The girl's name is Lori. I don't know the mom's."

"The mom's?" Ephraim plunked into a chair. So his second opinion of her was right. She wasn't a defiant teen. "The older one is her mother?"

"Yep. Nice too. Although she's pretty good at hiding from you."

"Hiding where?"

"In the silo."

"Are they living in the barn?"

He shrugged. "Didn't ask. But ain't no one gonna bother those pups with Lori and her mom there."

Ephraim ran his finger over his swollen lip. "**That,** I believe."

"Lori wants the solid black male if her mama will let her keep it. Her mom's really nice. When I complained about Mamm treating me like a baby, she said I should be glad I got people who keep me on a short leash, and if I want to live a long, happy life, I better listen to them."

He really didn't want to hear about any of the thief's alleged qualities. "When did you talk about all this?"

"The first time I saw her."

"When was that?"

"Saturday morning."

His head hurt, making concentrating hard. Maybe she was new to the area. Then why did she look so familiar?

None of her actions made sense. She'd stolen the dress last night, and tonight she'd hung money on the clothesline to pay for it. Why would she need a dress yesterday and then have money for it tonight? Had she stolen the cash from somewhere? That didn't make sense. No one used stolen money to pay for something they'd gotten away with stealing in the first place.

Deciding to pay another visit to the barn, he stood.

As he walked toward the barn, he noticed that his cornfield had been damaged by someone walking right over the sprouts. Before crossing Levina's driveway, he saw a thin beam of light. If he went into the barn right now, the woman would make excuses, lie, and disappear. He'd be better off making himself comfortable somewhere and watching. To his left, near the cornfield, lay a fallen tree. He took a seat and waited. A few minutes later someone turned off the flashlight.

Had they slipped out the back or gone to sleep? He kept watch. About thirty minutes later the woman came out of the barn, wearing her jeans and too-tight top. She leaned against the side of the building for a while, looking rather peaceful under the moonlight. Barefoot, she crossed the road and went to the tree. As she ran her hands across the bark of it, Ephraim felt chills cover him.

**It couldn't be.**

He leaned forward, watching as she climbed onto the lowest branch, caressed the dip in it, and then rocked back against the trunk. Was it possible?

She ran her fingers through her short crop of hair and then down the side of her neck.

"Cara," he whispered. Part of him wanted to yell her name and run over to see her. It was a foolish thought born from a childhood experience.

**Cara Atwater.**

Twenty years ago they'd spent the better part of a week building a friendship unlike any other he'd ever had. Her tomboy ways had made her more fun than most of the boys his age. Her eagerness to try everything, mixed with her excitement about life, had been permanently etched into his memory.

When he'd left Dry Lake during his **rumschpringe**—his time to decide whether to become Amish or not—he'd gone to New York, hoping to find her. He'd lived and worked there for two years. He called the number for every Trevor Atwater, her father's name, in the book. He watched for her in every park, restaurant, and store. Finally he gave up and moved to South Carolina.

It might have been fun to reconnect with her back then, but now she'd become her mother's child—returning with a daughter and obviously with a past that could bring nothing but heartache to Dry Lake.

Malinda had caused a lot of division in the community. He couldn't give Cara that same opportunity. Malinda left a legacy of grief—twice. Even Levina, Malinda's grandmother, died waiting to hear from her again. Now Cara had returned to what had once been her great-grandmother's place. Unsure what to think or feel, he watched her. What a mess her life must be in. No car, no house, no husband, no money.

He'd been so sure her mother was turning her life around when she'd left here twenty years ago. She had an Englischer husband, so the community couldn't make a way for her to leave him by giving her a place to live. Because she was desperate for a safe place for Cara, the community was willing to take in Cara. But Malinda had left here with her and never returned.

The young woman in the tree drew a deep breath and folded her arms, looking as peaceful as she was beautiful. But looks were deceiving. Peacefulness did not describe her, and her beauty masked the troubled waters just below the surface.

In spite of longing to talk with her, he wouldn't go to her. The community, especially his father, had to be protected. First thing tomorrow he'd go into Shippensburg and buy her a bus ticket. Then he'd fix her a box of things that would make life a little easier on her and her daughter.

# Eleven

As dawn eased the night away, Deborah stood in the laundry room, threading freshly rinsed dresses through the wringer before dropping them into the clean laundry basket.

A driver would arrive for her soon, and she had a lot of clothes to hang out before then. She usually did most of the wash on Mondays, but there had been so much work left over from Saturday's auction, she hadn't managed to get to it yesterday. Late Saturday afternoon she'd washed the clothes she and her family had worn during the auction to keep the mud from staining them. She'd meant to remove the items a few hours later, but she'd forgotten. So that'd caused her to do something she'd never done before—leave laundry on the line on a Sunday. It wasn't acceptable to have the appearance of having done laundry on a Sunday. Early Monday morning realization of what she'd done smacked her, and she hurried out to remove them, but her newly sewn teal dress was missing.

One of her friends was certainly playing a trick on her. When she found out who had masterminded this, that person had better watch her back, because paybacks were . . . fun. She'd begin by watching which of her friends blushed and who giggled the most the next time she saw them. That was a sure giveaway. Then she'd come up with a plan and get the rest of the girls to help her.

After wringing out the last item, she tossed it in the basket. Carrying the clean, wet load, she went through the kitchen on her way to the front door. One glimpse of the room made her stop. Kitchen drawers were open, and utensils were strewn across the countertops. Obviously while she'd been in the laundry room with the wringer washer running, someone had come in search of something. As she headed for the clothesline, she saw Ephraim loading a crate into his buggy. Without seeing her, he climbed in and left.

She grabbed a shirt and shook it. He must be trying to get a head start on the day too. She wondered what he'd been looking for in the kitchen. It had to be him. Almost everyone else in the household was still asleep.

Her stepmother's sister had arrived last night to help take care of the younger ones so Deborah could go to the hospital this morning. As she reached for a clothespin, she stopped cold. A ten-dollar bill dangled from the line. She laughed at the silliness of it before shoving the cash into her pocket. Money didn't grow on trees, but it appeared to grow on clotheslines. Whichever friend had come up with this prank had planned rounds for it—one day taking the item, the next day leaving money for it. Maybe she should **borrow** ten dresses from the instigator and leave one dollar.

Sunlight warmed her back, making the day feel as if it might be a good one. While she hung a pair of pants on the line, a horse and carriage pulled into her driveway. She'd hoped Mahlon would arrive for his workday in the cabinetry shop before her driver came to get her, but Ada was driving the rig. She stopped the buggy near Deborah, studying her but saying nothing.

Deborah dropped a pair of wet pants into the basket and walked closer to Ada. "Gut morning. What brings you out this early?"

"I thought maybe I left my roasting pan here on Saturday."

"I don't remember seeing it. You know that every year I have a box of lost-and-found items people have left at the auction. But the last time I added something to it, there weren't any pots or pans. We can go look, though."

She shook her head. "If you haven't seen it, I'm sure it's in one of the boxes of stuff I took home Saturday." Studying the barn and pastures, she seemed to be searching for something. "I guess while I'm here, I'll stop in at the shop and speak with Mahlon."

"Mahlon?" Deborah's heart jolted.

Ada wasn't looking for missing pans. She wanted to find her son, which meant he'd been out all night again, and this time she'd realized it. But Deborah hadn't seen him since yesterday when he came by the house after work. If he were already at the shop, his buggy would be parked along the fence nearest her house, and his horse would be grazing in the closest pasture.

She looked but saw no sign of either. "I saw Ephraim leaving a little while ago. Maybe they're meeting at a job site." Or maybe Mahlon had been out with Eric again.

"Oh, ya, you're probably right."

She hoped she was. She hated the concern on Ada's face. If Mahlon was going off with Eric behind Ada's back, Deborah would be tempted to tell him his mother deserved more respect than that. But Mahlon would say he wasn't a kid and he footed most of the bills. She hoped Mahlon didn't put her in this kind of spot once they married. She considered Ada a friend and hated not sharing what she knew to be true.

Mahlon was the kind of man who needed time and space to work through the things that bothered him. Deborah worked through her issues with the help of her friends and church fellowship. Over the years they each had allowed for what the other one needed. When he was ready, he'd tell her everything.

Her driver pulled into the driveway, and she didn't have the laundry hung out yet. Ada wrapped the reins around the bar on the dashboard of her carriage. "I'll finish that for you. Is there more to be washed?"

"Ya, but you don't have to—"

"I know. But I'm here, and you need to go, so shoo."

"Denki, Ada."

"Gern gschehne. Now go."

Deborah gave her a quick hug and climbed into the passenger seat. Unrest concerning Mahlon rode with her for the hourlong drive to the hospital, and she silently prayed for him.

Three hours later and with Becca's errands behind them, she was in the car on her way home with her Daed and Becca. Distant rain clouds moved across the sky, and she hoped someone had taken the laundry inside.

From the front passenger seat, Daed watched the scenery, making occasional remarks to the driver. He looked surprisingly well, and except for admitting to being very tired, he said he felt fine.

As they came closer to Levina's old barn, Daed pointed. "What's that box?"

Deborah peered through the front window, unable to spot it.

Daed tapped the glass. "Pull over and let me take a look."

She saw the wooden box with a piece of a blue tarp covering the top sitting outside the barn door. It looked like the one Ephraim had this morning.

Daed climbed out of the car, lifted the tarp, pulled a folded paper out of the side of the crate, read it, and returned it to the box. He replaced the covering and got back in the vehicle.

"What were you reading, Abner?" Becca asked.

He shrugged. "A note written by whoever left the box. Looked like Ephraim's handwriting."

Becca frowned. "Well, who was the note to?"

"It didn't say. Just boiled down to instructions to keep what they'd taken but telling them they couldn't live in his barn and they needed to leave Dry Lake."

# Twelve

Cara pulled Lori in the wagon her employers had loaned her. Scattered drops of rain caused her to head straight for the barn. Without a change of clothes for Lori, she wouldn't chance that the cloud would pass on by. Her muscles ached from her second day of deep cleaning the Howards' house. It was only Tuesday, and after leaving money on the line for the dress, she had ninety dollars in cash. It made her dream of having the comforts of her own place, one with books to read to Lori and beds with sheets and a pillow and a refrigerator with food and—

"Look, Mom, someone left us something."

Cara blinked, snapping out of her daydream. A hundred feet ahead, right at the barn door, sat a box. An uncomfortable feeling stole through her.

While on her lunch break today, she'd called half a dozen places, looking to rent something. The cost of living here didn't compare to the expense of New York, but it was still several hundred dollars. It would take two weeks of working for the Howards to earn that.

She didn't dare hint to them that she had no place to live. They seemed like nice enough people, but that didn't make them trustworthy. Still, they let Lori play in their backyard and didn't begrudge Cara fixing herself and Lori a little to eat when she prepared meals for Mrs. Howard. While Mrs. Howard slept, Cara showered and washed her and Lori's clothes. Hot water, soap, and shampoo had never felt so good.

She went to the crate and lifted the plastic covering. At a glance she saw blankets, cans of food, and a can opener. Someone had figured out they were staying here, which meant they had to get out. Quick.

A note caught her attention. While Lori

knelt beside the box, looking through the stuff, Cara read the note.

Whoever had written it had instructed her to leave Dry Lake and pick up two bus tickets that were already paid for. Destination: New York City.

Alarm pricked her skin. Someone knew they were from New York?

"Look, Mom, a cloth doll. She doesn't have a face. You ever seen a doll without eyes?"

"No, but I've seen men without hearts."

She laughed. "You what?"

"Never mind. Look, sweetie, we can't stay here. Whoever left this box of stuff said we have to move on."

"Why? We didn't hurt the puppies or break nothing."

"I know. But we have to go anyway."

"But my puppy!"

"Go tell him good-bye."

"No. He's mine! Simeon said I could have him."

"Lori, we don't even have enough food for us." She bit her tongue to keep from cursing.

Lori ran into the barn, crying.

She followed. "We don't have a choice, honey."

"Why? It's a stupid old barn, and we're not hurting nothing!"

Cara sat down next to her daughter and waited. When the tantrum eased up, Cara would tell her again that they had to go, and then they'd leave without hysterics. The one thing that had made all this bearable for Lori was the puppy she'd claimed as hers, and now . . .

The barn door creaked open, startling her. A police officer stepped inside. Her knees went weak.

"Ma'am, can you come out of the barn?"

She swallowed her fear and headed for the barn door.

"You, too, little girl."

Panic rose in Cara. "Is there a problem, Officer?"

"Just follow me, please."

Two police cars sat waiting outside. A female officer motioned to Lori. "Can I talk with you, honey?"

Cara's breathing came in short, quick spurts. The rain clouds skirted eastward, and she wished the threat of them hadn't caused her to carelessly hurry to the barn. If only she'd waited . . .

"You're on private property, ma'am." The man stood in front of her while the woman talked to Lori a few feet away.

"There are puppies in the barn, and my daughter's picked one out."

The woman kept trying to engage Lori in a conversation, and her daughter answered a few questions, but mostly her attention seemed fully on her mother.

"The owner asked you to leave, both verbally and in a written note."

"Yes, but . . . there's been a misunderstanding. I work not far from here."

"It's our understanding that you've been stealing from the residents around here."

"My mom doesn't steal!" Lori screamed at the man.

No matter what answer Cara gave him, he'd check it out, so lying would only add to her problems. "I did take a few things." She spoke softly, hoping Lori wouldn't hear.

"Where do you live, ma'am?"

Tears filled her eyes. It was over. They'd take Lori. "Please, you don't understand."

"Just stay calm, ma'am. Do you have an address?"

Tears threatened as she shook her head.

"Several homes in the area have been broken into lately." He pointed to her dress. "Amish clothing and quilts are among the missing items."

Cara looked at Lori. Her little girl deserved better than a mom who failed her all the time.

The man took a step back, and the woman moved forward and frisked her while he looked through her backpack. He pulled out the cash that Mr. Howard had paid for her work yesterday and today—nearly a hundred dollars.

He held it up. "All tens, just like the missing cash on the report."

"But I . . . I earned that. You have to believe me."

"You've entered people's unlocked homes and taken items."

"I said that already, but I didn't steal that money."

The man pulled handcuffs from his belt. "You've been breaking and entering as well as stealing. Before we go any further, I need to tell you that you have the right to remain silent . . ." The officer rattled off things Cara had heard on television a hundred times.

She tried to think of something that might get her out of this mess. "You can have the money. Please don't do this, please."

The woman placed her hand on Lori's head. "Unless you have a relative or someone who can keep your daughter, she'll have to be placed in protective custody."

Broken, she looked at her daughter. "I'm sorry, baby. I'm so, so sorry."

Lori tried to run to her, but the woman held her.

"Please turn around and place your hands on your head," the man said.

"Leave my mom alone!" Lori screamed and flailed against the woman's hold, but she didn't release her. In a minute Lori would be taken in one car and Cara in the other.

All her years of holding on in the face of hopelessness drained from her. "Lori, honey, listen to me, okay?" Trying to keep from crying, she blinked. "This feels scary, I know, but they'll take good care of you. You'll be okay, and I'll come for you soon. I promise."

"No!" Lori screamed. "Don't let them take me!"

When Ephraim topped the hill, he spotted two police cars in front of his barn. He slapped the reins hard against the horse's back, spurring her to quicken the pace.

As he pulled to a stop, he saw a policeman holding Cara by the arm—or at least the woman he believed to be Cara. Handcuffs held Cara's arms behind her back as her small body shook with sobs. The officer opened the door to the backseat of the patrol car.

"Don't take my mom!" The little girl kept screaming the same thing over and over as a woman officer held on to her arm.

"Lori, you have to calm down," the woman spoke firmly. Lori kicked at her, but the officer avoided being hit.

Ephraim jumped down from the carriage. "What's going on here?"

The male officer turned to him. "Are this barn and land your property?"

"Ya."

Lori couldn't catch a solid breath, but her wails were haunting.

"Then you're the one who called the police about a thief and trespasser?"

"No. Just let her go."

"We can't do that, sir. We need to investigate her for suspicion of child endangerment and neglect."

Cara turned to him. "Please . . ." Tears brimmed. "Please help us."

What a mess. If he did any more for her than just speak to the police, it was sure to open old wounds. People didn't trust Malinda when she last visited, and they'd be angry that he'd stepped in to help Malinda's daughter—someone they might have heard had been roaming the community, drunk and stealing from them.

She gazed into his eyes, silently pleading for him to help. He moved closer to her, wanting to ask so many questions. As he looked into her eyes, a moment passed between them. He knew she was not who she appeared to be—a worldly, troublemaking thief. He looked at the policeman. "This is all a mistake. The police never should have been called." A flicker of recognition came to him. "You're Roy McEver, right?"

The man nodded.

"Your father used to patrol this area before he retired. You rode with him some even as a kid. I'm Ephraim Mast. My Daed's Abner."

"Oh yeah, he's one of the preachers. And I remember you. While I was here with Dad one time, you invited me to play ball."

He'd taken quite a harassing from the

other guys for inviting an Englischer to play. Ephraim nodded, feeling like he might get Cara out of this fix yet. "She's not done anything to deserve handcuffs."

"She confessed to stealing."

Her honesty needed better timing.

Cara shook her head. "Only that dress, which I paid for, and a few items I borrowed from you. I swear it. Anything else that's missing—especially money—wasn't taken by me. You've got to believe me."

"Nothing was taken that I wasn't glad to give," he assured the officer.

"She had cash on her. Nearly a hundred dollars. In tens."

"I work for Mr. Howard, on Runkles Road. Ask him."

"You could check her story out and let her go, right?" Ephraim asked. "I think you'll find that someone else must have stolen whatever money or other stuff is missing from elsewhere."

The man sighed. "It's not that simple. I could let her go, but the girl has to come with us. This woman is homeless. We have to file a report and turn the case over to social services."

A sinking feeling of just how deeply Ephraim was getting involved nagged at him. He couldn't ask anyone in Dry Lake to let a stranger he couldn't vouch for stay in their home. If he told them he needed their help to keep her from being arrested, they'd never take her in. Still . . . he couldn't ignore her need for help—not and live with himself.

"She can stay at my place until she gets on her feet."

"Are you saying you'll take responsibility for the child's care?"

Ephraim nodded.

Roy hesitated, but then he unlocked the cuffs and released Cara. "Ephraim, I'll need your information. What's your address?"

Lori pulled free from the policewoman's grip and ran to her mother. She jumped into her arms. While Ephraim told Roy what he needed to know, Lori sobbed, clinging to her mother.

"Shh. It's okay, Lorabean. Everything's

going to be okay." Cara held her tight, looking pale and shaken while stroking her daughter's hair.

But Ephraim knew everything wasn't going to be okay. What would his father's reaction be? He could only assume he was the one who called the police. His Daed wanted this drunken thief, as he called her, away from their community.

# Thirteen

As the police cars pulled away, stress and strength drained from Cara. But even before she took in a breath of relief, suspicion about the man's reasons for helping crashed in on her. Sure, she'd begged him, but why was he really doing this?

She'd split his lip last night, the evidence of it still clear on his face. Did he intend to pay her back? Whatever his motives, she couldn't afford to defy the police. That would be a mistake Lori would have to pay for. Weighing her options, she tried to stop trembling.

He turned to face her. "You got things inside?"

His things, actually, and if he wanted them back so badly, she'd give them to him. She nodded, wondering if her legs would actually carry her. With Lori's arms wrapped firmly around her neck, she walked inside and jerked on the door to the silo. It didn't open. She tried to set Lori down, but her little girl started screaming, clearly afraid to be released.

Cara held her close, stroking her hair. "Shh. We're fine now."

He stepped forward, opened the silo door without any trouble, and grabbed a flashlight, an empty food container, and a blanket. "This it?"

He made no remark about it being his stuff. Everything they owned, including her change of clothes, was stuffed inside the backpack the policeman had left near the barn door. "And the little wagon that's outside with the backpack." Her words came out barely audible.

He motioned to the door. She went to the buggy, awkwardly climbing the high step with Lori in her arms. He placed the items in back, including the box of blankets and food, and then he went to the other side and got in. One slap of the reins against the horse's back, and they were off.

She'd been in this spot before, needing serious help from a man, only that was long before Lori. Anger churned. She'd been running from Mike then too. If she hadn't been in a similar predicament—desperate for help—there would have been no marriage and no Lori.

Feeling too many things at once, Cara rode quietly. Lori's breathing caught and jerked uncontrollably every few seconds. Her tiny hands clung desperately to her mother.

When they came to the street the man lived on, he kept going. She glanced at him, wanting to know his plan, but she kept her mouth shut. He had too much power for her to question him, to chance getting into an argument.

A few minutes later he pulled into a narrow lane. Unease wrapped around her throat. The path seemed to go on forever, with pastures on both sides and no other homes nearby. When his house came into sight, she realized that he'd brought her in a back way.

He pulled into a small barn. After he jumped down, he came around to her side. If climbing in while holding Lori had been difficult, getting out was worse.

"Can I help you?"

Lori clung to her tighter, locking her feet around her.

"No, thank you."

He backed away. Cara struggled to get out without falling as she toted Lori. Then she waited. Silently he unfastened the horse, hung the leather straps on a peg, opened a gate at the back of the building, and put the horse out to pasture.

"Let's go in and get you settled." He led the way to the door and opened it for them.

Still carrying Lori, Cara stepped into his home. The beige walls of the kitchen stood bleak and empty except for a lone clock. A small oak kitchen table looked sturdy and expensive, yet something about it made it seem hundreds of years old. Stacks of thick books sat here and there.

Late-afternoon rays stretched across the wooden floors.

Weak and shaky, Cara pried Lori free of her and set her feet on the floor.

The man removed his straw hat and walked toward them. Lori screamed. Cara moved in front of her daughter, shielding her from the unknown.

He leaned in and hung his hat on a peg. "I was just putting my hat up."

Feeling embarrassed and just as skittish as her daughter, Cara took a step back.

Bewilderment played across his face. "I won't hurt you. Surely you know that."

Cara didn't know that, and she kept Lori behind her.

Looking uncomfortable in his own home, he stepped away from them. "Are you hungry?"

Cara shook her head. "You wrote the note telling us to leave?"

"Ya."

"That means yes?"

He nodded.

"You bought us bus tickets to New York City. Why there?"

"Isn't that your home?"

Her heart turned a flip. "Why would you say that?"

He stared at her as if asking a hundred questions. "My name's Ephraim."

"Yeah, I heard you tell the policeman." She shifted Lori. "I'm Cara. This is my daughter, Lori."

He tilted his head, his eyes narrowing for a moment. "There's plenty of food in the refrigerator. Clean sheets and towels are in the bathroom closet." He grabbed a set of matches off the counter. "When the sun goes down, you can light a kerosene lamp if you wish. Since you've been staying in a barn, I guess the lack of electricity won't bother you much. I'd like us to talk, but that can wait until Lori is asleep. Or tomorrow if you're too tired. In the meantime if you and your daughter can stay out of sight, I'd appreciate it."

"Sure, I guess so."

"I just don't need my family to know about you, not yet."

She wondered who he was trying to kid. Himself maybe. He wouldn't want **anyone** to know she was there. She'd read it in his eyes as the police left. She was trash, and he was an upstanding member of his community.

He drew a deep breath, looking unsure. Not at all like a heartless man. "Lori, do you like books? I've got a few children's books in the storage room."

Lori looked at her mom before nodding.

He disappeared into a room and returned within a minute carrying a small stack of books. "They're quite worn but still just as good as the first time they were read. Books are funny that way."

Lori eyed the stack and eased closer to him until he could place them in her hands.

"Thanks," she whispered.

"You're welcome. Well, I guess that about covers it. I'll sleep in the shop." He started toward his hat but then headed for the door instead.

Lori flew toward the door and spread her arms out. "Don't leave us!"

Looking baffled, he stared at the little

girl. "You're safe here." He glanced to Cara as if it was his turn to beg for help. "She's both afraid of me **and** afraid of me leaving?"

Cara shrugged, unwilling to try to voice all that her daughter must be feeling. Besides, it should be obvious that her emotions were irrational right now.

He eased into a chair, rubbing his forehead. "I can't stay. I could be excommunicated."

"What?" Cara asked.

He shook his head. "Nothing. I shouldn't have said my thoughts out loud."

Lori moved to her mother's side. "Please, mister. Those policemen could come again."

Cara knew it wouldn't do either of them any good to try to explain why the police wouldn't return, not to a panicked kid and not when social services would show up again soon.

He sighed. "Okay. I won't go anywhere for now. Maybe Lori won't feel so strongly about me leaving after she has time to calm down, because I have some chores I need to do a little later. But for now I'll just be in the storage room. It's right there." He pointed to a door.

Clinging to Cara's dress, Lori nodded. Ephraim left the room and shut the door. Cara melted onto the floor and snuggled with her daughter. What an embarrassing, unpredictable mess.

# Fourteen

Disbelief rippled through Ada as she stared into her son's eyes. "You want time away? From what? Why?"

Mahlon shrugged before turning his attention to the bowl of potato soup in front of him.

Ada passed him a glass of milk. "You've talked to Deborah about this?"

"Not yet."

"We only have thirty-three days before we have to be out of here."

"That's more than a month, and it'll only take one day to move."

"Move to where? You haven't even decided on a place. We need solid plans. Not procrastination."

He looked up at her. "I think the Ever-sons' home is best. But they're asking too much for rent, so I'm waiting them out."

"We don't need a place nearly that big or expensive."

"It'll give all of us elbow room."

**Elbow room?** She'd worried for quite a while that he considered her a burden. It didn't matter that he'd been the one who hadn't wanted her to remarry because he hated watching all the adjustments Deborah had to make when her Daed remarried. Ada had thought she was doing the right thing when she agreed to remain single, so she had come up with a plan to support them. But to make her plan work, she needed to move to Hope Crossing. She could have made a decent living off her pies and cakes if they'd moved there. But he'd been stressed over that plan. To make up for his strong opinions, he'd come up with plans of his own. Maybe she'd been wrong to go along with them so easily. When she lost her husband, all she could see and feel was her love for the one child they'd had together. During all the years since his Daed had died, maybe what

Mahlon thought he needed and what he really needed were two different things.

Regardless of all that, nowadays he seemed frustrated that she needed his financial support. She hated to even think it, but maybe he'd be happier if she found a rental she could afford on her own. If it was in a touristy spot, she could sell her baked goods to local restaurants. He and Deborah could live alone.

"Why do you have to get away now?"

"Because it's now or never." He pushed the bowl back and stared at the table. "You know it is, Mamm." He gazed at her through those earnest hazel eyes. "I'm twenty-three, and I've worked full-time for nine years. **Nine years,** Mamm—eight of them for Ephraim. Come November I'll be married, and by next fall you'll have your first grandchild. And probably one every couple of years after that until I can no longer remember being young. I just need a few days away on my own. Is that so wrong?"

"Are you . . . unsure about getting married?"

He scoffed. "The only thing I know for sure in this whole stinking mess of life is that Deborah Mast means everything to me." Taking his bowl with him, he stood and went to the sink. "Little else makes any sense. Things I don't want to think about wake me at night. In the space between asleep and awake, I hear whispers about wars and homeland security, and I see the Twin Towers falling all around me again. When I'm asleep, every object in my hand turns into a weapon of some sort. And when I wake, I'm filled with a desire for . . . vengeance, I think."

Unable to bear the grief he'd just heaped on her, she sat. And in ways others wouldn't see, she wasn't sure when she'd ever get up again. "But a few years back you said the strength and number of the dreams had faded into nearly nothing."

"I know, Mamm. But they started back."

"Why?"

He shrugged. "It doesn't matter. But I think I can make peace between me and God if I have some time by myself."

She studied him, hoping words of help and comfort would come to her.

He turned his half-empty glass of milk round and round. "Eric's home for a while."

The pieces began to fit, and she had a few concerns as to what the image would be when the puzzle was complete. "Maybe the dreams returning has to do with your renewed friendship with him. I'm sure he came home with war stories."

"He came home to bury a mutual friend."

"Who?"

"Stewart Fielding."

Her heart ached with things she couldn't say. "He's one of the boys you and Eric used to hang out with, one that wrote you letters regularly from Iraq."

"Ya."

"Did you go to his funeral?"

He nodded.

"Does Deborah know you went?"

"No."

They'd been down this road many times

before. He wanted to follow the Amish way of life, but then he mingled with friends who pulled him in the opposite direction. Ada knew Amish folk who had Englischer friends and it wasn't an issue, but the way Mahlon's friends lived challenged the core beliefs of the Amish. That had to stir conflict in her sensitive son.

"Mahlon, I think seeds were scattered over you without your permission, and others you've planted without realizing it. But you have to know when to pull away from certain friends before—"

"Mamm, please. Just back off. I'll find us a new place. I'll do whatever it takes to keep the bills paid. Just trust me and help Deborah to do the same. I don't want her getting hurt. Not ever."

The sounds of a horse and buggy caused Ada to look out the window. "I saw Deborah this morning."

Concern etched across his face. "When you were looking for me?"

"Ya. I didn't tell her you went out last night and never came home, but she's bound to be wondering." Seeing Deborah driving the buggy down the road toward their house, Ada pointed out the window.

Mahlon glanced. "She'll think I was with Eric, which I wasn't. I was just walking, alone. Must have gone eight to ten miles. It helped, but not enough. I kept thinking someone I knew would see me, and Deborah would be embarrassed by my odd behavior. I need a couple of days someplace where no one knows me. Where no one expects work or help or answers. Can you understand that?"

Hoping he knew what he was doing, she hugged him. "Ya, a little."

"Denki, Mamm. I'll go for a ride with Deborah and talk to her."

Ada watched as her son left the house and climbed into the carriage next to his betrothed. If anyone had the power to help Mahlon navigate the muddy rivers within him, Deborah Mast did.

It pained her to watch him struggle. If he could just let go of trying to make life fit inside his understanding, his hands would be free to grasp the richness around him. She shouldn't worry. She knew that.

Maybe all he needed was a week to think things through and for her to find a home of her own. But she couldn't do that on the meager amount of money she could make inside Dry Lake. She'd have to move elsewhere if she hoped to make a living.

Deborah passed the reins to Mahlon when he climbed into the rig beside her. He guided the horse onto the road before shifting the reins into one hand.

"How's your Daed?"

"Adjusting to new medicines and feeling decent."

"Good." A slight smile radiated from his lips, and his hazel eyes bore into her as he patted the seat beside him. When she slid closer, he put his arm around her shoulder. They rode in silence, but the warmth of who he was filled her. Most of their evenings started out quiet unless she did all the talking, but soon enough he'd open up. And when he did, they grew even closer.

Finally he cleared his throat. "Mamm said she came by this morning."

"Ya. Looking for you, I think."

"I went out last night but not with Eric."

"All night?"

He nodded. "It was foggy and quiet, so I walked until the sun began to rise. I found a few answers, a bit of peace, but . . . mostly it seemed to only confuse things."

"I don't understand, Mahlon. I try. You know I do."

He fidgeted with the reins. "Remember when I went away for nearly a week about four years ago?"

"Ya."

It'd been one of their secrets. Ephraim had a week-long job out of town. So Mahlon told his mother he was going with Ephraim, and he told Ephraim he needed to stay at home with his mother. No one but Deborah knew the truth.

"I came back with my mind clear and all sorts of things worked out, ya?"

She shifted, staring at him. "You're going away again?"

"Just for a few days. I need a little time. That's all."

"I don't understand. What is it you want time to do?"

"Easy, Deb."

"Don't try to calm me, Mahlon. I have as much right to feel things as you do, and I don't like how you're acting. Less than a week ago we began telling our friends and family of our plans to marry, and now you need to get away?"

"This has nothing to do with you."

Mahlon told her about his nightmares and insomnia, but she also heard what he wasn't saying—that the responsibility of finding a home, getting married, and starting his own family had triggered old feelings of panic. When he lost his father at ten years old and took on the responsibility for his widowed mother, it seemed to dig a channel inside his soul, like the wheel of a buggy caught in a deep, muddy rut. Being in New York on September 11 during the terrorist attacks made it a thousand times worse, and now Eric's return seemed to have triggered questions inside him that he had no answers for.

He pulled onto Jonathan's long dirt driveway and came to a stop. "If this was happening to you, you'd need a lot of time among your friends and family. You'd spend hours and hours with your many friends, me included, talking until you unearthed the answers that put things in perspective and brought you peace. But that's not me, Deb."

Her heart twisted, and her eyes brimmed with tears. "You need time completely alone." She cupped his face with her hands. "I'm sorry I got aggravated."

He pulled her closer and placed his lips over hers. After the gentle kiss he studied her. "Sometimes I get mad at me too, but I'm still the same anyway."

"I love you for who you are. You go talk to yourself and God. And find peace."

He wrapped his arms around her, and

she felt him tremble. Whatever had been unleashed inside him was making him more miserable than he could bear. Silently she prayed for him, as she had every day for as long as she could remember.

"When will you go?"

"Saturday most likely. Ephraim has a lot of work scheduled for the rest of this week, and I can't leave yet. I'd like you and me to go out Friday night, and then I'll leave the next morning. I'll tell Ephraim tomorrow that I'm taking off a few days next week."

## Fifteen

The edge of darkness began to take over as Ephraim left the barn with a full and sleepy pup in hand—the one Simeon said Lori wanted. He'd taken clean clothes from the clothesline back to Cara and Lori over an hour ago before going to visit his Daed.

Cara had said nothing when he'd set the items on the table. He'd added a little more wood to the oven in case she wanted to scramble some eggs or fix a grilled cheese sandwich. Without experience on a wood stove, she wouldn't be able to cook much, but he assured her she could use any of the food in the house to fix her and Lori something to eat. He had no idea why, but an accusing look had returned to her eyes when he said the words.

It made him miss Anna Mary. Her friendly, easily understood ways were much more welcome than this mess . . . except he wasn't sure how well she'd take the news of Cara when the time came.

He stepped onto his porch with the full intention of tapping before walking in, but Lori sat in a ladder back chair in the kitchen, staring through the screen door. In that brief moment he saw a very worried little girl. She seemed to think if he didn't keep his word and come back, the police would show up again. Her wet hair hung about her shoulders, and her shiny-clean face eased into a slight smile at the sight of him.

Ephraim came inside and held out the pup.

"Mom, look!" She jumped up from her chair and scooped the dog from his hand.

Cara walked out of the bathroom, towel drying her hair and wearing one of his shirts over her jeans. Her eyes questioned him.

Ephraim removed his hat and hung it on the peg. "He's full right now, but I'll take him back to his mother in the morning."

Lori cuddled the puppy. "Whatcha gonna name him?"

"Name him?" He had no plans to keep the mutt.

"Mom said we don't have enough food for us, let alone a dog. But if you want him . . ."

Ephraim chuckled. "Well, I've been thinking maybe I need a dog around here." He noticed dozens of bug bites on Lori's arms and legs. He went to the kitchen cabinet where he kept some over-the-counter stuff, grabbed a tube of anti-itch cream, and passed it to Cara.

"Thanks." Cara read the side of the package and removed the lid.

"Not a problem." He patted the dog's head. "How about Better Days?"

A faint look of cynicism crossed Cara's face, but she said nothing.

Lori set the dog on the floor and walked across the room. "Here, Better Days." The puppy ran to her. "Look, he likes it."

Ephraim closed the front door. "Actually, he likes you, and he would have come no matter what you called him. But he'll get used to the name."

"Can he sleep on the bed with me?"

"I suppose for tonight. If it's okay with your mom."

She looked to her mom, who gave a silent nod. Contentment seemed to erase the last of Lori's stress, and she smiled.

Cara sat on the floor near Lori and dabbed spots of medicine onto bug bites. Ephraim grabbed yesterday's newspaper off a counter, took a seat at the kitchen table, and opened it. Half reading and half listening to the banter between mother and daughter, he felt the depth of the bond between them.

He'd been nineteen when his mother died, and although he hadn't realized how much he loved her until after she died, the pain of losing her wore on him night and day, slowly easing with time. Even now he had nights when he dreamed of her and heard her voice in his sleep.

The room grew quiet as Cara and Lori moved into the bedroom. Cara's soft voice rode through the silence of his home as she read from one of the children's books, not sounding anything like the woman who'd split his lip last night.

Hoping she'd come back into the kitchen when Lori was settled, he added a bit of wood to the cookstove and put on a pot of coffee to brew. After returning to the kitchen table, he read through a different newspaper. She came out of the bedroom, closed the door behind her, but remained near the doorframe.

Her eyes seemed glued to the table. Taut lines across her face had replaced the tenderness he'd seen there when she was with Lori. "I appreciate your kindness to my daughter." She lifted her eyes, staring straight at him. "I don't suppose you're ready to tell me the bottom line in all this."

Ephraim went to the stove and poured her a cup of coffee. He set it on the table. "That's percolated coffee, meaning it's boiling hot." He placed cream and sugar in front of her before pouring himself a cup and taking a seat. He motioned to a chair.

"Sit." She slowly moved forward and took a seat.

Without touching her cup, she stared at the black liquid in front of her.

He dumped a bit of cream and sugar into his cup. The clock ticked off the minutes. "Is it too late in the day for you to drink coffee?"

She shook her head.

"Do you take your coffee black?"

"I'll keep close tabs on what I use while we're here. You'll get what I'll owe you. I'll even pay for your kindness to Lori. But I won't use anything I don't really need, like coffee or cream or sugar."

Not liking her tone, Ephraim wondered if they would get along only when Lori was around. "So you're figuring on paying me for each thing, are you?"

"Are you saying I won't?"

Ephraim tried to steady his growing frustration. "I'm saying you couldn't possibly pay me for the trouble your presence is going to cause. I don't need your money anyway. But an attitude overhaul on your part might make this situation bearable."

She ran her hands across the edge of the table, and he noticed a slight trembling of her fingers. It dawned on him what she thought he might want.

His offense at her faded. Hidden inside her was a steely determination. He wouldn't be surprised if she'd fed her daughter dinner tonight but not herself.

He reached into his pocket, feeling the toy horse he'd dug out of the storage room. When he knew her as a child, she'd treasured it above all else, and then she'd given it to him.

She drew a shaky breath. "Did the policeman say how social services will contact me?"

"They could just drop in, but he thinks they'll call first because Dry Lake is a long way to drive just to find out no one is home."

"You drive by horse and buggy, but you have a phone?" She looked around, searching for it.

"Not in the house. The few Old Order Amish people who own a phone never have it inside their home. The church leaders gave me permission to have one because of my business. It's in the cabinetry shop. It has a loud speaker directed this way, so I can usually hear from this distance— except in winter when my windows are shut."

He went to the refrigerator and pulled out a coconut pie his sister had made for him. He slid it onto the table and grabbed two plates from the cabinet. "This is the best pie you'll ever have. And it has no strings."

She stared at the pie as he cut a piece and put it onto a plate. "I appreciate everything you've done for us. Unfortunately, I know how situations like this work . . . even if you don't."

He held the plate out to her. When she didn't take it, he set it on the table. He put some cream and sugar into her coffee and pushed it toward her. "Relax, Cara."

She stared at him with those bronze eyes he remembered so well—only back then they carried hope instead of cynicism. The only dare those eyes had carried as a child was the fun kind that lacked fear. She'd trusted him when he said she'd be safe to jump from a loft or drop from a rope into the creek. He motioned to the slice of pie. "It's free. I promise."

She didn't look like she believed him, but she didn't argue. "I've been looking for a place. I want to be gone within a few days at most."

"The sooner the better for me too."

She studied him without a trace of trust in her eyes.

"I want nothing from you except respect. I'm sure there are plenty of men who'd like more from you. I'm not one of them. It's angering that you can't believe that." He took a sip of his coffee. "But I understand it."

"It's angering?" She blinked several times. "You certainly don't look or sound angry."

Suddenly he remembered why her mother had come back—to find a place of safety from a man who'd grown too violent to control. She'd made arrangements with Levina to take Cara in. Even received permission from the bishop for her to give Cara up and for Levina to take care of her.

At the time he'd really liked Cara. Not as a girlfriend or anything, but as a pal who wasn't afraid to try things she'd never done before. He'd been glad the church leaders were going to allow her to live with Levina.

But her mother had never brought her to Levina as she'd arranged. What had her life been like because of that?

"Saying something directly is all it should take to get a point across. Don't you think?"

She gave a half shrug. "Most talk is a waste of time. Actions mean a lot more."

He nudged the mug of coffee and the plate of pie closer to her. "Then let my actions say I'm on your side in this."

After a few moments a half smile created a faint but familiar dimple in her cheek. She slowly took the cup in hand. Breathing in the aroma, she lifted it to her lips. Her eyes closed, and she took a sip. "Oh, man. If I had a cigarette, I might believe in heaven." She ate the pie slowly, as if savoring every crumb.

He had dozens of questions to ask and a hundred things he wanted to tell her, but he doubted if either held any wisdom. She needed time to get past the trauma of being kicked out of a run-down barn, of almost losing Lori, of begging for help. "So you've been walking to the Howards for work every day?"

"I've been thinking of firing the chauffeur. He never shows up on time."

He chuckled. At least she still had a sense of humor, even though it had turned rather bitter. "Cara, no one can see you leaving this house. My father's sick. He just came home from the hospital today. I need time before I can tell him you're staying here."

"I'll take Lori with me, and we'll go out the back way, through the fields. We'll leave before daylight and not come back till after dark. I need the money if I'm going to get out of here in a few days, and I just can't leave Mr. Howard hanging. If he loses more work hours, he'll be fired."

Her personality was an odd mix of sarcasm, humor, honesty, and courage. In some ways she seemed a lot like the girl he knew twenty years ago. If she wasn't such a danger to him, he could enjoy getting reacquainted.

"Fine. Use the same route I brought you in by, and try not to be seen."

She angled her head, questions etched on her face.

"You're not a prisoner. We're in this together."

He pulled the toy horse out of his pocket and laid it on the table. He thought he saw a shadow of recognition cross her face, but then she stared into the bottom of her empty cup. Either she didn't recognize it, or she didn't trust him enough to want to discuss any part of her past.

Leaving the toy on the table, he rose. "Good night, Cara."

# Sixteen

Consciousness tapped against the numbness of sleep. Waking, Cara snuggled on the softness beneath her, enjoying the luxury. Unlike when she'd slept in the barn, she didn't wish to hurry daylight along. The pleasure of a mattress beneath her and covers surrounding her caused a sense of dignity to return, even if she and Lori never had much.

She reached across the bed until she felt the warmth of her daughter's back. Her eyes misted. Waking could have been so miserably different for both of them if Ephraim hadn't come along.

Lori's breathing came in slow, rhythmic sounds, renewing Cara's strength for the battles ahead. Through all the haze of panic and shame yesterday, she'd not given much thought to Ephraim's actions. She'd only fixed on her unease about his hidden motives.

She put her feet on the clean wooden floors, grateful not to be in that cold, smelly barn. She eased into her jeans. The toy horse Ephraim had pulled from his pocket and left on the kitchen table now sat on the nightstand. She'd taken it with her when she went to bed last night. He'd acted like it should mean something to her, but she'd been too leery of him to ask and too drained to think straight.

She didn't mean to be so callous toward Ephraim. But she'd lost herself once. Her sense of self-respect had died a painful death. Buried the year she turned nineteen. Of all the things in life she grieved for, giving up her own self in exchange for food and shelter and safety was the worst.

American tradition lied. Black was not the color worn during loss and grief. White was. White lace. Tulle. Chiffon. Silk. But in spite of marrying Johnny when she wasn't in love with him, the life they built became one she cherished.

She took the toy horse in hand, studying it. Ephraim was not Johnny, and he wasn't helping her so she'd owe him a lifetime debt. He wanted her out of his life as much as she wanted out. And he deserved to be treated with respect, not jaded bitterness. As she clutched the horse in her hand, a vague memory moved through her like a shadow.

Standing barefoot on a creek bank, she watched a boy as he stared at the horse in the palm of her hand. Words were coming out of her mouth, but she couldn't make them out. Closing her eyes, she concentrated. **"You keep it,"** she heard herself say. Goose bumps ran over her whole body. **"Keep it until I return."**

Cara's heart raced at the memory. She wanted to remember more, but the scene ended right there. "Until I return," she whispered.

From the foot of the bed, the puppy responded to Cara's movements and waddled up to her. He licked her hands while she tried to keep him calm. Figuring he'd pee if she didn't get him outside quickly, she picked him up. She tiptoed through the dark bedroom and tripped over a stack of books. They fell like dominoes. With her free hand she put them back in place. Wondering if Ephraim collected books or if he actually read them, she walked through the dark kitchen, heading for the front door.

A movement flitted before her. She stopped short, her heart pounding.

"Cara?" Ephraim sounded startled.

"Yeah. Did I wake you?"

He drew a sleepy breath. "No. I was on my way to get a drink of water."

"I think the puppy needs to go out."

"Pffft. The whole point of better days is that they are supposed to come in and stay," he mumbled, trying to lift the puppy from her.

"What?" She didn't release the dog.

"It's a joke. We named the dog Better Days. Get it?"

Was it normal to make jokes when so much stress existed between them?

She passed him the dog. "I'm afraid I don't, but you should take the pup out before **you** get it."

He chuckled. "If Better Days starts peeing on us before the day begins, what can we expect next?"

She figured he must be a morning person. "Do you really want an answer to that?"

He went out the kitchen door. His laughter clung to her, and something about his movements made a memory jump into her mind. A cool breeze stirred the tall grass as water rippled over her bare feet. A boy grabbed a rope and swung out over the deep part of the creek, laughing as he let go.

Was Ephraim the boy in her memories?

The screen door banged as he walked in. She jolted, taking several steps back. As if he didn't see her, he went into the kitchen, set the pup on the floor, lit a kerosene lamp, and grabbed some milk out of the refrigerator. He tore off small chunks of homemade bread, tossed them into a bowl, and poured milk over them.

He set the container on the floor. "Another week or so and they'll be ready to be weaned. Guess I better start taking them some soggy food once in a while." He scrunched a few pieces of newspaper and placed them in the wood stove. He added small strips of wood on top, struck a foot-long match, and held it inside the stove. "If anyone from social services shows up here today needing to talk to you, I'll tell them where you're working." He dropped the match inside the stove and put the solid metal eye back in place.

She watched from the shadows. "Ephraim?"

He dumped coffee beans into a hand-crank grinder. "Ya?"

There were many things she wanted to know, but asking questions might start things she couldn't stop. Still, if she remained silent, she might never know any parts to her past. Having any sort of connection to people her mother knew could give her and Lori ties to family or friends or something. But could those connections do more harm to Lori than the lack of them? She wished she knew the safest thing to do.

He added water and coffee into the percolator and set it on the stove. "There's a lot going on inside that head of yours, isn't there?"

She swallowed. Why was he acting so easygoing? "Do . . . do you know me?"

"Ya, I do." He said it calmly, so matter-of-factly. "We met when we were kids. You were eight. I was twelve. Do you remember?"

Tears stung her eyes. "Some of it started coming back to me about a week ago. What I remember covers about five minutes of time."

"Is that when Malinda told you how to get here?"

"You knew my mother?"

Ephraim stopped all movement, staring at her. "Knew?" A few moments later he set two mugs on the table. "Only a little. Things I've heard. A few conversations I had with her that time you visited." The puppy finished his meal and began whining. Ephraim brought him to Cara. "When did she . . . die?"

Cara pulled the mutt against her, wishing Ephraim hadn't asked, hadn't moved in so close. Of all the things she hated talking about, losing her mother was the worst. "You don't have to say it so careful like. It doesn't matter when, does it?"

"I was nineteen when my mother died, and, yes, it mattered."

She scoffed. "There's a whole world of hurting people out there—starving, dying horrific deaths, being mutilated in accidents or by wars or by violent people."

He stroked the puppy's head. "If we're feeling sorry for ourselves, that type of thinking can help us get some perspective. But their misery doesn't stop my pain or yours. Losing a mother is tougher than it sounds."

His insight made it hard for her to respond. "People could lose themselves completely if they let it all start to matter."

"True. But a person can just as easily lose themselves if they don't let it matter."

"Great. Now I understand. No matter what we do, we lose."

He walked to the kitchen table. "There's definitely truth in that. So, if Malinda didn't tell you how to get here, your dad must have."

"Fat, stupid chance of that."

Ephraim watched her, looking as if she'd just cursed or something.

She rolled her eyes and huffed. "He went MIA a long time ago." His brows furrowed in confusion. "MIA," she repeated. "Missing in action."

"I know what it means, but . . ." He shook his head. "I'm sorry."

"Makes no difference. I'm sure I'd be in a worse jam if he'd hung around."

"How **did** you land here?"

Her heart beat as if a rock band drummer were pounding against it. If Ephraim knew she was running from a stalker, he'd kick her out. Now.

Lori came out of the bedroom, and Cara's nerves calmed. He'd already proved he wouldn't ask awkward questions in front of her.

Lori rubbed her eyes. "Morning, 'From."

"It's Ee-from, honey." Cara set the puppy on the floor. His little legs couldn't carry him to Lori fast enough as he ran across the slick floor, sliding and falling.

"'From will do." He set the milk on the table. "I want to drop you and your mom off near the Howards', so we need to head out soon. Do either of you want some eggs?"

Lori scooped up the dog, giggling when he licked her. "Me and Better Days like scrambled eggs."

## Seventeen

The moment Ephraim stepped out of Robbie's truck after work, he smelled food cooking. He headed straight for his house, hoping Deborah wasn't fixing him a meal at his place today. He'd cut the workday short because he had a plan, one that had nagged at him since it sprang to mind. And he had questions that he hated to ask Cara, but he needed answers.

As he drew closer to his home, he heard female voices. He looked through a window and spotted Anna Mary and Deborah in his kitchen. Since Cara and Lori couldn't come back here until after dark, he'd wanted to get some food to take to them. He'd planned to pick them up near the Howards' and find a suitable spot to stay until dark. But now he couldn't grab food, not without his sister and Anna Mary asking him questions he wasn't ready to answer. Cara had stuffed every piece of belongings she and Lori had into her backpack this morning. At the time he'd thought it a little odd, but right now he was glad she'd left no evidence of staying here last night. He had to tell everyone, but they didn't need to find out yet, and certainly not like this.

He changed course and went to the gate inside his barn that led to the pasture. Trying to spot his horse in the pasture, he wondered again how well Anna Mary would take the news of his dealings with Cara. The concern over his father's health and the need to find Cara a place to live was all he'd thought of since yesterday. He'd scoured the newspapers today and made several calls, but he'd found nothing, not even an empty room in some Englischer's home.

When he didn't see his horse, he whistled. Under a grove of shade trees, she raised her head, angling it as if wondering if she'd truly heard him. He whistled again, and she whinnied before breaking into a gallop.

Ever since dropping off Cara and Lori near the Howards' place that morning, he'd felt their presence. The first rays of dawn had spread their fingers across the land as he'd stopped his carriage just out of sight of the Howards. Cara thanked him, her voice barely audible and her mood invisible. She helped Lori out of his buggy, not glancing up even when Lori blew him a kiss. As he watched them go down the road, he knew he couldn't let them walk back to his place after a long day of work. But they'd need to stay somewhere out of sight until after dark, so he'd come up with a plan. A reasonable one. Except lurking inside was an emotion he didn't want.

His horse trotted toward him, and he opened the gate, letting her inside the barn. He bridled her and began connecting the leads.

"Ephraim." Anna Mary's voice made him pause.

He put the horse collar and hame over the animal's neck. "Ya?"

"Deborah helped me cook a meal for you on that awful wood stove."

One reason he didn't own a gas cookstove was to keep women out of his kitchen. Anna Mary knew that. If he ever grew serious about someone, he'd buy a gas oven. The wood stove was an unspoken line of defense against pushy women who wanted to win his fondness by showing what a great wife they could be. But he'd never considered Anna Mary pushy, and he'd actually been considering buying a gas stove.

He ran the harness traces through the whiffletree. "Sorry, but I have plans tonight. I'm heading out as soon as I hitch the buckboard."

"Won't you come eat something first? I've spent most of the afternoon cooking."

He shook his head as he fastened the leads.

She stepped forward and petted the horse. "I don't suppose I can go along."

"Not this time."

"I made fried chicken. Can I at least pack some to send with you?"

"No, thanks."

She touched his hand. "Are you leaving because I dared to cross one of your not-so-invisible lines?"

"No, but I have to question why you'd do such a thing if you thought I might mind."

She said nothing. He stopped what he was doing. After a year of courting, they knew each other pretty well, and they rarely argued, but he was being difficult, and he half expected her to tell him off and leave. Although he had no idea how he'd feel about that if it happened, he wasn't one to walk lightly.

She shrugged. "I figure the fact that you didn't tell me to never go in your kitchen is a pretty good indication of how you feel about me."

His blood ran hot. She'd been talking to her older sister. He'd courted Susanna years ago and had broken up with her over this issue. A year later she married someone else and now had three children.

Ephraim never regretted letting Susanna go. Or any of the other girls he'd dated. But Anna Mary was different.

"I just wanted to do something nice for you."

"That's not all you wanted. You're trying to figure out where you stand—if I'm the same with you as I was with Susanna. Or whoever. You told me once you don't want to be compared to anyone else, and yet you're testing to see if I'll react to you the same way."

She sighed. "Guilty, but I didn't know that until right now." She wrapped her hand around the buckle he was fastening on the horse and gazed into his eyes. "I promised myself that I wouldn't get this way over you, that'd I'd keep things light and easy. But I can't stand trying to figure out if I'll become just another girl you once courted."

Ephraim realized he'd become somewhat callous over the years; otherwise, he'd have recognized the spot she was in. He placed his hand over hers, seeing afresh that in some ways she was very tender-hearted and was willing to be vulnerable with him.

Taking her hands into his, he chose his words carefully. "You mean more. Only time will tell us what we both want to know."

She closed her eyes, looking both disappointed and relieved. He placed his hand on her shoulder, and she wrapped her arms around him. When they connected really well, like now, he hoped he'd never court anyone else. He longed to have a family of his own. To have the warmth of a woman in his bed. To make the circle of life complete by becoming a husband and father. But . . .

Anna Mary backed away. "Fried chicken is great for taking with you."

Ephraim couldn't help but smile. "It smells delicious. How much did you burn before figuring out how to regulate the heat?"

"Only a few batches."

He laughed. "You're teasing, right?"

"Ya, but if Deborah hadn't been with me, I'd be in tears, and your freezer would be empty of chicken."

"I guess we could eat a quick bite together before I head out. If it doesn't taste like burned grease," he teased, "I could take some with me too."

"You know, Ephraim, I appreciate honesty, but there are times when a bit less truthfulness would be appreciated."

"I see what you mean." Ephraim placed his hand on her shoulder as they walked across the yard. "I'll gladly take some chicken with me even if it does taste like burned grease."

She laughed and elbowed him in the ribs. "You're awful."

"I know. I'm just making sure you know that."

# Eighteen

With her backpack across her shoulders and Lori falling asleep in her arms, Cara walked back toward Ephraim's. Just as she topped one hill, she stared at another one. Her goal was to get a little closer to Ephraim's and then find somewhere out of sight to rest until after his family's bedtime. Since Lori got up before dawn and had been helping Cara clean out closets today, she needed this nap. Unfortunately, her taking one right now was quite painful for Cara. But if she knew her daughter, she'd be up and moving again in twenty or thirty minutes.

A horse and wagon came across the horizon, making her think of Ephraim. She'd spent most of the day wondering if he'd heard from the social worker. The idea unsettled her, making her thoughts as scattered as her emotions were raw.

She kept walking, the rig heading toward her at a steady speed. She'd never expected the man she'd dubbed Heartless to be so even-tempered and . . . pleasant. He didn't seem unfeeling or conniving, but she wasn't convinced he had no ulterior motive. She'd learned long ago to keep the walls around her firmly braced. People weren't trustworthy. It seemed they often wanted to be. But human weakness won out time and again.

The rig grew closer.

**Could that be Ephraim?**

Her heart beat an extra time. Was he in the area by coincidence, or had he come to pick them up?

"Whoa." Ephraim brought the horse to a stop, a warm smile hidden beneath a layer of seriousness or maybe caution. "Hi." He watched her, and for the briefest moment she thought she actually remembered those gray blue eyes.

He set the brake and climbed down.

Better Days stuck his head out from under the bench seat, wagging his whole body. Ephraim placed his hand on Lori's back. "Let's get you two in the wagon."

Half asleep, Lori raised her head, easily shifting from Cara's arms to Ephraim's. As the pressure of carrying Lori lifted, the aches and pains running through Cara's body eased.

Ephraim took her elbow and helped her onto the wooden bench. A paperback book titled **The Whole Truth** lay on the seat beside her. A bookmark peeked out about midway through the pages. She used to love reading before life took every minute of every day just to survive. Ephraim had to be a reader.

He climbed up easily with Lori and placed her in Cara's arms.

"Thank you." Her words came out hoarse.

"Not a problem."

For reasons that made no sense, tears threatened, and she licked her lips. Trying to gain command over her emotions, Cara rubbed her lower back. "I didn't know you were coming."

"Me either, at least not when I dropped you off this morning. I meant to be here earlier. Since we can't go to my place until after dark, I thought we'd go to a secluded spot near the creek. I brought some food and blankets."

"And a book." She held it up.

"Ya."

The dog nudged her with his nose.

"And Better Days."

"I figured it was about time somebody brought you better days." He chuckled at the joke and slapped the reins against the horse's back.

Cara stroked Lori's head, realizing she'd fallen back to sleep. "Any word from social services?"

"Not yet."

"What if your father sees them when they show up? Or someone else sees them and tells him?"

"I don't know. Like you, I don't have many answers right now."

"No wonder you keep toting the dog all over the place. You want Better Days to stick around."

The lines on his face curved upward, but seriousness made the hint of a smile fade. "We need to talk about a few things. Can I ask you some questions?"

A memory flashed in front of Cara. About two decades ago she'd stood in front of a boy who'd asked her the same basic thing. "The barn Lori and I hid in and the house that used to sit on that now-empty foundation—they belonged to an old woman, didn't they?"

He nodded. "Levina."

"Levina was the one Mama and I stayed with?"

"Ya, that's right."

"And you asked me if I was a boy or a girl."

Under his tanned skin his face flushed a pale pink. "Well, you were a skinny eight-year-old kid who wore jeans, and your hair was cut shorter than most newborns."

She ran her fingers through her hair,

tugging at the end of the short crop. She liked her hair like this, regardless of what he might think of it.

"Nobody would mistake you for a boy now."

"No, just a thief, a drunk, and a troublemaker."

He winced. "Sorry."

A small burst of laughter escaped her, catching her by surprise. "Well, I feel so much better now."

"Then my work is done, because I came to make you feel better."

"Don't quit your day job."

He laughed, and she understood why that sound had stayed with her all these years. But why had the memory of Levina's name returned to her but Ephraim's hadn't, even when she stood inside his home and he told her?

"Remember seeing the creek for the first time?"

"No. But I do remember cool water rushing over my feet. And someone . . ."

"If there's a boy in that memory, it

would've been me. I don't think you saw anyone else that week. Other than Levina and the bishop."

"What's a bishop?"

"The head church leader over several districts. He helps us stay strong in our faith and reminds us of the meaning of the vows we've taken."

"Like a guild master in World of Warcraft."

His brows crinkled. "Like what?"

"It's an Internet game. I've never played it, but I worked with people who do."

He chuckled. "The bishop would take exception to using the Internet or playing any type of war game."

His amusement skittered through her. "I remember your laughter. It was one of the first things that came to me last week. You laughing when you jumped into the creek or into a pile of hay in the barn."

"Do you remember our playing for hours in the trees?"

"Not really. Although part of me must, because I knew about the chains on the tree before I saw them."

"That was your favorite tree. We hung those chains there ourselves, wrapping them around and around the branch for you to use as reins. I'd say we did a good job since they're still there."

"I guess so. It just seems like I'd remember your name if we spent so much time together."

"You never called me Ephraim. You called me Boy, said it was something about a Tarzan movie."

She chuckled. "Ah, I probably came up with that because of the trees and rope climbing stuff."

"Makes sense." He pulled to a stop, got out of the wagon, opened a cattle gate to the pasture, and led the horse through it. After closing the gate, he climbed back in. "I'll park at the grove of trees near the creek bank. We can eat and rest there until it's dark. I . . . I'm sorry about needing to hide and sneak around."

She scoffed. "I've been hiding for as long as I can remember."

The wagon creaked as he drove over uneven ground. "I remember Malinda telling

Levina about hiding you from your dad." He drove to the far side of a stand of trees. "She tried her best to get you somewhere safe. I don't really know what stopped her, but I know she wanted you to have a good life."

Embarrassed at all he knew about her, she whispered, "Yeah, well, that didn't happen."

Ephraim drew a long, slow breath. "Cara, I can't afford to get caught off guard. I need to know. Is Lori's father likely to show up looking for her?"

Now she knew why he'd gone out of his way to pick her up. And why he was being so friendly. He wanted answers to personal questions.

"What you're really asking is whether I have a no-good boyfriend or husband somewhere, right?" She snarled the words, not caring how angry she sounded. The insult made her skin burn.

Without saying anything else, he climbed down, took a blanket from the wagon, and placed it in a clearing ahead of the horse before returning to her. As he lifted Lori from her arms, his eyes met hers. "I meant no offense."

She bit back her sarcasm, reminding herself that it didn't matter what he thought of her. Her mistake had been allowing the easy banter between them to make her think he had any sense of who she might be. But attitudes like his got old fast.

He took Lori to the blanket on the ground and gently laid her there. She didn't stir. He returned to the wagon and grabbed a basket from it. He held out his hand, offering to help her down. She turned and climbed out the other side.

When she glanced across the wagon, he was watching her, and she couldn't keep her thoughts silent any longer. "I was married to Lori's father. In spite of what your kind might think, he was a decent man. If he'd lived, I'd never have set foot in this stinking place."

"My kind?"

"Yeah, the ones who were born having it all. You dare judge the rest of us by a standard you claim to be God's. And just to prove your greatness, you create a God who favors you over us."

He stared at her as if sizing her up. She wanted to lash out until his high-and-mighty eyes opened. All humans were equal. Some started out with more because of their parents, but that wasn't through their own skill or worthiness. She'd started with nearly nothing and continually lost more as life went on. He'd been given everything. And yet he thought he was better than her?

"Mom?" Lori called, waking.

Cara hurried to her. "I'm right here, Lorabean."

She rubbed her eyes, searching her surroundings. "Where are we?"

"On a picnic." Ephraim set the dog on the blanket beside her.

"Better Days!" Every trace of fear drained from her, and she scooped the puppy into her arms. "Thanks, 'From." She grinned. "Me and Better Days are hungry. We got any food?"

Ephraim tapped the top of the basket.

"Fried chicken, potato chips, lemonade, and cake."

"You do way better picnics than Mom." The puppy licked her face. She giggled and jumped to her feet. "Can we go to the creek? Better Days would love it."

"I thought you were hungry," Ephraim said.

"First I wanna see if he likes the water."

Cara pointed to a sandy area that sloped to a shallow section. "No deeper than your ankles, and don't get out of my sight."

"Come on, Better Days." Lori took off running with the puppy dancing around her feet, half tripping her as they went.

Cara sat on the blanket. "You are better at doing picnics." She peeked into the basket. "All she's going to remember of her childhood is what I couldn't provide."

Ephraim sat beside her. "You're a good mother, Cara. She'll remember how much you loved her."

The gentleness in his voice made guilt run through her. All he'd requested were a few reasonable answers, and she'd been defensive and rude. Tears threatened, reminding her how weary she was. "Sometimes I can barely remember my mother. Other times the memories are so strong I can't break free of them. I think she died not long after we were here. Then life became an endurance test."

"Not long after . . ." The hurt in his eyes surprised her.

He dropped his sentence and looked out over the fields. While they rested on the blanket, waiting side by side for night to come, an unfamiliar pull to talk openly tugged at her. Her anger at him still rumbled, but she'd finally met someone who'd known her mother, someone who had enough honor to do what it took to keep her and Lori from being separated.

A leaf floated downstream, drifting powerlessly on the creek's current. That's how she felt—caught by a desire as normal and natural as water flowing and a fallen leaf. Rather than treat him like she did everybody else, she decided to ignore her offense and give in to her need. "I . . . I met Johnny when I was seventeen. He was a huge, burly man, and he became my shelter. Of course that safety came with a price, and we married a year later. He believed in your God too. Said he met him in prison." She shrugged. "Somewhere during the first years of our marriage, I fell in love with him."

Ephraim grabbed a Mason jar out of the basket. "I've never heard of anyone falling in love after they got married. Although I have known a few who fell out of love."

"We got married at the courthouse, but we went to upstate New York for a honeymoon in the Catskill Mountains. The first day we hiked and canoed and had a picnic. It was the most wonderful day I'd ever had . . . or at least remembered having. That night he said his stomach hurt, so he slept on the couch. Much to my relief."

"He knew how you felt, didn't he?" Ephraim loosened the lid on the jar.

"He knew. I guess he didn't care about the time it took to change my mind about him. By the fifth night of our honeymoon, he was still making up excuses to sleep on the couch, but I invited him to stay with me." In her mind's eye she could see him clearly as he eased into bed next to her. How many times since he'd died had she wished he'd come to her bed again or been there for meals or watching Lori grow?

Ephraim held the jar of lemonade out to her. "Sounds like you found a truly good man."

She took a sip of lemonade and passed the jar back to him. "I did. When I got pregnant a couple of years later, I thought he'd be furious. But when I told him . . ."

The memory haunted her, and regrets twisted her insides. "I watched all this worry cross his face, and I realized he really did love me. I mean, he'd said he did even before we were married. But I hadn't really believed it." She sighed. "We thought we could give our child more than either of us had growing up. But before her second birthday . . . he died." She rubbed her forehead. "I never have a cigarette when I need one."

Ephraim leaned back, propping his elbow on the blanket. "I'm so sorry. I . . . I just needed to know whether to expect someone to show up looking for you and Lori."

She bit back saying, **Whatever.** In spite of how badly his words had stung, her anger wasn't completely justified. As her bitterness shrank back, she realized the obvious. What he'd been asking was, did she have someone looking for her?

"'From, look," Lori called. "What kind of fish is this?"

He rose from the blanket and went to the creek bank.

Relaxing a little as he left, Cara exhaled slowly. She dug the toy horse out of her backpack, trying to remember owning it. But whether she ever remembered it or not, the past wasn't her goal. She only had today and the opportunity it afforded her to give Lori a better life than she and Johnny had.

Of course, she hadn't told Ephraim about Mike. But hadn't he earned the right to know the reason she fled New York?

Nineteen

A swath of crimson sky touched the horizon, signaling that nightfall was close at hand. Ephraim and Lori sat in the middle of a fallen tree that stretched from one side of the creek to the other. With their feet dangling several feet above the surface of the water, Ephraim passed the last bits of bread to Lori to toss below. Catfish circled, snatching the food as soon as it hit the surface. Better Days sat on the creek bank, watching their every move.

In spite of telling himself to do otherwise, his eyes kept returning to Cara. She sat on the blanket with her legs pulled to her chest, his sister's dress flowing around them like a large sheet. She watched the horizon as daylight drained from the sky.

She looked like something out of a movie or a distant dream—a curious mix of delicate softness and unyielding stone.

He should have waited until she'd rested and eaten before he asked her questions. Too little food and sleep, along with the trauma of yesterday and the work today, had overloaded her with stress. He should have known not to insult her dignity. She'd shared some of her life with him, so it didn't seem that he'd done any damage to whatever small amount of trust he'd manage to earn. But it really ate at him that she'd been right.

**His kind.**

Her bull's-eye remark wasn't a revelation. Even after his time living among the Englischers, he had a tendency to judge people unfairly sometimes . . . too often. After being raised by a very conservative group, he had no clue how to finish breaking the measuring stick. But if he wasn't careful, he'd only strengthen her disbelief in God.

" 'From, look," Lori whispered. She pointed to an area of tall grass. A swarm of lightning bugs circled, making quite a show.

He stood on the log and held out his hand. "Ever caught one of those?"

She took his hand, balancing herself as she stood. "No way."

He chuckled. "Your mama was the best bug catcher I've ever seen." They made their way across the log, and he helped her get on solid ground.

"Do they bite?"

"Lightning bugs? No. But if they did, your mom would've bitten them right back."

"Yuck."

Cara cleared her throat. He glanced up, realizing she'd moved from the blanket to the creek side. "Are you saying I eat bugs?"

Holding back a smirk, he hoped a little teasing might ease the tension between them. "Maybe."

The last of the anger faded from her face, and gentleness replaced it.

He stared at her, wondering a hundred things. He wished he could see inside her heart and **really** get to know her beyond the few sentences she shared about her past. Ephraim placed his hands on Lori's shoulders and angled her toward the meadow. "If you hurry, you might get to those fireflies before Better Days, and then you can be the one to scatter them."

She took off running, the pup scurrying after her.

Ephraim turned to Cara, but he had no idea what to say. He would never really understand how it felt to grow up the way she had. To marry for all the wrong reasons yet have it turn out right. And then bury the man she'd grown to love and raise a child alone.

She held out the toy horse to him as if it symbolized a truce. "I'm Cara Moore now, not Atwater."

He placed his hand over it, sandwiching it between their hands. "For years I was sure you'd come back for this. Then I gave up. But I couldn't make myself throw it out."

He removed his hand, and she stared at the horse. "Ephraim, I . . . I had a guy following me . . . for years. He's the reason I needed Johnny and the reason I came here. He won't find me now. I'm sure of that. Anyway, while he was camped out in front of my apartment building, I took what cash I had, and Lori and I boarded a bus. When I got to the bus station, I had no idea where I'd go. So he has no way to know where I am. And no way of tracking me—not this time."

**She has a stalker?**

He could still see the defensive bitterness inside her, but now he felt amazed that she carried as much hope and trust as she did.

She started walking toward the blanket. "I have one desire, Ephraim." Tears brimmed her eyes, and she cleared her throat. "To protect Lori. She's innocent in this mess that started so long before she was born. You asked me this morning when my mother died. I was eight. And my dad disappeared within a few weeks."

"Cara." Ephraim wanted to scream **no** long and loud. "You were raised in foster care?"

"Yeah, one of those homes is where I met Mike, the psycho teen who turned into a stalker."

A desire to understand her outweighed any need to proceed carefully. "When he started threatening you, why not go to the police?"

She sank onto the blanket. "Lots of years, lots of reasons. I tried to go to the authorities once while living as a foster kid under his parents' roof. Long story, but he won and I ran. When he showed up later, turning him in would've been the same as turning myself in. I was a fifteen-year-old runaway who served drinks and danced in skimpy clothes at a bar. I had to stay below the radar."

He sat beside her. "And after that?"

"By the time I was of legal age, I had Johnny to take care of me. He managed a diner, and I worked as one of the waitresses. He never told me what happened between him and Mike, but the other waitresses said he caught Mike skulking around one day and put a gun to his gut, saying he better not see his face again. Mike disappeared. I didn't see him again until a year after Johnny died."

"What happened to Johnny?"

"Brain tumor—an aggressive, high-resolution glioma. There were four months between the time he was diagnosed and the day I was standing by his grave. When Mike heard Johnny was dead, he came after me, and it all started again—changing jobs and moving apartments. I'd shake him for a while but never for more than a year."

"Why didn't you go to the police then?"

"I was afraid for Lori. I knew a lot of girls with terrible boyfriends or husbands, dangerous guys, and they'd end up really hurt sometimes, especially if they talked to the cops. I couldn't afford to provoke a crazy, violent man, and Mike is both. If I killed Mike and went to jail for it or if I made him angry enough to kill me, Lori would suffer either way."

As Ephraim understood, he found it hard to sound casual. "She'd go into foster care."

"Ain't life grand?"

Ephraim felt the sadness inside her, even though her face showed little emotion. "This last time Mike found me, he'd figured out too much—Lori's name, her school, her likes and dislikes. He threatened my roommate. She said he tore up our place. He wants me, and it seems he finally figured out that he'd never have me—unless he had Lori. I got lucky, really, that he didn't nab her at school while I was working."

A landslide of thoughts tumbled through him. While waiting for the right words to come to him, he spotted movement near the fence line. With dusk falling he couldn't make out what was moving. Maybe his father's cows were heading for the barn.

He returned his focus to Cara. "I'm glad you found your way back here."

Cara drew a deep breath. "As soon as we can get social services off my back, I'll be on my way. This place has nothing for me. I thought maybe I'd find some magical connection that would mean something special for us, for Lori. I should have known better. Levina must have been eighty when I was child. And if Emma Riehl, whoever she is, cared so little she never came for me, why did I think she might have some tie or relationship to offer me or Lori now? It was stupid."

**Emma Riehl?** His stomach twisted. Emma was Cara's aunt. She was married to Malinda's oldest brother, Levi. Why would Cara think Emma was supposed to come for her?

"Where does Emma Riehl fit in, Cara?"

She rolled her eyes, looking more jaded than her years allowed for. "A few weeks after my mom died, my dad took me to a bus station. He promised that Emma Riehl would come for me, and then he left. She never showed up. So the next thing I knew, someone from social services was hauling me off to the land of the lonely."

Why would her father leave her at a bus station if he didn't believe that Emma was coming for her? He couldn't ask Emma, not with Cara living in his house. He couldn't tell Cara either. Not yet. If she handled it wrong, the community would hold him responsible. It hadn't dawned on her that he probably knew Emma, or maybe it had and she just didn't care after the incident with the police.

Ephraim eased his fingers over hers. "You're exhausted. You need a few days of regular meals, rest, and some peace. Maybe I can get one of my sisters to go to the Howards for a few days."

She slid her hand free and ran her fingers through her short blond hair. "I appreciate the offer. But I need to work, to prove to social services I can support Lori and myself. I want out—out of your home, out of Dry Lake. If you didn't turn in that report to the police, someone else did, which means people around here think poorly of me and Lori already. I won't start a new life fighting a battle I've already lost."

Odd as it seemed, he didn't want her to leave Dry Lake altogether. She had family and roots. It wasn't the right time to tell her that, but it would be after she had her own place. Then the community would see her in a different light. Right now they'd only see her through the eyes of the rumors about a drunken thief. "Don't you want to know why your mother came here? Or how Emma Riehl fits into the picture? Or why your dad thought she would come for you? Or why she didn't?"

"I came here thinking that's what I wanted, but now I know none of that matters. I need to build a life for Lori. Her childhood matters. Not mine."

Behind the tough exterior, Cara was still the little girl who'd swum in creeks, jumped from haylofts, and looked at life through eyes of hope. He'd waited years for her to return, longing to see her again. To look into those eyes and rekindle the feelings of friendship that tied them. Cara shifted, glancing behind her. "Hey." She tapped his shoulder and nodded backward.

He turned to see Simeon and Becca walking toward him. Dread climbed onto his heart and clung there. The lay of the land kept this little area unseen, so Ephraim had thought it was a safe spot.

He came here often, and no one ever showed up.

He turned back to Cara. "Just sit tight, okay?" He stood.

"Hi, Lori!" Simeon pointed. "Look, Mamm, there's the missing pup we're searching for!" He ran to the spot where Lori and Better Days were chasing fireflies.

Becca came up to Ephraim, concern written across her face. Her hands moved to her plump waist. "What's going on?"

He'd broken many of the written and unwritten rules of his people by being alone with an Englischer woman. He had no defense for it, no excuse or rationalization that would be accepted by her or anyone else. "I know what I'm doing. I don't need a lecture."

Shock drained from her face, and accusation took its place. "News of something like this could kill your father."

Her words squeezed him like a vise. He'd known since yesterday that what she'd just said was true, but as he saw the fear reflected in her eyes, he realized he was caught between what was right for his Daed and what was right for Cara. No matter what he did, one of them could be hurt.

"This isn't about him. And it isn't any of your business."

She looked from Cara to Ephraim. The pain in her face was evident, even under the night sky. He let out a slow stream of air.

"This is wrong." She spoke softly, as if trying to keep Cara from hearing her. "Alone, after dark, sharing a blanket with an outsider. You're in serious violation of everything we hold dear, things you took vows concerning."

"This woman needs a little help for the next few days, maybe a week."

"Is . . . is she the one your Daed's been telling me about, the one Simeon said was staying in the barn and your Daed called the police about?"

"He shouldn't have done that. She's not the type of person he thinks."

Becca massaged her temples. "I want to trust your judgment, Ephraim. If you think she's a worthy cause, give her money and send her on her way, and I'll say nothing to anyone about tonight."

"She needs more than money. She needs . . . a friend."

"Ephraim, please, put an end to this tonight, before it's too late."

Stunned at her gentle threat, Ephraim saw that she cared about his choices the way any mother would. He knew she honored his sense of duty toward the family, but he hadn't realized she carried maternal feelings for him. "She stays. At least for a while. I'm sorry."

Becca's eyes narrowed, studying Cara. "If she's just someone who needs help, does Anna Mary know about her?"

"Not yet."

"Where is she staying?"

"I'm trying to help her find her a place. Until then I'm sleeping in the shop."

Becca clutched her throat, wavering as if she might faint. "She's staying in your home?" She drew several breaths. "I'll give you until Saturday to get her out of your place. Then you must go to the church leaders and come clean about what's been going on. After that . . ." She turned toward the creek. "Simeon," she snapped, "kumm." Without waiting, she stomped off toward the gate.

Ephraim turned to Cara, who stared up at him from the blanket. "None of this changes anything."

"I'm really sorry about all this. I had no idea the Amish had strict rules about such things."

"Being here with you is against what I vowed when I joined the faith. And for good reason. But right now we have no choice." He took a seat beside her and watched Simeon walk toward the gate, waving to Lori as he left.

"Is Anna Mary your girlfriend?"

"Ya. She's the one who made the fried chicken and cake we just ate."

"Then you'd better tell her what's going on."

What could he say to Anna Mary? That he'd allowed a strange woman to stay in his home and sleep in his bed overnight when he wasn't keen on Anna Mary cooking a meal in his kitchen?

# Twenty

The shrill of the hydraulic saw in Ephraim's hand didn't keep him from hearing the amplified ring of the office phone. Stopping the wood in front of the rotating blade, he glanced up. His foreman moved toward the corner office to answer it. Grey's lively steps gave no hint to the troubles he kept buried. Despite how long they'd known each other, the two never spoke about what weighed on him.

Tomorrow was Saturday—Becca's deadline day—and Ephraim had no more answers now than when she'd given him the ultimatum day before yesterday. Trying to focus on the piece of wood in front of him, Ephraim couldn't keep from thinking of Cara. She needed help, and he wanted to give it to her, but was Becca right? Was he going about this the wrong way? He'd taken a vow to live according to the Ordnung. Having a young Englischer woman in his home was in direct violation of the Old Ways. It wouldn't be considered wise by any Christian standards.

How could helping her be right if it had the potential to cause division between him and everything he believed in—if it separated him from his family and community? The Amish reached out to those who weren't Amish. But never like this.

The community would have issues with her living at his place, but the real problems would arise when they learned who she was—the daughter of Malinda Riehl Atwater. He didn't want to tell Cara that her mother had left a trail of devastated loved ones. Twice.

When he was twelve, he'd overheard the adults saying Malinda had broken her vows to the church. She left Dry Lake and her fiancé mere weeks before their wedding. All for an outsider. A drifter who'd come through and stolen her good sense. Was her daughter doing the same thing to him, coming to Dry Lake as a drifter and on a course to ruin his life? Even if she wasn't, would the community believe her innocent of that?

Sunlight shifted across the concrete floor, catching his eye. He glanced up to see Grey. Ephraim turned the saw off.

"Call for you. Someone from social services," Grey said softly.

"Thanks." He went to the office and closed the door behind him. The woman on the phone asked a few questions before telling him of her plans to conduct an in-home visit that afternoon. He thanked her and hung up the phone, his heart racing. His time was up for keeping secrets. Once the social worker pulled into his driveway and went into his house, the news would permeate the community like pollen in springtime.

He picked up the newspaper from his desk. A dozen large red **x**'s filled the little boxes on the for-rent page. He'd made calls for two days, searching for an apartment for Cara and Lori. He'd found nothing.

His Daed would take the news much better if Ephraim could say she'd be leaving in a day or two.

He studied each square he'd made an **x** in, wondering if there was any way he could get her moved before Sunday. Church was to be held at his place this week. If Cara could be gone by then, his punishment from the church leaders wouldn't be as severe.

By this time tomorrow everyone in the district would probably know he'd shared his home with a woman. He knew Becca hadn't said anything, not yet. She wanted to give Ephraim time to alter the situation. But he had to tell Daed before someone else did. Anna Mary needed to know too. But when he'd gone by her place earlier, her mother said a driver had taken her to her sister's last night.

He tossed the newspaper into the trash. His anxiety rose, as if a firestorm were headed straight for his house.

As Cara placed the clean lunch plates in the cabinet, the doorbell rang.

"Get that, please," Mrs. Howard called from her bed.

Cara glanced through a window into the backyard, checking on Lori.

After three nights of staying in a house instead of a barn, she could feel the effects of regular meals and sound sleep at night. It was midafternoon, and she still had a bit of energy, and her hands were steady.

When she opened the front door, a middle-aged man with red hair and freckles stared back at her. "Cara?"

A nervous chill ran down her spine. "Do I know you?"

He shook his head. "I'm Robbie. I work for Ephraim." He pointed to the front seat of his car, where a young woman sat. "That's Annie, Ephraim's fourteen-year-old stepsister. She's to take your place here, and you're to go back to his house. He said to tell you a Mrs. Forrester called, and she'll be at his home in about an hour."

Feeling as if she were suffocating, she nodded. "Okay, give me a minute."

"I'll be in the car."

Her mind whirled with disjointed thoughts as she went down the hallway to Mrs. Howard's bedroom. Ephraim's willingness to help her was unbelievable. She felt he wasn't the least bit attracted to her, but he did seem as honest and direct now as twenty years ago when he'd asked if she was a boy or a girl.

An image of him popped into her mind, followed by a thought that made her chuckle. Hollywood would love to get hold of him. She didn't know if he could act, but he was definitely a looker with that strawberry blond hair and those gray blue eyes. Six feet of pure drawing power, as Kendal would say.

When Cara entered the bedroom, Mrs. Howard looked up from her book.

"Remember when I told you I might need to leave during the day sometime this week?" Cara waited until she nodded. "Well, I need to go now. There's a driver outside, and he brought Annie, a young

Amish woman, to sit with you until your husband gets home."

"No problem, dear. Can she weed the garden?"

"Being fourteen and Amish, she's sure to be better at it than I am."

# Twenty-One

With only an hour before social services arrived, Ephraim dialed the number to his Daed's doctor's office. He finally had his Daed's nurse on the line. Because of privacy rules, the nurse couldn't tell him anything specific about his Daed's health. When Ephraim asked for general information concerning cardiomyopathy, she freely shared the information.

Listening intently, Ephraim tried to hear everything—spoken and unspoken. "Do you think his heart can withstand the stress of some difficult news?"

"Stress is a part of life. Patients who have cardiomyopathy can't rid their lives of stress. And bad news can usually be shared in a way that's not jolting or shocking."

"He seems more fragile with each passing year. I don't want to do or say anything that would cause an episode, but his symptoms continually weaken him."

"We often suggest that patients who have cardiomyopathy with symptoms similar to your dad's have a procedure called AICD. A cardiac defibrillator is implanted into the chest wall, and it causes the heart to reset its rhythm as needed."

"Has he been told about this procedure?"

"I'm sorry. I can share about diseases, but your question falls under doctor-patient confidentiality."

Ephraim thanked her and hung up. He needed to tell his Daed about Cara in a way that wouldn't shock him.

He left the office and entered the main part of the workshop. "I'm heading out for the day."

Mahlon set aside the carving tool in hand. "Did you put my time off on the schedule for next week?"

"Can we talk about it later? I have some other things I need to deal with."

"Ya. Don't forget Deb wanted you and Anna Mary to go out with us tonight."

"I won't forget. You and Grey be sure to clear the center of the room and put the paints up high. The bench wagon will be here tomorrow." Church met at his place only once a year, just like it did at everybody else's home in the community, but the timing of it being this Sunday couldn't be worse. Since his home was small, he and his family had to set up the benches in the shop.

Needing a few minutes to think, he went into the field. The pasture was thick with grass, the pond sparkled in the distance, and a breeze stirred around him. He closed his eyes.

An odd feeling nagged at him, as if he'd missed a step in planning the next few hours. What was stirring such unrest in him? **Have I missed something I should do?**

A little unsure if that was a prayer or him questioning himself, he was surprised when peace eased through him. He took a deep breath. Maybe this afternoon wouldn't be so bad after all. Lingering in the quiet moment, he welcomed more of God. Suddenly it seemed as if he were in church during one of those rare and special moments when His spirit seemed to rest all around him.

**Be me to her.**

The thought made his heart race, and he stumbled back. He couldn't be anything to Cara but a friend—for a very short time. She was fascinating, and under different circumstances they could enjoy being friends. But she was from a different world, an outsider—and the daughter of Malinda Riehl.

"Ephraim?"

He turned to face his Daed. "Good to see you out and about."

He propped his foot on the bottom of the split-rail fence. "I came looking for you. You've not been around much lately. Do you have that much going on with work?"

"Just the usual stuff. How're you feeling?"

"Pretty good. I'm watching my salt intake, hoping I don't get another bout of fluid overload."

"Daed, I need to talk with you about some things that are going on. Do you think you're up to it?"

Half of Daed's face lifted in a smile. "Sure."

"Maybe we should go back to your house and sit."

"You're not going to start mollycoddling me like Becca does, are you?" He laughed. "I don't think I could stand that. I know the woman doesn't want to lose a second husband, but if she doesn't lighten up, I'm going to quit trying to pacify her. She's got every daughter in the house following her lead. Don't you start too."

"Well, let's at least go sit in the side yard."

They moseyed that way, and each took a seat in a lawn chair. The breeze carried the aroma of one of Becca's suppers cooking.

Without telling his father who Cara was, he began explaining about the woman he'd found staying in the barn. "Daed, Becca said you called the police."

"Ya, I did."

Ephraim tried to keep his voice even, but he wanted to snap and growl. "You should have talked to me first."

"You wrote a letter, telling her to leave."

"It's my barn and property, and I was handling it. The police came and were going to separate her and her daughter, so I said she could stay at my place. She's been there for the last three nights."

"An Englischer woman and child, without a husband?" He looked more concerned than angry. "I can't believe you handled it this way. If she is destitute, why not bring her to our home?"

"For a lot of reasons." Not only would no one have wanted them, but Cara and Lori needed a quiet place to ease the harshness of what they'd been through, not the discomfort of being a guest in a houseful of people. "You'd just come home from the hospital. And your home is always bursting at the seams with children."

Lines of disappointment carved into stone around his Daed's eyes. "Better her in a bedroom with children than jeopardizing your soul." He stared at Ephraim as if he no longer understood him. "But years ago you came home when I needed you, and you've been more to this family and to me than I ever had the right to ask. I won't let the bishop forget that when he's talking with us preachers after you go see him."

"Daed." Ephraim paused. "I'm not taking this to the bishop. I'm just telling you what's going on, forewarning you about what's ahead."

"She's not gone?"

"No."

Daed stared, wordlessly lecturing him before saying, "You're not asking for forgiveness, ready to take your discipline from the church and put this behind you?"

"No."

"No?" His voice rang across the land, echoing back to them. "You have to put a stop to this. You need to repent—to the church leaders, to this community, and to

God, who you knelt before and vowed to keep the Ordnung and to live according to our ways."

Ephraim had taken that vow. And since returning to Dry Lake nine years ago, he'd always aimed to be a good influence on the younger generation, to help them learn to respect the Old Ways.

**Be me to her.**

The thought seemed to float on the wind, entering his soul from outside himself. "It's not against our ways to help someone."

"It's not against our ways to be with a woman either, but that doesn't make it right except in one circumstance, does it?"

"Daed, I'm asking you to trust me. Please."

He leaned forward. "I trust in God and in the Old Ways and in the authority of the church. The Word says every way of man is right in his own eyes. We have the Ordnung because man cannot allow emotions and quick decisions to guide him."

He knew his father's words were true,

but did one truth negate another? "We're also told not to withhold good when the power is in our hands to do it."

"You really think you're doing any good in this? You need to remain faithful to your oath." Daed rubbed the center of his chest. "Even as a preacher, I doubt I can cut down on the shunning time that's ahead of you."

Ephraim nodded. The night he chose to stay in his home for Lori's sake instead of going to the shop to sleep, he'd known he would be shunned.

Daed drew a long, tired breath. "Who is this woman?"

Ephraim shook his head, wishing he hadn't asked.

A knowing look went through Daed's eyes. "You knew her before she showed up in the barn. She's from your days among the Englischers, isn't she?" He pounded his fists on the arm of the chair, his face turning red. "You absolutely cannot continue this."

Ephraim had no choice. Telling him the truth of who she was would be better than his thinking an Englischer was seeking to renew some imaginary relationship. "She's Malinda Riehl's daughter."

His father's face drained of all color. "Cara?"

Ephraim nodded.

Daed's eyes filled with tears. "I thought I saw Malinda walking down the road with Cara beside her last Friday. I thought I must be imagining things. But it didn't dawn on me it might be Cara. I'll tell you what I did see—a drunken thief, or maybe worse."

"No, Daed. You saw someone who needed help. She's not a drunk. I'm sure of it."

His Daed looked toward heaven. "Oh dear Father." He focused on his son. "Listen to me. Malinda Riehl grew up one of us, was taught the same things you were. But when she ran off the first time, she left betrayal and brokenness behind her. You think her daughter's any better? I tell you, she'll be worse. Shunning will be the easiest of what's in store for you."

Ephraim closed his eyes, searching for peace as he listened to the birds sing and the wind rustle the leaves. "I don't know what happened the first time Malinda left, but the second time around wasn't by choice. I understand that she stirred a lot of negative emotions while trying to find Cara a safe place to live, but—"

"Don't tell me what happened," his Daed interrupted him. "You weren't much more than a child. I remember well the trouble she caused. It was only six months after I'd been chosen as a preacher. Her presence caused a rift between your mother and me, but the church leaders agreed that Cara could come here to live. Levina, Malinda's own grandmother, was willing to raise Cara. But we couldn't give permission for Malinda to stay. For dozens of reasons all three of us church leaders fervently discussed over and over again, we couldn't do anything that would make it easy for Malinda to run from her husband as she'd run from the community that loved her. Malinda said little in response to our decision except that she needed some time with Cara to prepare her. They went back to

New York, and she never returned. Never even called."

"Daed . . . she died. Had an accident not long after she left here with Cara, and it killed her instantly."

His father grew quiet. "If your mother were alive to learn of that . . ." He closed his eyes. "I'm sorry. I really am." He drew a jerky breath. "You'll never know how much I hate this. But the mess isn't our fault, even though I was the one who called the police. You can't risk your salvation because Malinda chose the world over God. Tell me her daughter isn't of the world too."

He couldn't. The weight of what was ahead settled over him. "I know you can't understand all this. I'm not sure I do. But my mind is made up. I'll do whatever I can to help her."

His father stared at him. "She's already caused you to turn your back on God and family. Don't let this woman stay. If you do, all that will be left for you is ruin and regret."

"My decision isn't out of rebellion. It's

the right thing to do, and I'm the right person to do it."

Daed placed his hand on Ephraim's shoulder and gently squeezed it. "You're wrong. But it seems I won't be the one to convince you of it." He stood and walked into the house.

Ephraim closed his eyes. "Be Me to her." He mumbled the words, wondering what they really meant.

# Twenty-Two

As they rode in Robbie's vehicle toward Ephraim's place, Cara felt like a voiceless child again. The words she would need jumbled into nonsense inside her brain. Through years of dealing with social workers, she'd always hated the meetings. Those she'd had experience with didn't see things that were clear and saw all sorts of things that weren't even there.

"You known Ephraim long?" Robbie asked.

Cara folded her arms, wondering if she owed it to Ephraim to answer this man agreeably. "Long enough."

He frowned and shrugged. "Where'd you get that dress?"

"Excuse me?" Cara tried to keep the snarl out of her tone.

"It's a Plain dress, but you're not Amish."

"The Howards insisted on extreme modesty, so I wear it when I have to. Can we just ride in silence, please?"

"I reckon so." He straightened his ball cap. "I was just trying to make conversation."

Who was he kidding? He was on a fishing expedition, hoping to reel in answers. But she wouldn't tell him so, in case that'd be disrespectful to Ephraim.

Her mind moved from thought to thought like fire on a wind-swept hill. What if the social worker didn't accept her living arrangement as stable enough? What if she took Lori because Cara had been forced to steal to feed her daughter? She was making enough money to keep them fed now. But Mrs. Howard would be out of her cast within two weeks. Then what would she do? If Ephraim stopped helping her, she'd be homeless again. How was she going to prove to the social worker that she was capable of providing for Lori when everything hinged on one man's generosity? Suddenly it felt as if she'd left one corner only to be backed into a different corner. And wouldn't Mike be pleased to know the misery he'd dished out?

She tapped her fingertips against her thighs, wishing she could relax. "You don't happen to have a cigarette, do you?"

"Sorry. I gave up smoking years ago."

Forcing herself to sit still, she tried to focus on something besides Mrs. Forrester. Ephraim had planned on seeing Anna Mary this morning to tell her what was going on. He didn't seem the least bit nervous, so she figured they must have a really good relationship.

Robbie barely tapped the brakes before pulling into the shop's driveway.

"Did Ephraim say to come in this way?"

He shrugged. "Didn't say."

"Then drive to the road that leads to Ephraim's driveway. Let's not use the shop's. Please."

"You should've said something sooner. It's too late for that now." He passed the main house and pulled up in front of the shop.

Wondering if the man came this way on purpose, she mumbled a sarcastic thanks. She hoped Ephraim's family hadn't seen them pass, but what was done was done.

She turned to her daughter. Haunting images of social services taking Lori sent a nervous chill through her. No one was going to take her daughter. Logic told her that social services wasn't looking for an excuse to separate children from their mothers. Still, her nerves were driving her up the wall. If she had nothing to fear, why were her emotions in overdrive?

When the engine shut off, she found her voice. "Lori, we're going across the field and straight to Ephraim's house. If you see him in the shop, don't call out to him or do anything that might draw attention."

Robbie scowled. "Guess I should've taken you the long way around."

"I guess so." They got out of the car, and she took Lori's hand in hers. Without a word they crossed the parking area and entered Ephraim's yard.

They went inside. The quiet beauty of his home whispered hope. Surely one look at this place would tell the social worker that Lori had a good place to stay now. Sunlight lay across the gorgeous hardwood floors, and for the first time she wondered if they were Ephraim's handiwork. The beige countertops were spotless, and everything except their breakfast dishes was neat and clean.

A breeze stirred the warm air as Cara set the backpack in a chair. "Remember when the police let us come home with Ephraim?"

Lori nodded.

"Well, because we were sleeping in the barn, they needed to turn our names in to someone who looks after little kids. They just want to make sure you're being taken care of. A woman named Mrs. Forrester is coming to see us today. She's going to ask questions, and we're going to be very polite and answer her."

"I liked it better in the barn with the pups than in New York. Can I tell her that?"

Wishing she knew how to instruct Lori to answer, Cara moved to the kitchen sink.

"Can I tell her about Better Days?"

Cara licked her lips, trying to calm her nerves. "Sure, but he's not your dog. You remember that, right?"

"He's just as good as being mine as long as you don't make us leave."

Cara turned on the hot water, trying to drown out the accusation in Lori's tone. To Lori, every move had been her mother's choice. Cara let Lori feel that way rather than have her believe a bogeyman was after them. She deserved to feel safe—even if she came to resent her mother in the process. That decision stood like every other decision she'd made: choosing the lesser of the two evils.

Desire washed over Cara. A longing so deep it seemed to have the power to pull her into another world. She ached to call upon a higher being . . . to ask some unseen life form to smooth things out, not only with social services, but with Ephraim's family.

Realizing she still had on an Amish dress, she dried her hands and went into the bedroom to change. It wouldn't do for the woman to ask any questions about the dress, like where she got it.

Lori followed her. "Can I go outside?"

"Not today." Cara slid into her jeans and sweater. Somehow she had to keep Lori pinned up inside until Ephraim's family had gone to bed for the night. "You can read a book or draw or play with the toys Ephraim brought you."

"Are we hiding again?"

Cara sank onto the bed. "Lori, I need you to stay inside today and be really, really good. Can you do that for Mom?"

Her daughter studied her. "How come I got butterflies in my belly?"

Placing her hand on Lori's head, she smiled. "Because I do, and you can feel it. But we'll be fine. Ephraim won't let anything bad happen to us."

She hoped that was true, but she hated herself for needing his help. Hated Mike for putting her in this situation. Hated relying on handouts. But she saw no other way. Not right now.

Someone knocked, making Cara jolt to her feet. She motioned for Lori to hop up, and Cara straightened the bed.

"Hello?" A girl's voice rang through the house. "Ephraim?"

Cara hurried out the bedroom door to find a pretty Amish woman with jet-black hair and blue eyes waiting by the door. The woman's eyes moved from the top of Cara's head to her feet and back up again. "What are you doing here?"

A second woman, the one who'd served Cara and Lori food for free at the auction, stepped forward. "Where's Ephraim?"

Unsure what Ephraim did or didn't want her to say, she stayed silent.

The blue-eyed one shrugged. "He doesn't seem to be here."

Lori moved in close to her mother. "I saw him in the shop when we came home."

"Home?" the blue-eyed one echoed, her face reflecting shock.

The screen door flopped open, and Ephraim stepped inside. One quick glance around the room, and he turned his focus to the blue-eyed one.

She offered a sweet smile, searching his face for reassurance before lowering her eyes. This girl was in love. She had to be Anna Mary.

"Mamm said you came by this morning to see me."

"Ya, I wanted us to talk." He glanced to Cara and Lori.

The blue-eyed girl kept her focus on Ephraim. "I spent the night with my sister."

He looked at Cara. "You doing okay?"

She forced a nod.

He gave her a half smile, but his eyes carried a look of stress. "Deborah, Anna Mary, this is Cara Moore and her daughter, Lori. They're staying here for a while."

Deborah stared at Ephraim, stunned into silence.

Anna Mary's eyes grew large. She

pointed both index fingers at the floor. "Here?"

Ephraim's face became stonelike. "Ya."

"She can't stay **here.**"

Lori hid behind her mother as the tension in the room became suffocating. A knock on the screen door made Cara jerk. Ephraim glanced to her, and the undercurrent of understanding that ran between them didn't need words. The social worker had arrived, and she'd overheard Anna Mary's proclamation.

With no hint of nervousness, he turned toward the newcomer. "Mrs. Forrester?"

"Elaine Forrester, yes."

"Come right in."

He let the thirty-something woman inside. She didn't look anything like the social workers Cara remembered. No funny-looking glasses or wild gray hair half pinned up and half falling down, and she wasn't peering down her nose at them. Holding a blue canvas briefcase in one hand, she looked straight at Ephraim. "You must be Ephraim Mast." He nodded and shook her hand.

"I'd like to talk with you too, but first I'm here to see Cara and Lori Moore."

Cara's skin felt like a pincushion as she stepped forward. "I'm Cara, and this is my daughter, Lori."

"Nice to meet you. You're living here now. Is that correct?"

"Yes," Ephraim spoke up. "For as long as they need."

His bold statement shocked Cara. Anna Mary clenched her jaws and said nothing.

"Mrs. Forrester, this is my sister Deborah and a friend, Anna Mary."

"Nice to meet you." She walked to the kitchen table and set her briefcase on it. After pulling out a leather clipboard, she tapped it. "I'm just going to look around the place." She faced Cara. "Then we'll chat."

Feeling almost as vulnerable as if Mike were looming over her, Cara nodded.

Ephraim motioned Deborah and Anna Mary to the back door. They filed out in silence. He turned to Cara. "You'll do fine. I'll be in the hiddy. It's the area inside the hedges. When she's ready to talk with me, just call."

"Thanks."

🌿

Ephraim followed Deborah and Anna Mary into his hiddy. He'd barely stepped through the narrow opening in the hedges when they came to a stop and faced him. Obviously Daed or Becca hadn't said anything to his sister about Cara. Deborah's eyes begged for answers, looking more worried than he'd seen her since their mother died. He hadn't expected that, or maybe he hadn't taken the time to really think about it.

Instead of looking jealous, Anna Mary seemed confused. "What's going on?"

He realized the news, all of it, had to come out within the next few minutes, but sharing it as slowly as possible seemed wise. He was on the brink of being shunned, and Anna Mary should hear the truth from him. "Cara needs help, and I'm giving it to her."

"Ephraim, where is she from? Who is

she?" Deborah demanded. "How do you know her?"

"She's from New York. Came here about a week ago. She was living in Levina's barn, and I gave her a place to stay."

"In the barn?" Anna Mary shuddered. "So where are you staying?"

"It's complicated. Her daughter, Lori, was afraid the police would come back for them, so I stayed in the storage room the first night. Then I spent the last two nights in the shop."

"The police? Were they after them?"

"No. Not really. It was mostly a misunderstanding, but they did show up."

His sister stared at him. "Why would you do this?"

"Sometimes doing the right thing doesn't look right at all."

Deborah angled her head, looking worried. "If this gets back to the bishop, you'll be excommunicated. And I can't think what this could do to Daed."

"Daed knows. I talked to him earlier. Healthwise, he took it well. I've made my choice."

Anna Mary took a seat on the wooden swing. "Without even talking to me?"

He squelched his desire to say that he didn't need her permission to help someone. Besides, there hadn't been time for a committee meeting, and she wasn't home when he decided it was time to tell her.

"You'd do this, knowing you'd be shunned?" Deborah wiped a stray tear. "This Cara person must be someone more to you than a stranger who hid in your barn. Who **is** she? And who is that Elaine Forrester?"

Ephraim took a seat next to Anna Mary. He wasn't willing to talk to them about Cara's ties to the community until he could first tell Cara that she had relatives here and that her mother had been raised Amish. "Elaine is a social worker. Cara's a friend from long ago, and she needs help in order to hold on to her daughter."

"Has she taken possession of your good sense?" Deborah asked softly.

Anna Mary sighed heavily. "Don't make it sound like he's interested in her. Do you really think he'd allow any girl this much access to his home if he was attracted to her?"

Thankful Anna Mary was thinking about this reasonably, Ephraim eased his hand over hers. "I've looked through ads and made calls, trying to find a place for her. There's just nothing out this way."

"There should be some jobs and apartments in Shippensburg," Anna Mary offered.

Like a stick being flailed into a hornets' nest, her statement struck him, stirring emotions and thoughts that stung. He didn't want Cara in Shippensburg.

Stunned at the feelings surging through him, he turned from Anna Mary's probing eyes and gazed out across the field. Answers to Cara's past were hiding among the Amish of Dry Lake. And whether anyone in his community liked it or not, Cara deserved to be treated as a treasure once stolen and now returned to them by a power not her own.

# Twenty-Three

Cara had replied to a hundred questions, including some probing ones about her relationship with Ephraim. Now she waited in the living room while Mrs. Forrester and Lori strolled through the home, chatting. She could hear Lori telling the woman about life in New York, being hungry some days since leaving there, and going on a picnic with Ephraim.

"Lori," the woman said, "what's your mommy like when she gets really mad?"

Without a moment's hesitation, Lori answered, "She gets on her knees in front of me and points her finger right here." Cara couldn't see, but she was sure Lori was pointing to her nose. "She calls me Lori Moore, real quicklike. Then she says, 'You stop.' " Lori mimicked her mother's voice. "Sometimes she says, 'Give me a break, kid. When you're the adult, we'll do it your way.' "

"Does she ever hit you?"

"No. But she hit a man at a bus station once. She wouldn't tell me why, and I didn't ask twice."

"Has she ever left you with anyone who hit you?"

They walked into the storage room, and Cara couldn't make out all their words. It sounded like Mrs. Forrester was going into more personal questions. A few minutes later the two reentered the room. The woman set the leather clipboard beside her and dug into her briefcase. Cara tried to catch a glimpse of her notes.

Mrs. Forrester tapped the legal pad where Cara's full name and Social Security number were listed. "If I run your info through the New York database, will I get a hit?"

Cara swallowed, not sure she was ready for Lori to know. "I was in foster care from eight years old until I was fifteen."

"Because?"

"My mother had died, and my dad . . . left."

"But you were only in the system until you turned fifteen? Why?"

"I ran away."

The woman pulled out several pamphlets and set them on the coffee table. "What made you leave New York?"

"Does it matter?"

"I won't know that until you talk to me."

Cara stood firm, not wanting to give an answer in front of Lori. "There are reasons. Good ones."

The woman leaned forward. "I'm not here because of an anonymous tip. This visit was initiated because the police filed a report based on what they had witnessed. Added to that, you removed Lori from school the first part of May. School doesn't end in New York until mid-June or here for another week. Technically, she's truant, and you're the reason." She tapped the pamphlets. "My gut says something's going on that has nothing to do with questions about your parenting ability. Although your decision-making process does seem questionable."

**Great.** More viewpoints from the clueless. Cara figured the woman might survive two weeks with someone like Mike hounding her, maybe less.

Mrs. Forrester shrugged. "I'm only here to help, but I want answers to every question."

Cara didn't want her kind of help, but she stood. "Come on, Lori. You can wait outside with Ephraim."

Lori took her hand and walked silently until they were outside. "Is she gonna put cuffs on you and take you somewhere?"

"No."

"You sure?"

"Yes." She wasn't sure of much else, but that part didn't worry her. They walked to the six-foot hedges and found the slight entrance. She spotted Ephraim on the swing with Anna Mary. They made a striking couple. "Can she stay with you for a few minutes?"

"Ya."

Lori clutched her hand tighter. "I wanna stay with you."

Ephraim stood. "How about if we walk to the barn and check on Better Days?"

Lori shook her head.

"We'll bring the pup back here." Ephraim held out his hand, but Lori didn't take it.

Cara pulled her hand free. "I'll be here when you get back. I promise."

"No." Lori clutched her mother's leg.

Cara pried Lori's hands free and knelt in front of her. "Come on, kiddo. I'm going nowhere. Can't you trust me on this?"

Lori wrapped her arms around her mother's neck. "I'll be good. Just don't leave me."

"You couldn't get rid of me if you turned into a whole gang of trouble. Never forget that." Cara hugged her tight and then stood. "I'll be here when you get back."

Lori swiped at her tears and took Ephraim's hand.

He moved in closer to Cara. "How's it going in there?"

"Good, I think, except I'm afraid she's going to ask questions about my life that I don't have the answers to."

Ephraim chuckled, but it sounded forced, making her wonder if he actually cared. She knew he had honor to him or he wouldn't be doing all this to help her. But that was different. Honor was what made people do certain things so they could live with themselves. Caring? Well . . . that meant she and Lori mattered.

When she went back inside, Mrs. Forrester was on the couch waiting for her. Cara went to the rocker and sat, ready to answer the toughest questions yet.

"Cara, what caused you to leave New York that you're not willing to talk about in front of your daughter?"

In spite of wanting to stonewall the woman, Cara described her years of dealing with Mike, and the woman took notes.

Mrs. Forrester tapped her pen on the legal pad. "Logically one would think he'd have given up stalking years ago. But when you were in foster care and told the authorities, somebody blew it, Cara. I might be able to do some investigating, but you need to contact the police."

"No."

"He could be doing this to others."

She cursed. "That's not my problem. When I tried to turn him in years ago, everyone ignored me. The only thing that matters to me is staying alive so I can keep Lori safe."

"Okay, okay." She took the pamphlets off the table. "There are programs that offer assistance. Lori's past the age to be eligible for WIC, but there are other policies in place to help provide food and shelter."

Cara held her hand up. "I don't understand. Am I in a battle to keep Lori or not?"

"Did you know your daughter saw Kendal doing drugs?"

Cara swallowed. "Yes . . . Lori told me. Kendal and I had a big fight about it. It didn't happen twice."

"Having no friends can be better than having bad ones."

"Oh yeah? When you have some maniac running everyone out of your life, let's see how you feel."

The woman sighed. "Cara, you have a new start now, and I see no reason to consider removing your daughter from you."

Hope hung frozen in the air. Afraid it might turn to vapor and fade into nothing, Cara didn't move.

The woman stood. "I'll do a follow-up or two. You need to get her enrolled in school before the next year begins."

"Is . . . is that it?"

"We're done for now."

Cara's heart danced inside her chest, some weird, excited tap she'd never felt before.

"I've seen and heard a lot in my years as a social worker, and overall you've handled a bad situation pretty well." She passed the pamphlets to Cara and explained how to get government help.

"I don't want assistance. I just want to be left alone."

"Your decision. If you change your mind, let me know."

When they stepped outside, Ephraim walked toward them. Cara's eyes met his, and she wondered if he knew what he'd done for her.

Mrs. Forrester turned to her. "Thank you, Cara. I'd like to speak to Ephraim alone for a few minutes."

Deborah and Anna Mary told Ephraim good-bye and left. Cara took Lori inside, hoping Ephraim would come talk to her as soon as he could.

"How'd I do, Mom?"

She knelt in front of Lori. "You were you." She licked her lips, trying to keep the tears at bay. "And that was absolutely perfect."

"Are the police coming back?"

She tugged on her daughter's dress. A week of wearing mostly the same dress day and night made for a very tattered outfit. It'd been a long journey to get free of Mike, but they finally had a new start. "Nope."

"We don't have to hide anymore?"

Cara gasped, fighting harder against the tears. "No, honey, we don't." She eased her arms around Lori, and the matchless comfort of the gesture swept through her.

She heard footsteps on the porch and looked up, not caring if Ephraim noticed her tears.

"Mrs. Forrester is gone." He opened the screen door and walked inside. "She likes you. She said she wished all moms were as determined to take care of their little ones as you are."

Cara laughed. "Who cares whether she likes me or not?"

His smile warmed her, and she rose to her feet. "You do, trust me."

The puppy whined, and Ephraim let him in. Feeling years of heaviness fall from her body, Cara felt giddy. The desire to dance around the room pulsed through her.

Ephraim leaned against the counter. "Seems to me this deserves a celebration."

Lori ran to the center of the room, Better Days nipping at her heels. "Let's dance! One, two, three." She clapped her hands as she said each number.

Cara laughed and hurried to her side.

Better Days ran around them, barking. She and Lori hummed "My Girl" and clapped and danced a jig as they often did when the tiniest bit of good news came their way. They raised their arms and twirled, a tradition that cost them nothing but always made Lori happy. How long had it been since they'd danced and laughed? They twirled around and around, laughing and making their favorite wild moves with their bodies.

When the dance was through, they gave themselves a round of applause. But suddenly Lori darted behind her, causing her to glance up. Two men dressed in black stood beside Ephraim. When had they come in? Lori pressed her body against Cara's leg, holding on tightly.

One man rubbed his chest. **"In dei Heemet?"** The man looked upset, and his voice wavered.

The older man pulled his stare from Cara. "Ephraim," he whispered, shaking his head. **"Kumm raus. Loss uns schwetze."**

Ephraim nodded, and the two men left the house.

He walked to Lori. "This is your home until we find something better suited to you with electricity and your own bedroom. No one is going to change that." He placed his hand on her head. "Trust me?"

Lori released her firm grip on Cara's leg, her body relaxing as she nodded.

The joy of a few minutes ago faded from Cara. "Is everything okay?"

"Ya. But I need to leave. I'll sleep in the shop tonight. I don't have time to start a cook fire. Can you?"

"Sure. Are you in trouble?"

"I'm not in trouble with the One who counts."

"What?"

"For you, the police and Mrs. Forrester counted. We all have someone we don't want to be in trouble with."

She laughed. "Maybe you should take her somewhere extra nice."

A puzzled look covered his face for a moment. "Oh, you think I meant . . ." He chuckled and tipped his hat. "Good night, ladies."

# Twenty-Four

Still fighting tears, Deborah slipped into a clean dress for tonight. She and Mahlon had made plans, but she was in no mood for going out. Part of her wanted to crawl into bed and pull the blankets over her head. But she hoped to get Mahlon to change his mind about leaving tomorrow, and she wouldn't pass up the opportunity to be near Ephraim. Maybe once she had time with him, she'd begin to understand why he'd done such a brazen, foolish thing.

Hearing men's voices outside, she moved to the window. The bishop and her Daed stood in the side yard, talking to Ephraim. She raised the window higher so she could eavesdrop.

"I understand how this looks," Ephraim

said, "but I've done nothing wrong. I'm just asking for some time to work with her, to help her get on her feet."

"She's worse than her mother," Daed said. "Malinda would never have dressed like that or stolen from us or dragged her child around, homeless. If you don't put a separation between you and her, you'll put one between you and God."

"It's not like that. She's on a path she didn't choose. It was chosen for her, and I want to help her get off it. And she's not a bad influence." Deborah heard the ire in her brother's voice as he defended himself. She couldn't imagine him giving in to any temptations with a girl, but she never would've believed he'd invite an Englischer woman, this Cara, to stay with him either.

"Did we not see her dancing in your home? In that tight clothing, with too much skin showing, even her belly." The bishop's voice remained calm as he tried to reason with Ephraim.

"She doesn't see things like we do. You see her ways as sinful. She sees them as normal."

"It doesn't matter how she sees them. Get her out of your life and away from this community," Daed added.

Deborah wondered why they wanted to get rid of the girl. She understood getting her out of her brother's house and away from him, whether he was sleeping in the shop or not. But why would they want her out of Dry Lake?

"I can't do that."

A knot formed in Deborah's stomach.

"Please don't do this," the bishop said. "If you refuse to submit, we'll have no choice but to be very strict on you until you're willing to follow wisdom. A shunning is always painful, but will I be forced to draw lines even more severe than is normal?"

Someone knocked on Deborah's door. "Kumm."

Anna Mary held out Deborah's black apron. "All pressed and ready to go."

"Denki."

The bishop stood near Ephraim, talking softly, and she could no longer hear him.

"What are you looking at?" Anna Mary moved to the window.

Deborah felt like a dress being run through the wringer. Why was Ephraim being so stubborn?

Anna Mary's face turned ashen. "The bishop knows?"

Deborah slid into her apron. There wasn't anything she could say that would make this better. The damage had been done.

Anna Mary slowly turned from the window and sat on the bed. "Don't worry so much about Ephraim. He wanted to help this girl, but I also think he wants to test me."

Deborah pinned the apron in place around her waist. "What do you mean?"

"He's been single all these years, goes for long spells without courting. He's been seeing me longer than anyone. We've been getting really close. I can feel his voice inside me even when he's working out of town." She pulled a pillow into her lap. "And now he does this? You can't tell me it's not odd."

Mulling over her friend's conclusions, Deborah placed her Kapp on her head. "If he's shunned, will you wait for him?"

"Of course. We'll be allowed to visit him, and we can take him special dinners. Singings and outings will be forbidden, but we can work around that."

Deborah sat beside her friend. "I heard what the bishop said. I don't think the normal restrictions will apply."

"Why?"

"Because Ephraim's refusing to remove Cara from his home or separate his life from hers. He intends to do as he sees fit."

Hurt filled Anna Mary's eyes. "For me there is no one else. But the waiting won't be the hardest part. The damage to his reputation won't fade for years."

Deborah grabbed straight pins from the nightstand and weaved one through the Kapp and strands of her hair. "It makes me feel sick thinking about it."

"Cara is nothing more than a trouble-making nobody . . . a . . . a tramp." Anna Mary tossed the pillow onto the bed. "He felt sorry for her and was willing to help. The idea of people thinking otherwise just makes me mad."

Taken aback by her friend's harsh view

of Cara, Deborah moved to the window. The yard was empty now, the conversation over. Ephraim and Mahlon were probably downstairs, waiting for them. "Excommunicated." She hated the feel of the word in her mouth. "Ephraim's doing this. Mahlon is getting away because he feels like it. Why do men have to be so hardheaded sometimes?"

Anna Mary opened the bedroom door. "I have no idea. And they say women are difficult to understand." She shrugged. "Maybe the bishop won't be so tough on him after all."

"Maybe." But Deborah didn't think so, not after hearing what the bishop had said to Ephraim.

As they walked into the living room looking for Mahlon and Ephraim, she caught a glimpse of movement in her parents' bedroom. "I'll be back."

She went to the doorway. Her Daed was sitting on the side of the bed, his elbows propped on his knees and his head in his hands.

Becca stood near him with her back to

the doorway. "He won't be allowed to work at his shop? That's never been part of a shunning before. Will the business survive without Ephraim?"

"I can't think of that right now."

"That shop puts food in our babies' mouths."

Deborah tapped on the door. "Daed?"

"Deborah." He stood, wiping his eyes. "You look nice, like a young woman ready for her beau."

She nodded. "Are you okay?"

"Ya. A bit rattled, that's all."

"Your brother . . ." Becca burst into tears. "All these children left to raise, and the oldest, who's been a man of faith for many years, now begins to waver?"

"He's not wavering." Deborah choked back the tears. "He's not. He stepped outside the Ordnung, but he'll take the discipline and go through the steps to become a member in good standing again. I know he will."

Her Daed brushed her cheek with his hand. "Of course he will. Now, what did you need to see me about?"

"I was looking for Ephraim and Mahlon."

"They've gone to the shop. Your brother needs to teach Mahlon a lot between now and Sunday."

She couldn't believe the procedure for a shunning was moving so quickly. "Sunday?"

Daed nodded. "The announcement will happen at church."

Her heart thudded against her chest. "Why so soon?"

"This situation with Cara is worse than Ephraim said."

The ache that settled inside her chest was familiar, like she was losing a family member all over again. "Oh, Daed."

"It'll be fine, Deborah. Just a little storm. We'll get through it."

But she knew he didn't really believe that. She could see it in his eyes and hear it in his voice. "I'll be with Ephraim, Mahlon, and Anna Mary tonight. I'll talk with him. Okay, Daed?"

He smiled, his eyes misting. "Sure. Do what you can." He rubbed his chest. "I . . . I think I'll lie down for a bit."

Deborah helped him get comfortable and kissed his cheek. "Please don't take this too hard. He's doing this because he's a good man, not because of sin."

Her Daed patted her hand. "I hope you're right."

She left, eager to try to talk some sense into her brother.

❦

Standing at his desk, Ephraim tried explaining unfamiliar things about the business to Mahlon: bookkeeping and ordering hardware, lumber, and various items from the paint store. Open in front of them was a color-coded calendar that mapped out daily goals as well as long-term goals. It all had to do with the business of cabinetmaking, including customer service.

Mahlon shoved his hands into his pockets. "I thought your roots and your respect for the Old Ways went deeper than doing something like this."

Ephraim tossed his pen onto the workload chart. "Are you hearing anything I'm saying about the shop operations?"

"I can't get all this by Sunday. You're the owner. Grey's the foreman. I just build cabinets and do what I'm told."

As the reality of the impending ban began to press in tighter, Ephraim couldn't stop wondering how his family and business would fare without him. He moved to a file cabinet and began searching for any records that might help Grey and Mahlon during his absence. He'd expected to be excommunicated, but he'd never imagined the kind of strictness the bishop had just imposed on him.

A shunning was a rare thing. When the bishop did see it as necessary, the disciplinary time usually included a few painful restrictions. People couldn't take anything from his hand, but they could give things to him and were encouraged to do so to show love. He wouldn't be allowed to sit at a table with others during mealtime. He knew his family; they'd simply choose not to eat at a table. Instead they'd share meals while sitting in the living room or outside in lawn chairs, and Ephraim could join them in those settings. Being under the ban would cause conversations to be awkward at first, but he and his family and friends would work their way through that discomfort, and inside a normal shunning he would have been allowed to do his job, even if he couldn't hand things to anyone Amish or tote one end of a set of cabinets.

Typically, the hardest parts about a shunning were the embarrassment and the fact that the person couldn't stay for any of the after-church meals and couldn't attend any kind of fellowships or singings.

**But this kind of shunning?**

**Be me to her.** The phrase returned, jarring him out of his self-centered thoughts.

With several files in hand, he turned to Mahlon. "Bills have to be paid for Daed's household and the shop." He tossed the information onto the desk. "Grey's going to need your help, and you have to try. You said you would stay next week instead of going on your trip. But will you stick around until I'm no longer being shunned?"

"Why are you letting this happen over an outsider? I could understand if your own heart pulled you to step outside the Ordnung, but some stranger coming through?"

Ephraim didn't miss that Mahlon hadn't answered his question. "She showed up and needed help. I couldn't exactly say, 'Could you come back next year when my Daed is better and when Mahlon gets his head on straight?'"

"Get my head on straight?" Mahlon mumbled. "Try being more direct next time." He leaned in. "Who is she?"

"Someone who's paying the price for her parents' choices—just like the church leaders always warned us about when we were growing up."

"She has Amish roots?"

Ephraim nodded. "She doesn't know. She thinks her mother had Amish friends."

"If her life is an example of what happens when relatives from the past have left the church, I'll hold on with a death grip."

"One would hope you'd hold on to the Old Ways because you believe in them."

"You're in no position to lecture me."

Ephraim changed the subject. "I hate to bother Grey at home, but I think we should go by his place tonight and prepare him for what's going to happen next week. It'll help Monday go smoother. If you need to know something, ask Grey. But he's going to need you to do your part plus some."

The shop door opened, and Deborah and Anna Mary walked in.

Anna Mary's eyes reflected worry. "Is it true? Starting Sunday?"

He moved to her and wrapped her in his arms. She'd handled hearing about Cara staying in his home pretty well. But learning that the shunning had been confirmed and that it'd begin so soon seemed too much for her. He hated it, but he had to warn her about the enforcement of his shunning, beginning Sunday, and she would barely be allowed to acknowledge his existence until the ban was over.

Mahlon went to Deborah and whispered something, causing her to nod. So much rested in Mahlon's hands over the next few weeks or months. Ephraim hoped he was up to it.

# Twenty-Five

The sound of rain against the tin roof pattered its way into Ephraim's dream, stirring him. The cement under his pallet and the aches running through his body assured him he was too old to sleep on the floor. The dream of God calling to Cara through thick clouds and strong winds slowly faded. How many times during the night had he dreamed of God calling to her? And how many times had she spit at Him and walked off?

He sighed. Right now Cara didn't even believe in God, so she wasn't spitting at Him. Maybe it was just a dream—more about his own fears than a hazy premonition.

He sat upright, waiting on energy to

start flowing. After today he'd have no job and no fellowship with friends and family. He missed his life already. Running the shop, baseball and volleyball games, church, community meals, singings, family—all of it was a part of who he was.

During the service the preachers would contrast his actions with the wisdom of the Word. The bishop would explain his decision and then share his edict, and Ephraim's life would become immediately and intensely silent.

A cup of coffee and a shower would feel really good about now. Instead he went to the half bath in his office and washed up in the mud sink. He wouldn't chance seeing Cara this morning. He didn't want her to catch a hint of what was going on. She had more than enough to handle without his adding guilt to it.

She deserved to know who she was and that she had relatives here in Dry Lake. And he intended to tell her when the time was right, but first the community needed to become more open and more tender toward her. They would, given time. But right now they were reeling from the news that the drunken thief Ephraim's father had warned them about had shared a night with Ephraim in his home. They would assume she was her mother's daughter and want to get rid of her. He'd tried to explain to both his Daed and the bishop about Cara's good points and why she needed a second chance, but they didn't feel they could trust his judgment. A few believed him—Deborah, Mahlon, Anna Mary, and a couple of friends—but no one else. Not yet. But they would. They were good people. Even the shunning was out of love and a desire to redirect Ephraim, not out of spite or anger. But they were letting fear help make their decision. The events with Malinda leaving Dry Lake the first time took place when he was a toddler, so he knew only some of the baggage through hearsay. What he had heard was hefty enough.

The scariest thing of all was that even if Cara had the means to leave Dry Lake right away, he didn't want her to. There was something about her, something as strong and fascinating as it was vulnerable and frozen. He'd never seen anything like it in another human. No wonder God called to her. Even He didn't like being shut out from such a rare being.

Since Ephraim wouldn't give the bishop a set date for Cara to be out of his home, the bishop refused to set a date for the shunning to be over. So today began a blurred journey with no definite end. He could still come to church, and he would.

He drew a slow breath, trying to dispel the weight of his reality.

After shaving and practically bathing in the mud sink, he put on his Sunday clothes and walked into the shop area. All woodworking equipment had been moved to the sides, and benches were lined up for the church meeting—the men's side to the right and the women's to the left—facing one another with the "preachers' stand" in the middle. In an hour people would begin arriving. Even though the bishop had been scheduled to be at a different church today, he'd come here instead. Just to carefully and gently declare Ephraim shunned.

Hating the hours that lay ahead, he felt more alone and nervous than ever. He sat on a bench. "God?" He whispered the word, wishing he knew what to ask. A thousand memories of growing up within this community flooded him. Even though he'd left for a while before officially joining the faith, he'd never hurt anyone—not like he was doing now. He'd been barely twenty and a nonmember when he headed for New York. Now he was a man, and he'd made his choice to join the faith long ago. So what was he doing in this mess?

The aroma of coffee rode on the air, and he looked up.

His father sat down on the bench beside him and held out a mug of coffee. "Did you sleep here again?"

Ephraim took the cup. "Ya."

"Son, what are you doing?"

He sipped the coffee, enjoying that his father knew the exact amount of sugar and cream to put in it. "I don't know, Daed. The right thing, I hope."

No one wanted him shunned, not the bishop or preachers or friends or family, but without discipline and holding one another responsible for following the Ordnung, their faith would have scattered in the wind long ago.

For Ephraim's refusal to adhere to correction, as the bishop called it, he wouldn't be allowed to work or have visitors come to his home, and he couldn't be spoken to until the bishop changed the boundaries of his discipline.

In spite of wanting to always submit to the Ordnung, he found himself at odds with it. But if that's what it took to offer at least a tattered, faded image of who God is to Cara and Lori, so be it.

"You said she doesn't see things like we do. But is she at least a believer?"

He shook his head.

"Whatever she does believe could have the power to draw you away from the one true God."

Ephraim stared at the caramel-colored liquid in his mug, wishing he had the right words. If he took days to explain everything to his Daed, he still wouldn't understand. He'd only warn his son with Scripture and fret over Ephraim's difference of opinion. There was plenty written in the Word to support both sides—avoiding those in and of the world and reaching out to them. Wrangling about it would solve nothing and only put more distance between them.

Ephraim wrapped his hands around the mug. "Why did Cara's mom leave?"

"Malinda was engaged to one of our own. He'd gone to Ohio to work for his uncle for the summer. Her father hired Englischers each summer to help with crops. That summer before the wedding season, she fell for one of them. The Amish man she was engaged to had no hint she was falling for someone else. A few weeks before the wedding, she took off with the Englischer. Malinda's fiancé said she was pregnant with the Englischer's child and had no choice. Your mother never believed it. I figured she must've been, though, because she never came back here—not until years later when she feared she couldn't keep Cara safe from her drunken husband."

They sat in silence, watching the rain. When the sounds of horses and buggies and muted voices filtered into the place, Ephraim knew his time to share anything with his Daed was drawing to a close. "I don't know what all happened with Malinda, but Cara was raised in foster care, and her life's been a nightmare. I feel God calling to her. Maybe I'm wrong, but I think He's asked me to show Him to her. That's all I want to do."

His father gazed into his eyes. "I believe most of what you said is truth."

"Most?"

He raised a brow. "That's **all** you want?"

Unable to continue looking his Daed in the eyes, Ephraim turned to stare out the open double-wide doors.

"I've seen the way you look at her, Son. She calls to you in ways you're not owning up to. And she'll break you in ways no one will be able to fix." His voice wavered.

Anna Mary stepped into the shop, looking pale. The skin around her eyes was puffy, as if she'd been crying for hours.

Daed shook his head. "Even she won't be able to repair what Cara will do to you."

Fear shivered through Ephraim. Was he tricking himself into thinking God wanted this of him? Were his own hidden motives pulling him?

Unsure whether to go to Anna Mary or not, he stayed put. She took a seat on the women's side. One by one families arrived, taking seats according to gender and age group without speaking. By sunset last night, news of what today held had spread throughout the community.

The service began as any other. Soon the songs were over, and the first preacher stood to share his message. Ephraim's father followed. The aroma of food cooking wafted through the air, and he knew Cara had started a fire and was baking something. Anna Mary's eyes moved to his. She knew it too. In spite of their reality, she offered an understanding smile.

He could only hope she'd hold on to that accepting spirit throughout this ordeal.

With the women's benches set to face the men's, his and Anna Mary's eyes kept finding each other. The three preachers, including his father, took turns speaking, each for nearly an hour. Children went to the bathroom and came back. Mothers who needed to nurse their infants went into a large storage room at the back of the shop, where chairs were provided, returning later with sleeping babes.

The bishop stood before the congregation, speaking in their own language about how the Amish couldn't afford to let the children of those who'd chosen to leave the church waltz right into the community and cause the baptized ones to disregard the Ordnung.

He held up a German Bible. "Scripture says to suffer not a man to touch a woman and to refrain from the appearance of all evil. How then can a man share a home—a one-bedroom home—with a woman, even for a night and be considered in submission to the Ordnung? Where the heart is, the flesh will follow."

He set the Bible down. "Ephraim is telling us that his heart isn't with this woman and that his flesh won't follow anything but God. But I think he's lying to himself. I don't believe he's committed the sin of fornication, not yet. But even so, can we allow such rebellion? Unless boundaries are set up and those under the submission of the church stay within those boundaries, our standards of accountability are no better than the world's. We have no choice but to offer discipline in love in hope"—he looked at Ephraim for the first time—"in great hope that he will choose to stop going his own way and instead follow the ways of his people. The ways of the Ordnung."

"Better Days, come back here." Lori's voice came through the open door and echoed within the tin building. The bishop continued as if he'd not heard her, but every eye started scanning outside.

"Better Days!"

The puppy ran into the shop, quickly followed by Lori.

"Lori Moore." Cara rounded the corner, wearing her jeans and tight sweater that showed an inch or so of her belly. She came to an abrupt halt, her eyes showing obvious alarm. "Lori," she whispered and motioned for her daughter to come back out of the building.

Every eye moved to Cara. Whatever relatives she had inside Dry Lake, those who knew or would soon know who she was, would not easily let go of their shock and offense at such inappropriate dress. Especially on Amish property during a church service.

Lori pointed at Ephraim. Cara shook her head, but the little girl walked straight to him and sat beside him. "Mom told me not to leave the yard. She's gonna be so mad at me. Can I stay here?" She whispered the words, glancing to her mother as she spoke.

He saw bits of Cara in her. Smart. Strong willed. Defiant. And alarmingly shrewd.

Cara studied him for a moment, and he gave a nod. Lori probably thought she'd won, but the look in Cara's eyes said her daughter was in plenty of trouble. The least disruptive course right now was for Lori to stay. Besides, how wrong could it be for a fatherless child to want to sit with a man— to feel the comfort of his presence, the way he had as a child with his own Daed?

Thankfully, whatever the bishop had to say about the shunning would all be spoken in High German or Pennsylvania Dutch. Lori wouldn't understand a word of it.

Cara left, and Lori crawled into his lap. Her cool skin reminded him that she didn't own a sweater for the warmer weather of springtime—only an adult-size hoodie that dragged the ground. The dampness from the earlier rain clung to her, and he wrapped the sides of his black coat around her. The shivering soon stopped.

By the time the bishop stepped forward to give his summation of Ephraim's wrong-doings, Lori was relaxed and peaceful in his arms and the dog at his feet. It was not an image anyone in the room approved of. But as the bishop explained everything to the congregation, Ephraim found Lori's presence comforting. His district would have to turn their backs on him, but he would not turn his on Cara and Lori.

The bishop asked Ephraim to stand. He shifted Lori to his left arm and stood. She watched, wide-eyed, but she didn't wiggle to get down. If she'd never been in church before, she might not think that much about what was going on.

The bishop gestured toward him, and from their seats the congregation faced him, each one seeming to stare at him with sadness and confusion.

"Until further notice you will not speak to him or do business with him. I want to encourage you to write him letters, reminding Ephraim of who he is to you and the calling God has placed on his life. Tell him how much you miss him, and share God's wisdom as you see fit, but there will be no visitations until he removes the woman from his home. Does everyone understand and bear witness to this act?"

"We do."

The echo of their agreement rang in his

ears. He glanced to his father, who had tears in his eyes. The stricken look on Anna Mary's face bothered him, and he hoped she had the strength to endure the rumors that were sure to circulate after today.

"Then as an act of obedience that we may cause him to submit to the teachings of our forefathers, we begin this journey with great grief, and we will pray for him daily."

Ephraim remained standing as the bishop prayed. When he said "amen," the muffled sound of loved ones leaving without a word spoken rocked him to his soul. Anna Mary wept softly, and she didn't budge until her mother placed her hands on her shoulders and guided her out of the building.

Lori watched the people filing out in stony silence. "What are they doing?"

"The service is over," Ephraim whispered.

When the place was empty, he sat. Lori leaned her back against his chest, asking nothing.

It was over.

And yet it was the beginning.

His head pounded worse than his heart, but he collected himself as best he could before heading for his house.

As he stepped inside, he heard Cara in the storage room. "Lori Moore, is that you?"

The little girl's eyes grew large.

Cara came to the doorway, wagging her finger at her daughter. "What did I tell you—"

Ephraim raised his hand. He'd had all the controversy he could stand for one day. "Don't. Not now."

Cara raised her eyes to his, clearly ready to challenge him. Understanding flickered through her eyes. "You okay?"

"Ya." He set Lori's feet on the floor. "And you obey your mother when she tells you something."

He'd spoken softly, but Lori's eyes filled with tears. He'd never been so weary of emotions battering like a tempestuous sea. He wondered how Cara had managed to cope all these years. She'd moved from one loss to another—always fighting to survive, always having people turn their backs on her or worse—and yet she did what needed to be done without giving up.

The puppy yelped, wanting inside.

A half smile of understanding tugged at Cara's lips. "Better Days is yapping to get in. I think you should be the one to open the door."

She couldn't know what was going on between him and his people, but she'd picked up on his stress. He drew a relaxing breath. If she could lose everything over and over again, surely he could stand the trial of being shunned for a season without carrying it on his sleeve.

He let the dog in. Then he stepped to the doorway of the storage room. She'd cleaned the whole thing. "Amazing."

"Yep, that's me," she teased, then pointed to rows of boxes along one wall. "You'll need to go through those, because most of it looks like junk. I've sorted the rest and labeled each box."

He looked through some of the possible rubbish bins. Old shoes, rusted lamps, and broken stuff. "Hey, this is definitely not trash."

She shrugged. "You still milk cows?"

He laughed, and for the first time in days, stress drained from him. "This has nothing to do with storing fresh milk. Although I guess I can see why you might think so." He lifted a silver cylinder. "This is an ice-cream maker, a hand-crank one."

"Yeah? When's the last time you used it?"

"Oh no. We're not cleaning out this room based on a woman's point of view. It's my stuff, and it stays if I say so."

"I'm beginning to see why you're still single. Women don't take too kindly to the 'my way or the highway' approach, you know." She shoved a sealed box onto the shelf. "Do people actually make ice cream at home? Or is that one of those things you bought 'As Seen on TV,' and it doesn't really work?"

"Ice-cream makers work. And how do you suppose an Amish man would buy something 'As Seen on TV'?"

She shrugged. "I don't know. Do they make a gas-, fire-, or kerosene-run television?"

Amusement stirred in him. "I'll get all the right ingredients together and make some. Then you'll see."

"Ice cream, hand cranked by a man whose idea of an oven is fire in a hole? As long as I can just see it and not have to taste it, you have a deal." Her golden brown eyes met his, calling him to enjoy the day and forget whatever weight demanded to be carried.

He longed to search the hidden regions of her heart and take his discovery into his own. Emotions pulled at him, causing feelings they shouldn't. He hoped his motivations for helping her were as pure as he'd thought. They'd started out that way. And he needed his drive to help her to be based on godliness and that alone. Otherwise everyone's greatest concern was rock solid.

And he was a fool.

# Twenty-Six

Cara slid most of her breakfast into a bowl and set it aside. She'd take it to the mama dog later. Lori was sprawled on the living room floor, reading and playing with Better Days.

Ephraim was nowhere to be seen. He came each morning in time to drive them to work, showed up at the Howards' each evening to bring them home, and stayed hidden in between. It'd been four days since that fateful church service, and except for eating a late dinner with Lori last night, he hadn't joined them for a single meal.

He had a nice home with plenty of food, but in spite of his words, she knew they weren't welcome here any longer. Since Sunday, when she'd accidentally interrupted the church service, she'd felt him pulling away.

As Ephraim took her to and from work, she'd seen people in their buggies, and they'd seen her. But the friendliest gesture she or Ephraim received was a nod. Like the smell of the musty barn clinging to her clothes, she carried the scent of their dislike throughout each day.

If that was how the rest of them felt, she could easily ignore it. But the opinions of his family and friends seemed to have affected Ephraim. Clearly her friendship with him was dying. She wished she could find a place of her own before he started resenting her.

Knowing they could have been good friends if things were different grieved her. Friendships were like food—each had its own taste, texture, and nutrients. She and Kendal were like a cheap dessert that shouldn't be eaten often and at its best was only so-so.

But she'd valued Ephraim's friendship like she'd valued food when starving.

After wiping off the kitchen table and drying her hands, she went into the bedroom. She peeled out of her jeans and sweater top and slid into the teal-colored dress, hating it more each time she had to wear it. She stuffed her dirty clothes into the book bag, planning to wash them at the Howards' today. The constant use of the clothes they'd left New York in was causing them to fray quickly, but that only made the jeans more comfortable. This weekend she'd walk into town and buy Lori a couple of outfits.

Ephraim knocked, making Better Days start yapping. "You ladies ready?"

Cara slung the backpack on her shoulder and hurried out of the bedroom. "Yeah." She grabbed the bowl of food. "Can we stop by the barn?"

Ephraim looked from the bowl in her hands to her.

Cara motioned for Lori to go on out to the buggy. Ephraim's eyes didn't budge from her as she headed out in front of him. "What?"

"Did you eat anything, or are you giving it all to the mutt?" He picked up Better Days and closed the door behind him.

"I had plenty."

They climbed into the buggy, and he and Lori began talking about the book she was reading. When he slowed the horse near the barn, he turned to Cara. "I'll feed the dog from now on. If you cook it, you eat it."

Ire ran through her, and she jerked her backpack off, took money out of it, and threw it in his lap. "Here. Does that cover it?" Without glancing at him again, she climbed down and went into the barn. The mama dog wagged her tail. Cara knelt, calling to her while taking the foil off the bowl. "I brought you some scrambled eggs."

About the time the dog was finished, the barn door squeaked open.

Ephraim loomed over her. "I don't want your money. I want you to eat."

She stood, realizing how short her five-foot-three stature must look to him. "Have some control issues, do you?"

"I have concern issues." He took her

hand and wrapped his thumb and index finger around her wrist. "You're losing weight."

She jerked away. "You have no idea what size I was before."

"How did your jeans fit when you left New York?"

"What?"

"Going by Englischer style, I'd say they fit snug. Now they must be nearly a size too big. Eat, Cara. Okay? I'll feed the stupid dog."

Wondering if the words he said and the words she heard were anywhere near the same, she nodded. When she first met him, he seemed bossy and haughty, so maybe the way she listened was the issue.

"She's not stupid." The sentence made her sound like a spoiled child, and she regretted not staying silent.

"Fine." He rolled his eyes. "I'll feed the highly intelligent dog."

"I'm not incapable, you know. I can take care of Lori and myself and even feed a stray dog here and there. I know it doesn't look that way."

"Mom, help!" Lori's scream pierced the air, and they both took off running.

Ephraim's horse, hitched to the rig, trotted into the street, following another horse and buggy. Lori sat on the driver's bench, staring back at them, wide-eyed with fear. The two people in the first rig looked behind them. Their buggy seemed to slow, causing Ephraim's horse to do the same.

Lori tried to make her way to the side of the buggy.

"No. Stay there," Ephraim commanded as he ran toward the runaway horse and buggy. Cara tried to keep up with him, but she fell farther behind every second.

"Lori, grab the reins and pull back on them," Ephraim instructed as he picked up speed. Cara couldn't tell if her daughter was following his instructions. The rig in front of Ephraim's slowed more, causing Ephraim's horse to follow suit.

Ephraim passed his buggy. He lunged across the base of the horse's neck and grabbed the reins. Within a few seconds he stopped the horse.

The people in the other buggy slowed,

almost stopping as they watched for a moment. When Ephraim gave a nod, they nodded in return and went on their way. Cara kept running for Ephraim's rig. She could see Lori crying and Ephraim talking to her. She finally caught up and climbed into the buggy. She drew her daughter into her lap. "Why would the horse do that?"

Still breathing hard, Ephraim took a seat on the bench. "That was Mahlon's rig. Just for fun my horse was trained to follow it. I guess I didn't set the brake."

"Why didn't your friend stop?"

"He slowed his rig in a way that kept my horse from running into the back of his buggy."

"Yeah?" She motioned toward the moving buggy. "And then he and your sister barely acknowledged us before they kept going."

"Let it go, Cara."

Frustrated but unwilling to argue, she rode in silence the rest of the way to the Howards' place. When she climbed out of the buggy, she muttered a thank-you. He nodded and left.

Something weird was happening between her and Ephraim, but she had no idea what.

The hours passed quickly as she cooked and cleaned and washed clothes, but she still had no answers to her questions as her workday drew to a close.

"Cara," Mr. Howard said when he came home, "we need to talk." He pulled his billfold from his pocket. She studied each bill as he placed it in her hand. "You've been great. Wish we'd had you before I used up all my leave time during those first weeks of Ginny's injury. You've gotten here earlier and stayed later than I dared ask of you. But we learned during her last appointment that her bone healed quicker than expected. I just spoke to her doctor's office, and rather than a regular checkup visit tomorrow, she'll have her hip cast removed. We'd love to keep you, but our budget says we can't. As much as we hate it, we'll have to make do on our own."

It was odd the way disappointment stung every single time it happened. "You don't know anybody else who needs help, do you? I can do almost anything with a little practice."

"No, not that I know of." He shoved his wallet into his pants pocket.

"Okay."

Lori was in the side yard, playing with dolls under a shade tree. When Cara went to get her so they could give Mrs. Howard a proper good-bye, she spotted something she'd noticed twice already this week—a horse and wagon a few hundred feet away with one of the middle-aged men she'd seen at Ephraim's. He sat on the open tailgate of the wagon, selling what looked like some type of vegetables. Probably asparagus and rhubarb since that was all that was ripe in the Howards' garden. But this road seemed like an odd place to try to sell anything. It had almost no traffic. And the man in the wagon appeared more interested in watching her as she worked the garden or hung clothes on the line than in selling.

She'd wanted to ask Ephraim about him, but he seemed in no mood to answer any questions about his people. Deciding it was time she asked the man directly, she headed that way. When he spotted her, he jumped off the tailgate, shoved the crates farther into the wagon, and hurried to the seat. He slapped the reins and took off.

Was it time for him to go, or did he not want to speak with her?

She and Lori went inside and told Mr. and Mrs. Howard good-bye. The Howards apologized again for needing to let her go so abruptly, and she knew their decision was based on something they couldn't control. She assured them it didn't matter and gathered all of her and Lori's clean laundry before leaving. Going down the front walk, she wondered if Ephraim would still pick them up after their tiff this morning.

"Wait," Mr. Howard called.

Cara stopped. "Yeah?"

"Ginny just reminded me of something. My sister lives up the road a piece. She bought paint a few months back. Started painting a room but never finished it, let alone the rest of the house. Don't know how good your painting skills are, but I could put in a good word for you."

"Thanks."

He pointed. "Straight that way about two miles. It's 2201. Two-story brick house, black shutters, pale yellow trim."

"Think she'll mind if I go by there now?"

He shook his head, chuckling. "You do that, missy. She should be there this time of day. I'll go in and give her a call."

Lori tugged on her hand, and they started walking again. In the distance a horse and buggy topped the hill, heading for them.

**Ephraim.**

Her heart beat a little harder. She'd never met anyone like him. In spite of their having a bit of trouble getting along and him being a believer in things that didn't exist, she liked who he was—determined, honest, and giving. The man had a lot going for him. And he was so attractive. If he wasn't Amish, she might even be tempted to fall for him. For her, that'd really be saying something.

"Look, Mom. 'From is coming."

"Yep, I saw him top the hill a few minutes ago."

"Think he brought Better Days?"

"He's brought him every day this week."

"It's Saturday tomorrow. Maybe he'll make ice cream for us."

"Tomorrow is Friday, honey."

Lori cursed.

"Lori Moore, watch your mouth."

"You swear."

"Yeah, well, when you're almost an adult, we'll discuss this again. Until then you talk like a little girl. Got it?"

She shrugged. "Why?"

"I don't know, kid. It's just the way it is."

" 'From doesn't curse."

"Good. Then take after him."

Ephraim pulled to a stop beside them. He had a bit of a smile on his face. That'd been a rarity since she'd interrupted their Sunday service.

"Afternoon, ladies."

Lori put her foot on the step and hoisted herself up. "Hey, 'From."

Ephraim looked beyond Lori, studying Cara with a serious expression.

She smiled. "Hi."

"Afternoon."

Better Days danced all over the seat, welcoming them.

"Mom said I need to take after you."

Ephraim rubbed his chin. "You need to start shaving? I can lend you my razor."

Lori slid closer to him. "She said I'm supposed to talk like you."

Cara sat down. "Hey, Lori, zip it."

Ephraim said something in Pennsylvania Dutch. The sincerity in his voice and reflected on his face added to her puzzlement. Was he annoyed with her intrusion in his life or not?

That aside, his words sounded like something he'd said earlier in the week. He gave Lori a half smile. "Is that what she meant?"

"Nope," Lori chirped. "She meant I'm not to curse."

Ephraim tilted his head at Cara. "We wouldn't want your mother to watch her mouth too, would we?"

Cara harrumphed. "Shut up, both of you."

"Be nice, Mom."

Ephraim laughed and slapped the reins against the horse's back.

"I'm careful what I say most of the time."

"Can you go a week without cursing?" Ephraim asked.

Cara raised her chin. "Shut up, 'From, before I'm tempted to say so much more than a few harmless curse words."

He chuckled.

She pulled her pay out of the pocket she'd sewn on the dress. "Today was my last day with the Howards."

"Did you know that?"

"No. Mrs. Howard is getting out of her cast earlier than they'd figured. Even so I'd thought they'd keep me working until she did a week or so of physical therapy and was able to get around better on her own again. Something must have come up with their finances."

He slowed the buggy to turn it toward his place.

"I got a lead on another job a couple miles straight ahead. Would you mind taking me by there?"

"What kind of job?"

"Painting."

"You ever painted before?"

"No. But before a few days ago, I never cooked on a wood stove either, and you weren't complaining about the meal I fixed last night."

He looked at Lori and rubbed his belly.

He'd come in late last night to get his telescope. That had been his mode of operation all week. When every trace of daylight was gone, he'd slip into the house long enough to get his telescope out of the storage room, tell them good night, and leave. But last night Lori had talked him into eating a second dinner with her.

"When your mom was about the same age you are now," he said, loosely holding the reins, "I asked her if she'd ever picked corn before, and she said, 'No, but I can learn.' And then she started helping me."

Confused by his sudden trip down memory lane, Cara stared at him. Maybe she should relax and enjoy the friendly mood he was in, but she couldn't shake the feeling that he was setting her up for something. "What's with all the nice banter?"

He sighed. "I can't win. If I'm concerned and say so, you tell me I'm being bossy. If I give too much, I must want something. If I give too little, I'm mean and can't possibly understand your situation."

His words bit, but she knew they were true. "You get stung every day of your life, and we'll see how you feel about bees."

"I'm not a bee."

Even as guilt washed over her, she knew he'd never understand. Life had trained her to regard every action with suspicion. And that a swarm of bees could attack at any moment.

# Twenty-Seven

Inside his hiddy Ephraim stared through the telescopic lens, seeing nothing except his own thoughts. He'd been a sky watcher since he turned twelve, but he'd taken up stargazing through a telescope over a decade ago.

Now the vast expanse of the night sky and the brilliance of the stars and planets were hidden behind Cara's face. Those golden brown eyes and soft features seemed to linger with him like his favorite nighttime view of the heavens in the fall—the harvest moon. In the right season the soft orange luminance of a true harvest moon outlined the terrain of bright highlands and darker plains, making them easily visible to the naked eye. And its beauty was a part of him. Too amazing to look away from, it seemed as if he could reach out and touch it. But regardless of how close a harvest moon appeared, it was more than two hundred thousand miles away.

A lot like Cara.

The couple she'd gone to see about painting for them—the Garretts according to the mailbox—walked outside with her as they said good-bye, and he'd overheard what they'd said to her. If she could find someone to help her move furniture and have the painting done by the end of next weekend, they'd hire her.

She hadn't declined the job, nor had she accepted. He'd expected her to ask him for help during their long ride home, but she hadn't. He refused to volunteer. Asking for help was one of the oldest biblical principles and one of the ways people showed each other respect.

Trying to focus on the sky, he adjusted the telescope. He didn't hear or feel anything, but he knew the answer. **Be me to her.**

When God loved people, He didn't

count what something cost Him. He only counted what it'd do for the ones He helped. His Son's life proved that. But Ephraim wasn't God. And Cara irritated him as much as she fascinated him.

The Pennsylvania Dutch phrase he'd spoken to her last week circled through his mind. **Die Sache, as uns zammebinne, duhne sich nie net losmache, awwer die Sache as uns ausenannermache schtehne immer fescht.** He hadn't intended to say it out loud, and he could never tell her what it meant. But one evening he was next to the buggy as she climbed out of it. She'd stumbled a little, and he'd helped steady her. As she stood so close to him, he'd spoken the truth, and some of the tension of the moment broke.

It wasn't like he was interested in her romantically. Certainly not. His attentions belonged to Anna Mary. She was cut from the same broadcloth fabric he was. But Cara—

A terrified scream came from the house. He bolted across the yard. As he entered the house, he heard Cara shriek, "No,

Ephraim!" The fear in her voice swirled feelings inside him like dust caught in a windstorm.

As he hurried through the kitchen, a shadow moved across the room. Cara ran into him, bouncing off his chest like a rubber ball. She staggered back.

Ephraim grabbed her arms to keep her from falling. "What's going on?"

Her labored breathing didn't slow as she gently splayed her hands across his face, touching him as if he might not be real.

"It's okay, Cara. You're awake now."

She backed away. The image of her in his shirt, swallowed in it like a teenager, burned into his mind. She slumped into a kitchen chair. His Bible lay open on the table in front of her. Had she been reading it?

Her hands covered her mouth, and the silvery moonlight reflected a lone tear. She lowered her arms to her side. "What are you doing here?"

"I was watching the stars when I heard you scream."

She glanced at the clock but said

nothing about it being after two in the morning.

Cara drew a shaky breath. Against his better judgment he sat down across from her. The moon's glow lay across parts of her body, shadows filling in the rest. Pages of the Bible rustled as a breeze crossed the kitchen. Tree frogs and crickets played summer's tune. She swiped the tear from her cheek and wrapped her arms around herself.

Ephraim waited for her to speak. But within moments her vulnerable side retreated, and she regained control of her breathing. The woman in front of him squared her body and became as unyielding as the day he'd met her.

**Be me to her.**

How was he supposed to do that? She didn't trust him, and he wanted to be trusted—at least in some distant, "I won't do any more damage to your life" sort of way. He angled his head, trying to make eye contact.

She pushed the Bible to the side, slid the chair back, and stood. "Good night."

"Wait."

Trying to think of something she'd talk to him about, he settled on her job situation. "What did the Garretts say?"

"Not much."

Wondering if anything short of the threat of losing her daughter would make her ask for help, he stifled a sigh. "Will you take the job?"

"I could make really good money. The kind that would help me get out of here."

Was his place that bad? He motioned for her to sit, but she didn't. He went to the kitchen cabinet. "So what's the holdup?" He grabbed a glass.

"I have to work a few things out."

"For Pete's sake, Cara. If you need help, just ask."

She stared at him. "You heard what they wanted?"

He drew water from the tap and set the glass on the table near her. "Ya."

"You have a full-time job. It's already a huge cut into your time to chauffeur us back and forth. How could I ask you for more?"

"You could ask me to help you find someone." His curt tone didn't seem to faze her.

She took a sip and leaned against the counter, seeming neither angry nor stressed. At this moment he'd give her his house if she'd open up and help him understand her. She wanted to make that money. He knew she did. It'd mean the start of independence for her and Lori. Why was she still afraid of him?

Frustrated with her, he couldn't keep his silence any longer. "Fine. I'll help. Thank you for asking."

"You?"

"You don't have to sound so confident in my abilities."

"But you already have a job."

"Actually, I'm off for a while."

"Off?" Lines of uncertainty creased her brows. "And you're willing to paint a house while you're on vacation?" The confusion on her face faded. "Oh."

"What **oh**?"

"If you help me do this, I can get out of here sooner. That's worth painting during your vacation." She looked pleased with herself, and he wasn't going to correct her.

"Here's the deal. I'll be your employee for a week, do everything you need. But you have to answer one question."

"Depends on the question."

"Words like **stubborn** and **mulelike** aren't strong enough to describe you."

She laughed softly. "Hey, your beliefs can't be turned off and on at will. When you have to be stubborn to survive, it becomes a part of you. And then you're its slave."

He wondered if she had any clue how much some of her thinking followed the teachings of God. "You were screaming at me in your sleep. What'd I do in the dream?"

Her fingers moved over her lips, across her cheek, and back again.

"I just want to know so I can help."

She opened her mouth three times before words squeaked out. "I was blindfolded, and you were leading me somewhere. When we got there, you told me to take off the blindfold because you had something special waiting." She placed the glass on the table. "This is silly. I'm going to bed."

He shrugged. "Fine. Go to bed." He wouldn't be out-stubborned by a woman—a featherweight at that.

She huffed. "There was a hot-air balloon with a basket. You talked me into getting in it. It went up and up. Everything below was gorgeous, and I felt free. Then I noticed a rope attached to the bottom of the basket. The end of it dangled inside a black hole that kept expanding, but with every inch of growth, it made the basket shudder and begin to unravel. I screamed for you to help me." She sighed. "The bottom fell out of the basket, and I woke right before I hit the ground."

Ephraim's heart thudded.

"Happy now?"

He shook his head. "I won't lead you to a place where the weight of the world can be defied only to watch you fall."

"It was a stupid dream."

"Or maybe it's your greatest fears surfacing while you sleep—fear of trusting a man, fear that when troubles come, no one can help you."

She lifted the glass, took a sip, and set it down. Then she shifted from one foot to the other, but she didn't respond to what he'd said. She pointed to the Bible. "That says some really odd stuff."

His mother had bought him an English version of the Bible when he was a teen. Reading a German Bible had been difficult, and she'd wanted to make it easier for him to turn to God's Word if he ever had a mind to. At the time he hadn't considered it much of a gift, but it'd grown to mean a lot to him.

"Ya, it does."

"You think so too?"

"Sure. Everyone does. Parts of it are thousands of years old. If you and I have trouble understanding each other because of cultural differences, imagine if we weren't from the same generation and country or if we didn't speak the same language."

"Do you honestly believe there's a God?"

"Ya. And I believe He sent His Son

Jesus and that He left His Spirit to help guide us."

"My mother believed in God. In his own way Johnny did too."

"His own way?"

She shrugged. "The diner he managed was open seven days a week, so going to church was out. I never saw him read a Bible, but sometimes I'd see him praying— not just at mealtime, but walking the floors, talking out loud to God. A lot of it seemed to be for me and Lori." She moved to the Bible and smoothed her fingers across the page. "I can see why people would want to believe in something stronger than themselves."

In spite of wanting to open a discussion on this topic, he decided to say nothing rather than the wrong thing. She didn't know it, but God was having a conversation with her.

She closed the Bible and pushed it away. "If you can be there for me for another week, maybe two, that's all I need." She ran her fingertips across her lips. "Can you?"

It was as if she'd calculated how much

inner strength he had to continue helping her, and all she could come up with was a week's worth, possibly two. "Yes. I promise you that much."

She nodded, but he didn't think she believed him.

# Twenty-Eight

Ephraim ran the paint roller up and down the Garretts' bedroom wall, listening to Cara and Lori in the next room.

Cara had begun to open up a little, even dared to ask a few questions about his beliefs. He'd started to tell her about her roots half a dozen times, but it seemed that sharing eternal truths was more important than factual ones, especially since the ones based on her mother were sure to cause pain and provide no answers. She thought her mother had been in Dry Lake to visit friends. And for whatever reason, her family's **friend** never came for her at the bus station. He hated how betrayed she'd feel when she learned the truth and realized he'd known everything all along. But to tell her too soon would take so many things from her, especially if she reacted like he figured and bolted—never to be seen or heard from again. But holding on to the secret sometimes made him feel as if the smithy was shoeing his insides.

He dipped the roller into the oversize bucket and carefully loaded it with paint before applying it to the wall. He had no doubts that the news of who she was had reached the Riehls. They knew she was staying at Ephraim's, but not one of them had come by to see her.

The thought of Cara finding that out hurt, and he longed to protect her from it. But if she stayed around long enough, he hoped the community would choose to do the right thing and stop ignoring her. They were trained to shut out the world and all its trappings, but sometimes, in trying to avoid ungodliness, they shut out the wrong things. Warming up to the idea of Malinda's daughter returning would take time, especially since she'd been seen wearing unacceptable clothing and short hair, living in a barn, and dancing inside his home.

But if they'd ever give her a chance, they'd see a remarkable person.

Cara's soft voice caught his attention as she chuckled about something. Five days of working twelve to fourteen hours, and he wanted more. More laughter, more sharing of lunches under the shade tree, more working until midnight, and more times of talking softly while drinking their first cup of coffee each morning.

Carrying the roller with him, he moved through the hallway. The Garretts had fully accepted the Howards' recommendation of Cara. Before they left for vacation, they'd given her a key to the house and permission to empty their belongings out of the closets so she could paint them. He stopped outside the family room. Cara propped her hands on her hips. The new overalls she'd bought in town last Saturday and washed umpteen times in his wringer washer before wearing them once were now covered in paint. She took long strides through the room.

"Walking," Lori said.

"You tried that one already. Come on,

kid, use your imagination." She moved her hips slowly. "Give me a good synonym for what I'm doing."

"Tripping."

"Tripping?" Cara laughed. "Remember the words in the book we read last night? How about swaggering or sashaying."

Ephraim cleared his throat. "Or shuffling like an old lady?"

She wheeled around, a look of surprise in her eyes before she shook the paintbrush at him. "Is that bedroom finished?"

"No ma'am."

"Then I suggest you shuffle back in there before I sashay over and whack you upside your Peeping Tom head."

He stood his ground. "I think the title of boss has gone to your swaggering head."

Lori giggled. "Earlier she tried to make me learn about idioms."

"Oh, I agree. Everyone needs to be warned about idiots."

" 'From,'" Cara fussed, threatening him again with the loaded paintbrush, "idioms, not idiots."

"Where'd you learn about idioms?"

"Ninth-grade grammar. Clearly it wasn't your favorite subject like it was mine. An idiom is a type of phrase, as in 'I walk all over you.'"

"I'll say it again; this boss thing has gone to your head."

She raised her eyebrows. "Get back to work."

He shook his head. "It's Friday afternoon. We've done enough. We'll be finished tomorrow and have everything back in place before the Garretts get home."

"I don't know."

During the nights, while he slept at his house, she'd stayed here at the Garretts, sleeping a little before getting up to prepare the next room to be painted. She'd emptied closets, applied painter's tape, and edged paint along the ceilings, baseboards, and corners. When he arrived, the room was ready to be rolled. "You've stayed here all week. You need to spend tonight at my place, where you'll actually sleep. And I'm making ice cream again."

Lori started dancing around the room. "Yes! Yes! Yes!"

"If you can get your mother to leave work, that is."

"You're using my child's love of ice cream to manipulate me." Cara held the paintbrush under his chin like a sword. "You cheat."

"Yep, and I win too."

She laughed. "Fine. After we rinse out the brushes and rollers, we'll leave."

"Nope, we'll put them in a bucket of water and take them with us. I'll rinse them out later."

She frowned and huffed and then left the room, mumbling under her breath. After being around her all week, he knew her venting and teasing were rolled into one. He found it amusing. He'd caught glimpses this week of the woman she was when life offered a bit of security and dignity. Now he understood why he'd waited for her to return to Dry Lake. Why he'd gone to New York in hopes of seeing her. He'd never had a friendship like hers. He couldn't define it, but it seemed she carried magical powers to remove the calluses from his heart and cause him to see life in a refreshing way.

Lori tugged on his pants. " 'From?"

He ruffled her hair. "Is that ice cream calling your name?"

She nodded. "And the puppy's name too."

"Guess you better go get him from the backyard and put him in the wagon."

He went to the bedroom and placed the roller in the paint tray beside the bucket. He'd never considered it important for a woman to be able to earn money, to have that same sense of power he got from running the cabinetry shop. He'd been a fool in that, and he wondered what else he'd been wrong about all his life.

He heard her moving about in the kitchen and went to join her.

She glanced up while rubbing her lower back. "Grilled cheese tonight okay?"

He nodded, wishing he had a better stove. Aside from breakfast food, there weren't many dishes he could prepare on the stove either. It worked decently enough, and he had other reasons for owning it, but cooking on it hadn't been important. Before the shunning he ate half his lunch and supper meals at his Daed's place, and Deborah provided him with the other half.

His Daed needed him to share a meal at his table as often as he could. It gave them time to talk business and relieved his Daed from the guilt of requiring so much help. Concern flickered through him as thoughts of his Daed, family, and the business pushed to the forefront again. He missed sitting around the supper table with his family, but it hadn't left a hole inside him like he thought it would.

Cara snapped her fingers, a lopsided smile on her face. "Do I have to lug the buckets of water with rollers and brushes out to the wagon myself?"

"Sorry."

It didn't take long before he was loading the last of the items into the wagon. Cara locked the house and then placed her backpack on the floorboard. She stretched her back several times, clearly achy and stiff.

"Ephraim, who's that?" She nodded at

the buggy stopped on the side of the road ahead of them.

He glanced that way and saw Rueben Lantz. "Anna Mary's Daed."

"Oh. I guess that explains why he's been watching me."

"You think he's been keeping an eye on you?"

"I'm sure of it."

"Maybe it isn't you he's watching. Maybe he doesn't trust me." Unfortunately, right now Ephraim didn't blame him. He never thought he'd feel such a bond to any woman he'd known for only a couple of weeks. Still, it wasn't romantic feelings. Cara was a friend, and that word had taken on new meaning lately.

Ephraim hoped Rueben would move on before they passed him, but he didn't.

"Aren't you going to stop and speak to him?" Cara asked.

"No."

"At least wave?" She studied him as if waiting for some piece of information to make sense.

"He wasn't looking our way."

It did seem a little odd that Rueben hadn't made eye contact or acknowledged them, but in a way Ephraim couldn't blame Rueben for being angry with him.

Thankfully, she dropped the matter. Soon they were entering his driveway.

He slowed the horse as he pulled into the barn. "I haven't been home before dark all week."

She rubbed her thumb and index finger together, mimicking what she'd told him represented the world's smallest violin.

"Slave driver."

"Rich boy."

She slid the strap of the backpack onto one arm and climbed down. He unhitched the horse and put it in the field. Better Days ran after the horse, and Lori took off.

She gazed beyond the gate that led to the pasture. "Look at that pond."

He'd seen it a million times, but today the golden amber shades reflecting the almost-setting sun reminded him of the harvest moon. "Want to walk that way?"

"Yeah, I do."

As they strolled, Cara seemed to soak in

her surroundings, studying the trees and wildflowers as they drew close to the pond.

"'From, look." Lori ran up to them, holding a stick. "Watch this." She tossed it, and Better Days raced to it. He stared at it before running back to Lori.

"Here, boy." Ephraim whistled. The puppy ignored him, but the mama dog came running from nowhere. Lori giggled and grabbed another stick. While Cara gazed at the pond, Lori tossed the stick, and, surprisingly, the mama dog fetched it each time.

Cara tucked her arms around herself. "It's gorgeous."

"A night sky is better."

She went to the water's edge, and he wondered what she was thinking. And feeling.

The leaves on the trees that lined the upper banks whispered in the breeze. A group of mallards landed on the water in front of her, causing ripples.

Lori ran toward her mother but couldn't stop in time to keep from pushing her forward. Lori fell back on the bank, but Cara almost landed in the pond. While regaining her balance, the mama dog crashed into the back of her legs, making her knees buckle. Cara fell headfirst into the shallow water.

Ephraim ran in, grabbed her by the arm, and helped her to her feet. Mud dripped from her arms and chest. Her white sneakers were hidden under the soft, gooey mud.

"You okay? The dog—"

She slung filth from her hands. "I'm well aware of what happened."

"Come on, let's get you out of here." He held on to her arm as he took a step toward dry land.

Cara tried to move forward, but she seemed stuck. She yanked on one leg. Her bare foot suddenly jerked free, and she jolted against Ephraim, and they both began to topple. As he reached for her other arm to steady her, the dog jumped on him, sending both of them into the water.

He got to his feet, feeling the slimy muck seeping through his clothes. He grappled for better footing and then took her by the arm, trying to help her stand. As she pulled against him to get upright, he slipped and took her down with him.

Cara sat in the shallow water, looking at him as if he'd planned all this. "We can do this, right?"

He laughed. "We haven't been successful so far. But I don't think we can give up." He stood and reached for her.

She put both hands in the air like a stop sign. "Oh no. Not a chance. You've helped me enough, thanks."

Every moment he spent with her seemed to make him crave more. Suddenly he realized they were in far murkier waters than the pond.

She pulled herself to her feet and dug in the mud until she found her shoe. Tossing it to the bank, she almost fell again.

With her feet and hands in the shallow water, she half walked, half crawled onto dry land and sat on the grass. "I smell like fish and sludge. Yuck." She glanced up to see tears in Lori's eyes. "If you cry, kid, so help me I'll push 'From back in the water."

"What'd I do?" He took two giant steps

out of the water and flopped onto the ground next to her. "Let's throw the dog into the water. This was all her fault."

The tension in Lori's face eased. "You're not mad, are you, Mom?"

"Yes, yes I am."

Lori laughed. "Seriously?"

"I'm also wet and muddy." She stood. "One bathroom for two adults to get cleaned up. Now, how's that supposed to . . ."

She let her sentence trail, and Ephraim looked to see why. On the hill above them stood Mahlon, Deborah, and Anna Mary. They stared. His sister looked as if the scene in front of her made no sense. She turned away. Mahlon waved and then followed her. He knew what was happening. They'd heard the ruckus and had come to see if someone needed help, but now they had to leave without talking to him. Anna Mary didn't budge.

"Tough crowd," Cara mumbled. "What's going on?"

He shrugged, watching as Anna Mary came toward him. Was she going to side-step the ban and talk to him?

Cara got to her feet and started up the hill. "Anna Mary, hi."

Anna Mary didn't respond. She focused only on him. "This is wrong, Ephraim. Are you trying to make her think you could actually be interested in someone like her?"

"Someone like me?" Cara's voice took on an edge.

She faced Cara. "I'm not blaming you. He should think. But men don't, you know."

"Someone like me?" Cara repeated.

He wasn't surprised at Cara's seething tone. But he didn't understand why Anna Mary wasn't sounding at least a bit jealous. Since they began seeing each other, she'd had times of flaring with jealousy over girls he'd spoken to or taken home from a singing umpteen years ago. And none of them meant anything. Never had. Yet his feelings for Cara were multiplying faster than made any logical sense.

"While he's been **helping** you, his business didn't meet its scheduled work load."

"That's enough, Anna Mary." But it was

too late. He saw in Cara's eyes that she understood more than he wanted her to.

Anna Mary clenched her jaw. "Then we need to talk. Privately." Cara snatched the backpack off the ground and held her hand out for Lori. When they were out of hearing range, Anna Mary turned back to him. "The bishop gave me permission to be here."

Ephraim's heart rate increased. "What's going on?"

"The shop is already getting behind on orders, and you've only been gone a week. Grey and Mahlon tried to keep up, but your Daed had to step in. It's too much stress for him. His arrhythmia went wild, and now he's in the hospital."

As if the past week had been a fling and now reality had closed in around him, he couldn't catch his breath. "I want to see him."

"The bishop said he's willing to lift the ban concerning your Daed."

"Good. And I want to talk to his cardiologist."

"Becca's been trying to see the doctor

too. Last I talked to her, she said he's supposed to be making hospital rounds tomorrow morning."

Ephraim's heart twisted. Cara couldn't
finish that painting job by herself, not before the Garretts came home. But he
couldn't let himself be sidetracked any
longer. The last time he spoke to Daed's
nurse, she hinted there might be an option
concerning his heart problems. He needed
to check into that before his father's heart
failed altogether.

Trying to plan a dozen things at once,
he felt as if he were trapped inside the old
dark silo where Cara once hid. "I need
you to do several things for me. One, ask
Mahlon and Grey to help Cara tomorrow.
She's wrapping up a painting job. If either
of them will go in my stead, I'll head
straight to the hospital."

"They'll do it. You know they will. But
I have more that I need to tell you."

He wasn't sure he could handle more.

"My Daed, the bishop, and a few members of the community have found a place
for Cara to move to—in Carlisle."

"Your Daed got involved?"

"He's more upset than I am about that woman being here."

With his mind lingering on Cara day and night, Ephraim could see why Rueben felt concern. The emotions churning inside him alarmed him at times. Maybe he should let the wisdom of the men in the community prevail over his current choices.

"The twenty-mile distance will more than satisfy the bishop's desires that she move on, but it's not so far you can't keep up with how she's doing. Daed and some others pitched in to cover three months of rent plus the deposit. The bishop also has a list of potential jobs within walking distance of the place."

Duty to his family and community and desire to be with Cara warred within him.

"Let her go, Ephraim. Stop trying to be her answer to everything, and do what's best for your family. For the business and community. For us."

He knew she was right. With his Daed sick and the shop struggling, he had no choice. Besides, finding Cara a place and making sure she and Lori weren't separated was his goal—that and getting the community to accept who she was and treat her right. If the bishop, Rueben Lantz, and some others had gone through all the steps to find her a place, they must be willing to accept her—at least somewhat—in spite of the rumors concerning her and her mother.

Ephraim made himself respond. "Ya. It does seem to be time."

Cara's friendship seemed to fade, like a dream he couldn't hold on to once he awoke, leaving only longing in its stead.

# Twenty-Nine

"How could he do this?" Deborah fought against tears. "It's like he's enjoying being shunned. Did you see him laughing and horsing around?" She stopped at the clothesline and yanked a towel from its clips.

Mahlon slid his hand into hers. "It was a funny situation. That's all. They'd both fallen into the water."

"What was he doing at the pond with her anyway? Having a stroll has nothing to do with giving her a place to live." Deborah half folded the towel and dropped it into the basket. "And what if Daed had seen that? Does Ephraim understand what it could do to him?"

Mahlon picked up the laundry basket

and held it for her. "Your Daed wasn't there. Don't borrow trouble."

She took a dress off the line and folded it halfheartedly before tossing it in the basket. "I wanted to be the one to talk to him."

"I know. But the bishop was right. If Ephraim was going to feel drawn back into the fold, it'd be Anna Mary doing the pulling. If a woman in love can't make a man see and hear what he needs to, no one can."

"Mamm could've gotten through to him. If she were around, he'd not have done any of this."

"You can't know that. Come on, Deb. Ephraim deserves a little room. He's stepping out to do something he feels is right. Do you really think he's that wrong?"

Without answering him Deborah pulled more clothes from the line and wiped at tears. This past week had been miserable. And knowing Mahlon wanted to get away by himself only added to the hurt she carried.

Seeing Anna Mary coming toward

them, Deborah stopped messing with laundry. "How'd it go?"

She gave a nervous shudder. "I've never been so bold with Ephraim. But I told him what he needed to do, and he agreed."

"He's going to do it?"

Anna Mary nodded.

"Did Cara agree?"

"I didn't talk in front of her." Anna Mary crossed her arms. "But I told Ephraim it's not right to act so friendly around her. She's gonna get the wrong idea about how he feels toward her."

Deborah sighed. "I just hope Daed doesn't find out that Ephraim's not keeping his distance from her as he should."

Ephraim knocked on his own front door, waited a few moments, and entered. How would he explain to Cara that his family and business needs dictated his life? They had for years.

She was standing beside the double

kitchen sinks, still wearing the wet, muddy clothes. Her face and arms dripped with clean water as she grabbed a hand towel. The backpack sat in one of the sinks. She turned to face him. "You've been lying to me."

"I have not."

She ran the rag over her face and bare arms, keeping her eyes fixed on him. The hurt she tried to hide sliced into him. "Fine. Don't be honest with me."

With no clue what to say, he wrestled with everything that had to be said.

"I can't believe this." She slung the towel into the sink.

"Look, it's complicated, and I can explain it."

"You lasted a little over a week. It's more than I should have expected. And I appreciate it."

Her calm, matter-of-fact tone belied the betrayal reflected in her eyes. The walls between them that had been removed now reappeared like a magic trick gone bad.

"You need to work at your shop tomorrow. I'll finish at the Garretts' on my own and bring your share of the money once I get paid. Then Lori and I will move on."

"You caught wind that something's not right, and that's it? You're done?"

"I may not dress appropriately or wear my hair just so or know anything from inside that Bible you read every night, but I don't play people."

"I wasn't playing you." He walked toward her, feeling his shoes and socks squish with mud and water. "I've kept a few things from you but not to trick or deceive you. I was trying to protect you until the time was right."

"What things?"

"Why don't you get a shower, and we'll talk after we eat."

She shook her head. "It doesn't matter anyway. I'm not about to trust anything you have to say now."

He'd done a horrible job of trying to be God to her, but he had to make her understand. "For a dozen reasons I can't make you see, I was trying to do the right thing.

There are more people involved in this than just you, Cara. People I care about."

She made a face. "What are you talking about?"

He pulled a chair out for her. "I think you should sit."

"No." She gazed into his eyes, once again looking as defiant as the day he saw her at the barn. "I have things to do." She went into the bathroom, closed the door, and turned on the shower.

He couldn't help but wonder if some sliver of this was how God felt sometimes. God gave up things He didn't have to. He cared so much it hurt, and at the first sign of a perceived wrong, His people stopped trusting Him or even trying to hear Him. But as the thought came and went, he knew this wasn't about who God was to her. It was about who she was to God. Wondering if that's how relationships with God always started out, he prayed for her.

The door to the bedroom creaked as Lori opened it. "Can me and Better Days come out now?"

"Sure. Are you hungry?"

Lori moved to a chair, her brown eyes reflecting concern. "Mom's mad, huh?"

"A little."

"Does this mean we gotta leave?"

He hoped not. He wanted to give her a promise, but he had no control over Cara. She could pack her things and walk out at any minute. Maybe he should have talked to Cara earlier in the week while they painted and Lori slept on the couch, but it'd been easier to put the ugliness of the truth to the side and let Cara enjoy the progress she had made. Now he needed to talk to her without Lori nearby. "I have an idea. Would you like to meet my sister?"

"You got a sister?"

He laughed. "Lots of them, but the one I want you to introduce yourself to is Deborah."

"Can Better Days come too?"

"Ya. Kumm."

They walked across the yard, through the parking lot of the shop, to his Daed's place. Deborah stood in the yard, talking with Mahlon and Anna Mary. None of them noticed him.

"Go to the girl in the blue dress and tell her you want to show her your puppy and stay with her for a bit."

"I gotta stay?"

He knelt in front of her. "Just for a while. I want to talk to your mom, okay?"

"That's all you guys have been doing all week."

"I know, but this is different. If you do this, I'll make ice cream later tonight, even if it's midnight."

She studied him, looking unsure. "Mom won't like me staying here without her."

He had a feeling Lori was the one who didn't like the idea. "She won't mind. I'll make sure of it."

Lori hugged his neck. In spite of having so many younger sisters, Ephraim was surprised by the tenderness that washed over him for this little girl. He placed his hand on her back, hoping he could make a significant difference in her life. But it wasn't all up to him. Cara's will and choices could override everything.

Lori walked toward the group, a muddy Better Days running alongside her. All three of them glanced to Lori when she said something. His sister immediately responded to the young girl with kindness. Deborah bent, petting the dog in spite of his wet fur. While kneeling on the ground and chatting with Lori, she noticed Ephraim and held his gaze, her warm smile assuring him of her loyalty before she lowered her eyes.

Anna Mary gave him a cold look, as if warning him to follow through on his agreement. He turned for home but decided to wash up and put on something clean. Since he'd been staying at the shop at night, he had several sets of fresh clothes there. And the workers had left for the day.

After a quick cleanup, he hurried back to his house. It wouldn't do for Cara to think Lori had slipped outside and off the property while she was in the shower. As he entered the house, she came out of the bathroom, barefoot and in Deborah's dress, towel drying her hair. Whether she was covered in mucky pond water, paint-covered jeans, or Amish clothes, her beauty was evident. Her hair was as short as his, and it grated against everything he'd been taught about a woman never cutting her hair, yet he liked it.

She barely looked at him as she headed for the bedroom. "Where's Lori?"

"She's with my sister."

"You had no right—"

He held up his hand, stopping her short. "I need to tell you some things, and you aren't going to want her to overhear them."

She went to the sink, where the grubby, wet backpack sat. "I told you, forget it." After opening it, she pulled out its contents. The soggy clothes she tossed in the sink, but when she pulled out a thick leather book, her movements became slow and gentle. She flipped the pages, checking the water damage.

"After you and your mother left, I climbed our tree every day, waiting for you to come back."

She tossed the book onto the table as if

it didn't matter, but he'd already seen that it did. "So what's your point?"

"You were supposed to come back. Malinda intended for you to be raised by Levina. That's what she was doing here that week—getting permission."

The taut lines on Cara's face melted as every trace of emotion drained. "She wouldn't send me away."

"She didn't want to. I was finishing up some chores for Levina really late one night, and I overheard your mother through an open window, sobbing like her heart was breaking. The plan was to take you back with her and prepare you for what needed to be done."

"That's ridiculous." She snatched up the book. "I've heard enough."

He stood and blocked her exit. "Cara, listen to me. The church leaders decided they couldn't provide a place for your mother. She'd joined the church, but then she left here with a man who wasn't Amish. When she came back with you, she was married to that man. They wouldn't support her leaving him, but they were willing to take you in because you were a child, and she was willing to give you up."

"My mother wouldn't have passed me to some friend to raise. She used to hide me from Dad sometimes, but—"

"Levina and Emma Riehl weren't friends. They were relatives. Riehl was your mother's maiden name. And Levina was your great-grandmother."

She froze, seemingly unable to catch her breath.

He touched her arm, and she jerked.

"The old woman?"

"She was your mother's grandmother. She died a number of years ago."

"But I . . . I have relatives here?"

He nodded.

"Why didn't you tell me?"

"Whatever bad feelings your mother caused in Dry Lake still cling to most."

"Meaning they know who I am and don't want anything to do with me?" Pain and utter disbelief reflected in her eyes.

"At first no one knew you were here. When they found out a woman was staying at my place, most didn't know who.

Now, among other reasons, they need some time to adjust."

"Adjust?" She tried to bury the hurt from his sight. "They need time? After leaving **me** in a bus depot?"

"I don't know why that happened. Maybe your dad just thought Emma was coming."

She rolled her eyes, looking disgusted. "Yeah, right. It had to be him. We can tell that by how welcoming those same people are now." She stared at him. "Why are they being like this? You know something you're not saying."

"They've heard things about you. Rumors."

"Enlighten me."

"They believe you're a thief and a drunk. I never said a word about you taking anything from me, but—"

Her brown eyes bore into him, and he could almost see the puzzle pieces fitting together. "The man who saw me coming out of that home must've started people talking." She slammed her palms on the counter. "I only took what I had to.

And I wasn't drunk. Exhausted and clumsy, but—"

"I know, Cara. I get it. And they will too if given time."

"So now they think I'm worse than my dad, who ruined the life of an Amish girl."

He nodded.

She sidestepped him and left the house, letting the screen door slam behind her.

He went after her, surprised she wasn't going to his Daed's house to get Lori. Instead she went the back way toward the cornfield.

"Cara, wait."

She turned to him. "All this time I've shared parts of my life with you, and you knew more than I did. Go away, Ephraim. Go back to your tight-knit community and leave me alone."

He followed after her. She didn't stop until she stood on the empty foundation of Levina's place.

He moved onto the platform with her. "I'm sorry. If I could have prevented this, I would've."

Her eyes brimmed with tears. "All

those years of having no one was easier than this."

"I know it's hard to understand, but it takes rules, restrictions, and avoiding the ways of the world to live as we do. Our boundary lines don't change because someone wants more freedom. A person either agrees to live by the rules of being Amish and joins the faith, or they leave. Your mother joined the faith and then left. She didn't return until she was trying to protect you."

"So it didn't really matter what I did. They would've been set against me anyway because of what she did."

"Not exactly. Whatever trouble your mother caused is only part of the wall. The half-truths going around about you have done a lot of damage. And you carry an aura of the world, and that makes you suspect. We slept in the same house together. When the church leaders stopped by, you and Lori were dancing. Still, if you'll give the community a little time, they'll come around. Their attitudes toward you are already changing."

"What makes you say that?"

"The bishop found a place for you to live. It's not too far from Dry Lake. And the rent is already covered for three months."

"They're paying me to leave?"

He hadn't thought of it like that. "Cara, I'm sure that's not how they meant it."

"So is that what your girlfriend came to tell you—that the community has a plan for getting me out of Dry Lake?"

"No, the real news is that my Daed's in the hospital, and I need to go see him."

"What? I'm sorry. I'll get Lori right now, and we'll stay at the Garretts for the night."

"No, I didn't mean that. He's stabilized, so it's not an emergency."

"Why didn't they tell you sooner?"

He rubbed the back of his neck, realizing he'd just stepped into another pile of horse manure. "I made the choice, Cara."

"What are you talking about?"

"I'm under the ban."

"In English, please."

"I'm being shunned. I can't talk to or be talked to or work with any Amish person around here—not even family."

"On vacation, huh?" she mumbled as she walked to the far end of the foundation. A few moments later she squared her shoulders slightly. "Do I need to do something to help set all this straight for you, or is just getting out of here enough?"

"I don't want you to go, especially not like this."

"Yeah, and I didn't want to grow up in foster care. But life happens, 'From."

Her use of his nickname told him her anger was gone. Resignation had seeped into her, and she was ready to make amends and leave.

He moved to the edge of the foundation and sat. "I went to New York about a year after my mother died. I went looking for you. I actually thought I had a chance of finding you."

She sat beside him. "I'm sorry I called you a liar. You've been nicer to me than anyone could expect."

"I'm glad we **had** to get to know each other. I'll never see life the same since seeing it through your eyes. But being Amish is who I am, and my family needs me. Especially with my Daed's health as it is. I provide for the family."

"And your God wouldn't want it any other way, right?"

His heart felt as if it might plummet to his feet. "Die Sache, as uns zammebinne, duhne sich nie net losmache, awwer die Sache as uns ausenannermache schtehne immer fescht."

"Back atcha." A half smile tugged at her lips as it had half a dozen times this week when he'd said that to her. "You ever gonna tell me what that means?"

Gazing into her eyes, he longed for more time. "The things that bind us will never loosen, but the things that separate us will always stand firm."

She eased her hand over his, sending warmth and loneliness through him. "And what doesn't separate us allows us to be friends . . . at least for now."

He held on to her hand. "We'll pace what needs to be done. Take the time to get Lori used to the new place and to find yourself a job."

Cara gazed at the horizon, looking

peaceful in spite of the storm. He didn't push for her to respond. Plenty had been covered for now. They waited as daylight faded into dark and a few stars became visible.

# Thirty

Before getting out of bed, Cara pulled Lori's warm body closer and kissed the back of her head.

She slid into her jeans, leaving Ephraim's shirt on. It hurt to know she had relatives in Dry Lake who didn't want to talk to her. But she couldn't dismiss what Ephraim had done to improve their situation. Lori's life was better and would always be better because of the path he'd cleared for them. That alone was enough to soothe the Grand Canyon–size ache in her chest.

She tiptoed out of the bedroom as daylight loomed. The idea of seeing Emma Riehl ran through her mind. Maybe if she understood why her dad had left her at the bus station and told her that Emma was coming, and why she hadn't, Cara could lay it to rest.

Heat radiated from the cookstove. A percolator prepped with coffee and water sat next to the sink, ready to be placed on the stove. Ephraim must've slipped inside at some point and started the fire and fixed the percolator for her. On his own, without his community pulling at him, Ephraim was quite a man. He had integrity.

And something beyond that.

He'd captured a piece of her heart. She wasn't sure why it had happened. Maybe because he was a truly nice guy or maybe because she felt connected to him since he'd known her mother. Whatever the reason, her heart had really poor judgment and timing. But he'd taken only a sliver. She'd move on and get it back.

Moving as quietly as she could, she placed the percolator on the stove. She'd had a lot harder wallops in her life than learning her relatives wanted nothing to do with her—losing her mother, growing up in foster care, dealing with a stalker, and marrying a man she didn't love. This latest hit had her staggering, but not for long. She'd start new and find something she was really good at. Maybe she should start her own painting business.

The Bible lay open on the table. The two men she'd been closest to had beliefs founded in that book. A shred of hope that strength could be found inside those pages drew her to it.

She sat down and pulled it in front of her. The words were barely visible in the dim glow of dawn. She lit the kerosene lamp and flipped pages, pausing here and there as a phrase caught her eye. Its beautiful prose and imagery were fascinating, even without believing in its origin. As she turned the thin, delicate paper, she remembered her mother loving this book. She had scribbled verses inside Cara's diary, along with thoughts of love and short lectures of wisdom from mother to child.

**Daughter.** The word caught her eye, but she'd already flipped past it. Turning back through the pages, she began scanning each one.

**Daughter.** The word popped from the book. She placed her finger under it and traced back a few words.

"I will be your Father, and you will be my sons and daughters."

The longing to be a beloved daughter hit so hard she couldn't breathe.

**If only it were true.**

❧

Ephraim sat on the bench swing in his hiddy. Concern for his Daed's health pushed in on all sides, but that wasn't enough to keep his mind off Cara.

The top of the sun edged over the horizon, bringing stronger rays of daylight with it. The green fields sparkled with dew. Horses and cows grazed on nearby hills. Mist rose from the valley and from the shop's roof. Everything he saw spoke of a promise—the best this earth had to offer. The pursuit of happiness. Peaceful living. And freedom.

But all he could feel was emptiness and duty.

He'd hardly slept last night. His whole body ached for things he never knew existed before Cara. She woke the sleeping parts of his soul, just as she had as a child. Existence before her was shallow and only satisfying because he didn't know anything different.

Now he knew. Part of him wished he didn't. The other part longed for there to be answers.

Was he falling in love with her? It didn't matter. It couldn't. He tried to think about something else.

Since the house was quiet, he wondered if Cara and Lori were still asleep. After Cara had picked up Lori from his sister, he'd made ice cream as promised. Then he'd gone to the shop. Cara probably hadn't slept much either. Or maybe she had. She was certainly more used to upheaval and grief than he was. Did she feel grief over him? Or was he the only one who felt so stirred by their friendship?

He knew she needed to get to the Garretts' this morning to finish the job, but he hesitated to wake her. He went to the clothesline in his Daed's yard, where he'd created a trough of sorts using a sheet strung between two lines. He'd placed the freshly washed paintbrushes and rollers inside. It must've been about midnight when he remembered he needed to finish cleaning the soaking items. He placed the tools into a bucket he'd scrubbed for this very purpose.

The door to his Daed's home swooshed open, and he glanced up.

Anna Mary looked as weary as he felt. With Becca at the hospital with Daed, Anna Mary must've stayed to help Deborah with the younger ones. She headed for him without hesitation, apparently confident in continuing the special privilege granted to her by the bishop.

She came to a halt, her bare feet wet from the dew. "Mahlon and Grey both offered to help Cara today. The bishop gave permission, provided one of the elders can visit at will. I told him that wouldn't be a problem. One of the men will be here in about an hour to drive them over."

"Why the big production? Cara isn't going to try to seduce them, for Pete's sake."

"That's not the point. The bishop is our head, and we submit to his word. Have you forgotten the ways of your people so quickly?"

Chafing at her tone, one she never would have used before the shunning, he put the last two paintbrushes in the bucket.

"Robbie will be here to take you to the hospital about the same time. I want to go with you."

"I'm sure Deborah needs your help around here. Besides, I'd hoped to talk to Daed alone."

She moved in close and laid her hand on his chest. "Look, this is hard on both of us, but I have to know that you care about us—that when this is over, you'll be ready to commit to me the way you have to that woman and her child."

Like a spring rain, drops of realization fell on him, and he understood what his heart had been trying to tell him. He placed his hand over hers and removed it from him. "I'm sorry. But I can't do that."

He doubted if he ever could have, not without settling. But now that he knew what it meant for someone to connect with his soul, for someone's very presence to make a difference in how he perceived a day, he had to let Anna Mary go.

"What are you saying?"

"You can tell people you ended things between us. That you're tired of me. Ashamed of me. They'll sympathize. Probably even think you've done the right thing."

Her face turned red, and she burst into tears. "But why?"

"You don't really want an answer to that. If it helps, I don't want an answer to that either."

Her face scrunched with confusion. "Maybe you're just irritable from all the stress. Or angry at all that's happening and taking it out on me."

"Have I ever taken anything out on you?"

She used her apron to wipe her cheeks. "Then I need you to explain this to me."

She really didn't know? He removed his hat, fidgeting with it. Then he realized. She thought so little of Cara that she couldn't imagine Ephraim might have feelings for her. "I'm not in love with you."

"But . . ."

"I really am sorry."

She jerked the bucket from the ground and slung it across the yard. "I can't believe this. You should be begging me to stay in your life."

"I agree. But I'm not." He heard Lori chattering and looked that way. Across the field Cara stood basked in sunlight, a complete array of the forbidden. And all he wanted was more of her. She wasn't just an Englischer with her short hair, worldly dress, and permissive ways. She lacked every element inside her soul to become Amish. And still he longed to spend time with her.

Anna Mary squeezed his arm. "Look at me."

When he did, he saw the pain he'd inflicted. He hated it, but he couldn't change it.

"Her?" She sounded incredulous. "She's seduced you, hasn't she?"

"No. She has no idea how I feel. I'm not even sure how I feel. I may die a lonely bachelor. But that doesn't change anything between you and me."

She tightened her hands into fists before bolting across the yard.

As guilty as he felt, relief washed over him. Whatever discoveries within his heart lay ahead, they wouldn't involve betraying Anna Mary on any level.

# Thirty-One

Cara stood at the kitchen counter as Joe Garrett wrote out a check. With his hand blocking her view, she couldn't see the amount. She heard Lori in the next room, talking with the Garretts' little girl.

Mr. Garrett paused, holding the payment in his hand. "You did an amazing job. Not a scratch on any of the floors or furniture, closets not only painted but organized. Every room painted beautifully. And no spatters of paint anywhere to be seen. I never expected all this. And in a week? You must've been logging some major overtime."

"I'm glad you're pleased."

He passed her the check. "I think that should say how impressed we are."

She glanced at the amount and nearly choked. Five hundred more dollars than they'd agreed on. All she'd hoped to do was ensure the Garretts were happy to pay her fee.

Heather Garrett motioned around the room. "I love it. Absolutely love it." She took the checkbook from her husband. "I've been threatening to clean and organize forever."

Cara's heart pounded like crazy. She had money, real start-up money. She was so excited she wanted to dance. Instead she folded the paper and slid it into her pocket. "There's a box of stuff in the garage, things that seemed obsolete when I cleaned out the closets."

"I'll go through it later this week."

Cara went upstairs to help Mahlon and Grey finish. They were busy moving pieces of furniture back into place. In spite of her being a stranger and an Englischer to boot, they'd let her manage the day without complaint. She liked both of her co-workers, which surprised her. They weren't at all what she'd thought they'd be—stuffy, judgmental, and difficult.

With a check in her pocket, her portion of it worth more than a month's pay, she felt hope buoy her again. "I really appreciate all you've done today." She peeled a strip of painter's tape off the baseboard.

Grey straightened his shoulders, working the kinks out of his neck. "Glad to help. The brushes, rollers, and most of the drop cloths are clean and loaded in the wagon."

Cara tossed a wad of tape into the trash. "We need to gather up the remaining supplies from the basement and walk through every room together to make sure we covered each item on the checklist, and then we're ready to go."

Mahlon pulled tape from a different section of the room. "Maybe you could help Deborah paint after I find us a place."

"I thought I was taboo."

Looking a bit uncomfortable, Grey set a lamp on the dresser. "I'll tell you plain out. You've made some huge blunders. Surely many Englischers would see it that way too, no?"

As much as she hated to admit it, he was right.

"See, among the Amish certain lines are not crossed. Ever. But if you move out of Ephraim's place and show yourself trustworthy, folks will come around eventually—if you're interested in that."

She peeled off the last bit of tape and reeled it in. There it was, staring her in the face again—the need to move out of Ephraim's place. "Except for Ephraim, I don't care what the rest think."

Grey set another lamp on the nightstand and plugged it in. "Right or wrong, he hid things from the church and community where you're concerned. He joined the faith years ago, and it's against our ways for him to open up his life to a woman who's not Amish, so you'll never be allowed much leeway with Ephraim."

She appreciated Grey's honesty. It stung a bit, but his tone and facial expressions said he wanted to help her understand. She longed to look in the faces of her relatives

just once to see what they were like. The
desire grew, and thoughts of going to
the Riehl place tugged at her.

Mahlon threw a wad of tape into the
trash. "Ephraim can do as he pleases if he's
willing to turn his back on everyone and
live shunned the rest of his life."

**What?** Feeling the room grow smaller,
she leaned against the dresser. That's what
had happened to her mother, wasn't it? And
not only had her mother paid a price, she'd
suffered too. And now Lori was paying a
price as well. "Being friends with me will
cause continued division? I don't want that."
Should she walk away and never look back?
"Isn't there some middle ground here?"

Grey slid the curtains back onto the
rods. "Maybe. If you dress modest, watch
your mouth, and behave in reserved ways
so it's clear you're honoring our lines of
morality."

"That's a tall order."

"For us too." He snapped the curtain
rod in place. "But God gives us strength.
And the church leaders set good examples
and hold us accountable. Our ways cause

bumps, bruises, and misunderstandings that get pretty heated sometimes. But after everything settles back down, we all learn from the mistake."

She couldn't imagine the type of management it took to keep an entire Amish community together for hundreds of years. The understanding Grey had just opened to her eased the pain of the people's stance against her. But like Ephraim said—the things that bound them would never loosen, but the things that separated them would always stand firm. Suddenly, for Ephraim's sake, she wanted to get out of his life so he could begin repairing the damage she'd caused. And she needed to get out as soon as possible.

But first she wanted to look in Emma Riehl's eyes and ask what happened.

Ephraim sat next to the hospital bed. His Daed had slept most of the day. His breathing was fast and shallow, his legs, ankles, and feet were swollen, and his fingernails had a bluish tint. The progression of the cardiomyopathy seemed rapid of late, and in spite of what Scripture said about trusting God, Ephraim worried.

The midafternoon sun reflected off the walls. An emergency had interrupted the doctor's rounds this morning, so he hadn't been by yet. Just as well, Ephraim supposed, because when his Daed was awake, he expressed reluctance to let him talk to the doctor. He kept saying he didn't need his son to treat him like he was a kid. But there was more to his objections than that; Ephraim was sure of it. With Becca finally gone to the cafeteria for lunch, he intended to find out what.

"Daed." He touched his arm, waking him. "We need to talk." He gave him a minute to wake before he passed him a glass of ice chips.

"I'm thirsty, and all they allow are ice chips? This is a lousy hotel."

He hoped his father's bit of humor was a good sign.

"Daed, I need to be here when the doctor comes to talk to you. I want to hear what he has to say."

"We discussed this already. I'm fine. There's nothing to know."

"Then let the doctor explain that to me."

"Did you come to visit or to wear me out?"

"I came to see if there's anything that can be done about these episodes. Your heart condition is worsening, landing you in the hospital time and again. What aren't you telling me? I think you owe me the truth."

"Owe you?" His father stared at him.

"Yes."

"You're the one who owes me. Letting that girl sleep at your place. I'm being dishonored in front of the whole world."

The turmoil inside him eroded every semblance of peace he'd found among his people over the years. If his father had an inkling how Ephraim felt, he might need to be moved to ICU. "I'm sorry for the stress the situation has caused you. But right now I want to discuss your health. Nothing else."

His father set the glass on the tray table. "I don't like being treated like a child."

"Me either. But you're treating me like one. Shouldn't we act more like business partners? We don't have to always agree, but we can love and respect each other as equals."

His father picked at the tape where the IV was stuck into his arm. "The meds that improve my heart's ability to pump aren't working like they used to. We've tried a lot of different things, but the symptoms are just getting worse. There's nothing to be done."

"I talked to a nurse a couple of weeks ago, and she said there's this thing called an AICD."

Daed's eyes misted. "Not acceptable. It requires a blood transfusion. And I refuse to mingle my blood with that of a sinner. I'd rather die."

Weary of rules and constraints and family needs, Ephraim's frustration peaked. "We need to consider all the medical options."

"You're asking me to ignore my convictions. All those years of working by my side, and you still don't understand me?

Where is the respect for everything I've done for you? I built that business up and practically gave it to you."

"When you asked me to come home because of your illness, I came and took over supporting the family. So don't even start about **giving** me the shop. I work twice as hard as I should so I can give you and your family more than half of all the profits. Now, I want to discuss your medical options, and we'll decide together."

"I won't be put to sleep and have my chest ripped open. Those doctors aren't God. My life is in His hands."

Grinding his teeth, he tried to temper his answer. "He's not the one you've been relying on to support you. I've been carrying that burden. So if there are ways to ease the symptoms, we need to consider them. Don't let your illness be worse than it has to be."

His father gazed out the window, and Ephraim watched the minute hand above his bed circle the clock twice. "You didn't need to be **draus in da Welt.** If God wanted to use my health to get you home, I'm not arguing."

"Whoa." Ephraim jumped to his feet, a dozen arguments against that nonsense running through his mind. "You were bad off, and I had to come home. But you can't hold my life ransom unless you have no other choice. I won't stand for it—not any-more."

"Not anymore?"

Ephraim looked out the window, seeing miles and miles of a world he didn't belong to. "I gave you my life, Daed. Too freely. Too easily. I'm not sure why, except I loved you and I respected what you wanted more than what I wanted. At the time it made sense to become who you needed me to be. But you've taken it too far. And I've let you."

His father held his gaze, seemingly stunned at the turn of the conversation. "You want your freedom to chase after that woman, don't you?"

Bright sunshine illuminated the earth, but Ephraim's thoughts and feelings sus-pended inside him like thick fog. "I want you to stop controlling my life. You've made choices, and I carry the weight of them. You chose a wife more than ten years younger than you. You chose to continue sleeping with her even after you were too sick to support the children you already had. She brought two children into the marriage, and you had three more after you became sick. I should have realized this long before now, but doesn't it seem wrong that I have to pay for your choices?"

The muscles in his father's throat constricted. Minutes droned on, and his father's eyes misted. "Are you saying you're leaving the faith?"

"No. I'm saying if there's a possibility of you getting well by trying certain things, then you should try them."

"If I allow a surgery, I'll have to sign papers to accept a blood transfusion if the need arises." Tears moistened his eyes. "Besides, part of me wants to see your mother so badly."

As the layers of Daed's thoughts unfolded, Ephraim saw there wasn't just one issue stopping him from pursuing his medical options. He had a tangled mess of reasons. "Daed, it was more awful to lose Mamm than we could bear for a long time."

"I still miss her."

"Me too. One of the first things I remember after you married Becca is her standing at the kitchen sink, washing dishes. Because she wore her hair the same way and had on the Amish garb, she looked a lot like Mamm. She put good meals on the table for us, just like Mamm had. She packed my lunch like Mamm. She even sat on the couch reading to the little ones, kissed them tenderly, and tucked them in like Mamm. There wasn't one physical act Mamm did that Becca couldn't do. But she wasn't Mamm. And our hearts knew it."

"I'm sure Becca would understand. She ached over losing her husband too."

"I know." He sat next to his father and placed his hand on his arm. "You fill a place in our family that I can't fill. If I have to, I can make the necessary decisions and earn the money to pay the bills. But we all want and need you. You've got to fight. If not for yourself, for your youngest children who won't even remember you if you give up now. For Deborah, who adores you more than you know. And for me. I'm tired of trying to be you but more than ready to be your son again."

Someone tapped on the door while opening it. "How are you feeling today, Abner?" He nodded at Ephraim. "I'm Dr. Kent."

Ephraim stood and introduced himself. "I've been talking with my Daed, and I'd like you to explain his options to both of us."

The man looked to Daed. When he nodded, the doctor took a seat. "Sure. I'll cover a few basics, and we'll go from there. To begin with, your father doesn't have heart disease. Years ago a virus moved into the organ and caused physical damage. He's been on medicines for a long time, and that worked for a while. But this past year their effectiveness has been waning, and he's having more episodes. His thyroid has suffered a lot of damage, which is stealing his energy. Monitoring his diet is no longer enough. His heart rate is becoming more difficult to control, as is the fluid retention in his body. He's not bad enough to be eligible for a heart transplant. And I hope he doesn't get to that point, because the waiting list is longer than most can survive. But we've had good success with AICDs. It will be able to decrease his heart rate when needed, and I believe implanting one is the best treatment plan for Abner, though it's not without problems."

"Will he need a transfusion for that?"

"Unlikely. But I won't operate without blood from the bank already in the OR. His blood doesn't clot well, so I'm particularly cautious." He glanced from Daed to Ephraim and back again. "Is that a problem?"

Ephraim nodded. "It's a pretty big obstacle for my Daed."

"Why?"

Ephraim waited on his Daed to speak up, but he didn't. "He's uncomfortable with the thought of having a stranger's blood going into his body."

"Abner, I had no idea that was part of the holdup. As long as the blood type matches or is compatible, you can have friends and relatives donate blood for you."

His father didn't move for several moments. Then he looked at Ephraim. "I didn't know that."

Irritation pounded inside him. Ephraim had suffered years of unfairness, and it threatened to turn into deep-seated anger. His father should have been slower to stand against the unknown and quicker to ask every possible question.

"Ephraim, are you convinced I should do this?"

Ephraim couldn't be sure his father would fare better after the procedure or even that he'd survive any possible complications. "I won't take on the responsibility of deciding for you."

His father shook his head. "I've been wrong. I can't begin to make it up to you unless I try to gain my strength back." He looked to the doctor. "I'll do it."

## Thirty-Two

Standing at Ephraim's stove, Cara stirred the pot of beef stew she'd slow cooked at the Garretts and then brought here.

"Are you sure about this?" Ephraim's eyes held such concern she had to look away.

"I have to know why my dad told me Emma was coming and why she never showed."

"Cara." He whispered her name, but she refused to look into his face. He moved beside her. "Once you start asking questions, you're likely to hear things about your mother that you may not want to know."

"Look, I already figured that out." She waved the wooden spoon at him. "Maybe she wasn't a good person when she left here, but she was a good mom to me. I've got proof of it in my memory and more in the diary. She wrote things about God and Scripture." Her heart raced, feeling the rush of secrets her mother had probably hoped she'd never know.

Ephraim opened the cabinet. "I'd forgotten until just now, but I remember her talking to me during your visit. She said something about trusting God. Oh, and being good to you when you came back."

Her eyes stung with tears. "Pity you didn't remember that before I had to give you a fat lip."

He took three glasses from the shelf. "I'll drive you over there, if you want, and wait near the road."

"I can walk, thanks. News flash. I survived the streets of New York, alone and with a stalker. I'm not weak, Ephraim."

He passed her three bowls. "A blind man could see that. I just don't want to wait here alone, wondering how it went. How will I know if the conversation is over at seven, nine, or twelve o'clock?"

She took a ladle out of a drawer. Clearly

he didn't want her facing this alone and then walking back. He cared . . . maybe more than just as a friend. A tremble went through her. Too much separated them for them to become more involved than they already were. And whatever relationship they did have had to end. Or at least move to more distant ground.

She dipped up a bowl of stew. "I'm leaving tomorrow."

"What? Why?"

"I have some start-up money. And you have to get unshunned from your family, community, and friends as quickly as possible."

"We talked about this."

"It's time, Ephraim. We both know it. And I'm not going to that apartment your people picked out for me."

"But it's already been paid for."

"I won't be paid to leave. And if it wasn't for you, I'd tell them so myself in not-so-nice terms."

"Where will you go?"

"Jiminy Cricket, you ask a lot of questions."

"The social worker, remember her?"

"When I get settled, I'll call her." She swallowed, trying to hide how much she was hurting. "We accomplished our goal. I have money now and can stand on my own two feet."

"A thousand dollars won't go far."

"I'll get another job."

"How?"

She slammed the bowl on the counter. "What do you want from me?"

"Time. You just found out about your relatives, and you're ready to bolt. I'm not ready for you to leave. Besides, Lori needs—"

"Ephraim," she whispered, "the things that separate us will always stand firm."

He clenched his jaw, staring down at her.

"Let's eat. Then you can drive me to Emma Riehl's place."

She couldn't swallow a bite, and she heard none of the chatter between Lori and Ephraim, but soon enough all three of them were in the buggy. The sun slid behind the mountains, and darkness eased over the earth—deep purple faded to a dark blue, and then the very air itself seemed to go black.

Ephraim pointed. "There, to your left."

A bonfire blazed in the side yard. Two or three dozen people sat around in lawn chairs. Children played freeze tag, and teens played volleyball near the barn.

"The American dream lives." The bitterness in her tone surprised her, but Ephraim didn't flinch.

"Half the community is here. We don't have to do this now."

"Yes I do."

He tugged the reins to slow the buggy. "Maybe you should try being stubborn for a change, Cara."

"Sarcasm doesn't suit you, 'From. You should leave that to experts like me."

Before he came to a complete stop, a broad-shouldered man with a beard left the crowd and walked toward them. She couldn't tell in the dark, but he appeared to have gray hair around the edges of his hat.

"That's Levi Riehl. He's Emma's husband and your mother's oldest brother. He might not like that I'm here."

"Good, then I won't be the only one who wishes you'd stayed home. I'll be back." She stepped down from the buggy, wondering if she should have worn Deborah's dress instead of her jeans. But it seemed wrong to put on an Amish dress, as if she were pretending to be part of something she wasn't. Besides, she hated that thing. It made her look heavy, old, and frumpy.

The man looked at Ephraim and waved. He started to turn back toward the house, but then he caught a glimpse of her. He stopped all movement. "You're Cara."

She nodded.

He studied her face. "You favor your Mamm, even under the night skies."

"I don't really remember what she looked like. But I remember other things."

**Her hands, her voice . . . her love.**

He stood there without saying anything else, and she thought she'd suffocate under the stiltedness of it. "We didn't have any hint that she might have passed away until ten years after her death. I'm sorry for how hard growing up without her must have been on you."

"You didn't know?" Her mind tried to process that detail. "Emma—she's your wife, right?"

"Ya."

"My dad said she'd come for me."

Levi stared at the ground. "We had no idea where you were." He shook his head. "If we'd known your mama had died and how to get you, we would have."

Children's laughter from the side yard surrounded her like a cyclone. She could have grown up here? Since that never-ending day at the Port Authority so many years ago, each day had carried pain and loneliness. Now all those years of grief stacked on top of her, squeezing her until she couldn't breathe or think.

He glanced behind him. "I need to get back."

Her legs shook, and her head spun.

"Levi?" A woman walked from the bon-fire area. When she spotted Cara, she gasped. **"Ach, es iss waahr."**

Levi went to her side and whispered something in her ear.

"Enough." The woman pulled away from him. She stood directly in front of Cara and touched her cheek as if making sure she was real. "Oh, dear child." She burst into tears. "God forgive me."

"You did nothing wrong, Emma." Levi put his arm around his wife, supporting her. "Kumm."

Shaking her head, Emma wiped falling tears from her cheeks. **"Nix meh. Schtobbe."**

Whatever she'd said, she appeared to be waiting on Levi to answer. After a pause that seemed to last forever, Levi nodded. "We've talked about coming to see you, but it's just so complicated with Ephraim being shunned because of . . . of . . . your being there." He shrugged. "I could explain a dozen honest reasons, but none of them seems worthy as I stand here."

Emma stepped closer. "Your father called our phone shanty about twenty years ago. His words were slurred. He ranted about Malinda wanting you to be raised

Amish. Kept mumbling that I had to come get you. I tried to reason with him, telling him he was asking too much. That Levina was going to raise you. The agreement was that Malinda would bring you back to Dry Lake, not insist we come get you. Levina was too old and unfamiliar with traveling to go by bus. I was pregnant with twins and mostly on bed rest. Levi was working overtime to make ends meet. And your Daed's words were that of . . . of a . . ."

"A drunk." Cara finished the sentence for her.

"He never said Malinda had died. He only said he'd found our number in her personal phone book and we needed to come get you. Finally I agreed and wrote down the details about where you'd be and when. As I thought about it over the next few days, I discounted the conversation. He was drunk, and I figured if Malinda wanted you here, she'd have brought you."

"So you just dropped it?"

Tears choked Emma when she tried to speak, and she looked at Levi.

He rubbed her back. "A few days later

we tried reaching him by phone, but the line had been disconnected. I called information, trying to find another number for Trevor or Malinda Atwater."

Teary-eyed, Emma drew a breath. "We decided Malinda must have changed her mind about giving you up but that your dad wanted you gone from there." She rubbed her hands together, looking as nervous as Cara felt. "We thought she was still alive. I knew she didn't want to give you up."

"We didn't hear from him again until a decade later when he sent a package here, addressed to you," Levi said. "That's when we realized Malinda might be dead, and he thought you were living here."

"But . . . Ephraim had no idea my mom had died."

"We shared what we suspected with just a few people—mostly your uncles. There was no way to be sure she'd died, and . . . and the news would only have stirred guilt and conflict in our district again."

Emma moved in closer. "When your dad called here, if we'd thought for a moment Malinda had died . . ."

Cara's knees gave way, but she didn't sink to the ground. Someone seemed to be holding her up. Ephraim? When did he get down from the wagon? Would he be in more trouble for this? Her thoughts jumped as if her mind were a Polaroid, registering isolated scenes here and there.

Children held marshmallows on skewers over leaping flames. Moms passed out graham crackers and chocolate bars while guarding the children so they didn't get too close to the fire.

The next thing Cara knew she was in the buggy. Warmth from Ephraim's hand seemed to be her only anchor to reality. The clip-clop of the horse's hoofs echoed against the night. Lori's faint voice spoke to her, but she couldn't make out the words.

Slowly a few solid thoughts formed. "My father didn't follow through long enough to put me into safe hands. What kind of man does that?"

Ephraim said nothing.

"Why would my mother marry someone like that?"

He pulled into his driveway. A buggy

stood nearby with a man in it, staring at them.

She waited for Ephraim to guide the horse around back, but he sat still, watching the man. She recognized him. Rueben Lantz, the one who'd seemed to watch her for more than a week. She sat up straight. "What? You got something to say to me?"

He didn't respond, not even a shake of his head.

She jerked the reins from Ephraim and slapped the horse's back. He lunged forward, coming dangerously close to the man's rig. Both horses whinnied and pranced skittishly. Ephraim pried the reins from her hands and guided the animal away from the other one. Rueben drove off, and Ephraim didn't stop the horse until they were in the barn.

Feeling like her heart had been trampled under a dozen horses, she got out and went to the gate.

Ephraim helped Lori down.

"I want to be alone," she growled at him.

"Not yet."

She moved in close, whispering, "Please.

Take Lori inside before her mother turns into a lunatic in front of her."

He nodded and took her daughter into the house.

The silhouette of the rolling hills and massive trees, the silvery glow of the pond, the calls of night—all of it mocked her. These would have been her childhood memories. Instead her life was filled with concrete and asphalt, as unyielding as the people she'd grown up with—people whose names she didn't even know anymore, except for Mike Snell's family.

The ache that rolled over her threatened to steal her good sense, and she started walking. She went through the cornfield and soon stood next to the trees. Memories washed over her freely. She wished she could stop them. Wished she'd never come here.

A horse and buggy stopped on the road. "Hello." The warm, friendly voice reminded her of her mother's. Tears began to flow. The woman drove the carriage beside the trees. "I was at the Riehls' place. I saw you leave. I was hoping I'd find you."

Cara wiped her tears. "Whatever you want to say, don't. I can't stand hearing one more thing."

The woman stepped down from the buggy. "I'm Ada. I've been praying for you since before you were born."

"And what a great job your mighty God has done."

She placed her hand under Cara's chin. "You made it back here against all odds. You have a few stout supporters in this community who want to set things right. I'd say He's been quite busy. He's had a few obstacles to work around, ya?"

Cara wanted to lash out about the community's "support." She also wanted to turn and walk away. But the softness in Ada's voice, the tenderness in her touch called to her, and she fell against the woman, sobbing.

# Thirty-Three

Cara woke with rough fabric against her skin, a sheet over her, and a hard pillow under her head. The aroma of coffee filled the air, and she remembered walking back to Ephraim's last night with Ada.

Streams of sunlight made it difficult to open her eyes. She splayed her fingers across the cloth and sat upright, realizing she was on Ephraim's couch. The warm stuffiness of the room said it was at least midmorning. Soft voices floated from the kitchen. She headed that way.

Ada sat in a chair at the table, and Ephraim was leaning against the counter near the sink. A shoebox-sized package wrapped in brown paper and yellowed packing tape sat on the kitchen table.

He glanced out the window. "She's dead set against moving into the place some of the men have paid for."

"Do you blame her?"

"No, but that little bit of money in her pocket isn't enough."

"I'll talk to her. Maybe she'll agree to—"

"Cara." Ephraim pulled a chair out for her.

She rubbed her temples, desperately wanting a pain reliever. "Where's Lori?"

He pointed out the window. "She and Better Days and her dolls are having a picnic."

"Did I miss something? I thought you were shunned."

"He is," Ada offered. "I spoke to the bishop, told him I wanted a chance to talk some sense into Ephraim." She smiled. "Made for a good excuse. Besides, I didn't want you staying alone last night, and I didn't want Ephraim to get in even deeper trouble with the church leaders, so I slept over."

Cara took a seat. "I feel horrible."

Ephraim placed a mug of coffee in front of her. "This will help."

"Do you have any pain reliever?"

He pulled a bottle of ibuprofen out of the cupboard. "Cara, Ada has something she'd like to talk to you about."

She shook her head. "I'm not staying in Dry Lake, no matter what she says. I'm leaving today. I'm going to get a shower and soak my aching head. If I'd known crying gave a person such a headache, I'd not have done it. Great lotta good it did. Everything's the same, except now my head hurts."

Ada slowly pushed the package toward Cara. "Levi and Emma brought this by earlier."

The box looked well kept, yet the yellowed tape that sealed it made it appear quite old. It had no return address, only a name. Trevor Atwater—her father. She angled the box so she could see the faded date stamp. It'd been sent a few days before her birthday ten years ago. She would have been eighteen.

Pushing it away from her, she rose. "Idiot. He leaves me at a bus station and assumes I'm living here ten years later. I'm getting a shower." She walked off.

"You have family," Ephraim called out to her.

She turned to face him. "I've had family here my whole life. Big fat stinking deal. It made no difference when it could have. And none of them want me here now. Open your eyes, Ephraim. I meant so little to these people that Emma Riehl never called anyone to check on me. Not the police or social services or even the place where my mother worked. They didn't want to know the truth about where I was, how I was. And I'm sorry for what I know about them. I wish I'd never come here."

Cara stormed into the bathroom and slammed the door. She flicked on the shower. In spite of her exhaustion, tears trailed down her face. Emma and Levi had cared less about her than Simeon did for those stray pups. It seemed impossible right now to accept that fact, but the pain would fade eventually. She stayed in the shower until the water turned cold. She dried off and slid into the only piece of clean clothing she had—Deborah's dress. When she came out, Ada was at the stove, loading pancakes onto a plate.

The sight only made her hurt worse. If her father had made contact with Ada instead of Emma, everything would have been different.

Cara walked to the table.

"Ephraim and Lori have gone for a walk by the creek. Lori said they're going to teach Better Days to be a better dog than his mama and not to knock people into the water." Ada chuckled. "Wonder who the guinea pig for that will be." She set the plate of pancakes on the table, clearly offering them to her.

"I'm not hungry. Thanks, anyway." She picked up the package, walked to the trash can, and threw it in.

"I'm a few years younger than your mother would be. One summer we were hired to work the cornfields, detasseling. You know what that is?"

Cara shook her head.

"The pollen-producing tassel on top of the cornstalk is removed by hand and placed on the ground. It's really hard work, but the pay is great. We began before sunup, took a short lunch break, and worked until suppertime. Mr. Bierd handled his workers differently than most farmers. He gave each worker a section to get done according to age and height. If you didn't finish your section by the end of the week, you were given half pay and never hired again. I needed the money bad, but each day I got further behind. The day before time to get paid, your mother realized I was behind. She asked a few others to stay and help, but they were too tired. She stayed with me, and we worked until nearly dawn. That's the kind of person your mother was, Cara. Over and over again." Ada went to the trash and pulled out the package. "Don't be afraid to look."

The desire to run had never been stronger than at this moment, but Cara took the package from her and forced herself to open it. On top was an envelope. She pulled out the card. In jagged heavy cursive, it wished her a happy eighteenth birthday.

My beautiful daughter, you deserved to grow up with someone as great as your mom. I figured sending you to live with her brother would be the next best thing. I wasn't much of a dad, or a husband, or a human for that matter. For that, everyone I loved has suffered. I'm winning over the addiction for now. I'm ashamed to even think about how hard and how often your mother tried to help me overcome my dependency.

I've sent you a few items, along with a letter explaining the story between your mother and me. I didn't sweeten it. At times you'll probably wish it was more gentle, more like how parents should be. But we didn't start out as parents. We started as two reckless nineteen-year-olds.

If you can find it in your heart to see me, I'll be staying at the

Rustic Inn on West King Street in
Shippensburg for a week, beginning
on your birthday.

> Happy Birthday,
> Dad

She searched through the box, finding
photos of her and her mother at various
stages of Cara's infancy and childhood.
Until Cara was eight.

Deeper in the box she found a few
stuffed animals, a Bible, her birth certificate, and her parents' marriage license. At
the bottom was a stack of letters with Cara's
name written on the envelope of each one.
She set them on the table next to her.

The last item was a green spiral-bound
notebook with the words "The Book of
Cara" scrawled on the outside. The bottom
right corner of the cover had her father's
name on it.

Unsure she wanted to know the
**unsweetened** story, she laid the book on
the table.

"May I?" Ada tapped the birth certificate.

Cara shrugged. "Sure."

Ada unfolded the document. "This doesn't make sense." She pointed to the date of her birth.

"Why not?"

Ada shook her head and opened the marriage certificate. "Something's wrong. This says your parents were married fifteen months before you were born."

"I don't see the problem."

"That means she wasn't pregnant when she left here. Or if she was, you aren't that child."

"So? She wasn't pregnant when she married my dad. If you'd ever read the entries my mother wrote in my diary, things about honoring God and always trying to do right, that wouldn't surprise you."

"Your mother was engaged to an Amish man. He told us she ran off with an Englischer because she was expecting his baby."

"With the reception I've received here, I figured something along those lines. They must've had it wrong . . . or maybe Mama changed after they knew her."

"The rumors don't fit the time line. That's for sure." She read the dates again, as if triple-checking her facts. "She left so quickly. As far as I know, she didn't return or write or call or anything until about ten years later when she showed up with you." Ada waved the papers at her.

"Maybe I'm not the child she was pregnant with when she left here."

She tapped the book. "I bet the answers are in there."

Cara laid it to the side. "Later."

Ada slid her hand under Cara's, holding it palm to palm. "You know what I think?"

Cara didn't answer.

"I think you need some mulling-over time. You want out of Dry Lake. Ephraim thinks you should stay. I think we need to find a solution." She rubbed her neck. "My son, Mahlon, is supposed to be finding me and him a place to live. But he hasn't really tried. I think he'd like it if I wasn't living with him. So, instead of hitting him upside the head, I started looking for a place on my own."

"I didn't think the Amish believed in violence."

"Oh, honey, nobody **believes** in violence. Some think the outcome justifies it. Amish don't. I was only joking. Even Amish people joke about things."

"I guess I don't really know the Amish, do I?"

"No, and they don't know you." She placed a hand on Cara's back. "Maybe that will change with time. I've got an appointment to look at a certain place tomorrow afternoon. I've been told it needs a lot of painting and fixing up, but it has plenty of bedrooms, bathrooms, and a huge kitchen. The Realtor says it's a bit rough, but the owner is interested in exchanging work for rent, which is where you could come in. Mahlon says you're quite good at painting. Maybe you can live and work there with me."

"I . . . I . . ." Searching for the most respectful way to refuse, Cara fiddled with the edges of the letters.

Ada looked at her as if reading her thoughts. "Just think about it. Okay?"

"You're very generous. But wouldn't you get in trouble for that? I mean, Ephraim's been shunned over his dealings with me. What'd happen if I moved in with you?"

Ada drew a deep breath. "I won't lie. It might be an issue even though I'm not a single Amish man. You've got quite a reputation of being worldly, and the bishop's going to have lots of reservations. But I can work it out. I think."

"I have money now. And I really think I should leave. I've caused enough trouble in everyone's life."

She tapped the notebook. "You should read that. Your dad took the time to write it, and it's been sitting here in Dry Lake for ten years. Seems to me it's begging to be read." She stood. "I need to go, and you need to think." She headed for the door and then paused. "Could I take your birth certificate and your parents' marriage license with me?"

"Why?"

"I have an idea." She looked unsure about saying more.

Cara held them out to her. "Sure. Why not?"

The screen door banged shut as Ada left. Cara lifted the spiral-bound notebook and stared at it. She didn't really want to read it. Not anytime soon. The desire to pack her things and get out of Dry Lake was so strong she thought it might lift her straight off the chair.

But more than any other feeling was the desire to see her parents, if only through the eyes of a man who admitted he struggled with addiction. Torn between curiosity and resentment, she opened the thin cardboard cover.

I met your mother when she was
nineteen years old. She was the most
striking woman I'd ever seen, with
brown eyes and blond hair that she
parted down the middle and wore in
a bun with the white prayer Kapp. I
was an Englischer by her standards,
and she was in love with another
man. She was more loyal and honest

than anyone I've ever known, but she wasn't perfect. Neither of us was. She'd had her heart broken and was desperate to leave Dry Lake, so I took her away from there. She regretted that decision, and I understood, but by then we were married, and neither of us could undo the choices we'd made. I hope—and at times dare to pray—that you found Dry Lake to be as wonderful a place to grow up as she remembered from her childhood.

The words released a lifetime of bottled sentiments, and she closed the book. When she'd longed to feel something besides cold and emptiness during her teen years, this overload wasn't what she had in mind. Confusion swirled in a dozen directions, pulling at her to believe different things. Desperate to escape before she suffocated under the swell of emotions, she went into the bedroom and stuffed her and Lori's things into the backpack. Ada's mothering voice washed over her, making some tiny fragment of Cara wish she could stay.

When she went outside, she heard Ephraim and Lori talking in the hiddy. She walked to the entryway. "I'm ready." His eyes met hers, causing a fresh surge of tormenting feelings. He'd been a good friend in spite of the trouble her presence had caused him. "Will you take me, or do I need to hire a driver?"

He slowly rose, looking disappointed in her decision. "I'll take you."

"Where are we going, Mom?"

As Ephraim headed toward the barn, Cara moved to the bench swing and patted the empty place beside her. Lori snuggled against her.

"Are we going to the Garretts' again?"

"Tell me about your walk."

Lori shared her excitement over what Ephraim was teaching Better Days. " 'From and me are going to find a home for all the pups next week."

"Lori, sweetie, it's been great staying here, but Ephraim needs his home back, and we need to find a place of our own. We have money now, so we'll find a good place, okay?"

Lori jumped to her feet, fists tight, hurt and anger etched across her tiny body. "No."

With the backpack on her shoulder, Cara lifted her daughter's rigid body and toted her out of the hedged area. Ephraim brought the carriage to a stop. Lori arched her back and screamed, causing Cara to nearly drop her as she eased her feet onto the ground.

"Get in the buggy, Lori."

She ran to Ephraim and grabbed his hand. "No!"

Cara refused to look in Ephraim's eyes. They said the same thing Lori's did—that Cara was wrong. "Don't say no to me again."

"I won't go. So there. And I didn't say the word **no.**"

Cara had forgotten how sassy her daughter could be. Lori clung tighter to Ephraim's hand. "I got 'From and a dog, and I'm not leaving!"

"One . . . two . . ."

Lori began a panicked cry, afraid her mother would reach the number ten. Cara had no idea what was supposed to happen if she reached it. Lori had never disobeyed past the number four.

"Stop." She held up one hand, still clinging to Ephraim with the other. "There ain't nobody after us, and I'm not going."

Cara's world tilted. Her daughter knew they'd been running from Mike? She looked to Ephraim before sinking to her knees. "All right. I hear you." She looped her daughter's hair behind her ears. "Who do you think would be after us, Lorabean?"

"The police. That lady that came here, Ms. Forrester, said they wouldn't come looking for us."

Cara's heart skipped several beats. Lori didn't know about the stalker after all.

Cara looked to Ephraim, searching for answers he didn't have.

He placed his hand on Lori's head. "Take Better Days inside and get him a bowl of water, okay? I need to talk with your mother."

"You better listen to him." Lori shook her finger at her mother. "Or I'm never talking to you again."

The screen door banged shut, and Ephraim helped Cara to her feet. "She's not ready to leave."

"She'll be fine. And we can't stay here. I'll only make things worse for you. Your people aren't talking to you. You can't work. You can't even see your family or Anna Mary. You should be shoving me into that buggy and promising Lori it's the right thing to do. She'd believe you."

"I won't lie to her to make you feel better."

"Then lie to her for her sake!"

"You're being stubborn."

"You're being just as bad, insisting I stay when we both know I should go."

"I've plowed the fields with mules more cooperative than you."

Chafing with frustration and hurt, Cara glanced to Ephraim. If he had an inkling how betrayed she felt by her relatives, he'd help her get out of here before she lashed out at them and caused him more trouble in the process.

Images of Ephraim climbing the tree

with her as a child floated across her mind. "I can't stand the churning emotions inside me. It's like someone opened a dam and I'm stuck in the pool at the bottom of the falls."

"I don't have to imagine it. I feel it." He took her hand and placed it on his chest. "It's enough to rip an ox apart, and I don't want you facing it alone."

Her eyes burned with the threat of tears, but she willed them away. She pulled her hand free. "Whatever it is you want from me, I can't give it."

"We're not talking about what anyone wants here. That passed by so long ago nothing can repair it. You need help getting your feet under you, emotionally and financially. I give you my word, I'll ask for no more than that."

She closed her eyes and listened to the sounds of spring: wind, birds, the distant mooing of cows. Wishing she could pray, she took a deep breath.

Ephraim placed his hand on her shoulder. "Think of the difference this could make for Lori."

Unable to reject his reasoning, she nodded. "Okay. For a little while. But not here in your house."

"Ada's determined to find a place to rent. She really likes the idea of you staying with her."

"I'll help her get settled and paint whatever rooms she wants. But when the painting job is done, it'll be time for me to find a place away from here."

"In the meantime I'll do my best to help Lori accept that and adjust." His eyes said he meant it. "I'm sure she won't be mad at you if we do it right."

The need to cry seemed to vanish, and she couldn't help but smile at him. "Using Lori to get your way? You cheat."

"Yep, and I win too."

But she couldn't hold on to the faint smile. It wouldn't be long before she'd regret going with this plan; she was sure of it.

## Thirty-Four

Ada opened the oven and removed a pie. Haunting questions kept looping through her mind, but she had no answers. Not yet.

She set the pie on a cooling plate and turned off the gas stove. Her baking was done for today, and, like always, every bit of space on her kitchen table, chairs, and countertops was covered in baked goods. The bakery's courier would come by soon, but Ada had too much to get done to wait. She scribbled a note and taped it to her front door, telling the courier to let herself in. They'd handled it this way a few times over the years.

With Monday's orders filled, she changed into a fresh dress and apron and headed out the door. It was three thirty by the time she had her horse hitched and was on her way. But she didn't want to hire a driver. She needed time to think, and for her the gentle speed and rhythmic sounds of a horse-drawn carriage always helped.

She'd let Mahlon make decisions for her for so long that her desire to put a stop to it had her thoughts running in circles. If she could just understand herself and why she'd made the kinds of decisions she had in the past, maybe she could find a few answers for her future. Baffled or not, she had to keep moving toward helping Cara. And she knew if she wanted to ease Cara's pain and make a difference for her and Lori, it'd begin with the church leaders and Cara's uncles. So when she left Cara yesterday, she'd gone to see the bishop. She'd talked to him about finding a place of her own and having Cara move in with her. He listened patiently, but then he told her that her plan wasn't a good idea, which meant no.

It would be impossible for Ada to become a church member of the Hope Crossing district without being a member in good standing in the Dry Lake district, so she couldn't ignore his stance. After talking with him for nearly an hour, explaining that people's reactions to Cara were based more on rumors than facts, she showed him the documents Cara had loaned her. He said little, but he decided to have a districtwide meeting tonight. In a little over four hours, everyone would gather at Levi Riehl's farm.

But Cara was only one issue weighing on her.

Ada gently pulled on the reins, bringing the rig to a stop as she stared at a fork in the road. To her left the road headed straight out of Dry Lake. By steering right, she could stop by Israel Kauffman's before heading to Hope Crossing.

She couldn't keep living based on what Mahlon thought he wanted from her, but if she wasn't that woman, who was she?

The Realtor would meet her at the rental place in an hour and a half. And here she sat, feeling almost as confused as the day her husband was killed. Israel's wife died that day too. Did he ever have times of feeling as lost now as he did then?

He probably didn't. Grown children and even a few grandchildren surrounded him on all sides. He'd freely admit he had strong support that kept a smile on his face most days. His middle daughter, Lena, was his biggest help, not just because she handled the chores and was so good to her younger siblings, but because she radiated happiness and humor all the time.

Lena and Deborah were cousins, and aside from Amish traditions they'd been raised very differently, but both took pleasure in trying to bring joy to others. Deborah's sense of humor was subtle compared to Lena's more boisterous approach where she tried to make people roar with laughter. Ada remembered one night at her home when Deborah, Mahlon, and Lena were playing board games. As out of character as it was for Mahlon, Lena's wit kept him chuckling for the entire evening.

Worry for Mahlon nagged her. He continued to search, for . . . something. Peace? Stability? Something that would stop him from wavering like wheat in a field. Whatever it was, Ada had begun a search of her own.

She'd never considered herself a strong woman, one who knew what she wanted and went after it. Whatever her husband had wanted, that's what she wanted—even down to the flavor of ice cream she chose at the local creamery. After he died, her personality type had made it easy for Mahlon to lead her in whatever direction he wanted.

What had made her be someone who never trusted her own thoughts or desires or dreams? Why had she feared being wrong so much that she let others be wrong for her?

She didn't know, but she had a fresh chance to follow her heart, especially where Cara was concerned. It was time to trust her gut and find a way to follow her heart.

If she went to every Amish home in Dry Lake and asked their opinion of what she should do next, some would think one way and some the other.

But what did **she** think?

Finally ready to trust her own desires, she slapped the reins against the horse's back.

It was time to talk to Israel. As a former homebuilder, he knew housing structure and probably some of what it'd take to expand her business. He had a way of giving sound advice when asked without trying to sway the person one way or the other. That was Israel—state the facts and let the person decide.

When she pulled onto his driveway, she saw him and several of his children sitting on the porch, casually visiting on this warm Monday before suppertime. She knew his family tended to have an early meal and then he'd return to his work of building furniture.

He rose from his chair and walked to her, studying her face intently.

"Ada." He nodded. "This is a first."

"You may wish for it to be the last too."

He cocked an eyebrow, looking rather amused. "Doubtful. What's up?"

"I know this is awfully bold of me, but

I got some things on my mind, and I need a man's . . . No, I need **your** opinion."

"Of course. I thought maybe you'd come by to make sure I'd heard about tonight's meeting. Care to come inside?"

She shook her head. "I'm going to Hope Crossing to look at a place. I was wondering if you might go with me."

"You're thinking of moving to Hope Crossing? That's quite a piece from here."

"About an hour by carriage."

"You want to find a home that far away?"

"I'm aiming to do what I should have done ten or more years ago—find a place where I can expand my baking business. Better to get started at forty-three than not at all."

He smiled and took a step away from the buggy. "Lena, I'm going with Ada. I'll be back in about three hours."

"Supper will be ready in twenty minutes." Lena stood. "Do you and Ada want to eat with us first?"

Ada fidgeted with the reins. "The Realtor is meeting me there in about ninety minutes."

He looked back toward his house. "We need to go on, Lena."

"Can I fix you some sandwiches to take with you?"

He looked up at Ada. "Are you the least bit hungry?"

Although she'd spent her day baking, she'd eaten almost nothing. As she began to make her own decisions, she already felt stronger. "Ya, I think I am."

"Good. Wait right here." Ada stayed in the buggy while Israel went inside. It wasn't but a few minutes before he came back out with a basket in one hand and a toolbox in the other. As he set the items inside the wagon and climbed in, she noticed he'd changed from his more casual clothes into pressed ones.

Tempted to pass him the reins, she clutched them tighter. She needed to steer her own buggy, even if she made mistakes and didn't handle it as smoothly as the person next to her would. Then again, maybe she'd handle it better. When she thought of all Cara had gone through—fighting to hold on to Lori and not caring if people misjudged her and yet seemingly remaining tender-hearted in so many ways—it did something inside Ada.

Israel propped his arm on the back of the bench seat. "So Mahlon's up for moving to Hope Crossing?"

Ada tapped the reins against the horse's back, trying to gain some speed for the upcoming hill. "I didn't ask him. I'm doing this on my own. And even though I'm not sure what **this** is, I want Cara Moore, Malinda Riehl's daughter, to be a part of it. When I have a set plan, I'll talk to the bishop again about allowing Cara to live with me."

As he asked a few questions about Cara and she answered, he pulled a couple of sandwiches out of the basket and passed one to her. The conversation flowed easily although Israel acted a bit nervous. He'd never seemed that way before. Maybe she should have let him guide the rig.

Once they were in Hope Crossing, Israel read the directions to her until they stopped in front of the saddest-looking house she'd ever seen. It sat on a large corner lot, with roads and sidewalks on two sides and a cornfield on another side. She couldn't see what was behind the home. It was huge; she'd give it that much. Two stories of unpainted clapboard with crooked black shutters and one half-fallen column holding up a wraparound porch.

"You say that girl paints?"

Ada nodded. "With a brush and roller, not a magic wand." They stepped out of the rig. Israel grabbed his toolbox, and they headed for the front porch. It only took her a moment to find the hidden key the Realtor had told her about. "The windows and doors have been redone recently, don't you think?"

Israel nodded. "Ya, I do."

When she pushed the door open, she saw newspapers and boxes scattered everywhere. A ladder stood near a half-painted wall. "Somebody began renovating the place."

"Ya. And left it worse off for it, I think."

They slowly climbed the wooden stairs,

which had a swatch of old carpet running down the center. At the top of the landing, they found four bedrooms and two baths—all with the most hideous wallpaper she'd ever seen.

Ada ran her fingers along a broken strip of wainscot. "Look, somebody tried painting over the wallpaper."

"I can't say as I blame them."

Ada laughed. "The Realtor said it was bad, but I hadn't expected this."

Israel got out a flashlight and some odd-looking tools before he stepped inside one of the bathrooms. "The tub is filled with junk." He went to the faucet. "And there's no running water."

After he'd poked around under the sink of each bathroom, he grabbed his toolbox, and they walked downstairs. When she opened the swinging wooden door to the kitchen, chills ran over her skin. "I . . . I had a dream about this kitchen years ago." She looked inside the sink and saw the pipes were missing.

"You sure it wasn't a nightmare?"

Ada opened a door to discover a huge walk-in pantry. "That's bigger than my whole kitchen."

"Ada." He pointed to the glass on the back door.

She walked over to him and stared at what appeared to be a trash pit. "The barn at the far end of the yard and the pasture behind it come with the house."

"I'd bet this place belonged to an Amish family at one point."

"That's what the Realtor said. But that was a long time ago." She moved to the center of the kitchen, feeling hope run through her in spite of the reality surrounding her.

Israel opened the back door. "I want to take a look under the house. I'll be back in a few."

As she ambled through the house, a sense of expectancy grew, defying all logical reasoning. Israel came back inside. "It's in bad shape as far as how it looks, but it's structurally sound.

"I want to do this."

"It's a lot to take on. You'll need plumbers first. I got an Englischer neighbor who does plumbing."

"The Realtor said the owners will pay to get the plumbing working. And she said they are willing to subtract from the rent all the cost of supplies and most of the cost of work done. All we have to do is submit the receipts and let them verify every so often that the work is being done. And we have the opportunity to buy the house at a set cost, regardless of the amount of fix-ups we do."

He set the toolbox on the deeply scratched wooden floor. "Whether you know it or not, I've seen you make success out of more difficult situations than this, Ada Stoltzfus."

"Me?" She watched to see if he was trying to be funny, but he looked serious. "You really think so?"

"I know so. You work in a closet of a kitchen with an apartment-sized stove and sink, and yet you've supplied desserts to that Shippensburg bakery for a decade. Just imagine what you could do with a kitchen this big and a full-size stove and double sink."

"Hello? Ada, are you in here?" the Realtor sang out.

"In the kitchen." She stepped closer to Israel. "You can't believe how much I want to do this for both me and Cara. But even if I sign a contract, I can't begin to make the kind of difference I want to for her without getting her uncles to see her another way."

"And since she's the reason Ephraim is shunned, I'm sure she can't move in with you without the bishop's approval. We'd better get you home so you're not late for tonight's meeting."

"I'd like to put a deposit down first."

He looked fully entertained by her as he gave a nod. "Then do it."

Inside Levi Riehl's home, Ada's palms sweated as she set up another folding chair. The warmth of the early-June air had nothing to do with the perspiration trickling down her back or the palpitations of her heart. Through the open windows and doors, she could hear carriages as they arrived and people chatting with one another.

A quick glance out the window let her know that most people were leaving their horses hitched to their buggies, which meant no one expected to be here long. When she'd arrived, her horse had seemed as worn out as she was, so she'd put him in the Riehl pasture.

She'd stopped by her house on the way here, thinking she might catch Mahlon and tell him of her plans, but he wasn't there. Despite feeling antsy and exhausted, she kept praying. She needed tonight to end with Cara's uncles—Levi, David, and Leroy Riehl—seeing the situation as she did. Levi seemed uneasy as he moved to the far side of the room and set up the last chair. He glanced at her several times as if he wanted to ask her something, but instead he just straightened the rows of chairs.

The bishop intended to separate rumors from truth tonight, and then he'd make a decision. But he told her that whatever he decided, it had to settle the issue. No more appeals. No more trying to change his mind. Ada agreed. And now she was miserably nervous.

Levi strolled over to her, looking as uncomfortable as he might with a stranger. "How's Cara?"

"I gave her the box you and Emma brought by. Mostly she's shaken, angry, and hurt."

He nodded. "Emma is pretty shaken too. Having to face Cara was heartbreaking for her."

"I think—"

"Mamm," Mahlon interrupted, hurrying toward her through the growing crowd. "What are you doing?" he whispered.

"What do you mean?"

He held up the papers she'd signed on the house in Hope Crossing. "I found these on the kitchen table."

"Can we talk about this later?"

"Are you picking out a house for us?"

His tone was stern, but his words were barely audible.

"No, of course not. You know I wouldn't do that."

She saw in his eyes some undefined emotion that looked a bit like . . . hope.

"Then what are you doing?"

"You and Deborah should go on with your own plans. That's what I need to do. I'm going to move to a place where I can sell baked goods to local restaurants and maybe to another bakery or two."

While Mahlon stared at her, David and Leroy, two more of Cara's uncles, strolled through the door, chatting with Rueben Lantz. She'd hoped Rueben, Malinda's former fiancé, wouldn't be here for this. It'd be so much harder for her to say what she needed to with him in the room. She wasn't interested in stirring up conflict, but if that's what had to happen . . . she prayed for courage.

"Why would you do this without talking to me?"

"I intended to tell you, but things are happening fast. Look, all it means is that you and Deborah make plans that don't include me living with you. Do you really mind?"

Mahlon studied her, looking unsure and pleased and terrified all at once. She'd seen these emotions in her only child many times over the years but never mingled into one confusing array.

"I guess I didn't realize you had that much independence in you . . . not to be disrespectful or anything. You really think you can make a go of this?"

"I do. It's what I wanted years ago, but you wanted to stay in Dry Lake. You're a man now, about to take on a wife, and I'd like to do this with your blessing."

He smiled. "My blessing?"

She nodded.

He looked past her, and she turned to see Deborah standing across the room. "I only wish you'd told me how important this was to you years ago, Mamm. If you'd done it then, things could be different."

"What things?"

He lowered his eyes, staring at the floor. "It doesn't matter."

But she had a feeling it mattered a lot. "Mahlon?"

Looking to Deborah again, he shook his head. "How can I be so in love and at the same time so restless for what might be or could have been?"

"Ada." David spoke from several feet away, interrupting her and Mahlon. "You came without your famous coconut pie." He shook the bishop's hand while he teased her.

His broad grin and easy ways didn't indicate the temper that tried to get the best of him at times. Leroy stood near him and gave Ada a nod. He was the quietest of the Riehls and probably the one who'd grieved the most when Malinda took off.

"What I've come for is a bit more serious than that."

A few nearby conversations stopped.

"Is this about Cara?" David asked.

Ada nodded, and Mahlon touched her arm, letting her know he was going to where Deborah stood.

Three of the men's wives—Anne, Susie, and Rueben's wife, Leah—entered, talking comfortably and keeping Ada from needing to say anything else right now. She moved to a chair and reached into the hidden pocket of her apron, assuring herself that the documents were still there. She wanted to get them back to Cara tonight.

Mahlon's eyes focused on her, as if he was trying to figure something out.

His reaction to her news confused her. Then again, his responses to daily events were often difficult to understand, and she hoped Deborah was better at figuring him out than she'd ever been.

As more people entered, Levi clapped his hands once. "Okay, whoever would like a drink of water or lemonade, help yourself and take a seat. It'll make it easier for those coming in behind you."

The volume of friendly banter decreased as people made their way to a chair. Most perceived Cara as a troublemaker who needed to be avoided. Rumors about her unacceptable behavior were fresh in their thoughts. Few knew why Ephraim had shared his home with Cara. They didn't know much about her, except that she was

Malinda's daughter and was a homeless thief with a daughter and no husband. Oh, and that she caused Ephraim to be shunned. But none of that really told them who Cara was. If Ada could convince them to give her a chance, maybe healing could begin for all of them. The Howards would probably put in a good word for Cara, but Englischers were never a part of Amish meetings—not this kind.

Emma hurried inside, wiping her wet hands against her apron. "Levi, those grandbabes of ours had the hose out, watering each other to see if they could make themselves grow." She wiped her brow. "I passed them to their mothers."

Everyone chuckled as Emma took a seat.

Ada said a silent prayer that the Riehls would set aside every obstacle that separated them from Cara.

The bishop moved to the front of the room. "Rueben and I found Cara a place in Carlisle. Thanks to the donations of everyone here, we paid the rent for three months. Cara chose to turn it down."

Murmurs floated throughout the room.

"What happens to the money?" one man asked.

"We made sure beforehand that we could get the money back, so no problem there. More important is why Cara turned it down. Ada said that Cara feels we were trying to pay her to leave. At first that sounded ridiculous, but after thinking about it, I realized there's some truth in that. It's possible we've reacted to Cara out of misunderstandings and unfair judgment. And a lot of that is because of rumors and who her mother was."

Levi stood. "Ephraim's had the most contact with her. Maybe he should be here."

The bishop took a seat. "What he did crossed the line, and he'll remain under the ban. Ada, will you tell everyone a little about Cara and what brought her to Dry Lake?"

Ada stood. Her voice shook as she explained how Cara grew up, why she came to their town, and her plans to leave. "She has no family outside of Dry Lake. Do we not bear some of the responsibility for what's happened to her? With only a few scattered memories from her childhood, she found her way back here. Will we let her slip through our hands a second time?"

The bishop stood. "In order to separate rumor from fact, I'd like to hear from those of you who've talked to Cara or seen her do anything firsthand. That means we set aside what you heard Abner say he saw."

Various people took turns sharing information about Cara. They told of her using drugs, smoking with Amish teens, and letting cows and horses out of pastures. The bishop took the time to look for an eyewitness for each rumor, and everyone soon discovered that no one had actually seen Cara doing any of those things.

When Anna Mary entered the room and took a seat at the back, Ada feared the damage she could do.

"Deborah had a dress go missing," one young man said. "I know 'cause she asked if I took it."

"I sure did," Deborah said. "If you'd taken it, I wanted to see you wear it."

Ada chuckled along with everyone else. If anyone knew how to bring humor and peace into a room, her future daughter-in-law did.

Deborah folded her arms. "Whoever took it left money for it the next night."

Ada figured Deborah knew at this point that Cara had taken her dress, but true to her nature, she wasn't going to make matters worse by adding that kind of information to the meeting.

Levi explained the conversation he'd had with Cara the night before. Then he added, "She didn't seem at all like the rumors have said. I'd like to help her, but I won't go against the bishop's wishes."

A man stood. "We offered her help, and she turned us down."

When he sat, a woman spoke up. "I wasn't living in Dry Lake when her mother was here, but I saw Cara at the auction. I don't like the way she dresses, and it's easy to believe the rumors about her. We can't afford to welcome someone like her."

Trying not to look as angry as she felt, Ada measured her words and tone carefully. "Have you once looked her in the eye and talked with her? I have. She's not to be feared. We might even learn a few things from her."

"Ephraim looked in her eyes," a man from the back of the room said, "and now he's shunned."

The group started murmuring, and Ada knew she was losing.

"I've wondered if maybe it was God's will that she didn't make it here as a child," David Riehl said over the crowd.

"David." Emma gasped. "She's your niece, and the mix-up that left her alone wasn't her fault. It was mine and Levi's and even yours. All of us talked about what to do, and we made careless mistakes and didn't try to find out what was going on."

"That's because she's Malinda's daughter," another man said, "and everyone in this room over the age of forty knows what that means."

The room vibrated with disagreements, and Ada feared the night would end without anything being settled. Cara would leave Dry Lake, and it'd be over.

Anna Mary stood, and silence soon fell. "I have more reasons to distrust her than any of you. And she's caused me to ask myself a thousand questions. But I have only one question for all of you." She cleared her throat. "Will Ephraim be the only man to stand up for her?"

Ada watched people's faces, witnessing many attitudes begin to change. Rueben's face went ashen as he watched his daughter.

Shaking and teary-eyed, Anna Mary took a seat.

Ada gave a nod. "Thank you, Anna Mary. Last night Levi and Emma brought a box for Cara. It was one her father mailed to her here for her eighteenth birthday."

Rueben started coughing as if he'd choked. "But . . . I . . . I thought you'd tossed it without looking at what was inside."

"We didn't open it, but we saw no reason to throw it out," Levi said. "Ada, what was in it?"

"Letters, journals, Malinda's Bible, and

documents—her marriage license, Cara's birth certifi—"

"Wait." Rueben stood, interrupting her. He fidgeted with the hat in his hand. Leah, his wife, tugged on his arm, gesturing for him to sit down. He shook his head. "Before this goes on, I need to speak with Malinda's family and the bishop . . . alone."

The bishop cleared his throat. "I think Rueben's right. We've cleared up all we can as a large group. Thank you for coming. May we all be reminded that rumors cause trouble and are usually based on lies. Along with Malinda's brothers and their wives, I'd like Rueben, Leah, and Ada to stay, please."

Within minutes everyone had left the room except the folks the bishop had named.

The bishop took a seat at the kitchen table. The rest of them followed suit.

He drew a deep breath and bowed his head in silent prayer. He opened his eyes. "Before I begin, is there something you wanted to say, Rueben?"

He stared at the table. Children's voices from outside filled the room, but not one adult uttered a word.

Rueben wiped his brow several times and finally spoke. "Malinda's leaving didn't go exactly as the rumors have it."

"Just how did it go?" Levi's voice had an edge to it.

Rueben struggled to speak. "Your sister didn't break up with me. And she wasn't pregnant when she left here."

Levi jumped up. "What? You told us she'd been seeing Trevor while the two of you were engaged and that she ran off with him after breaking up with you."

Breathing deep, Rueben stared at the floor. "I never actually said that. You just believed it."

Emma looked at Rueben's wife. "Did you know this?"

The stricken look on Leah's face said that she did, although all she managed was a shrug and half nod.

David glared at Rueben. "You make this make sense—now." He shoved his index finger against the kitchen table with each word.

"Well . . . I was working about an hour from here. That's where I met Leah. I'd been there most of that summer. When I didn't return home for a few weekends, Malinda hired Trevor to bring her to me. She . . . saw me kissing Leah. We argued, and she left with Trevor. She begged me not to say anything."

"How convenient for you." David smacked the table.

"It sounds like she wanted to leave with some shred of pride intact," Leroy said.

Emma scrunched a fistful of her apron and then released it, over and over again. "She was nineteen with a thousand broken dreams. She always felt abandoned by her Daed because he gave her to Levina to raise. She must have been devastated to be rejected by another man."

David shrugged. "I still say that Daed did his best when Mamm died giving birth to her. He couldn't take care of a newborn and the rest of us while holding a job."

The pain in Levi's eyes went deep as he put his head in his hands. "We shouldn't have left her in our Grossmammi Levina's care all those years. But our house never seemed like a good place for a girl to grow up—all boys and no mother?"

"Malinda made her own choices," David said.

Several started talking loudly at the same time.

The bishop raised his hands, silencing everyone. "Let's not forget that Malinda joined the faith, and then she ran off. She broke her vows, regardless of the reason. Still, it sounds as if shock and hurt were the reasons for her decisions, not rebellion."

Levi stood and began pacing. "For nearly thirty years we've believed she lost faith, that she ran around like a tramp. I questioned you, Rueben, because I'd never seen any signs of her being wild, even during her rumschpringe. And you led me to believe we simply never knew her."

"You decided that on your own. You told me she called not long after leaving and said that she was too ashamed to come home but that Trevor wanted to marry her. According to you, the next and last time you heard from her, she'd written to say she had a little girl."

Levi pointed at him. "By words or silence, sounds to me like you've been lying to us for years."

"I wasn't trying to lie."

"You weren't trying to tell the truth either," Leroy said.

Rueben gestured with his hands. "Look, I met Leah that summer, and we . . . we fell for each other. We were going to tell her, but she found out first. Those of you who knew Malinda know how high-strung she was."

"High-strung?" one of her aunts rang out. "I remember Malinda getting permission for one of her Daed's hired helpers to drive her to Ohio to see you. The wedding was only three weeks away. Trevor was the driver, and he brought her to you, didn't he?"

Rueben nodded.

Emma sobbed. "She never returned home after that trip. We assumed she'd planned to run off with Trevor and used visiting you as the excuse to get away. And you helped us believe that. You know you did."

"You were mean not to tell her how you felt **before** you kissed someone else." Leroy shot an accusing look at Rueben. "You and Leah didn't get married for a year after that. Was that just to make yourself look good? Now that we see who you are, we all know the answer to that. And don't you tell us our sister was high-strung after nearly three decades of letting us think she left here pregnant."

"She didn't have to leave the way she did," Rueben said. "And she didn't have to stay gone or marry Trevor. Even when she came back years later, looking for a safe place for Cara, I tried to get her to tell everyone what happened. I wanted to clear it up."

"You talked to her by yourself when she came back to Dry Lake with Cara? Without me or anyone?" Leah's tone said it all. She didn't trust her husband's heart when it came to Malinda. Ada wondered if Rueben had really been in love with Leah, or if once Malinda discovered him and Leah kissing and left, he felt compelled to marry her. Maybe waiting the year to get married had been more of a grieving time for Rueben than anything else.

Rueben didn't answer his wife, but Ada figured he would . . . for a long time to come.

"When Malinda returned with Cara, she didn't want it set straight. She said it wouldn't change that her father and brothers didn't want her returning to Dry Lake and that anything I said would only cause trouble for me and Leah."

Levi turned to his wife. "She thought we didn't want her even if we knew the truth?"

David slammed his hand down on the table. "We can't believe what Rueben is saying about Malinda not wanting to set things straight. He talked to her privately, and we'll never know what was or wasn't said, will we?"

Leah stood and folded her arms, her face taut with embarrassment and guilt. "When she came to Dry Lake with Cara, you had just as much opportunity to go talk to her as Rueben did. But you chose not to. All of you. So don't lay this mess fully on him."

Ada pulled the documents from the hidden pocket of her dress. "Finding all the right people to blame will not solve even one of the problems facing Cara." She unfolded the papers. "Trevor and Malinda married several months after they left here. Cara was born fifteen months later. If it's true that Malinda always felt rejected and you wish you could change that, I'm asking you to start with her grown daughter. And don't hold what Ephraim's done against him."

The bishop looked over the documents again, as if verifying what he'd read earlier. "The ban will not be lifted from Ephraim. We cannot ignore a single man allowing a woman to stay in his home overnight. But we need to do what we can to set things right with Cara, try to heal some of the hurt we've caused."

Ada interlaced her fingers. "I don't think trying to speak to her face to face is the answer right now. She's not one to trust people's motives. She'll want to know why you're coming to see her now and not a few days ago. When she figures out that we've met to decide what to do and she was the topic of a district meeting, we'll never get past her defenses."

"Sounds like she's as stubborn as her mother," Leroy said.

The brothers chuckled, breaking some of the tension in the room.

"Ada, you know her better than anyone here," Emma said. "If she won't trust us and doesn't want to speak with us, how do we break through that?"

"Letters, for now. But more than anything, I'd like permission for her to move in with me. I've found a place in Hope Crossing."

Questions came from several of them all at once.

The bishop held up his hand. "You have my approval, Ada."

# Thirty-Five

The sounds of night—mostly crickets and tree frogs—echoed hour after hour. The kerosene lamp sputtered beside the bed, and Cara's eyes grew heavy as she read the letters her mother had written to her father. Other correspondence was stacked on the nightstands—ones from her mother to her, from her dad to Cara, from her dad to her mom. She studied them again and again, trying to piece together the missing parts of her life. Through the open window, a summer breeze carried a sweet scent of flowers. Silvery moonbeams lay across the bedspread.

The differences between here and the Bronx were vast, and she could understand why her visit as a child had been chiseled into the recesses of her memory. Compared to the continual sirens, loud neighbors, and locked windows of her place in New York City, this was a vacation spot— except, just like New York, the people had issues. Not the same ones she'd been used to seeing, but problems nonetheless. She had them too. Clearly both her mom and dad did as well. But she'd expected more from a people who avoided worldly goods.

She skimmed a letter she'd read several times before. It seemed her mother had married her father without knowing he was an alcoholic. A lot of the letters were from her mother to her dad while he was in rehab. But her father's problems weren't the only ones her mother carried. She wrote about a horrible pain from childhood, but Cara hadn't yet discovered what it was. Trevor's father had been bad news, and Trevor came by his addiction honestly. Her parents were two hurting people who united in hopes of easing their pain. In some ways their relationship seemed to work . . . part of the time.

But reading these notes, letters, and

journal entries was like catching the tail end of a conversation—confusing—and she wished she understood more. But right now she was tired of trying to sort out her parents' past.

Ready to get out of Dry Lake, she tried to temper her restlessness. It'd been three days since she'd agreed to move to Ada's house in Hope Crossing. Between Ada needing to square the rental agreement with the owners and Ephraim's dad's surgery, Cara was still stuck here. Ephraim hadn't been around much since Sunday, and Lori constantly asked for him.

A slow cooing sound eased across the night air. Whatever bird made that noise, it was her favorite sound—soft and gentle as nightfall in the country. She placed the letters inside the box and slid into her jeans. From the foot of the bed, Better Days jumped up, wagging his tail. She picked him up and headed outside. It seemed the puppy would be fairly easy to housebreak, which would be important to Ephraim since the dog wouldn't be under Lori's watchful eye once they moved. After setting the dog on the grass, she studied the landscape.

The quiet beauty of Dry Lake contradicted her inner turmoil. She wondered if all Amish communities were this closed or if it simply seemed closed to her because of who her mother had been and who they thought Cara was. A whisper carrying her name floated through the night air, and she turned to see Ephraim in the entry of his hedged sanctuary.

She walked toward him. "How's your dad?"

"Doing well. He'll be released tomorrow. Actually, that'll be today. What are you doing up?"

"I've been reading letters my mom wrote to my dad when he was in rehab." She looked across the fields and to the pond. "I want out of here so badly, and yet there is something about this place. I can see why my mother missed it so much. Where did she live as a kid?"

"With Levina, but the rest of the family lived in the house next to Levi and Emma Riehl. Leroy Riehl and his wife live there now. Your grandmother died giving birth to your mother, and Levina, her grandmother, raised your mom. Fifty years ago we didn't have a midwife in or near Dry Lake, and hospitals were a long way away. I heard your grandfather talking to some other men one time. He said your grandmother was a tiny woman and had a lot of difficulty with each birth, and she didn't survive the night Malinda was born. Levina's children were all grown, and she welcomed Malinda into her home. I've always heard there was bad blood between your mom and her dad—as if she resented him for giving her to someone else and never asking her to come home after she was no longer a baby. She didn't move into her father's home until Levina had some health issues and couldn't take care of her. By that time your mother was sixteen or seventeen years old."

"And my mom's dad?"

"Your granddad died in the same car accident as my mother, and Mahlon's dad, and Becca's husband, and several others from the community. Three vanloads of Amish had hired drivers to take them to a wedding in Ohio. The driver of their van was going too fast and not paying attention to the road, and they slammed into a concrete highway divider."

"Ephraim, I'm sorry."

He stared at the night sky. "It was a huge loss, and I think it's part of the reason the community is so defensive about outsiders. None of the adults in the community trusted the driver of the van that crashed, but everyone ignored their gut feeling and paid a really high price. Now they're overly cautious about anything to do with outsiders."

She could understand some of that. Breaking trust only took a moment, and regaining it could take a lifetime or more. "Maybe my mom felt abandoned by her dad and that had a lot to do with why she took up with an Englischer and left."

"Maybe."

Cara moved to the bench swing. "It all seems like such a lie."

"All what?"

"How picturesque life can look. You get this quick view of something, and it looks appealing and wonderful—like the quaint appearance of being Amish. But it's all a lie."

He took a seat beside her. "Sunday evening you and Lori were near the huge trees by the pond as the sun was setting, and if someone had taken a snapshot of that, it'd warm the heart of every person who saw it. But the struggle for food, shelter, and safety is huge. That fight doesn't discount the truth seen in that flash of time. Love is real, and it's worth the battle. That's not a lie, Cara."

"Maybe you're right." She rubbed the back of her neck. "I'm so tired of thinking about all of it."

He reached into his pants pocket and pulled something out. Dangling a key in front of her, he smiled. "Maybe this will help. Paint and tools have been delivered. One bathroom is now in working order. The kitchen sink will be fixed tomorrow. A gas stove and refrigerator will be delivered early next week at the latest."

She placed her palm under the key, and he dropped it. Clutching the key in her fist, she relaxed against the back of the swing. "You were right, you know."

"Well, as my **Daadi** used to say—"

"Your who?"

"My grandfather."

"Okay."

"He used to say that even a blind squirrel finds a nut every once in a while."

She laughed. "You're weird, Ephraim. Who cracks jokes before sunup?"

He suppressed a smile, making slight lines around the edges of his mouth. "You were saying I was right about something?"

"I needed this transition, a place to live while coping with all I've learned. But what does my leaving mean for you?"

"That I get my bed back."

She elbowed him. "How long before you're not shunned anymore?"

"The bishop hasn't put a set time on it."

"But I'll be gone."

"It's a discipline for past actions, similar to grounding a teen or taking away certain privileges. Only unlike getting in trouble with your parents, none of your friends thinks it's cool."

"You know what I think?"

"Do I want to know?"

She huffed and pointed at him. "I think if God were real, he'd make that bishop apologize."

Ephraim started laughing and seemed unable to stop.

"What?"

"You're only going to believe He's real if He makes the bishop own up to something he's not really wrong in?"

"Not wrong? We didn't do anything close to going against that Bible of yours." As soon as she said it, she lost her confidence. "Did we?"

"Well, ya, sort of. Godliness asks us to abstain from the appearance of evil, and you staying in my home overnight . . . well, you know. There's nothing wrong in being held accountable, Cara."

"It's ridiculous. With all the bad in the world, you're shunned because you did something that **appeared** wrong? Where's the proof of your God's love in that?"

"You love your daughter, but you can't hold something in your hand as proof of that. Love is action on her behalf all the time. God's love is action on our behalf all the time. But we're in the middle of a battle. Part of life is 'fighting the good fight' to keep the faith. If there were no evil coming against us, we wouldn't have to fight to keep the faith, right?"

A feeling of being offended jabbed needles at her, yet chills and confusion washed over her. "I like you. And I think you like me. So let's do our friendship a favor and not discuss this God issue again, okay?"

He stood. "Do you believe in nature?"

"Well, of course."

"Then come look at its glory through the telescope."

When she shook her head, he held out his hand. "I'm not going to chance messing up our friendship by trying to convince you about God. That's His job. I only want to show you some spectacular things in the sky."

Cara placed her hand in his. They walked the few steps to his telescope.

She looked through the lens. "I don't see anything but my own eyelashes."

Ephraim made a few adjustments. "Here, try again. But don't blink right before you place your eye against the eyeglass frame."

Cara tried again. He stood right behind her, showing her how to adjust the finder scope and focuser. She wondered how many times he'd done this with Anna Mary. Had she felt like Cara did at this moment?

"Cara?"

She blinked. "Sorry. What'd you say?"

"Place your eye near the rim, and then adjust this until you can see."

"Okay."

She could barely think with him so close—the softness of his tone as he spoke, the warmth radiating from his skin, the gentleness in every move. But then she saw a view so breathtaking she couldn't believe her eyes. A strip of stars hung in the sky on a backdrop of gold and silver dust. She'd always heard there were way more stars in the sky than were visible to the naked eye. Suddenly every problem she'd ever faced took on a different perspective—as if it were a fleck inside earth's time line.

# Thirty-Six

Deborah studied Mahlon as he guided the horse and buggy toward Hope Crossing. It'd take them the better part of an hour to get there, so he'd slipped away from the shop before closing, hoping they could ride there and back before dark. They both wanted to see the place Ada would move into this Saturday.

The only noise was that of the horse's hoofbeats and the creaking of the buggy. Deborah felt that Mahlon had grown quieter with each day that had passed since Ephraim's shunning, and he seemed to be sharing less and less with her. He hadn't even noticed when she came out of her house with something behind her back or when she tucked a package under the seat of the carriage. Maybe he just needed to find something to laugh about. She certainly did, especially after going by Anna Mary's last night and finding out she and Ephraim had broken up.

A night out together before the weekend arrived would probably do both her and Mahlon some good. It had to be upsetting him that his mother had made a decision about a house without his approval. Now that her father was home from the hospital, the hardest thing for her to accept was that Ephraim and Anna Mary were no longer seeing each other. The shunning would end in time, but Ephraim had never changed his mind once he stopped seeing a girl. She held on to the hope that he would this time.

Ada had told her a little about what took place at the meeting last Monday after the bishop dismissed most of them. She wouldn't say too much about that, but she told Deborah all about the house in Hope Crossing and that Cara was moving in with her. Knowing all the odds Cara had beaten to find Dry Lake, Deborah couldn't wish she hadn't come, but she was glad that in two days she'd be moving away from her brother.

Drawing a deep breath, she tried to relax. She touched Mahlon's cheek, hoping to pull him from his thoughts too. "Where are you?"

"Thinking about all the changes happening in Dry Lake. It's like everyone's suddenly chosen to follow their own heart."

"Everyone's trying to do what's best. Even your mother."

"Maybe."

"So what's bothering you the most?"

"I stayed because I didn't feel she could make it on her own. And now . . ."

"Stayed?"

He said nothing.

"As in stayed in her house or stayed Amish?"

He shook his head and sighed. "Stayed with her."

"It didn't hurt anything for you to live at home these extra few years, did it?"

"No." He shrugged. "Do you ever wonder if after all this Ephraim will stay Amish?"

"Too often and too much. I think that's the main reason I'm not more upset that your mother has decided to move to Hope Crossing. She's getting Cara out of his place and out of his sight. I'm really sorry Ada's moving so far away from our community, but maybe he and Anna Mary can work things out once Cara's gone."

"I had no idea Mamm had that kind of independence in her. I only wish I'd known it years ago." He lightly slapped the reins against the horse's back.

"Well, you're free now. And you can find a place just for us. I'm so excited, but I'm nervous about all of it. Can you find us a place in ten days?"

"Just trust me. I'll handle it." Mahlon looked at the directions in his hand and brought the buggy to a stop in front of an old house.

"This is it?" Deborah asked.

He looked at the address on the paper in his hand and then to the mailbox. "Ya."

They sat in silence, staring at the place. It looked like a haunted mansion. The absolute worst home in Hope Crossing. Mahlon pulled around back and into the driveway.

Deborah scanned the surrounding area. The place sat on a corner lot, with a cornfield to one side of it and houses nearby but not too close. "It has a nice little barn, pasture for her horse, and a huge backyard."

"Ya, and a backyard so full of junk and fallen limbs she can't use it for anything."

"That can be changed with a bit of work."

They both got out, and Deborah held his hand as they followed the sidewalk around the side of the home, up the front walk, and onto the wraparound porch.

The gray paint on the six-foot-wide porch needed stripping and redoing. The white clapboard sides held so little paint it wouldn't require much cleaning, just fresh coats.

"No wonder your mother could afford this place."

"She says she gets money taken off the rent for every bit of work done to the place."

"I guess with Cara here to paint, your mother will be living free of charge for a while."

"One would think."

Deborah slid the key into the lock and turned it. "I love the door. The old-fashioned mail slot, beveled glass, and tarnished brass knobs. They're perfect."

"Perfect for what?"

"For fulfilling your mother's dreams. The old place looks full of potential."

They crossed the black-lacquer floors. Wallpaper peeled from the ceiling, musty boxes of junk sat everywhere, and newspapers were strewn all about. They walked into the kitchen.

Deborah studied the room. "It's certainly big enough for her to do her baking."

Mahlon looked down the sink. "This place is just a hull; even the pipes are missing."

"Ada said the plumber will return tomorrow, and the owners are covering the cost of that."

They walked through the rest of the house.

Mahlon shook his head. "I can't believe she wants this. It needs so much work."

"Don't all dreams need lots of work?"

He gave a half shrug. "Most dreams need to be ignored."

An uneasy feeling came over her. "Ignored?"

"Forget it." He motioned toward the front door. "I've seen enough. You ready to go?"

"I love this place, Mahlon. Can't you see that it's something she's always longed for? You wanted to stay in Dry Lake while growing up, and she did so. But now she's ready to try some things on her own."

"Great. She's making her dreams come true while I'm stuck doing Ephraim's job."

"Mahlon." Deborah stopped. "Are you angry with your mother over this?"

He shook his head. "I'm just tired of it all. Aren't you?"

"Tired of what?"

He closed the front door behind her. "I wanted to take one week to get away, and Ephraim needs me, and Mamm goes out and gets a run-down place, and . . . I . . ."

"You what?"

After locking the door, he shoved the key into his pocket. "Never mind."

"Never mind? It's like you're trying to tell me something without having to actually say it." As they walked down the porch steps, Deborah tugged on his hands. "I don't want to get into an argument just because you're in a foul mood, but if you keep dropping hints and saying they don't mean—"

"Okay," he interrupted and then slid his arms around her. "You're right." He kissed her forehead. "I just need a few days away, but I shouldn't take that out on you." He kissed her again. "Sorry, Deb."

She climbed into the buggy, hoping her present would help him feel better. She pulled it out from under the seat. "I special-ordered a gift for you from the dry goods store. It came in today."

He smiled. "And how did you manage to hide it from me?"

"You're not with me all the time. I've barely seen you the last few weeks."

He lifted it from her hands. "You shouldn't have done this."

"You're going to provide me a home soon. I think I can buy you one thing to go in it."

He tore the paper, saying nothing as the clock came into view. It was the most gorgeous clock she'd ever seen and exactly like the one he'd pointed out to her a year ago, saying he hoped to own one like it someday.

"It plays music on the hour."

"It's beautiful, Deb," he whispered as he removed the cardboard from around it.

"Flip that button, and we can hear every tune. There are twelve of them."

He notched the button to On. The tinny music seemed to grab him, and he didn't move. "That tune . . ."

"I don't know it, do you?"

He nodded. "It's everywhere I go lately.

Every store. Every client's home. In my sleep."

"What do the words to the song say?"

"It's based on a scripture: to everything, there is a season. Only the song says 'turn, turn, turn' a lot."

"It's a good tune, ya?"

He shrugged. "Except sometimes it feels like God is trying to tell me something. How do we get it to play another tune?"

"Press that little gadget."

He did. The same tune started over again.

"That's odd." She pushed the button again. "The clock was working when I wrapped it."

The same tune played every time she pressed the button. Chills ran up Deborah's arms and down her back.

Mahlon passed her the clock. "Let's just turn it off for now, okay?"

"Sure." She flipped the knob to Off, but the music didn't stop.

He retried the same switch, but the song played faster. "Try removing the batteries."

She turned the clock over, removed the

plate for the batteries, and paused. "What happens if it keeps playing?" Forcing a smile, she couldn't ignore that her heart was thumping wildly. When she removed a battery, the music stopped.

"We just won't turn the musical part on, okay?"

"But that is the special part. We can pick songs to mean certain things over the years, and then no matter where we are in the house, when we hear it, we'll remember our love."

Mahlon's hands trembled as he removed his hat. "Wherever I go, whatever I do in life, I'll never forget your love. Ever."

The oddest sensation ran through her.

He took her hand into his and kissed her fingers. "I love you more than you'll ever know." He stared into her eyes as if trying to tell her things he couldn't find the words for. "Let's go on home. I have work tomorrow, and you need rest so you can help Mamm pack."

Feeling more anxious than ever, she jolted when Mahlon put his arm around her.

"I think I'll take a few days off. Will you be okay if I do that?"

"But the shop needs you. It'll get even further behind. And you've got to find a place and get moved."

He rubbed her back. "I have relatives in Dry Lake I can live with for a week or two."

"You always hated that idea before."

"Things have changed. And the shop's going to be behind no matter what I do. I can't go from being the provider for Mamm to doing so for your Daed and all his children. That responsibility shouldn't have been laid in my lap."

"But that's how things work with family. You know that. What about your mother? Have you told her?"

"No. I'll write to her and explain. She'll be so busy settling into that place, having work done, and building this dream business of hers, she won't even think twice about it."

"Where will you go?"

He shrugged. "Somewhere quiet where no one knows who I am." He pulled her closer and kissed her head. "Your Daed is mending, and you'll be busy helping Mamm and Becca. You won't even have time to miss me."

"Well, I've been missing you for a while now. And I'd love to see you return with . . . you. Okay?"

"You are the most amazing girl any guy could have."

"Now see, that's the man I agreed to marry. So when will you leave?"

"Saturday."

"When will you be back?"

"Wednesday, probably. That next weekend we'll finish packing up my belongings that are still at the house."

"Okay. But someday, when you're ready, let's talk. I want to know what you've been thinking about."

"When I figure it out, you'll be the first to know."

She chuckled. "Fair enough."

# Thirty-Seven

Ephraim bowed his head in silence, trying to block out thoughts of Cara during the meal prayer.

When he opened his eyes, Lori smiled at him. "I got done praying first."

Ephraim chuckled. "I don't think that's the point."

At a table several feet away, Ada took a piece of fresh-baked bread and passed the basket to Cara. She rose from her table, walked over to his, and set the container near him.

Ephraim took a roll. "Denki."

"Gan gern?" Cara asked.

He laughed. "Gern gschehne."

"Yeah, Mom, gern gschehne." Cara

made a funny face at her daughter and returned to the other table. Lori giggled.

He studied Ada for a moment. Something weighed on her, something written in that letter he'd seen her read a hundred times. He didn't know who it was from, but she kept it tucked inside her apron, and he'd seen her shed a few tears when she thought no one was looking.

From the moment Ada had left his home after spending the night helping Cara nearly two weeks ago, she hadn't been allowed to talk to him. Between her writing to him and them sharing a conversation with each other through Cara, they talked fairly easily. He understood why the bishop had added unusual restrictions to his shunning, but the hardest part was a normal restriction—not being allowed to sit at a table with her. Cara came up with a plan that made the rules easier to live with. She and Lori took turns sitting at either his or Ada's table during mealtimes.

Ada's place in Hope Crossing was an hour from Dry Lake by horse and buggy, because the rigs couldn't use the highway, but it was only ten to fifteen minutes by car. So Robbie drove him here each morning and picked him up around ten or eleven each night.

In between those hours he and Cara worked to restore the home, then talked and kidded until the exhausting efforts felt like a game. Every morning they sat on the steps of the front porch and drank coffee. Each evening when it was too dark to work by kerosene or gas lamps and Lori was asleep, Ada stayed here, and he and Cara went for a long stroll. It's what he'd longed for when they finished painting the Garretts' place—more time with Cara.

He watched her as she ate, enjoying how quickly she'd begun to heal. The shock and grief of learning about her roots had quieted, but her heart hadn't changed toward her family. Several had written letters to her, but she'd not opened even one of them. She'd accepted their past indifference, not forgiven it.

When she caught him staring at her, she frowned. "You got a problem, mister?"

He had one all right. And he was looking straight at it. Everything about her fascinated him. The way she ate bread by
tearing off a small piece at a time. The way
she tried to tuck her hair behind her ear
now that it was growing a bit, but it was
still too short to stay. The way she whispered in early mornings and spoke deep
and soft in late evenings. And the thousand
other movements she made throughout a
day. All of it had captured his thoughts.

When he didn't answer her, she stuck
out her tongue and made a face. He didn't
allow the smile he felt to show on his face.
Even though he wasn't sure what he
wanted from life anymore, he kept that
confusion to himself. The shunning hadn't
convinced him of the things the church
leaders had hoped.

Without going to any Amish person's
place, he and Lori had found homes for
every puppy. After he paid to have the
mama dog fixed, they even found a great
family for her.

Even though living without modern
conveniences seemed silly to Cara, she was

clearly interested in trying to understand the whys of their religion. Each day she asked questions about living Amish. And despite her arguing against those ways, she grew to understand their culture a little more. Her insights were remarkable, but it was head knowledge to her. She seemed to accept none of it as a reasonable way of life.

Still, he was convinced she needed to see the good parts of the Amish way of life before she'd find peace and acceptance of her heritage. So he guarded his words and never spoke of his frustration with being shunned. According to the restrictions of the shunning, he probably shouldn't be doing anything that helped Ada build her new business, but it seemed to him he could get away with doing things that helped Cara, who happened to share the same home.

He was four weeks into a shunning that the bishop hadn't set an ending date to. It might last five more months or longer. Ada's dilapidated place seemed like the perfect solution to his problem of having too much time on his hands. It wasn't the painful situation the bishop had intended—not for him or Cara—and Ephraim figured he'd get a visit from the church leaders when they realized it.

"Hey, 'From." Lori took a drink of milk and set the glass on the table. "Does Better Days miss me when you take him home at night?"

"Ya, he does. Just last night he was telling me all about it while I was trying to sleep."

"Can he stay here tonight?"

"Lori—"

"Actually," Ephraim interrupted Cara, hoping to stop her from issuing a firm no, "I've been wanting to talk to your mom about that."

"Really?" Lori's eyes grew big.

"Yeah, 'From, really?" Cara raised an eyebrow. "Before or after you cause trouble for a busy single mom?"

He knew that each day took a lot of strength. Between painting and helping Ada bake, she worked long hours, and as the summer temps climbed, the lack of air conditioning and fans seemed to wear on her more than it did on him and Ada.

"I have a plan."

"One that works? Or one where we work, but it doesn't?" Cara teased.

His eyes defied his will and stayed focused on her as he soaked in who they'd become since meeting. Love was weird—and he no longer doubted that he loved her. No matter how much he gave or helped, he wanted to do more. He didn't know how she felt about him other than seeing him as a good friend whose company she enjoyed. But he did know she was happier now that she was out of Dry Lake, had a stable place to live, and had lots of work to do.

"What's the plan?" Lori asked around a mouthful of fresh-baked wheat bread.

**I wish I knew.**

He cleared his throat and looked to Lori. "I'm going to clean up the backyard so an adult doesn't have to put a leash on Better Days and take him to a side yard every time he needs to go out."

Lori looked pleased as she took another bite of her sandwich. Cara's face was not readable.

Yesterday afternoon when she corrected Lori for nearly knocking over a can of paint, he heard it in Cara's voice: she needed a safe place for her daughter to play **outside.**

With town shops close by and traffic as busy as it was, Cara didn't let Lori go outdoors alone. Part of the reason was because Better Days had to be kept on a leash, and if he pulled free of Lori's hand, she'd take off after him. But when Cara wouldn't trust Lori to play on the wraparound porch, it dawned on him that her caution was magnified because her mother had died from being struck by a car. That's when he decided to stop his repair work on the inside of the house and clean up the junkyard out back.

"Can I help?" Lori asked.

"Maybe later, after I've shoveled the broken glass into trash bags and mended the fence so little girls and puppies can't walk right through it, okay?"

"Okay. Me and Better Days will be in my room playing when you're ready."

Cara rose and began stacking plates. "She thinks you'll get that done before supper."

He scuffed Lori's hair. "I will, just not before today's supper."

He stood. "Guess I better get started."

Ephraim put on work gloves and began loading lawn bags with broken bottles and trash. The mid-June heat bore down as he lifted a half-rotted log and carried it to the wagon. He'd picked up all the large pieces of glass he could, but he knew there were hidden shards. The worst of it was in two corners that'd been used as trash piles. He wasn't yet sure what he could do about that.

While lifting another oversize log, he saw two men in a horse and buggy coming toward him. When the rig stopped near the carriage house, he recognized them. Two church leaders, the bishop and a preacher. He'd known this speech was coming, was surprised it'd taken a full week for them to make this visit. What he didn't know was if his father realized how much time he was spending here. Normally, as a preacher, his Daed would be with the other two church leaders during this type of visit. But the bishop's wisdom probably caused him to shield his Daed from the news.

Hoping to keep Cara or Lori from hearing what Sol and Alvin would have to say, he weaved around the trash and junk until only a wire fence separated them at the back part of the yard.

"Ephraim." Sol shook his hand, effectively reminding Ephraim that brotherly fellowship was heartily waiting for him as soon as he took the right steps to bring an end to the shunning.

Alvin moved to stand next to the bishop. "We regret the need for this visit and that we had to travel so far in order to connect with one of our own."

Robbie took him home each night, but that wouldn't count for much.

The bishop studied him. "Because of the vows you've taken, this is like flirting with betrayal. You've promised to marry within our sect, and Cara is not a part of us."

"She might be if everything had been handled right."

"If she'd come to us at the age of eight, she **might** have joined the faith. Big difference. And is that why you're spending so much time here, to set right a wrong? I think not. You are here because you let desire take root, and now it controls you."

Alvin opened the gate and came inside the messy yard. He placed his hand on Ephraim's shoulder. "You can't get free of the ban living like this, and you have a duty to your family."

"If that's your argument, it's a weak one. I've fulfilled more than my share of family obligations. I've worked for eight years to provide for my father's family."

The bishop came inside the fence too. "We've tried to give you a bit of flexibility, thinking you'd help Ada and then return to safer ground for your soul. But you haven't. One is not Amish because their parents are or once were Amish. Cara's an Englischer. Will you forsake God, family, and your business to follow this . . . this lustful path?"

"My being here has nothing to do with

lust." It had plenty to do with desire, but Ephraim knew himself well enough to recognize when lust tempted him.

The bishop placed a hand on his shoulder. "Anything that pulls you away from your walk with God, from the principles you believe in, or believed in before, is lust. If this was happening to someone else in our community, you'd be able to see it for what it is. Trust us, Ephraim. And come away." He spoke softly. "Let us do our job in correcting you. Please, for the love of all God has done for you, don't turn your back on Him."

"I haven't turned my back on God."

"No, you haven't," the bishop said. "But one who's been raised as you have doesn't turn his back on God overnight. It will happen slowly, until one day you realize you've lost all faith and you don't know when or how it happened. But I can tell you this: it began the day you took that woman into your home unsupervised. And it will continue as long as you come to Hope Crossing each day to work beside her."

"She needs someone to tell her of our

faith, to show her all the good parts of being Amish. Her mother wanted her raised with us. That opportunity was stolen from her. She's been asking questions about our ways. Will you prevent me from sharing that with her?"

"Most Englischers will ask questions about our beliefs, given a chance. It doesn't mean they're remotely interested in doing what it takes to live as we do. And what happens if, after all her questions are answered, she's uninterested in living Old Order? What then?"

Ephraim stared at the lush green hill, wishing he had answers. Cara had a few favorite spots she liked to walk to in the evenings. He was looking at one of them. They'd go through the pasture behind Ada's house, across the footbridge, and up that steep hill to a dilapidated barn and outbuildings. He had no idea why she found the half-ruined structures so interesting, but that's where they walked. They'd sit on a fallen tree or jutted rock or sometimes a blanket and watch the night sky. He could talk to Cara there, tell her about parts of himself that were hidden from everyone else. She shared things with him, and that only served to make him want her more. The only secret he kept from her was that he was no longer seeing Anna Mary. Surely, if she thought about it, she'd know that. But telling her would shift the relationship and add to all the confusion going on inside her.

"Ephraim," the bishop called to him, "what if she's uninterested in becoming Amish?"

"I don't know."

The bishop stared at him, looking deeply concerned. "Will you leave the faith? Will you make the same mistake Malinda Riehl made? You've lived a solid Old Order Amish life since your father needed you nine years ago. You did that out of love, but love is not always enough to accomplish what we want it to."

Ephraim held the man's gaze, unashamed of what was happening within him. His heart belonged to Cara. At thirty-two he'd finally experienced the connection he'd always longed for. "And there are times when it is."

The bishop drew a deep breath. "Ephraim, listen to me. Even if she chooses to join the faith and goes through all the right steps, if her decision isn't based on the right reasons, she is likely to leave after some time."

"She wouldn't do that."

"You care for her. That's clear. Does she return those feelings?"

He shrugged. "I don't know."

"If she gets so caught up in her feelings that she goes through all the steps to marry you, then she might only stay because she's married. But if you back off, she'll have a chance to choose for herself, not based on a life with you, but based on our faith."

Ephraim shoved his hands into his pockets and gazed at the sky. "You may be right about that."

"Ya." The bishop smiled. "I am right. I learned much of my wisdom from you over the years before you became all **verhuddelt.**"

Was the bishop right? Had he become confused?

Alvin shifted. "We don't want to lose you or add any more punishment. But as much as it grieves us to say it, this is your final warning. You have until Monday to decide. You must keep away from Cara at all times until we see progress in her. If she makes a decision to accept our ways and become Amish, that will change everything."

The bishop removed his hat, looking peaceful and confident. "You can't be the one to help her, not without jeopardizing your own soul. Let Ada do as she has permission to. Cara is out of your home now. If you'll return as we ask, I'll repeal the extreme restrictions of your shunning within a week. If you'll show some willingness to follow our wisdom, it won't be long before I'll end the shunning altogether. Then you will be a member in good standing before you know it."

Each man placed a hand on Ephraim's shoulder and bowed for silent prayer. "Be wise, Ephraim. There is much more than just your soul at stake. Many within the younger generations of Dry Lake are now questioning the ways of our people."

Feeling the weight of responsibility smothering him, he looked to Ada's house. Inside was a woman who possessed more of him than he did.

"Did you know Mahlon has been gone all week?" the bishop asked.

"What? He said he'd wait until I returned to work before he took time off."

"He left last Saturday and told Deborah he'd probably be back by Wednesday. Today is Saturday again, and she's not heard a word from him. She doesn't even know where he went. He's supposed to be out of his place by tomorrow at midnight, and from what we can tell, he made no plans for where to live."

The news quaked through him. His sister's heart would break if Mahlon didn't return. Was the letter Ada had been reading over and over again from Mahlon? He could think of a few reasons she wouldn't say anything yet and felt fairly confident she'd only speak up if she was positive what her son was up to.

"Can I talk to my sister?"

The bishop shook his head. "I'm sorry. I've made enough exceptions already. I let you talk to your Daed when he was in the hospital and to Ada several times when Cara found out she had relatives in Dry Lake."

Ephraim looked to the clear blue sky with its streaks of white clouds and golden sun, knowing that right where he looked there were the stars he couldn't see—not until darkness fell. "What you'd really like to tell me is that if I keep seeing Cara, I'll live under the weight of my choice for the rest of my life." He took a step back and began putting on a work glove. "Well, that's a price I just might be willing to pay."

## Thirty-Eight

Cara blew out the flame to the kerosene lamp on the kitchen table, gathered several letters that her mother had written, and walked to the back door of Ada's home. Ephraim moved through the darkness, repairing the gaps in the fence as if fixing it tomorrow would be too late. She'd seen two men in black suits arrive in a buggy and talk with him hours ago. He hadn't come inside since—not even for supper. She'd left him alone, knowing there were times when work did for a man what talking did for a woman.

Robbie had arrived an hour ago, spoken to Ephraim, and then left by himself. Whatever was going on, she'd bet the roof over her head that her presence was still making his life harder. She stepped onto the small back porch. Ephraim stopped cold and watched as she walked to him.

"I knew they'd come for you—those men in black. And yet you're still here."

"Faith in God is required. Remaining Amish is not."

She wanted to ask if he meant that he was willing to leave the Amish faith. If he said yes, part of her wanted to throw herself into his arms. But with the weight of her mother's past resting inside the letters she carried, she steadied her emotions. "Faith." She made a small gesture toward the sky. "I have faith that night will come and day will follow, again and again." She looked back at the house. "I have faith that either a need will be met or I'll have the strength to survive if it's not. Of late, I even have faith in you. But, Ephraim, I have no faith in your God, and I never will."

His eyes moved over her face, but he said nothing.

She held out the letters. "In my mother's own handwriting, in letters meant for me when I came of age, she confesses that she was never the same after leaving Dry Lake. She latched on to a different life for all the wrong reasons—out of hurt, betrayal, even out of my dad's need of her. So she stayed and married him. When she realized who she truly was and what she'd given up to marry him, her loyalty would not let her leave."

She stared at the letters. "Go home, Ephraim. Live as you need to, repair whatever damage has taken place. You've seen Lori and me safely through the storm, and we're fine now. My guess is you and Anna Mary are not so fine." She slid the letters into her back pocket. "She loves you, Ephraim. Don't throw that away because of a few crazy weeks with an outsider. I'm sure she's not happy that you spend so much time here with me. But given a chance, she'll forgive you. Go, make the right choice—not just for you, but for your children and grandchildren and all generations to come."

Crickets chirped, and the beauty of night seemed to move around them, but he said nothing. After long minutes of silence, he motioned for them to walk. They went through the back gate, across the wooden footbridge, and up to the top of the hill.

The darkened landscape surrounded them—the silhouette of rolling hills, trees, and valleys. A few stars shone through the hazy summer sky. They moved to the fallen tree and sat.

"Mahlon took a few days off starting last Saturday and hasn't returned." He pointed to the edge of the wood nearby, and she spotted three deer slowly entering the open field. "Since he was a teen, I've known he has a deep restlessness inside him—the kind that makes a man either leave or always wish he had."

"What will the community do?"

He sighed. "Grieve. And wait to hear from him."

"You need to be there for Deborah."

"I can't even talk to her." He rose. "It's all so frustrating. My sister's probably sick over Mahlon's absence. If any woman around is worth coming back for, it's her."

"Is there anything I can do to help?"

He removed his hat and ran his hands

through his hair. "It's possible. I don't know if it'll work, but maybe Deborah could talk to you while I'm nearby."

"And you could talk to her through me, like we do with Ada."

"I need to see if she's okay. And I know she'll draw strength from you."

"From me?" Cara scoffed.

He smiled and put his hat on. "Yes, you. If anyone knows how to take what a man has dished out and become stronger, you do."

"You're strange, you know that? Who else would see a homeless woman with a child and call that strong?"

"Possessions don't make a person strong—decisions do. Although I never thought about that before knowing you. While you were in the midst of the battle, you decided what you were and were not willing to give up, and you never let go. Deborah needs to see that."

"I don't think she'll see what you see in me, but I'll go. When?"

"Ada's hired Robbie to come by around eleven in the morning and take her to Dry

Lake for a Sunday visit since there's no service. You could ride with her. Go to my Daed's house and ask to talk to Deborah in the hiddy. I'll meet you there."

"It won't cause you problems for me to be there again?"

He shook his head. "It shouldn't, but I don't care if it does."

It seemed Ephraim had changed inwardly even more than her life had outwardly. He wasn't the same man who'd asked her to get off his property the first time he saw her, or the one who'd paid for two bus tickets to New York, or the one who'd tried to hide her from everyone he knew. But like he always said, the things that separated them would always stand firm. That's why she had no choice but to send him home to Anna Mary.

She cleared her throat, wishing she could undo the damage she'd caused him. "Does Ada know about Mahlon?"

"She hasn't said so, but I think she does."

"I got the mail from the box a few days ago. I think he'd written to her, but I don't know what the letter said. It didn't seem to be good news, though. Why wouldn't she tell anyone about it?"

"Whatever he wrote, I'm sure she doesn't want to alarm anyone."

"I came here and totally disrupted your life. You chose to ignore the Amish rules and are being shunned. Mahlon's mother decided to move out of Dry Lake and take me with her. Is it possible Mahlon's absence has something to do with me?"

"No. Although I see why it could look that way. Mahlon's been odd since the day we lost so many members in the car wreck, his Daed among them. He got worse after being in New York the day the Twin Towers fell. Deborah says he felt the earth shake, saw the smoke rise, and heard the screams of those trapped inside. His mother had been in the towers the day before. The experience did something to him."

"That would affect anyone."

"Deborah has loved him since she was a child." He sighed. "I have no idea what this might do to her."

Cara stood. "You need to go home tonight, 'From, and start acting like the Amish man you are."

He stayed on the log, looking up at her. "Ya. I know."

When he rose, mere inches separated them. Regardless of the Amish stance against electrical energy, it ran unrestricted between them.

Afraid to keep lingering, she turned away and started walking. But she wasn't ready to go back to Ada's. Tonight was all they had, and so they'd walk.

Ephraim stayed beside her, saying nothing for a long time. Finally he cleared his throat. "Since I didn't leave with Robbie, I'll use Ada's horse to get back to Dry Lake. I'll put the mare in the pasture, and tomorrow Israel Kauffman or Grey or someone will recognize her, realize I borrowed her, and see to it she's returned to Ada by tomorrow night."

She appreciated his effort to make small talk. "How can you know all that?"

"Too many years of experience among my people." His half smile looked more sad than happy, but she knew he was right—the Amish were **his** people.

❦

Deborah sat on the floor of Mahlon's bedroom, too weary to cry anymore. She held his shirt to her face, breathing in his aroma. Except for the occasional headlights of passing cars, darkness surrounded her. She kept telling herself to light a kerosene lamp or walk back home, but she continued to sit here hour after hour, trying to make sense of it all and figure out a way to fix it.

She longed to hear from him, to know he was safe. But if something hadn't kept him, if he hadn't been in an accident of some sort . . . if he'd chosen to leave like this . . . she wasn't sure she wanted to know that. And yet, not to know the truth meant living in limbo every second of every day. She couldn't stand that either. So she'd prayed until she was sick of it, but she kept praying anyway.

Israel Kauffman and Mahlon's cousin

Jonathan had come here with her long before dark. She'd emptied his dresser, footlocker, and nightstands. They'd dismantled his bed and moved all the heavy furniture. She'd asked them to go on home and let her pack his huge, messy closet on her own. They'd taken the grandfather clock with them, so she didn't know what time it was. But it didn't matter. It was somewhere between yesterday and tomorrow.

The closet was empty, and boxes were scattered throughout the room. Her prayers had changed shape and purpose since four days ago, when he should have come home and didn't. But her feelings had not altered. She was scared, and more than that she felt like a fool. Who lets a loved one go off without knowing where or how to reach him? Who lets someone talk in jumbled circles without insisting he make sense?

Car lights shone on the wall, but rather than moving around the room as they did when a vehicle passed the house, they stayed in one spot. Then they disappeared. She got up from the floor and moved to the window. Through the blackness of night, she saw a car parked on the shoulder of the road a hundred feet or so from the house. A light came on inside the car, and the door opened.

**Mahlon!**

She wanted to scream his name and run to see him, but neither her voice nor her body would obey her. He moved to the side of the car and leaned against it. Staring out at the field, he lit a match, and soon she saw smoke circle around him. A man got out of the driver's side and sat on the hood of the vehicle. They just stayed there, smoking and talking as if nothing mattered—not her pain or worry or anything.

Another vehicle headed toward them. Mahlon glanced at it before tossing his cigarette to the ground. He walked to the cattle gate, opened it, and called for his horse. A truck with a trailer attached to it pulled up beside the car. While Mahlon harnessed his horse, his friend opened the tailgate of the trailer. After the horse was loaded, the driver of the truck held something out the window. Mahlon went to the man, took whatever it was, and stepped away before the man left.

He stayed in the middle of the road, looking at the place where he'd grown up. As she stood there too bewildered to move, realization bore down on her like a merciless drought. She longed for a man she clearly didn't know. No matter how she tried, she couldn't put together the pieces of her childhood love and the lonely stranger she was now watching.

He was safe. But her heart broke anyway.

The man she'd willingly give herself to had no intentions of returning to her. Somehow she was seeing what he couldn't tell her—as if she was meant to be here, meant to see the truth for herself.

When he got into the car, she ran down the steps, out the back door, and toward the road.

As the car came toward her, she waved her arms. "Mahlon, wait!"

Mahlon looked straight at her, but the car kept going.

"Mahlon!" she screamed as loud as she could.

The brake lights glowed bright red, and then small white lights shined as the car backed up. It stopped. When Mahlon opened the door, she saw Eric in his military uniform. Mahlon got out and closed the door, but Eric didn't drive off.

"Why?" She choked on her tears.

He studied her as he'd done a thousand times before, but his face was a mixture of uncertainty and hardness. "I'm sorry."

"Sorry?" she yelled. "I didn't ask for an apology. I asked for an explanation."

He shook his head and held out an envelope. "I was going to leave this in your mailbox. It's for you and Mamm."

Wondering what could possibly end the twisting confusion inside her, she snatched it from him and looked inside.

"Money?" She gasped. "You're leaving me, and you're going to fix it by giving me money?"

He stepped toward her, his hands reaching for her shoulders, but she took a step back. "I can't do this, Deb."

"Can't do what?"

He said nothing, but she saw a tear trail down his face.

"You have someone else?"

"Never, not in a million years. I swear that to you."

"Then why?"

"I joined the faith, but not all of me did. Parts did, slivers too small to find most days. You were all that held me here, and finally I know that I can't live like this."

His words were short, and she should understand them, but her mind couldn't grab on to any of it. "I . . . I believed you. All this time I thought you really loved me. But you don't, do you? Why? Why can't you love me like I do you?"

"Don't do this to yourself, Deb."

"You're the one doing this! And what about your mother? You're her only child. She gave up everything to raise you."

"That's what parents do."

"You promised to always be here for her, and now you do this?"

"She'll be fine. She's already proved that. And eventually you will too. But I never will—not if I stay."

Deborah's legs shook, and she feared she might fall over. "This can't be. It just can't."

"Take the money. I'll send more when I can."

She thrust the money toward him. "I don't need anything from you, Mahlon Stoltzfus. Absolutely nothing ever again!"

He closed his eyes, and fresh tears fell onto his cheeks. When he turned to get into the car, she threw the envelope at him, and money scattered everywhere. She left it there and hurried down the road, glad her home was in the opposite direction from the way his vehicle was headed.

"Deb, I'm sorry!" Mahlon yelled, but she refused to turn back.

Unable to see for the tears, she kept running until her legs and lungs were burning. She thought she might pass out, but she refused to stop.

The sound of hoofbeats came from in front of her. Dizzy and confused, she couldn't make out who got off the horse that stopped somewhere ahead of her. Then Ephraim filled her view.

When he tried to reach for her, she shoved him away. "He was here, and he . . . he left." She sobbed. "Why, Ephraim? He doesn't love me. Why doesn't he love me?"

Her brother stepped forward. When he placed his arms around her, she was too weak to lash out. She melted into his arms and wept.

# Thirty-Nine

Cara looked at herself in the mirror, wondering if wearing the Amish dress and apron was a matter of respect or hypocrisy. Although she hated the style, she loved the teal color. It seemed a shame to cover most of it with a black apron, but Ada thought she should wear both to Dry Lake today. The purpose of the apron was to hide a woman's curves. Thing was, she had no problem showing her figure. She was petite but well built. It was part of who she was, so why hide it?

People were so odd—not just the Amish, but people in general.

Some men paid big chunks of their salary to see half-naked women or prostitutes, while others lived in celibacy, hoping

God would bring them the right woman. Some women did anything for fun or money, while others denied all temptations to remain loyal to men they didn't even like. Most people fell between those two points. Right now she'd like to know where she landed on that imaginary line. Had she become more of a teal-dress girl than a short-top, bare-belly one?

If there was a God, was he ever confused by the choices people made? Or disappointed? It seemed to her that even among the most religious, there was error that caused division and hurt as much as any sin did.

Ada came to the doorway. "You look nice."

"I feel like a bag lady."

Ada's eyes reflected a deep sadness, but she smiled anyway. "Would you rather stand out for men and women who only want to please their eyes or for those who see beyond this life into the next?"

Cara shrugged. "Jeans are comfortable."

"I'd guess men's flannel pajamas and clown suits are comfortable too. When you're willing to wear those in public day in and day out, I'll believe your rationalization about those tight-fitting clothes you wear."

By an act of determination, Cara didn't roll her eyes. "I'd rather live free and make my own choices than be told what to wear."

Ada stepped inside the room and motioned for Cara to turn around. She adjusted the apron ties. "We all submit to something. Athletes submit to the rules of their game. Lawyers and judges submit to the laws. The highest court in the land submits to the Constitution. Even the most rebellious person is submitting to something, usually the darkest part of their sin nature. The Amish choose to submit to the Ordnung in order to be strong against desires that want no boundaries. The preachers, deacons, and bishops help us keep those written and unwritten rules. If you don't want to submit to that, you don't have to, but don't believe that you're free." Ada's voice cracked, and when Cara turned to face her, she saw tears in her eyes. "No one is, Cara. And those who think they are just haven't thought about it long enough."

Cara constantly balked at Ada's explanations about anything Amish. Maybe she'd gone too far. "Is something wrong?"

Ada pulled an envelope out of the bib of her apron. "This had been pushed through the mail slot of the front door when I woke this morning." Ada passed it to her, then went to the window and stared out.

Cara read the writing scrawled on the front. **Mamm, this is the hardest thing I've ever done. I'm not coming back. I'm sorry. Take care of yourself, and help Deborah to forgive me. Love, Mahlon**

The words twisted inside her. At times the endless rules seemed enough to run anyone off. And yet, for most, their way of life came with an undeniable strength against all that the world sought to steal— a person's soul, family, and faith.

She didn't have to believe in God to know that her soul could be trampled on and that right and wrong existed. So why would someone like Mahlon give up the power of the good parts to get free of the weakness of the bad parts? It was a little like what Ada said about everyone submitting to something. Every way of life had frustrations and error.

Ada sat on the bed, looking hurt beyond description. "He sent a letter earlier this week that made me think this might be coming, but I kept praying it wouldn't. I did my best raising Mahlon. There wasn't a day when I didn't put real effort into being a good Mamm and a positive influence."

Her words reminded Cara of something her own mother had written to her dad. She went to her dresser and flipped through the letters. When she found the right one, she took it to Ada and sat beside her. "Mama once wrote that the reason she gave her all to help my dad get free of his addiction was because she had to know she'd done her best, and then she could accept whatever came of it. But she writes it much better than I can say it." Cara passed her the letter.

"Denki." Ada ran her fingers over the folded pages. "I can remember from our school days that Malinda had a special way of saying things."

Cara went to the dresser and gathered a large stack of letters. "Then read these as it suits you."

A horn tooted, which meant Robbie had arrived.

Ada held on to the letters as if embracing a delicate teacup. "I can't go visiting, not today."

"Those men in black—"

"The church leaders aren't men with guns from an Englischer film. They are servants of God who are doing their best, whatever may come of it."

For the first time Cara understood who the men were and why. "You're right. I'm sorry. The church leaders told Ephraim that Mahlon might have left, and he's concerned for his sister. He wants me to come to Dry Lake today and be a go-between for him and Deborah so they can sort of talk."

Ada nodded. "Go. I'll keep Lori here."

"Better Days is still here. The backyard needs more work, but it's safe enough for them to play in. Ephraim roped off two corners that have a lot of glass shards down in the grass. Tell her not to go inside those areas."

"I'll take good care of her." Ada wiped a stray tear. "I don't think Deborah will ever want to see me, so it's just as well I live so far from Dry Lake now. But will you tell her I'm sorry?"

"I will."

The horn tooted again. Cara hurried down the steps and out the front door. The awkwardness between her and Robbie wasn't as miserable as their first ride together, but returning to Dry Lake was difficult enough without trying to hold a conversation with him. After they shared a polite hello, she settled back in her seat, glad he was staying quiet.

"The Masts are good people." Robbie startled her when he spoke. "Abner, Ephraim's dad, just doesn't know who you are. One day you're in jeans, stumbling around like you're drunk, and the next you're wearing a dress you stole off his clothesline. You lived in a barn his son asked you to leave, and then you moved into his son's home. I think that's enough to stretch anyone's trust."

"You know too much."

"I shoot the breeze with Abner pretty regularly. Unlike Ephraim, he's a talker. So, were you stealing from the Swareys and drunk the day he saw you on the road?"

"Good grief." She rolled her eyes. "Yes. I stole a pair of shoes and some stuff for Lori's blisters. And I'd do it again if need be. But I wasn't drunk."

He shrugged and said nothing for a few minutes. "I know that most of the Amish in Dry Lake are sorry for how they treated you. The rest don't know what they think, not yet. So you just say very little and nod a lot when you're around a group of them. Almost all of them know Englischers they like. The Amish are extremely careful who they let have an influence on their children. You seem to have a lot of influence on Abner's child—a grown man, but still Abner's child."

"You know, you actually make sense when you're not being obnoxiously nosy."

Robbie laughed. "At first I didn't trust you being in Ephraim's life either."

"And now?"

"He doesn't care whether I like it or not. And I can't stop you from being in his life. Since I can't get rid of you, I'm trying to keep you from making things worse between him and his family."

"Denki."

Robbie smiled and held up a small plastic bag. "This is for you."

Cara took it and looked inside. He'd bought her a pack of cigarettes. "You know these things kill a person slowly. So if your goal is to get rid of me, that's a poor plan."

He chuckled. "No. I had to stop to get gas on the way here, and I remembered you wanted a smoke last time we rode together."

She held the bag out to him. "That was thoughtful, and I'm impressed. But I'm fully detoxed, by no choice of my own, and I don't intend to re-tox."

"Smart woman." He pulled into the Masts' long driveway. There had to be twenty people under the shade trees, and most of them were looking right at her as the car passed by.

"What was Ephraim thinking?"

"He wanted you to come?"

"Yeah."

"That's interesting. They're here to support Deborah, but I don't see her. She's probably in no mood to be seen, but they want to make a statement to her by their presence." He clicked his tongue in disgust. "I worked beside Mahlon for a lot of years, and I never saw this coming. Leaving is one thing. But to go after joining the faith and asking someone to marry you is just not done—and never like this."

"I need to keep my mouth shut and nod a lot, you say?"

"Yep."

"I don't think I'll be more than a few minutes. I'm going to see if Deborah will come to the hiddy and talk to me. Will you wait?"

He stopped the car. "Abner's under one of the trees behind us. I'll go talk to him for a bit."

"You're welcome to come and go among the Amish as you please?"

"It took a few years of being a good neighbor and a good employee to have this type of ease. But I'm still an outsider, so the rules of play are different. Mahlon could repent and return tomorrow, and it'd take him a decade to be truly welcome in many of the homes."

"And Ephraim?"

"I don't really know. It's different with him. He crossed a line, to be sure. Now that they know who you are, some admire what he did. Others think the two of you probably, well, you know."

"Slept together."

"Yep. And they're offended that he let you stay the night. After the shunning is over, it'll take years to regain most people's respect. He'll never have everyone's."

"You know, there are perks to not having a family or community."

"Yeah? Is it worth it?" He opened the car door.

As soon as they got out, several men and

women headed their way. She recognized Emma and Levi Riehl.

"Cara." Levi stepped forward. "You remember my wife, Emma."

Looking unsure of herself, Emma held out her hand. "Welcome."

**Welcome?** Who was the woman trying to kid?

But she remembered Robbie's advice, so she shook the woman's hand and nodded without saying anything.

"I have some people I'd like you to meet," Levi said.

The names flew at her as Levi introduced aunts, uncles, and cousins. She only nodded and smiled as each person shook her hand, either apologizing to her or welcoming her. Looking past the small crowd, she saw Ephraim leaning against the side of the house, a gentle smile revealing his thoughts. He'd paid the price for this day, and he continued to pay. Had he known this would happen when he asked her to come to Dry Lake today?

To her left, Robbie stood talking to the

man she'd seen in the pasture her first day in Dry Lake and who'd come to Ephraim's the night she and Lori were dancing. He slowly walked toward her.

Levi didn't introduce them as he had with everyone else.

"I'm Abner, Ephraim's father. I . . . I was wrong to tell everyone to beware of you—that you were drunk or on drugs when I'd only caught a glimpse of you."

Cara swallowed, wishing a simple nod would do as an answer. "I'm sure I looked as odd to you that day as you did to me. Besides, soon after you called me a drunk, I called your son heartless." She stole a glimpse of Ephraim. "It seems we were both wrong."

Abner held out his hand, but when she placed hers in his, he didn't shake it; he patted it. "Denki."

"How's Ada?" A woman's voice came from somewhere above her.

Abner looked to a spot at the side of the house, and Cara followed his gaze. Deborah stood at a second-story window, looking out.

Cara stepped closer. "She said to tell you she's sorry."

Without saying anything else, Deborah moved away from the window.

Levi motioned to a chair.

Cara took a seat. Women were whispering. Some were crying.

"We don't understand why he left." Emma sat in a chair beside her. "It just doesn't make sense."

In her mind's eye Cara could see how much sadness they must've felt when her mother left. It struck her that when she left a place, no one cared—except Mike. Maybe living under a set of rules that helped hold families together was worth it.

"When your mother left, we thought we understood. It wasn't until recently that we found out her real reason."

Cara wanted to ask what Emma meant, but she kept nodding. Besides, she didn't want to get all friendly and comfortable with these people. They felt remorse and pity. That wasn't good enough. She'd outgrown taking scraps of affection from a family's table a long time ago.

Deborah came around the side of the house, barefoot and no apron. Wisps of hair dangled around her face and neck, and her white cap sat a bit off center on her head, but no one seemed to mind. Her face held little of the gentle beauty Cara had seen at the auction. Right now her complexion reminded Cara of a puffy gray storm cloud. "I want to go to Ada, Daed."

Her father studied her. "Of course you can go to her. She needs a visit from you."

"I want to be her Ruth."

Abner shook his head. "Child, listen to me."

"No." Deborah broke into tears. "You listen. Please, Daed."

Confused, Cara turned to Emma. "Who's Ruth?" she whispered.

Emma leaned closer to her. "She's talking of Naomi and Ruth. From the Bible."

Cara was tempted to tell her she wasn't into fairy tales, but she simply raised her eyebrows like she understood. Vapory thoughts floated to her, ones that doubted her doubts rather than God. It did seem that sometimes that book spoke clear and honest truth about who people are—not that she'd read it very much.

Abner looked to Cara, studying her. If she knew about the story of Naomi and Ruth, she might be able to piece together what he was thinking.

"This is your home, Deborah. We need you. But if you want to spend a night or two away, you should."

"Ada needs me. Her only child has left. Your health is much improved since the surgery. And even if I leave, you have six children still living at home—five of them daughters. Can't you spare one for a woman who has spent her life being a good Mamm but now has no children at all?"

Cara realized that Deborah was asking to live with Ada. Forever. Abner looked to Cara again, and she almost read his thoughts. He was afraid of losing Deborah altogether if she lived in the same house as Cara. She couldn't blame the man. Cara had little allegiance to this faith of theirs, and she'd done damage to Ephraim's life without even knowing it.

Anxiety crept over her as she realized

that for Deborah to move in with Ada, Cara probably needed to move out. They wouldn't want her to have that much time or possible influence with Deborah. Cara looked to Ephraim. He'd done so much to see that she had a roof over her head and could sit among her mother's people and talk with them like this.

"I can move out." She said it softly, but enough people heard her that they began to pass the word along to those who hadn't.

Deborah stepped closer to her father. "That's not what I want. Ada's rental agreement is based on the work Cara is doing." She turned to Cara. "And she believes you're meant to be beside her. I don't want to take anything from Ada. I want to make up for what's missing now."

Abner sighed—a deep and weary one— as he took a seat beside Cara. "My first wife, Ephraim and Deborah's mother, loved your mother as much as Ada did. Were you aware of that?"

Cara shook her head.

"It's the reason Ephraim was allowed to spend so much time with you that summer your mother brought you here. My wife took one look into your eyes and trusted who you were. But I was so wrapped up in my fears of what Malinda would do to this district that I believed all the wrong things. It was easier to believe Malinda got what she deserved than to take a chance on reaching out. So we told her you could return but she couldn't."

Deborah moved a chair beside her father and sat.

He took Deborah's hand in his. "I've spent years too afraid of losing what's mine to see who anyone else really is. As a preacher I encouraged people to build an invisible fortress around themselves and their families. But that caused us to start carrying so much suspicion toward outsiders that there was no way for a stranger not to look guilty over the slightest thing. Then it became easy to turn to each other and say, 'I knew they couldn't be trusted,' or 'I knew they'd cause trouble.'"

He looked to Ephraim, who stood at the far edge of the house, an outcast inside his family's yard. "Ephraim and Deborah take after their mother." He turned to his daughter. "And Ada has a good heart like your Mamm. If you want to reach out to her like this, you do it, child. I won't stop you."

Deborah broke into tears and hugged him. "Denki." She stood, and several women surrounded her and walked with her back into the house.

# Forty

In spite of the open windows, the humid late-August air didn't stir. The aroma of Ada's baking filled the house as Deborah steadied the ladder for Cara while she rolled the wallpaper-piercing tool over another section of the wall.

Ada's telephone rang loud and long. The bishop had approved the installation of the phone for business purposes. Soon the screen door slammed, and Cara knew Ada was scurrying across the backyard and to the barn in hopes of catching the call.

It'd been two long months since Mahlon had left. Deborah's grief and confusion seemed to have no bounds most days, but Cara tried to keep her moving. Ada's grief was quieter and maybe deeper, but Deborah's presence seemed to help by giving Ada someone to tend to. Cara struggled with a sadness that had nothing to do with their loss, but she wouldn't tell them. Mahlon was gone and not coming back. Ephraim was in Dry Lake, with Anna Mary, she guessed, but she tried not to think about it.

Lifting the hem of her dress, Cara moved up a rung. With Amish coming in and out of Ada's home, Cara decided to stick to wearing dresses. Deborah had lots of clothes to share, and Cara hoped that her choices might reflect well on Ephraim. It couldn't hurt, and if it made any difference in how the church leaders looked at him, she'd wear the not-so-quaint garb without argument.

She passed the piercing tool to Deborah. "This area of scoring is done."

Every move Deborah made was slow, like that of a woman bearing thick, heavy chains. She lifted a bucket of warm water and vinegar to Cara. "Here you go."

Cara dipped a thick sponge into the solution and began soaking the walls with it while Deborah continued to hold tight to the wobbling ladder.

Many a night after Deborah first moved in, Cara lay atop the covers beside her and held her while she cried. Those first few weeks Cara had to prod both women to keep moving toward an unknown future. Now, with the help of the Amish communities in Dry Lake and Hope Crossing, Ada and Deborah even had times of laughter. And they'd expanded their business by selling baked goods to a local hotel for its restaurant and continental breakfast bar.

Cara stepped off the ladder. "Let's move to that segment. It should be ready to peel."

They slid the ladder to the right spot, and she climbed it again.

After one of Deborah's rare visits to Dry Lake, she came back saying that Ephraim's ban was over. Once he'd proved his intention to live as the church leaders wanted, the bishop reconsidered his shunning. Since the first part of July, Ephraim had been considered a member in good standing, and he'd returned to work.

She'd seen him just three times since June, when he'd cleaned up the backyard. Even then he came in with others from Dry Lake, and she only saw him in a room full of people. Their quiet mornings over coffee, humorous banter during the workday, and long walks at night were gone, but she'd remember them forever.

Would he?

Even though she still wished things were different for her and Ephraim, she'd found a bit of peace with her past and had chosen to stop blaming those who may or may not have been guilty of anything. And now she tolerated, maybe even enjoyed, getting letters and visits from her aunts, uncles, and cousins.

"You might want to hold the ladder from behind me, Deb."

Deborah gasped. "Oh my, you're right. That Amish dress does nothing for modesty when a girl is on a ladder."

"Red silk bikini—is that the view, Deborah?" Cara grabbed the top edge of the wallpaper and slowly pulled it toward her. "Cross your fingers."

"And let go of the ladder?"

"Which is more important, this wallpaper coming off in one piece or me not falling?"

The rare sound of Deborah chuckling warmed Cara's heart. "Do I have to choose right now?"

A thick splat of wallpaper remover hit the floor. "Sorry. Nothing's harder to get off than ancient wallpaper. What'd they use on this stuff?" Cara stepped down a rung on the ladder.

"I've decided it's elephant glue."

Peeling the wallpaper slowly, Cara came down another notch. "What's elephant glue?"

"You know, the kind of stuff that would make an elephant stick to the walls."

Cara peered down at her.

Deborah made a face. "It made sense to me when I thought of it."

Cara pursed her lips, suppressing laughter. "Was that one of those thoughts you have when you're half asleep, half awake?"

"Why, yes it was."

"I like those. They're amusing. Not

much help, but always worth a good chuckle. My favorites are the ones you mumble right before falling asleep."

"So, are you going to the Hope Crossing church meeting with me and Ada this Sunday?"

"Once was enough for me, thanks."

"Girls," Ada called, "lunch is ready. The deliveryman called, and he can't do his pickups today, so I've got my pies all loaded up in the buggy to take to the bakery, hotel, and diner. I'll be back in a couple of hours. Lori's going with me."

"Okay, Ada. Thank you."

"Denki." Deborah shifted to the side. "Was it the backless bench or the length of the service?"

"Neither." Cara tugged on the last part of the attached paper and stepped down to the floor. "In spite of your great efforts over the last month to teach me your language, I have no clue what's being said. Why sit through it when I need you to do a summation afterward?" Cara took the wallpaper to the tarp in the corner and dropped it, then wiped her hands on the black apron. She slid her arm around Deborah and guided her out of the room. "So, what does **geziemt** mean?"

"Depends. It can mean suitable, as in a suitable mate. Or it could mean becoming, as in beautiful to God in dress and behavior." They walked down the stairs. "Where did you hear it? Maybe I can figure out which meaning was intended."

"I heard it at church."

"The pastor was talking about living true to who God made you to be and not seeking to be who the world wants to make you into."

"Why is it so important to you to go to church? It's an off day. Why ruin it?"

"Because—"

Cara held up her hand, interrupting Deborah. "I meant that as a rhetorical question."

"Meaning you didn't really intend for me to answer?"

"Exactly." Cara pushed against the swinging door to the kitchen. Heat smacked her in the face. "Living Amish gives new meaning to the phrase 'If you can't stand the heat, get out of the kitchen.'"

"Let's sit under the shade tree out back."

"I vote let's buy an air conditioner."

"An air conditioner wouldn't be much use without electricity, my dear Englischer. But a battery-operated fan is an idea I could go for, not that our bishop would."

They grabbed the plates with their sandwiches, chips, and fruit. "How does Ada stand it during summer months?"

"I'll take that as a rhetorical question. It'll save me trying to explain it." After they sat at the table, Deborah bowed her head for a silent prayer, and Cara waited.

Deborah lifted her head. "A couple of girls from this district asked if I'd go with them to the singing this Saturday. I'm not sure I'm ready. Just thinking about going makes me start crying all over again."

"Why?"

"Because Mahlon leaving me like he did was equal to a public flogging. Everybody knows he not only broke my heart, but he humiliated me."

"Pffft." Cara rolled her eyes. "If they

have any sense, they're thinking of how insane he is for leaving you. What he did was about him, Deb. If I were you, I'd lift my head and dare them to think less of me because of someone else's stupidity."

"If you're right, why am I the one who feels like a total idiot for loving him?"

"Because he sucker-punched you."

"He didn't do it on purpose."

"And he didn't do it by accident either."

Deb shrugged. "Maybe you're right. If I go to a singing, do you want to come with me?"

"No way. It's for singles, not widows, right?"

"Ya. To me singings are for so much more than finding someone. It's a time for making friends who'll still be friends fifty years from now. The walls vibrate from the songs and laughter. I think I'm ready to make some real friends in Hope Crossing."

"Then you better start inviting people over more often."

Deborah sat back in her chair, smiling. "So you're saying you're not a friend?"

Cara blinked. "I . . . I . . . me?"

"I like your humility, Cara. It'd serve you well as an Amish woman."

"It's hard to be Amish if you don't believe in God, don't you think?" Deborah opened her mouth to speak, but Cara held up her hand. "Just take it as a rhetorical question, Deb."

Thunder rumbled, and the smell of rain hung in the air as Cara snuggled with Lori on the bed, reading to her. When Ada found this children's book in a box of things while moving here, she gave it to Lori. At first **Shoo-Fly Girl** seemed harmless enough. But it was all about a little girl growing up Amish, and Lori loved it.

"She loved going to church, huh, Mom?"

"Yes. Now nestle down and go to sleep." Cara got off the bed and laid the sheet loosely over her daughter, wondering how anyone slept in this August heat.

"I want to go to church with Ephraim again."

A dozen emotions washed over her at

the mention of his name, and the ache of missing him stirred again. "I'm not sure sneaking in to sit in his lap that one time could be considered **going** with him." She kissed her daughter's forehead. "Besides, you can't even understand what's being said."

"I know some of the words now. Deborah's been teaching me. I don't have to know all the words. But I can feel what they're saying, can't you?"

She brushed strands of hair away from Lori's face. "Yeah, sometimes, I guess."

Hearing the thunder grow louder, Cara hoped Deborah's night out with her new friends in Hope Crossing didn't get rained out.

The longing to believe in something other than what she could see had wrapped around her heart lately. Sometimes it seemed God was everywhere. And yet, at the same time, she didn't know if she could really believe that. Santa Claus and the Easter Bunny seemed real too when she was little.

"Shoo-Fly Girl loves being Amish."

"It's ridiculously hard, living as they do. There are more rules than bugs in a barn."

She giggled. "But there's rules to everything. You told me that lots of times before we even met the Amish."

"Yeah, I guess I did. Go to sleep. Do you want me to leave a low-burning kerosene lamp on the dresser tonight?"

"Nope. I'm trusting God like Shoo-Fly Girl. Do you wanna pray?"

No, she didn't. Not now. Not ever. She had prayed when her mother died, begging him to give her back. She had prayed when in foster homes, crying out for someone to care. But one day she realized no one was listening to her prayers.

"I'll close my eyes, and you say the words, okay?"

Lori shut her eyes tight. "Dear God, forgive me for doing wrong, and help me do right. Amen."

"Amen."

Cara picked up the kerosene lamp. "Good night, Lorabean."

"Mom?"

"Yes?"

"Do you trust God?"

"You need to go on to sleep now, okay?"

"Okay. Night, Mom."

"Good night." Cara patted Better Days and then pulled the door shut behind her.

She stood at the top of the stairs, tempted to read the same diaries and letters from her mother that she read every night. But it seemed she should use this time to do something else. There was nothing new inside that box her dad had sent her, but she made her way down the steps and to the hall closet anyway. After setting the lamp on a side table, she reached to the top shelf and grabbed her gateway to the past. With the box in hand, she picked up the lantern and went into the kitchen. Once seated at the table, she opened the box.

She set her mother's Bible to the side before opening all the letters and spreading them out on the table. She'd read every one and all of the journals a dozen times.

The stairs creaked, and Ada walked into the kitchen, carrying a lantern. She ran her hand across Cara's back as she passed her. "Can I fix you a glass of ice water?"

"No thanks." Cara leaned back in her chair. "Ada, if your district had never learned the truth about why my mother left Dry Lake, would they be writing to me or visiting?"

"I think so, but it's hard to know." With a glass of water in hand, Ada took a seat.

"It had to break my mom's heart to discover her fiancé's secret just weeks before the wedding."

"Rueben's been in a lot of trouble for the secret he kept."

"But not shunned?"

Ada shook her head. "He might be later on, but the bishop hasn't decided what to do yet. He's in a bad spot—needing to issue discipline to a man who did something wrong more than thirty years ago. If he's not careful, a lot of the youth will look at another shunning, along with Ephraim's and Mahlon's troubles, and not want to join the faith."

"It still makes me mad. It'd be okay with me if they shunned both Rueben and his wife forever."

"And it's harder to take since it's Anna Mary's parents, no?"

Cara nodded. "Too hard sometimes."

"You remind me so much of your mother. You've helped me and Deborah survive the worst thing imaginable. I couldn't have handled the last couple of months of bearing what Mahlon's done without looking at what God brought out of your heartache. And that awful imaginary whip you keep cracking to make me and Deborah stay focused on building a business. I'm actually glad you've been a jaded little taskmaster."

Cara's eyes stung with tears as she looked at one of her mother's letters. "Sometimes I almost feel whole again, like I've found answers that make sense out of some of my crazy life. At other times I feel so confused, bitter, and lost I can't stand myself." She dropped the letter onto the table. "I keep going over every piece of writing as if trying to verify that life's worth it."

She looked at her mother's closed Bible.

Of all the items her dad had sent that she'd read and reread, she hadn't yet opened that book. She'd stolen a few minutes with Ephraim's or Ada's but not her mom's. It always gave her an eerie feeling, as if it contained more of her mother's heart than her letters.

Ada slid her hand over Cara's. "Only God can redeem life and make it worthwhile. Without His worth covering us and being in us, man's history carries only faded hopes and broken dreams." She picked up the Bible from the table and handed it to Cara. "He can redeem your past and all the pain that awaits in the future."

Cara held the Bible between her two hands and let it fall open. The pages fluttered, and a yellow piece of paper caught her attention. She laid the book on the table and looked through it. After a few moments she found the paper and pulled it out. Unfolding it, she immediately recognized her mother's handwriting.

**I will be your Father, and you will be my sons and daughters.**

The words flooded her heart.

Choking back tears, she stood. Her heart pumped against her chest as thoughts and understanding pounded against her. "He's real." The room seemed to be shrinking, and she felt desperate for time alone. "I need to go for a walk. You'll stay with Lori?"

"Sure I will."

She hurried out the back door. Mist fell from the sky as she walked as fast as she could. Pain flooded her heart as if she were reliving every loss she'd ever sustained. Fragments of her past ripped at her, begging for answers. But there were none. There was only a dark hole in her soul, draining her of strength. The rain fell harder as she followed the narrow trail to the top of the mountain.

Looking out over the valley below, she clenched her fists. "Why?" she screamed into the rain. "I want to know why!" Her tears mingled with the rain, but no answer returned to her.

Thoughts of being inside Ephraim's barn, hungry and miserable as she sought refuge, filled her view more than the rain-drenched sky. She'd landed there out of desperation. The long journey began because she had pieces of memories and her mother had hidden a message inside her diary. But most of all, she'd landed there because something inside her, something beyond herself, had led her.

As if watching a movie in her mind's eye, she saw Ephraim standing at the door of the barn, holding out his hand. He didn't offer answers to all she wanted to know, but he gave her a way to a better life. He offered help and strength and himself, as a shield of sorts—but not the kind of protection she tried to give Lori, where the sharpness of reality was hidden until she was older. The shield didn't hide reality or pain; it simply absorbed the impact of each blow before it made its way to her.

Suddenly he changed, and a man she didn't recognize held his hand out to her. He was dressed even more oddly than the Amish, with darker skin, hair, and eyes. But most of all he had compassion for her and a love so deep she couldn't begin to understand it.

It had to be Jesus. As He looked at her, it seemed she was no longer the woman she thought herself to be. It was as if she was part of something bigger, and yet she knew she was nothing. She felt fully accepted, like a member of the family, but only because He'd opened the door—similar to the way Ephraim had.

Her earlier question of why didn't matter. The only question that mattered now was what she would choose from this point forward.

She sank to her knees.

Forty-One

With a book open and a mug of coffee in hand, Ephraim sat on his couch, listening to the rain.

He'd spent thousands of quiet evenings by himself since building this house nine years ago. Before Cara none of those times had been lonely. Well . . . maybe a little. But he'd never been lonely for someone in particular.

Then Cara showed up, and without her knowledge she passed on to him a long and healthy life of true loneliness.

The lonesomeness tempted him to . . .

He stopped himself cold, growled softly, and went to the kitchen. Lightning flashed across the sky, immediately followed by a loud boom of thunder. He thought he heard a phone ring. Setting his mug on the table, he cocked his head, listening. He did hear a phone ring. Three. Four. Five rings. Then silence.

Inside his dark home he waited. The phone rang again. He grabbed his black felt hat and flew out the door. Five rings, a pause, and then more rings meant it wasn't a business call or a wrong number. It was someone trying to reach him. He bolted across the soaked field and driveway. Fumbling through the dark, he grabbed the phone.

"Hello."

"Ephraim." Ada's voice held concern. "I'm in a little fix."

"What's up?"

"Cara went for a walk, but then the skies opened up. She's been gone over two hours. The creek's flooded. I'm watching Lori, and Deborah's not here, so I'm not sure what to do."

"I'll hire a driver and be there as soon as I can. Whatever you do, don't leave Lori, and don't try to cross that creek with her in tow."

Ephraim called half a dozen drivers before finding Bill at home. He arrived within ten minutes. In another fifteen Ephraim was climbing out of the car at Ada's house. She opened the door for him.

"Has she returned?" Ephraim had to yell to be heard over the pouring rain.

Ada motioned him in, leaving the door open for Bill to follow. "No. She was pretty upset when she left here."

"Why?"

"We were talking, and she had her mother's Bible in hand, the one her dad mailed to her. She found a note in it. I think she was shaking when she looked at me and said, 'He's real.' Then she bolted."

Excitement poured into him, making his head spin for a moment. But if learning she had relatives in Dry Lake was stressful, realizing God was real had to be hundreds of times more emotional. "Where was she headed?"

"I don't know, but she went through the pasture where that winding creek is sure to catch her. As a city girl, will she understand how dangerous the currents get in weather like this?"

Ephraim knew where she'd gone, but Ada's question worried him. "I'll take your horse."

"You want help?" Bill asked.

"No. We only have one horse, and it's too dangerous on foot. I'll find her." He hurried down the steps.

"Ephraim," Ada hollered through the pouring rain. He stopped. She motioned to him and then disappeared back inside. When he reached her door, she passed him a quilt and a two-way radio. "Let me know the minute you find her. If I don't hear from you within an hour, I'll call the police."

Ephraim spoke what he prayed would be true. "You'll hear from me."

Riding bareback, he spurred the horse along the muddy trail. Thunder rumbled in the distance as the rain slowed. When he came to the creek, he found it had flooded its banks and spanned into the lowlands of the pasture. As he carefully guided the horse through the shallowest area, he tried to block thoughts of Cara struggling to cross and being swept downstream. Soon the horse was on the other side. "Cara!" He cupped his hands around his mouth and called to her.

He wondered how she felt about her discovery. The problem with believing was it changed everything inside a person without altering the past. And sometimes it didn't change the present either—only the person's heart.

Even under the canopy of trees, large scattered drops pelted him. He pulled his felt hat down tighter and kept the horse moving forward along the slippery trail. "Cara!" he called against the rain, but his voice didn't carry far.

Through a clearing he spotted the old barn she loved so much. Hoping he'd find her safe, he felt peace warm him. When he came within a hundred feet of the barn, a flash of lightning illuminated the fields briefly, but he didn't see any sign of her. He spurred the horse onward. "Cara!"

The barn door opened. She stood in the

entryway with dripping wet hair and clothes. He urged the horse toward the barn. She stepped back, giving the animal room to enter the rugged structure. He tugged on the reins and came to a halt.

When she looked up at him, hope and longing tempted him to say things he knew he shouldn't.

"He's real." Her tone sounded both certain and surprised.

Too emotional to speak, he pointed to a wooden cattle gate behind her, and then he held out his hand. With the rain pouring and the creek rising, they needed to get to the valley and cross over before the currents grew too strong, or they could end up stranded on this side for the next day or two. She climbed up several rungs of craggy gate and took his hand. He pulled her onto the horse behind him.

He passed her the blanket and waited while she draped it around her. He shifted so he could look into her eyes.

Using the blanket she wiped rain off her face. "Just for a second I saw a man. He . . . He died so that no one would be separated

from Him the way I was from my family."
In spite of her proclamation, confusion was
reflected in her eyes.

Ephraim placed his hat on her head and
brushed one finger down her cheek, feeling
more connected to her than to his own
self. He squared himself on the horse. She
wrapped her arms around him and laid her
cheek on his back. He pulled the two-way
radio out of his pocket. "Ada."

"I'm here. Have you found her?"

"Yes. We're heading back."

He slid the two-way into his pocket.
With one hand he guided the horse, and
with the other he kept his hand on hers,
glad the darkness and rain hid the tears
that stung his eyes.

She was safe.

And she believed.

The creek water swirled higher and
faster when he crossed the second time, but
soon they were in Ada's barn, and he was
helping Cara off the horse. She passed his
hat back to him. The place smelled of fresh
hay. Bundled in the wet quilt, Cara leaned

against a stall, watching him wipe the horse down with an old towel.

He tossed extra oats into the horse's trough. "I . . . just want you to know you shouldn't feel the need to be Amish." He tossed hay into the stall and closed the gate. "You're free to go wherever. Join wherever."

"Thank you, 'From. For everything."

He wrapped her in his arms, feeling her tremble even through the blanket. "You scared me." He propped his cheek against her head, and they stood, watching the rain.

Forty-Two

Deborah put the finishing touches of frosting on the last cake, hoping she and Ada had enough goodies for tonight. It seemed the perfect way to spend Labor Day— baking and preparing for company. Ada was out front, tending to her flower garden, and Cara had gone for a long walk with Lori. All of them giving Deborah a few minutes alone before she had to greet a houseful of people—friends, family, and near strangers who knew about Mahlon running out on her.

Even though longing for him still held her prisoner some days, she'd grown weary of being embarrassed over what he'd done to her. She talked to Ada about the shame they both carried, and they admitted to only going out when necessary. So they decided to have an open house, welcoming Amish from both districts—Dry Lake and Hope Crossing.

Cara was right; it wasn't Deborah's or Ada's fault that Mahlon hadn't cherished them or the Old Order lifestyle.

The word **cherished** made her thoughts turn to Ephraim. Since the church leaders had lifted the ban from him, he'd probably come tonight too—if for no other reason than to catch a glimpse of Cara. It wasn't always easy, but Deborah said nothing to either of them about the other. They'd asked that of her, and she'd stuck to it. But she didn't need a conversation with Ephraim to know he was in love, and Cara didn't seem to know it.

The church leaders had insisted Ephraim return to Dry Lake in mid-June, and it was now early September, yet he'd already returned to the status of being a member in good standing. Deborah agreed with the bishop's point on the matter—it'd be hypocrisy to continue punishing Ephraim for handling Cara's situation wrong when all of them had been wrong concerning her in one way or another. Even though Ephraim had permission to see Cara, he'd yet to do so. He didn't want to influence her decision of whether to choose the Old Ways or not, so he kept his distance. But he'd told Deborah it drove him crazy.

Thankfully, Daed's health was still improving, so he had been some real help to Ephraim after Mahlon left without notice. That took some weight off Ephraim and gave Daed some of his self-respect back. With business booming like it was, Ephraim was looking to hire Amish men outside of Dry Lake.

When Deborah heard a horse and buggy stop near the house, she glanced at the clock. Whoever had just arrived had come much earlier than expected. She looked through the window and saw Lena heading for the house. Her beautiful cousin never seemed bothered by the blue birthmark across her cheek. Deborah was slowly and painfully adjusting to the idea of being alone, but she couldn't imagine what Lena felt—twenty-three years old and had never been asked out. Warmth wrapped around Deborah as she finally grasped what Lena always said—it's not about what's on her face that makes people whisper or the men avoid her. It's about what's in their own hearts.

Mahlon left because of his heart, and Deborah was ready to admit she'd never really known him. But now, nearly three months later, she knew a time would come when she'd be grateful to be free of him. But her love for Ada grew with each passing week.

The back door opened, and Lena stepped inside. "Oh my, it smells good in here." She held the door open, and Jonathan soon appeared, carrying a keg on his shoulder.

He set the barrel on the floor. "Hey, Little Debbie. I made a batch of the good stuff. Thought you might want a strong drink to get you through the next few hours."

It seemed odd that he understood

tonight wouldn't be easy for her. "How strong?"

"Extra lemons, less sugar."

She puckered her lips and made a smacking sound. "Jonathan's famous lemonade gone sourer just for me."

He dipped his finger in the almost empty bowl of frosting and placed it in his mouth. "Man, I miss you and Ada being right up the street from me."

"Ya, but we make a profit now."

Lena laughed. "You say he kept eating the profits?"

"Hello?" Anna Mary's voice echoed from the back steps.

"In here." Deborah stepped to the doorway and saw Rachel, Linda, Nancy, Lydia, Frieda, and Esther. They were all together again, and it'd never felt this good.

"Hi." Anna Mary hugged her. "We rode with Jonathan, but we got off the wagon out front and talked with Ada for a bit."

"We all came early to help you and Ada get ready," Rachel said.

Anna Mary looked around the room conspiratorially. "And to make sure we're in place early to scope out any single men who come from Hope Crossing."

The girls laughed, but Deborah knew it couldn't have been easy for Anna Mary to come tonight either. Cara lived here, and if Ephraim showed up, which he was likely to do, it'd be tough on Anna Mary. Yet here she stood.

Strength seeped into every part of Deborah, and she passed a ladle to Jonathan. He opened the lid to the keg while Deborah grabbed a stack of plastic cups and passed one to each girl.

Deborah set a bowl of ice on the table. "So, Jonathan, you brought eight girls with you, four of which are totally single, and it sounds like not a one of them is interested in someone from Dry Lake."

"That's okay." Jonathan dipped a ladle into citrusy liquid. "I'm not interested in anyone living in Dry Lake either."

Lena chuckled as he filled her cup with the shimmering yellow juice.

Ada walked into the kitchen from the front hallway. "So where are Cara and Lori?"

Deborah passed a cup of lemonade to Ada. "They went for a long walk. Cara wanted to be sure Better Days was tired so he'd stay settled as people come in and out."

When everyone held a cup of lemonade in hand, Jonathan raised his. "To Ada's house—"

"Ada's House!" Deborah interrupted him. She turned to Ada. "That's what this place needs—a good name, ya?"

"Ada's House?" Ada looked a little unsure, and then she broke into a huge smile. "Ada's House." She lifted her cup toward Jonathan.

He smiled. "To Ada's House. May God bless it beyond all they can ask or imagine."

Deborah knew well Jonathan's favorite Bible passage, the one he'd just spoken a few words from—Ephesians 3:20. She'd never been touched by those words like he always had, but this time they took on new meaning. She took a sip of the lemonade as the words filled her with hope and dreams of what lay ahead.

Ada placed her arm around Deborah's back. "He already has blessed me above what I'd asked or dreamed, because of you," Ada whispered.

Deborah raised her eyebrows, playfully. "But I'm open to even more. Ya?"

Ada laughed and nodded. "If you are, I am."

Ephraim ran his hand across the wood in front of him, removing the dusting of sawdust. Thoughts of Cara lingered continually. And rumors about her swirled like mad. Some said the church leaders intended to welcome her into the Amish community. Others said that there were two single Amish men in Hope Crossing eager to court her and that the Riehls were trying to build a relationship with her.

He'd love to be first in line to court her. Actually, he'd like to be the only one in line. But he wouldn't pursue her.

When she first entered his home, she'd made it clear she didn't want to owe him anything. He understood what had happened with Johnny—Cara marrying him for protection and a roof over her head without being in love with him. But even as he reminded himself of his stance, every part of him longed to see her, to tell her how he felt.

She wasn't the same person she would have been if she'd been raised Old Order. Innocence and trust had been stripped from her, one bad experience after another. Still, he found even her less-than-trusting attitude fascinating. She beckoned him so much it scared him.

He drew a deep breath and set the tools in their place. Maybe he should go to Deborah's gathering and at least get a few minutes with Cara. She should know he wasn't seeing Anna Mary anymore, shouldn't she?

Was that too self-serving?

Still unsure what he should or shouldn't say to her, he went into his office and dialed Robbie. No sense in taking an hour to get to Hope Crossing when Robbie could have him there in ten minutes.

In her caped dress, black apron, and bare feet, Cara spoke to Deborah's visitors before she walked past them and to the front porch. They seemed like a nice group, even Anna Mary, who was clearly uncomfortable around Cara—not that she blamed her. A lot had taken place between Cara and Ephraim, and whether he'd told Anna Mary about it or not, she had to sense it.

The sun danced through the leaves as the late-afternoon shadows of September fell across the yard. It didn't matter how hard she tried not to, she missed Ephraim just as much now as when the church leaders came here to reason with him and he returned to Dry Lake in mid-June.

She'd talked to him briefly and only a couple of times since the night she was caught in that rainstorm. Had anything ever felt as powerful and right as being in his arms while they watched the rain? But if he came tonight, he'd spend his time with Anna Mary.

Regardless of Ephraim or anything or anyone else, Cara was close to joining the faith. A few things nagged at her. She'd talked to Deborah and Ada about putting down roots of her own in Hope Crossing after she finished working on the house. Ada said that'd be quite a while, but then she said if Cara wanted to stay near them and yet live as an Englischer, the storage rooms above the carriage house could be refinished for her, and electricity and a phone could be added.

They were of the same mind-set as Ephraim—joining the Amish faith wasn't necessary to being a part of their lives. She leaned back against a porch column and closed her eyes. With each passing week more of her wanted to join the faith. It had aspects she wouldn't find easy—like never cutting her hair, wearing black stockings even in summer, answering to a church leader as her authority, and trying to understand the language. But she'd grown accustomed to most of their ways.

A man cleared his throat, and she jolted. Two men in black suits stood in front of her. Since the hitching posts and space for the carriages were around back, she hadn't expected anyone to come in or out the front door. She recognized one of them and realized she should greet them more properly, so she jumped to her feet.

The familiar man held out his hand. "My name's Sol Fisher. I'm Ephraim's bishop."

She wondered how odd she must look to them with short hair and no Kapp but in an Amish dress. She shook his hand. "I'm Cara Moore. Malinda Riehl's daughter."

"Yes, we know." He gestured to the man next to him. "This is Jacob King. He's a deacon in Hope Crossing."

She shook his hand too. "Ada's inside, as well as Deborah. Others too. Did you want me to call one of them?"

"We'll visit with them in a bit. First we'd like to talk to you." Sol ran his hand down his gray beard. "Ephraim was wrong to have you in his home unsupervised. Do you understand that?"

**More than ever.** She nodded.

The man drew a deep breath. "That's a serious matter. But I ask you to forgive me for being so upset with him that I didn't see you—the one who needed our help. I didn't look beyond your outward appearance or the rumors. If he hadn't reached out to you, none of us would have. I apologize for that."

Remembering her words to Ephraim— that she'd believe there was a God if the bishop apologized—she had to suppress her amusement. "Thank you."

Jacob stepped forward. "You need to say, 'I forgive you.' It's the Amish way."

Trying to say the words, she realized how humbling some of the Amish ways were. "I forgive you."

He held out his hand again. "I stand before Him forgiven. Thank you."

"Is it that easy?"

"No, but it's the first step. I'll wrestle with regret and you with feelings of resentment at times. But we've begun the journey by an act of our will and faith. If you need to talk about it more, my door will always be open to you."

Jacob nodded. "A fine first step you've taken, Cara."

Feeling awkward and out of place, she couldn't think of anything to say.

"We've been keeping an eye on you since you moved in with Ada," Jacob said. "You've come to a few services with her and Deborah."

"Yes."

"Since your mother was Amish and she wanted you raised in our faith," Jacob continued, "we feel you should know that we have no reservations if you want to consider becoming one of us. I brought you a schedule and a map to each home where services will be held."

Sol nodded. "It's not easy to live as we do, and it should not be considered lightly, but we're here to answer any of your questions."

"Thank you."

"And you're welcome to visit and move about either community. Of course we will come see you if an issue of improper behavior arises."

She had come to accept that rules were a part of every society and that if they accomplished a lofty goal, they were worth it. And it was clear that living Amish had more promise than it did restrictions.

A desire to see Ephraim swept over her. She wanted to tell him the bishop had apologized. Far, far more than that, she was tired of missing him. The men went inside, and Cara sat on the porch again, thinking everything through.

Lori would love joining the faith. It was all she ever talked about. She already wore Amish dresses to public school and didn't care what the other kids thought. She'd never liked wearing pants, which used to frustrate Cara. Once Cara went through all she needed to in order to join, Lori could go to the one-room Amish schoolhouse not far from here. She'd love that too. But none of those things were why Cara wanted to join the faith.

It was an odd way to live, but she understood the value of it.

Robbie's car pulled to the curb, and Ephraim got out.

The hardest thing in becoming Amish would be knowing it'd make no difference between her and Ephraim. But if Deborah could see her future without Mahlon, Cara could find a way to see hers without Ephraim. Even so, she wanted to tell him about her decision to join the faith before she told anyone else, and she wanted to tell him about some of the Amish skills Deborah and Ada had been teaching her.

Anna Mary would just have to deal with her talking to Ephraim.

He ambled up the sidewalk, a half grin across his handsome face. "Hey."

"Hi."

He stopped at the foot of the steps. "What are you doing out here by yourself?"

"Wishing you were here to talk to. Got a minute?"

His gray blue eyes mesmerized her, and she tried to slow her heart.

He took a seat beside her. "I have all evening."

"I don't think Anna Mary will appreciate that sentiment."

He propped his forearms on his knees. "Well, that's sort of what I came to tell you. Anna Mary and I have stopped seeing each other."

Her heart went crazy. "What? Why didn't Deborah tell me?"

"Because I asked her not to."

"Why?"

"Reasons we should probably talk about in a few months, okay?"

"Yeah. I knew Anna Mary would be hurt and angry, but I didn't think she'd dump you for being friendly to me."

"She didn't, and can we change the subject?"

"Not yet. When did you two break up?"

"Before you moved out of my place."

"Three months ago?"

He nodded. "So what did you want to talk to me about?"

She blinked, trying to gain control of her emotions. Could he read in her expression the hope she felt? "Oh yeah. Uh. The bishop came by. Not only did he welcome me to attend the church meetings and to consider joining the faith, he apologized."

Ephraim chuckled. "So does this mean you believe in God now?"

She laughed. "Can we go for a walk?"

"Sure."

"Give me a minute to check on Lori and make sure Ada will watch her for me. Last I checked, Lori was in the kitchen sitting in Deborah's lap." Cara hurried into the house, made arrangements with Ada, grabbed her sweater, and bounded out the door.

Without a word spoken she and Ephraim headed for their favorite spot. "If Anna Mary's not the issue and I'm not taboo anymore, why are you staying away?"

Laughing, he tilted his head heavenward. Then he mocked a sigh. "Why don't you just say what's on your mind?"

"Obviously one of us has to."

"You know why. I don't want to pressure or influence you in the choices that lie ahead."

"That was good thinking, but I've already made my choices."

Ephraim stepped in front of her and stopped. "Well?"

"Ah, so you left me hanging for months, thinking you still had a girlfriend, but you want my answer right now?"

"I'd have preferred an answer long before you even knew you needed to give one. And I've been unbelievably patient."

"You word things in a way that's very hard to argue with."

"And yet it never stops you, does it?"

"Shut up, 'From. I'm trying to tell you something." She pinned a lock of hair behind one ear. "I intend to join the faith."

He didn't smile or move or anything.

"The world has nothing to offer that could ever mean anything to me like being a part of a community that holds the same values."

His eyes moved over her face. "How sure are you?"

"Completely."

He studied her, and slowly a lopsided smile hinted at what she wanted to know—hope for who they might be was the reason he'd stopped seeing Anna Mary.

"I've missed you so much, Ephraim."

He took her hands into his, looking oddly shy. "Everything is empty without you. I'd like to start coming here more, and maybe one day you'll feel comfortable coming to Dry Lake."

Cara finally had one untarnished moment of complete happiness. "Like dating?"

He nodded. "What's the English word for when you're not seeing but one person?"

"Exclusive."

"Ya, that's it."

"Worried about me becoming interested in other Amish guys, are you, 'From?"

He released one of her hands and brushed her cheek with his fingers. "Maybe a little."

Forty-Three

Cara washed the supper dishes while Lori dried them and passed each item to Deborah to put away. Ada stood inside the walk-in pantry, going over the list of tomorrow's baked goods and matching that against the ingredients.

The bishop had come to see her last night, and she was bursting with news to tell Ephraim. It'd only been three weeks since the bishop had visited on Labor Day, and yet he'd been back to tell her good things.

Deborah placed a dish in the cabinet. "I miss Ephraim being here tonight. He hasn't skipped a day of coming since Labor Day."

"I know. All of us going to the top of the

mountain and stargazing every night has been so great I feel spoiled." Cara barely wiped her wet hand against her black apron before she tucked a wisp of hair behind her ear. Even with a hair net, pins, and a prayer Kapp, her short hair found its way free.

"Don't think I'm climbing that mountain again tonight." From inside the pantry, Ada half griped and half laughed the words. "Where is he, anyway?"

Cara rinsed a glass. "He's working late, something about hardware for a set of cabinets didn't come in on time. I'm a bit tempted to just show up and help him. Anyone up for the drive to Dry Lake?"

Deborah took a plate from Lori. "I need to visit Daed. Ada, you want to ride with us?"

She stepped out of the pantry. "I told Lori I'd teach her how to sew some doll clothes tonight."

"We're gonna make my doll an Amish dress just like mine."

Deborah put the last item in the cabinet. "Ephraim will be surprised to see you in Dry Lake. I was beginning to think it'd be six months before you crossed that border."

"Ephraim says I'm stubborn. Sometimes I think he's right."

Ada dropped her list and mocked complete shock. "You? He had to be mistaken."

Deborah pulled her lips in, trying not to laugh. "I'll go pack to stay at Daed's for the night. You can share my clothes and my bedroom. You get the horse hitched."

"We're going **and** staying the night?"

"It'll be good for you. You need some time around Daed and Becca."

Cara dried her hands and tossed the towel into the dish drainer. "I guess. I mean, if you say so."

Deborah put her arm around Cara and hugged her. "You and Lori have family and friends in Dry Lake. Get used to it." Deborah smiled, but tears brimmed. "Go get ready. Ephraim will love being surprised. You do know none of us have ever seen Ephraim so . . . well . . . I've never seen him even slightly crazy about anyone. I always figured it was just who he was—unable to care passionately about anyone."

Lori grabbed Ada's notepad off the floor. "He loves me and Mom."

Cara's heart startled, and she looked to Deborah and then to Ada. "He said that?"

"Yeah," Lori said. "And he hopes we'll be a family someday. But he doesn't think you're ready to talk about that yet."

Cara chuckled. "I guess I better keep you around, kiddo, so you can keep me posted on things."

Lori helped Cara hitch the horse to the buggy. Her daughter and Ada waved as Cara and Deborah drove out of sight. It was freeing to have people in Lori's life that she fully trusted. She asked Deborah a dozen things about the Amish lifestyle as they spent more than an hour getting to Dry Lake—things like how a preacher, deacon, or bishop was chosen, how the Amish always seemed to find work among their own, why some of the younger girls wore the aprons and some didn't. Soon they were nearing Levina's old place.

"Hey, Deb, why don't you let me off here at the conjoined trees?"

"Okay." Deborah pulled the buggy to a stop. "But whatever you do, don't go to my brother's place and fall asleep."

"Very funny. Just tell him someone's hanging around the barn with a batch of puppies. That'll make him head this way."

"It could make him run for the hills."

"Then I'll be in that tree waiting all night." She jumped down from the buggy and ran to the tree. A dozen memories flooded her as Deborah drove off. Wishing she had on jeans, she managed to climb it, then she rocked back against the trunk and waited.

❧

Ephraim glanced up from the wood in front of him, catching another glimpse of his sister. She looked better every time he saw her. He wasn't naive enough to think the grief was totally behind her, but it didn't own all of her anymore. Cara had been very good for her. A little of her New York, in-your-face toughness could go a long way in helping someone like his sister.

Deborah stood in the doorway of the shop. "You need to go to Levina's barn." She'd said the same thing a few minutes ago. He ran the plane across the flat surface, removing a bit of wood. "I'm busy."

His sister huffed. "If it wasn't important, I wouldn't have mentioned it."

Her tone startled him, and he laughed. "I do believe I just heard Cara in your voice."

"Ya, I think you did. G'night, Ephraim." The screen door to the shop slapped loudly as his sister left.

He drew a deep breath and set the tools in their place. Maybe he should check out what was going on at the barn. Walking through the dried cornfield, he thought of the first time he'd met Cara. If she'd lived in Dry Lake as she should have, they'd have married years ago. He probably wouldn't have courted anyone else. She spoke to his soul like no other. They fit.

The more time they had together, the more time they wanted. And he knew it'd be that way for the rest of their lives.

As he came out of the edge of the cornfield, he saw movement in the tree.

"A girl could spend a lot of time up here waiting for you to come by."

His heart filled with pleasure as he stepped forward. "It's almost too dark to see you, and I started not to come this way at all, but like my Daadi always said, even a blind squirrel can find a nut every once in a while."

"Are you calling me a nut, Ephraim?"

He moved closer. "What are you doing up there?"

"Waiting for you."

He propped the palm of his hand against the trunk. "I'm here. Are you coming down?"

"Nope. I have things I want to know first."

"Like how hard you'll hit the ground if you fall out of that tree?" Wondering if she had any idea what she'd done to his heart, he leaned back against the tree. "Fire away."

"I'll be allowed to go through instructions this spring."

"Really? The bishop said that?"

"Yep. You know what that means, right?"

"Ya. You'll be a member of the Old Order Amish faith come summer."

"That too."

"Too?"

"As in **also.** Meaning not the main thing."

"So what's the main thing, Cara?"

She shifted her body until her stomach was on the branch. As she clung to the thick branch and lowered herself toward the ground, Ephraim wrapped his hands around her waist and helped her make a soft landing.

They stood face to face, but he couldn't find any words.

Sliding her fingertips against the palm of his hand, she leaned against the tree.

"That you can marry me next fall, or technically winter if we choose to wait that long."

Ephraim wanted to ignore prudence and kiss her, but he forced himself to think logically. "I know you're aware most Amish have large families, but have we discussed the fact that the Amish allow God to choose how many children they'll have? That's usually a breaking point for those who've been raised as Englischers."

"Are you trying to talk me out of a marriage proposal you haven't even given?"

Soft laughter rose within him. "You're something else, Cara Moore. And I want nothing but more time with you and more of your heart. But you've got to understand some things."

"I understand. You hope to get lucky often enough to have lots of children, and you're trying to make sure I agree to that now."

"You know what I really think?"

"No, but I bet you're going to tell me."

He placed one hand on her waist. "I think you're in love with me."

"You **think**? You mean you don't know?"

Could his heart beat any faster? "I hoped."

"You'll still have to wait like thirteen or so months from now." She pointed a finger at him. "But you will wait for me."

He cupped her face in his hands. "And why would I do that?"

"Because you're in love with me."

He brought his lips to hers, feeling the power of things he'd always hoped for. "I am. You're absolutely right about that. I think maybe I always have been, so waiting until the next wedding season isn't all that bad."

# Ada's House Series
## Main Characters

**Cara Atwater Moore**—twenty-eight-year-old waitress from New York City who lost her mother as a child, was abandoned by her father, and grew up in foster care. Cara has been stalked for years by Mike Snell.

**Lori Moore**—Cara's seven-year-old daughter. Lori's father, Johnny, died before she turned two years old, leaving Cara a widow.

**Malinda Riehl Atwater**—Cara's mother.

**Trevor Atwater**—Cara's alcoholic father.

**Levina**—Malinda's grandmother who raised her from infancy.

**Ephraim Mast**—thirty-two-year-old single Amish man who works as a cabinetmaker and helps manage his ailing father's business and care for their large family.

**Deborah Mast**—twenty-one-year-old Amish woman who is in love with Mahlon Stoltzfus. She's Ephraim's sister.

**Abner Mast**—Ephraim and Deborah's father, Becca's husband.

**Becca Mast**—Ephraim and Deborah's stepmother, and the mother of two of their stepsiblings and four of their half siblings.

**Anna Mary Lantz**—Ephraim's girlfriend.

**Rueben Lantz**—Anna Mary's father.

**Leah Lantz**—Anna Mary's mother.

**Mahlon Stoltzfus**—twenty-three-year-old Amish man who works with Ephraim and is Deborah Mast's longtime beau.

**Ada Stoltzfus**—Forty-three-year-old widow who is Mahlon's mother, and she's a friend and mentor to Deborah Mast.

**Better Days**—a mixed-breed pup: part Blue Heeler, black Lab, and Chow, resembling the author's dog, Jersey.

**Robbie**—an Englischer who is a co-worker and driver for Ephraim's cabinetry business.

**Israel Kauffman**—a forty-five-year-old Amish widower.

# Glossary

**ach**—oh
**as**—that
**ausenannermache**
   —separate
**awwer**—but
**da**—the
**Daadi**—grandfather
**Daadi Haus**—
   grandfather's
   house. Generally
   this refers to a
   house that is at-
   tached to or is
   near the main
   house and be-
   longs to a grand-
   parent. Many
   times the main
   house belonged
   to the grandpar-
   ents when they
   were raising their
   family. The main
   house is usually
   passed down to a
son, who takes
over the respon-
sibilities his par-
ents once had.
The grandpar-
ents then move
into the smaller
place and usually
have fewer re-
sponsibilities.
**Daed**—dad or
   father
**dei**—your
**denki**—thank you
**die**—the
**draus**—out
**duhne**—do
**Englischer**—a non-
   Amish person.
   Mennonite sects
   whose women
   wear the prayer
   Kapps are not
   considered
   Englischers and

are often referred to as Plain Mennonites.

**es**—it

**fescht**—firm

**gern gschehne**—you're welcome

**geziemt**—suitable or becoming

**Grossmammi**—grandmother

**gut**—good

**Heemet**—home

**immer**—always

**iss**—is

**Kapp**—a prayer covering or cap

**kumm**—come

**letz**—wrong

**liewi**—dear

**losmache**—loosen

**loss uns**—let's

**Mamm**—mom or mother

**meh**—more

**nie net**—never

**nix**—no

**raus**—out

**rumschpringe**—running around. The true purpose of the rumschpringe is threefold: give freedom for an Amish young person to find an Amish mate; to give extra freedoms during the young adult years so each person can decide whether to join the faith; to provide a bridge between childhood and adulthood.

**Sache**—things

**schtehne**—stand

**schtobbe**—stop

**schwetze**—talk

**sich**—themselves
**uns**—us
**verhuddelt**—confused
**waahr**—true
**was**—what
**Welt**—world
**ya**—yes
**zammebinne**—bind

## Pennsylvania Dutch sentences used in The Hope of Refuge:

**Die Sache, as uns zammebinne, duhne sich nie net losmache, awwer die Sache as uns ausenannermache schtehne immer fescht.**—The things that bind us will never loosen, but the things that separate us will always stand firm.

**Ich bin kumme bsuche.**—I have come back.

**Ich hab aa die Cara mitgebrocht.**—I have brought Cara with me.

**In dei Heemet?**—In your home?

**Kumm raus. Loss uns schwetze.**—Come out. Let's talk.

---

\* Glossary taken from Eugene S. Stine, **Pennsylvania German Dictionary** (Birdsboro, PA: Pennsylvania German Society, 1996) and the usage confirmed by an instructor of the Pennsylvania Dutch language.

# Acknowledgments

Each novel is a journey filled with long months of writing alone, but if it weren't for the following people, Cara's story would never have become worthy of publication:

To my husband, who continually opens many more doors for me than the physical ones of a car, home, or business. I'm grateful you've shared over three decades of reality with me—the fulfilling, the satisfying, the difficult, and the yet unseen.

To my dearly beloved Old Order Amish friends who wish to remain anonymous. Your honest answers, insights, and determination have caused me to write Cara's story with great authenticity, which means so very, very much to me. From the most difficult questions during our first sit-down meeting to your review of the finished work, you've been good friends and willing co-workers. Thank you.

To Marci Burke, who always finds time

to do critique rounds even in the midst of a continually growing, successful career. As vital as your input is in each story, your friendship means numerous times more.

To Timothy A. Scully, MD, FACC, Northeast Georgia Heart Center, PC, Vice Chief of Staff, Northeast Georgia Medical Center, Gainesville, GA, who shared his knowledge and insight into medical conditions that affect the heart. You wove your expertise in with my story line until I had solid medical advice for every situation. Thank you!

To my editor, Shannon (Hill) Marchese, who works diligently so readers can share in her love of books. I'm continually amazed at you.

To WaterBrook Multnomah Publishing Group—marketing, sales, production, and editorial departments—who used their expertise, talent, and energy to get this novel into readers' hands. It is an honor to work with you!

To my line editor, Carol Bartley, who always helps me see the story through fresh eyes. Your task to help me find a balance between realistic-sounding characters and grammatically correct prose is never an easy one. Denki!

To my agent, Steve Laube, who always understands the heart of a writer, offers perfect solutions to the influx of issues, and who stands sentry at all times. My family sends their gratitude.

# About the Author

CINDY WOODSMALL is the author of **When the Heart Cries, When the Morning Comes,** and the **New York Times** bestseller **When the Soul Mends.** Her ability to authentically capture the heart of her characters comes from her real-life connections with Amish Mennonite and Old Order Amish families. A mother of three sons and two daughters-in-law, Cindy lives in Georgia with her husband of thirty-one years.